She is a stunning beaut...
to get back what the je...
Will she commit *The Perfect Crime...*

the *Heistess*

A Crime Thriller

by Lex Sloot

Media Center LLC

Hazle Township, Pennsylvania

Cover refinements by: Tracy Grover
Book layout by: Robin Wrighton

ISBN-13: 978-1-73794-642-7

Sloot, Alexander (Lex)
The Heistess; A Crime Thriller
First Printing, September 2023

Published by:

Media Center LLC
308 West 36th Street
Hazle Township, PA 18202
www.lexsloot.com

Other books by Lex Sloot:

The TOOLS to XEL (Excel)   978-0-97526-790-5
VIABILITY… The Essence of Existence   978-0-98642-876-0

Printed in the United States of America

For my family

Gerson ◆ Solomon ◆ Sloot

CHAPTER 1

Ariella and Her Motivation

Ariella Gerson decided to break into a jewelry store which was in downtown Averton, a small city in the north-western part of New Jersey where she lived. It was her belief, once her plan was put together, this could well be *The Perfect Crime* and she might never be caught.

Why would she even think of committing a heinous theft like this? It was to exact revenge on the man who stole a fortune from her unsuspecting grandmother, Rachel Gerson. He robbed Ariella's nana of her valuable diamond rings, emerald brooches, strings of pearls, diamond necklaces, heirloom watches, gold coins, and much more. This man, Huntington Barnwell, was the owner of the Fourth Street Jewelers and Gold Exchange. It was a third-generation family business, started by his grandfather. Hunt was now the owner.

He and his wife had been married for twenty years, both were in their mid-forties and had three teenage children. But unlike his father and grandfather who were both impeccably honest, Hunt was unscrupulous. If one looked the other way for just a second, he would rip you off. He was also having affairs with two women, one in her twenties and the other in her thirties. His wife suspected something but decided not to say anything to him just yet.

He would think nothing of stealing from his customers and misleading most about the value of their items or short-changing them wherever and whenever he could. It was because of this many despised him, and even Ariella felt that he must be stopped. More importantly, she needed to get back her grandma's jewelry or other items of equivalent worth and try to make him pay for his improbity.

It was back in mid-April when Rachel made the mistake of calling the Fourth Street Jewelers and Gold Exchange after their phone number appeared in an advertisement on TV. She was simply curious to know the value of all her gold, diamonds, and other jewelry.

Hunt went to visit Rachel right after receiving her phone call and took the items to his store 'for assessment'. He returned a few days later with a check for $5,000 saying the jewelry was worth only that much money. The grandmother insisted he bring everything back because she was not selling any of it, she just wanted an evaluation of it all. He left her with the check and never returned.

And so it was on Sunday, May 22nd when visiting her granny, Ariella found out the jewelry had been stolen. Yes, about five weeks had passed since Hunt brought in the $5,000 check. Her grandma was too frightened to say anything for all this time but finally got around to telling her what happened, and this news shocked Ariella. She decided to meet very soon with the owner of this store and find out how to get all the precious items back.

On Wednesday, May 25th Rachel had a heart attack mainly because of all the stress and she passed away. Ariella was extremely upset and remained in mourning for many days after the funeral.

As she slowly got over this sad event, Ariella vowed revenge, feeling that Barnwell was responsible for her nana's untimely death. It was on Tuesday, June 7th she took time off from work and went to the Fourth Street Jewelers and Gold Exchange to confront Barnwell. He said it was his understanding that all was for sale, and he paid more than he should have.

Ariella knew everything was worth well over $500,000. She even spoke to the insurance company, and they said there was nothing they could do because too many weeks had passed from the time when the goods were taken and when Ariella informed them as to what took place.

There was no way to prove the content of the conversation between Hunt and the old lady, and it was impossible to show how much expensive jewelry she possessed. No adequate records existed other than a very dated and incomplete insurance policy.

Ariella got into a shouting match with Hunt in his store that day. "You took advantage of my grandmother and stole a boatload of stuff, giving her only a tiny amount for a host of items you know are worth hundreds of thousands!"

"I did nothing of the sort," said Hunt angrily. "Just about all her stuff was costume jewelry. We see this all the time. Maybe *you* long ago swapped out the real items for fakes!"

Ariella went ballistic and screamed at him, vehemently denying she would ever do something like that to anyone. Other clients who were there looked aghast. Hunt yelled to his security guard, "Get this mad woman out of my store and if she does not leave, call the police and have her arrested!"

As Ariella was being dragged out, one of the customers came to her defense by pulling on the coat of the security guard saying, "Leave her alone! Stop treating her like that!" The man relaxed his grip on her arm.

Thankful this woman came forward to assist her, Ariella stormed out seething and mumbling under her breath, "I will get even with you! You will regret this!" She marched down Fourth Street hardly able to see where she was going because her eyes were filled with tears. About halfway down the block this customer, the other woman who came to her aid, caught up with her.

"Wait," she said. "I saw and heard everything that went on there and I think you are right. Mr. Barnwell is up to no good."

Ariella stopped walking and drying her eyes with a tissue said in a soft voice, "Thank you for helping me."

The other young lady was about Ariella's age, and holding out her hand said, "I am Barbara McKenna. This man also stole from me in the past, but nowhere near as much as it appears he took from you, I mean from your grandma."

"Hi, am Ariella Gerson. I really appreciate you standing up for me."

"Come," said Barbara, "Let me buy you a cup of coffee."

The two were in front of a supermarket with a food counter, so they walked inside and sat down. They chatted quietly, getting to know one another a little bit better while sipping on their hot beverages. Ariella went into detail about how Barnwell made off with all her grandma's valuables and paid only a pittance of what it was all worth.

After some forty-five minutes, the pair exchanged phone numbers and agreed to be in touch with each other soon. Barbara said she needed to go, and left Ariella at the coffee bar now drinking her second cup and thinking about getting even, or how to steal a pile of jewelry from Barnwell's store.

What made Ariella continue to ponder repeatedly about robbing the place was that her nana, who was in her early eighties and in very good health should never have died so suddenly. She should have lived for many more years.

Besides its monetary worth, some of the jewelry was of sentimental value, having been passed down through multiple generations as family heirlooms.

Ariella, still grieving over Rachel's death, understood she was the only heir. Her grandmother was her closest family member other than a few cousins who lived a couple of hours from her.

While the Ariella was due to receive about $25,000 and an old Buick automobile in the Will, the vast makeup of the estate would have been the jewelry and that was now gone. She still had a bit of college debt and inheriting gold chains, diamonds, rubies, and more would have gone a long way to help her if a decision was ever made to sell some select pieces. It was true that her earnings were quite good these days, but the house mortgage, car, and other expenses consumed most of her monthly income.

Ariella came from a stable family environment. Her mother, Sharon, taught high school math and history for many years and all the kids loved her. She worked very patiently with her daughter in the evenings to coach her in every aspect of her schoolwork. All this attention really paid off and Ariella became an outstanding student.

Her father Louis was the owner of a small construction business, and he specialized primarily in home repairs. Occasionally he would buy small run-down houses, renovate, and then flip them. He did quite well, and more than adequately provided for his family. Louis had two people who worked for him, but they were often unreliable, so he tended to do a lot of the work himself.

From the time she was about fourteen years old, Ariella assisted her father in his business after school and on weekends. She did much of the office-related paperwork including typing quotations, sending correspondence to customers, invoicing, and weekly bank deposits.

Besides being involved in administrative tasks, she helped with some of the physical work as well. At first, it was basic stuff such as passing tools, nails, screws, and other items to Louis, especially if he was up on a ladder. Her projects also included cleaning paintbrushes and packing things away at the end of each day. But as she got older, Ariella learned how to install drywall, and spackle, sand, and paint it.

Before too long she progressed to bricklaying, plumbing, and handling some minor electrical connections. Ariella became a huge help to her father, especially when school was out during the summer. He paid her well, so she was able to buy many new clothes, a small car, and other teenage necessities to keep her happy.

But Louis Gerson was not in good health, and when Ariella was twenty years old and in college, he succumbed to mesothelioma. Her mother did not fare too well after that and a year later she passed away. It was these two sad events that brought Ariella much closer to her grandmother.

When Ariella turned twenty-three, she graduated from college and got a good job at the technology firm where she was currently employed.

A year later it was time to buy a house, and this was done without needing any help from Rachel with the down payment. Her life was now stable, and things were going well until recently when Huntington Barnwell showed up and disrupted it all.

Breaking into the store would take a lot of organized planning on Ariella's part, to get back what was taken, and being caught would not be an option! Perhaps Mr. Barnwell could somehow be dealt with in the process and held to account.

◆◆◆◆◆

It was Wednesday, June 8th, the day after her encounter with the owner of the jewelry store when Ariella asked her immediate supervisor at work about having a longer lunch period, and he said that would be okay. She made her way to the local police precinct and told the desk sergeant she wanted to report a theft. He took her into an office where he sat her down and began asking questions.

After a couple of minutes, he realized this theft was not a recent occurrence but took place over seven weeks before during the month of April. He told her to wait there and said he would find the right person for her to speak with. Five minutes later she was escorted into a room where three men were seated. She was introduced to Detective Leyland Wakefield, his assistant Charles Weston from the crime lab, and Captain Brian Morley. A very agitated and upset Ariella told them her story. After listening to her, all three in one way or another and in condescending tones told her there was "nothing they could do" because there was no way to prove anything and too much time had gone by.

Detective Wakefield then spoke up, "We have heard rumors over the past few years that the owner of this store has fraudulently cheated a number of people out of significant amounts of jewelry but we never came across any definitive proof, just like in your case. If you can verify beyond doubt the value of what he took from your grandmother, prove he robbed others, if you can find a way to identify these individuals, figure out a way for them to get restitution, and if you can bring Mr. Barnwell to justice, then you go ahead and do so because we have been unable to."

Ariella was frustrated and enraged. "You people are the police! You should be able to solve crimes and not suggest to citizens they do your work for you!" Teary-eyed and annoyed, she got up, stormed out of the meeting, and headed back to work. She said quietly while getting into the Uber car, "So *they* have asked me to bring Barnwell to justice. I will show them how it is done! I will make him pay and I will see to it other victims get compensated!"

◆◆◆◆◆

Ariella was an attractive twenty-eight-year-old, tall and slim with long blonde hair and piercing blue eyes. After graduating high school, she went to a quality university, achieved a five-year degree in Computer Science and a minor in Mechanical Engineering, and was now back living in the small semi-rural city of Averton, New Jersey.

She was somewhat of a whizz kid regarding electronics, computers, and programming, and was totally fascinated by things mechanical including drones and related technology. As a result, she custom-built various versions of toy radio-controlled cars and other small vehicles. At one point she constructed a couple of small walking robots as well as many different types of flying machines from large ones to miniature.

In addition to being so technically oriented, Ariella was good with tools and carpentry work due to years of experience as a teenager helping her father. She had also taught herself how to design and make costume jewelry including necklaces, earrings, pendants, bracelets, and more.

In fact, this bright beauty knew a lot about precious metals like gold and silver and quite a bit pertaining to diamonds. Because of this knowledge, she understood much relating to the value of her grandmother's sparkling collection of family heirlooms.

In high school, languages were among her strong points, she spoke Spanish fluently and had a good working knowledge of both French and Italian. She was also proficient at speaking in different accents including being an ace at mimicking a good English accent. Some of this training came from acting in many school plays especially Shakespeare, where authenticity required using English-sounding speech.

Little did the amateur actress know then, how much being able to speak like a 'foreigner' would help her in the future. Yes, this was an exceptionally smart single girl who had a wonderful job working at a technology company, which created some highly complex electronics for their clients.

She had been employed there for the past five years since graduating from college and lived in a house owned by her, on which there was a moderate mortgage. It was enjoyable for her residing in the suburbs, and having a garden adorned with beautiful flowers. More importantly, she had a wonderful cat called Purdy. He was a loving, friendly, and appreciative companion.

While Rachel was alive, Ariella would visit her about once a month. The old lady was very independent and drove herself wherever she needed to go in her ten-year-old Buick, and being so self-reliant, did not require her granddaughter to be at her side too often. Ariella really understood the biggest problem about Barnwell taking all the jewelry was that Rachel held off saying anything until about five weeks after the $5,000 check was given to her. There was no doubt, that to get back any of what was stolen would require action against the dishonest Mr. Barnwell.

After her grandma passed away, Ariella asked the building's superintendent if the Buick could be parked there for a few weeks, until certain elements of the estate were sorted out. The man was very cooperative and told her to "take her time." Of course, in terms of the Will, she inherited the vehicle.

It was left there for a short while until she called Harry Woodward her car-repair mechanic from Woodward's Auto Center and asked him if he would store the automobile at his garage. Harry, who was married with grown children, was infatuated with the beautiful Ariella. He would do anything for her, so he told her she could leave the car at his garage.

CHAPTER 2

Saturday, June 11th

Some important household repairs needed to be done, and so on this Saturday while doing these chores, Ariella did not have time to think about robbing the jewelry store. Being a very 'handy' gal there was little she could not make, build, or fix. With only one car in her double garage, there was room for this vehicle and a well-equipped workshop. An assortment of tools and materials could be found here, and this allowed her to accomplish various fix-up projects.

There were three distinct tasks requiring her attention that day.

▪ The shaky steps and landing going into the kitchen from the backyard were to be tightened and stabilized.

▪ A repair was overdue for a leaking pipe in her basement wall.

▪ A small tree in the front yard which died over the winter needed to be removed.

Her first project would be the loose wooden step-treads. Using a star screwdriver-bit in her rechargeable drill she removed the old screws which were barely holding down the top piece on each of the steps, and these were replaced with longer screws. The treads were now firmly secured.

The small stairway ended at an unsteady wooden platform, which was about 4' x 4' square. The steps and this plywood panel were originally installed onto a concrete pad many years before so at least it was all on a firm base and not just sitting on dirt. Ariella removed the three screws which were holding this planking down and saw that eight were really required. No wonder it was so wobbly to walk on!

With the screws out of the way she was able to lift this ¾" thick plywood piece, but it was rather unwieldy to hold because of its size. She was relieved to see that overall, it was not in bad shape, so it did not need to be replaced. The hollow area under the landing was dirty and full of cobwebs, so with an old broom from the garage these were all swept away.

Taking her Shop-Vac, all the dust and dirt including the area under the steps was vacuumed out. The concrete base was now spotless, and the thirty-inch-high walls on which the platform rested were also cleaned by her. Ariella found a large U-shaped metal handle in her workshop, and this was screwed to the underside of the wooden panel. It was done carefully so that none of the screws poked through. This now gave her a handle to grasp, which would make it easier for her to lift the platform as she reinstalled it. Using eight new screws she secured the plywood landing back into place. The job was completed after barely two hours of work.

She went inside, drank a glass of water, made a peanut butter and jelly sandwich, and was ready to tackle the next project. This was the leaking pipe in the basement, and for this she took her toolbox downstairs. The drywall in one corner was still damp just like a week before when the problem was first noticed. But this time the wet patch on the wall had expanded considerably. In her head, she mused about how 'drywall' was also called 'gypsum board' and also 'sheetrock'. The funny names people think of!

Taking a utility knife and a straight edge, she slowly sliced a portion of this gypsum board approximately 2' x 3' ending just beyond the damp areas. By moving the knife multiple times over the same lines, this was done until she was able to pry it out: It bent and all but crumbled because of the wetness. She removed the screws which were remaining in the studs because these would be in the way when the segment was replaced. Looking through the opening, the plastic water pipe was visible, and one could see it had a tiny split in it.

Behind the studs, there was a large gap of more than twelve inches to the block wall and Ariella thought, "An excellent place to hide things."

The main water valve for the house was in a corner of the kitchen, so she went upstairs and cranked this to its 'off' position. Going back down into the bathroom in the basement, she turned on a cold water tap and let it run into the sink. After a few minutes, all the household water was drained out. Using a hacksaw, two cuts were made to the top and bottom of the split in the water pipe, and the damaged length was removed.

In her workshop, she found a similar diameter component of PVC pipe, plus two joining collars. This was cut to a measurement of 6" and, using the correct adhesive and the necessary purple primer, she glued the collars and the new 6" piece into place and thus repaired the leak. The main water valve was then turned back on.

There were all sorts of materials in her workshop, so finding a partial sheet of drywall was easy! She cut this to 2' x 3' which was the exact size of the gap created after the removal of the wet and crumbling section. The piece of gypsum board was taken downstairs, screwed to the studs then taped and spackled around its perimeter. This would have to dry before it could be sandpapered and painted. Another chore was done.

And now for the dead tree. The eight-foot-high sapling in her front garden died after the recent harsh winter, and Ariella wanted to get it out of the ground. At first, she tried to dig around it with a shovel and a pickaxe, but the roots were too deep, and little progress was made after working at it for a while. It could be that using her car might be best. In her garage was an old but very strong thirty-foot towrope with large silver hooks, one on each end. She pulled this around the base of the tree and looped it through one of the hooks. Ariella then brought her Subaru to a suitable spot on the driveway. Under the rear bumper, there was a towing ring into which the other hook was placed. By driving her car forward, as the vehicle moved, the cordage around the tree tightened in a lasso effect.

She began to cautiously proceed on the driveway, checking in her rear-view mirror that all was still okay. Suddenly the car lurched forward as the tree came loose and was pulled out of the ground. When the auto stopped, one could see the dried-out trunk and roots lying in the flower bed. There was a large hole left behind. With a handsaw, she cut the tree into a few pieces and dragged these to the backyard.

While there, she took a shovel and dug out a pile of earth which was put into her wheelbarrow and brought to the front garden to fill in the hole. Next season something else could be planted in that space. Her third household task was now completed. The towrope was carried back into the garage, coiled, and hung up. Her car was at that point driven inside and the garage door was closed. Now she could take it easy, relax, and get back to planning the theft of the jewelry store!

CHAPTER 3

Ariella was in her office all day completing a complex project, and now the weekend was finally here. It was almost a week since the home repairs were done by her, and about ten days from her confrontation with Hunt Barnwell in his jewelry store. Normally it would be a bus ride at this time of day to get home, but tonight she and Barbara were going to meet for cocktails after work.

As Ariella was leaving the technology company where she was employed one of her co-workers, Jason Myers, was getting into the elevator with her.

"When are you going to join me for a drink?" he asked, staring at her fine features and bright blue eyes.

"Oh, come on Jason," said Ariella, "We both know you are married, and you are not my kind of guy."

"Well, what is your type?" He was tall, quite handsome, and hoping to win her favor.

"Right now, it is no one." She kept thinking of her recent romance and break-up with her ex-boyfriend Patrick.

The elevator reached the lobby, and she walked out boldly. "Have a good evening Jason, and enjoy the weekend with your wife and children!"

"Good night." He looked wistfully at her striding confidently away from the building. How he wished he could be dating Ariella, sleeping with her, and making a life together.

Jason was a football star in high school and in college. Girls swooned over him, and he was always the center of attention. But these days, at thirty-three years old, he regretted being married and tied down. How his life had changed! It was now all about his twin six-year-old girls and his ever-complaining wife! But she had every right to grumble. The conceited, self-indulgent young man helped with little or nothing around the house. All he wanted to do was to hang out with his single friends.

Ariella set out for Tyler's Tavern on Second Street. Walking inside she made her way past many end-of-week revelers because this place was always packed on a Friday night. As she got close to one of the high-tops in the back corner, Barbara waved to her. Whew! How great that her friend arrived early enough to get a good table!

At twenty-nine, Barbara was a year older than Ariella. She worked for an importing company doing mundane but essential clerical work, but it was a job with not too much of a future and so she was constantly on the lookout for other opportunities. This career woman had been divorced for about three years and was pleased to be out of a disastrous two-year marriage, in which fortunately, there were no children. She too was tall and slim, with long straight brown hair, and this contrasted with Ariella's blonde mane. Together, the two made a striking pair.

When Ariella got to the table, Barbara stood up saying, "It is good to see you again. You look a lot better than the day we first met and had coffee in that supermarket."

These two beauties, both of whom were a bit fed up with men, sat down at the high-top and ordered martinis. Their night of fun had just begun. The conversation went immediately to the recent passing of her grandmother and Ariella explained how Rachel died so suddenly. She was thankful to now have someone to lean on who could console her during these difficult times.

"That awful lying, cheating man Barnwell, caused my granny to have a heart attack."

"I understand. I wonder if there is anything that can be done to help you get some restitution? What can we do?"

"I am working on a few ideas," said Ariella. "I know in time something will come to me, but this is just so difficult. There is no way we can ever prove that bastard to be wrong! It was his word against my nana's. I wish she did not see his advertisement and never invited him to her apartment or showed him her jewelry." She appeared exasperated. "I should break in and steal it all back!"

"What? Enough with this type of wild conjecture! I am sure between us we can come up with a plan where he will make good, or somehow get the authorities to look into his business practices." But Barbara knew in her heart it would be extremely difficult to bring this slippery Huntington character to justice.

"The sad part is he has no doubt done this before and he will certainly keep on taking advantage of others in the future." Ariella was misty-eyed as she spoke.

"I know, and as I told you, he already scammed me out of some prized possessions. I was in the store that day when I met you, just looking for bargains to try to make up for some of what I lost." Suddenly her face lit up. "I have an idea. Maybe we should advertise online asking for others to step forward, people who feel they were harmed by Barnwell. You never know, we might be able to build a case with enough witnesses and victims."

The pretty blonde smiled, "Oh please! You are starting to sound like a lawyer! Tell you what, why don't you begin formulating a course of action along those lines and see if you can find others who were wronged by him? Then let me devise a different kind of approach. In the not-too-distant future, we can sit down together and discuss our plans and jointly decide in which direction we should go."

"Okay." She was now concerned her gal pal would want to do something brazen, feeling that miss blue-eyes would look for a very practical or physical way to handle the situation, and was worried about what sort of scheme might be presented. But hey, whatever Ariella thought about, it would only be a 'plan' and it would be subject to the two of them debating it.

Barbara was brought up in a rather refined household. Her mother was a practicing attorney, and her father was a well-renowned doctor. They wanted their daughter to become a lawyer, but college was not for her. She felt the way to handle Barnwell would be to take proper, lawful, legal steps, and hoped Ariella would not simply go out and buy a gun!

And then the subject changed. Each spoke about their past week at work, the good moments, and the frustrating ones. Ariella relayed how a co-worker of hers, the handsome, married, Jason attempted to ask her out for a drink. They both laughed at the frustration he must be feeling, having been a king in high school and at college. Now he was driving around in a minivan with a wife, two kids, two dogs, a huge mortgage, and owing a lot on his credit cards!

"Not for me!" Both said this in unison clinking their glasses. It would likely not be the last time they would sing out similar words together.

"It's eight thirty, so we should leave," said Barbara suddenly. "We can go to my apartment for a light snack to eat. I am growing tired of those two guys sitting in that booth over there looking in our direction and leering at us!"

"Well, we know what they are talking about."

"Yes. They want to get us into bed!"

"C'mon. We are out of here," said Ariella.

The girls had been paying cash for their drinks. They left a generous tip, then made their way outside into the warm evening air. Because Barbara drove herself to work every day, her vehicle was in a garage nearby. The two walked there, got into the white Toyota, and off they went to where she lived. When arriving there, Barbara left her car in the open parking lot which was adjacent to her apartment building. At that moment Ariella did not realize how important it would be for her in a few weeks' time to know what type of auto her new friend owned and exactly where it was parked when she was at home.

Barbara slid her apartment key into the lock, and they went inside closing the door behind them. Before too long both were in the kitchen and Barbara started putting together a plate of cheese and crackers. She defrosted some frozen shrimp while Ariella opened a new bottle of cocktail sauce. Barbara got out a can of palm hearts, cut these into bite-sized pieces, and put them onto a plate.

"I know we have been at Tyler's Tavern for the past two hours, but we can have a glass of wine, right? You are not driving home because you said you would get an Uber ride."

"That is correct, and I would love some wine!"

They now relaxed in the living room and continued chatting about various aspects of their lives. Since they spoke about it earlier, the subject of the jewelry store and any revenge tactics did not come up again.

It was just after ten thirty when Ariella decided it was time to go home. They took the elevator down to the lobby, hugged each other, then said their goodbyes. It was a great 'getting-to-know-you' evening, and once in the Uber car, Ariella thought about how thrilled she was that finally, there was someone with whom she could socialize.

CHAPTER 4

Saturday Morning, June 18th

The sleeping beauty woke up at eight o'clock to Purdy meowing like crazy because he wanted attention. He was hungry, so he was given his food, his litter box was changed and then Ariella went to take a shower. She got dressed, put on her usual sparse amount of makeup, and was now ready to go out. Picking up her laptop, she drove downtown and after parking at a meter, strolled to a coffee shop located across the road from the Fourth Street Jewelers and Gold Exchange.

The night before was enjoyable and the newly found friendship was making her feel happier than she had been in ages. But now it was time to get back on track with her big idea. Barbara would not be told anything about the heist, at least not just yet, or not until it was over… or maybe never.

Ariella walked into The Jolly Java and sat down at the long bar-like counter which faced onto the street. She ordered a latte and a scone, then opened her laptop and pretended to be busy in it, but her brain was really trying to formulate a plan regarding how to break into the bling boutique and more importantly, how to get away clean. There were a few other people there each sipping on a cuppa-joe and some were doing work on their electronic devices.

Hunt Barnwell's business was located on the ground floor of a small four-story building with commercial rentals at street level and residential apartments on the three floors above. There was a large address designation sign on the outside of 101 Fourth Street. Immediately to the right of this property was another identical four-story commercial and residential structure at 125 Fourth Street. This low-rise also featured various sidewalk-access retail spaces and the three floors above were apartments.

Averton New Jersey was a hilly city and Fourth Street itself was a steeply inclined road. The observant gal noticed something interesting when looking across the way. The ground floor of 101 Fourth Street in which Barnwell's business was housed sat about four feet higher than the next-door commercial/residential edifice, number 125.

The Fourth Street Jewelers and Gold Exchange was the last store at the edge of the 101 property and it virtually butted up to a small clothing boutique at the 125 address. As was the case with so many buildings constructed early in the twentieth century, these two were only inches apart… with their side walls almost touching each other.

While sitting there, sipping on her hot beverage and seeing this, Ariella noticed a 'For Rent' sign in the window of the apartment above the jewelry store. Her eyes grew wide. A plan was starting to formulate in her mind but then it quickly dissipated. Even if she leased that space, there would be no way to bore through what could be a solid concrete floor to break into the shop below. Not only would this take forever to do, but people would hear equipment hammering or grinding away. And in any event, if she was the one renting above and a drop-through hole was made in the ceiling of the store, who would be the obvious culprit?

She ordered a second latte and another scone while continuing to glance at her laptop and play with the keys, but her real concentration was outside. Similar to the 101 Fourth Street property, above the ground level commercial rentals at the 125-Building, there were three floors of residential spaces.

She wondered who could be living directly on top of the clothing shop. This apartment was next to the 101-Building and its floor level could possibly line up with the ceiling area of Barnwell's place. The pretty planner sat there for another fifteen minutes scrutinizing the scenario outside. She took out her phone and snapped a couple of pictures of these two properties. She finished eating her scone, closed her laptop, left the payment in cash with a tip, and went out into the sunlight.

Ariella remembered there was a party store nearby. It not only stocked all kinds of fun items such as different color plates, cups, streamers, and so on, but all year long and not only at Halloween, one could also buy disguises, wigs, special make-up and more. She went inside and twenty minutes later left with a bag of 'change of appearance' necessities. Her idea was slowly being put into motion. She walked to her car and drove home. There was much work to be done.

◆◆◆◆◆

Ariella had been in a few relationships over the years and the last one was a serious three-year event where her boyfriend, Patrick, asked her to move in with him. But that didn't work out because of his infidelity. Thank goodness she did not give up her house for the brief period when they were living together.

For now, she was temporarily done with dating and was turning down the advances of most would-be suitors. This was therefore the perfect time for her to be working on the heirloom retrieval plan. She had no attachments and no people around who would question her absences during the day or after hours as her scheme got underway.

She needed to make sure nothing was revealed to Barbara. While hoping in the future her new friend could become a confidante, keeping the notion of the heist close to the vest at this point would take a lot of self-control.

It was 1:30 p.m. this Saturday afternoon, June 18th and Ariella was back at her house. She was interested to find out who resided in the apartment above the clothing shop at the 125-Building on Fourth Street. At the same time, she was keen to see what could be done with some of the wigs and other items. So, the creative make-up artist began experimenting with the new disguises purchased earlier. The short, dark, straight-hair look seemed intriguing and when her blond hair was tied up and hidden, this black wig gave an appearance bearing no resemblance to her normal self.

This would become her 'Mandy Moore' getup. She darkened her eyebrows with a makeup pencil. Yuk! This natural blonde always loved the way her eyebrows were lighter in color which added to her attractiveness.

She glanced at a couple of other headwear disguises. While the curly, charcoal-grey hairpiece would provide an 'older' demeanor, she felt today it should be the short, dark-hair look. The curly one would be used another time. There was also a scraggly grey wig with a grey beard, a disguise that could be handy if the image of an older man was ever needed.

With an eyebrow pencil, a distinctive beauty mark was added to her left cheek, on the point of her cheekbone. Its position would be easy to duplicate each time this 'character' was put together. In her make-up drawer was a pair of brown contact lenses which were used by her before. Her optician had provided a few sets of plain brown contacts to her for an office costume party last Halloween. She remembered how her co-workers were startled when they saw her baby blues had changed so dramatically. Trying to freak them out really worked!

The few sets of contact lenses were still in their boxes. In less than a minute her vivid blue eyes were a totally different color. Ariella took one last gander in the mirror, then removed the wig and stuffed it into her shoulder bag, knowing this would be put on after the Subaru was parked.

Wearing a pink blouse, navy slacks, and patterned sneakers she went into the garage, got in her car, and drove directly to the downtown area. About three blocks away from her destination she pulled over on a quiet side street and gazed around. It was three o'clock and there were only a handful of people outside. Two were walking their dogs and they seemed to take no notice of the newly arrived vehicle.

Ariella tied her hair up, then quickly and skillfully donned the short black wig. Looking in the visor mirror all seemed to be okay, so on went her sunglasses. She got out of the car, locked it, and went in a roundabout way to the apartment building located at 125 Fourth Street.

The Heistess waited outside the front entrance doors acting like she was gabbing on her cell phone but observing everything going on around her. Good, no doorman, just a small vestibule where there appeared to be a stack of mailboxes on the right-hand side. At the end of this foyer, there was a glass door, and it was very likely locked. She felt sure a person would need to get buzzed in if they did not have a keycard.

Right at that moment a taxi pulled up, an older gentleman emerged and walked up the steps directly toward this attractive young lady who was busy on her phone. When he got to the top of the three steps, she opened the outside door for him. Nodding and smiling, his gaze lingered on her finely featured face.

He strode through the entranceway, and she followed him inside as he moved directly to the far end of the foyer. Walking behind him she was able to read one of the names from the bottom row of mailboxes which belonged to residents on the first floor and noticed that apartment 1002 was occupied by Kayla Dixon. Ariella immediately began repeating the two words to herself so as not to forget the name of that tenant.

The older gentleman glanced back and seemed pleased this beauty was right behind him as he walked to the interior glass door. Still holding her phone to her ear, she acted as if fumbling with her one free hand in her shoulder bag to get her plastic keycard. She was standing right behind him as swiped his card and walked through. He immediately reciprocated her actions from moments before and he held the door open for her.

The charming chick gave him her best dazzling smile revealing her perfect teeth, mouthed a 'Thank You' to him, and continued talking in her best English accent sensibly to 'her brother' on her phone. This projected a conversation of stability and family to a man who had just broken the rules. Ariella stepped into the elevator with him saying a quick 'goodbye' and then put her phone into her bag.

"Where to?" asked the gentleman.

Responding in her English accent, "I need to go to the first floor, please." She was gambling on him not being headed there and that he lived higher up in the building. He pressed number one for her and number three for himself.

"Hi," he said holding out his hand, intrigued by her accent and her beauty. "I am Evan Sutton. Are you visiting from England?"

"Hello, I am Mandy Moore. Yes, I am on holiday from London and staying here for now with my cousin Kayla Dixon." Using the words 'cousin' and 'staying here for now' would sort of justify her fumbling for a keycard when she was not really a resident. Family members do tend to give their close relatives access to these types of tenanted buildings without raising eyebrows. She said 'holiday' and not 'vacation' just like someone from England would say.

"I am pleased to meet you. I hope you enjoy your visit." The elevator stopped. It did not take long to get to the first floor.

"Cheerio!" said Ariella as she walked out. While the doors were closing, the man was staring at her. Even with the short dark-hair disguise, her loveliness shone through, and Evan Sutton could not take his eyes off her.

"Good," she whispered. "Let everyone only remember a woman with dark hair, brown eyes, a beauty spot, and an English accent. Any cameras in this building will record my appearance in that manner."

Once in the passageway, she went to the apartment at the far end, the one closest to the 101-Building where the jewelry store was located. This would be the residence directly above the clothing shop. At the end of the hallway, the number on the door in front of her was 1015, and she rang the bell.

After about twenty seconds, the voice of a woman asked, "Who is there?"

Once again in her English accent, she said, "This is Mandy. Kayla is that you?"

The door suddenly opened, and a sweet white-haired old lady peered out at her. "If you want Kayla Dixon, that will be at the other end of this floor."

"Oh, I am dreadfully sorry to disturb you." Ariella flashed her sweetest smile, and looking past the woman added, "What a charming apartment."

"You are such a pretty girl. Are you from England?"

"Yes. I am visiting from London."

"Would you like to look around?"

She could not believe her good fortune. This place could now be evaluated to see if the heist of the shimmer shop could be carried out from here. "I would love to come in!" Obviously, the woman was very lonely... and trusting too.

"Do you know Kayla Dixon?" asked Ariella proceeding to walk inside.

"No, but her name is on the mailbox downstairs, and I understand her apartment is at the far end of this hallway. By the way, my name is Dora Jenkins. And what was your name again, dearie?"

"I am Mandy Moore." Ariella was very relieved. At least the old lady did not know Kayla Dixon.

"Would you like a cup of tea?" asked Dora.

"Thank you, that would be nice. You know us Brits... we enjoy our tea!" Now inside, Ariella's antenna went up. She was very careful not to touch anything such as the glass coffee table, the wide wooden arms on the edges of the couch, or other flat surfaces. If this place was to be a staging area for the heist, there was to be no trace of her ever having been there.

They chatted for some forty-five minutes and then Dora brought out photos of her late husband, her daughters, and her grandchildren. Ariella in turn used her cell phone to show pictures of her grandmother. She did not tell Dora her nana recently passed away because it was better to build rapport than to upset her.

Ariella asked to use the powder room and Dora indicated with her hand its direction. As luck would have it the bathroom was at the end of the apartment and its back wall was located right next to the 101-Building. It was very exciting to discover this, and a great opportunity for her to take a few cell phone pictures.

Climbing onto the edge of the bathtub and opening the window, she looked down onto Fourth Street and took a few photos. Again, inside the bathroom, Ariella clicked some snapshots of the large square tiles which covered all the walls. Taking a small tape measure from her purse she measured these tiles and found them to be 8" square. It all appeared very promising for getting into the ceiling of the jewelry store in the adjacent building. All this scouting around took less than two minutes.

From her coffee shop observations, it was apparent that the 125-Building was about four feet lower than the 101-Building. This put the floor of Dora's bathroom about in line with the space above the ceiling of the place she intended to rob. Hopefully, the store had a suspended or 'dropped' metal framed commercial-grade ceiling.

The Heistess was in that retail establishment only once, when confronting Hunt Barnwell about her grandma's valuables. But being so incensed that day, no attention was paid to any structural details, and a trip back inside was essential to verify her suppositions.

Ariella flushed the toilet, ran one of the taps in the sink, and with a tissue wiped down every spot which may have been touched, to avoid her fingerprints being left behind. These included a small area on the bathtub, the window catch above the tub, the faucet, the toilet handle, and the handles on both sides of the door. Gloves would certainly be worn if this was to be the base for the break-in. Before too long she emerged and once again took her seat on the living room couch.

The old lady really took a liking to Ariella and eventually, when she was getting ready to leave, Dora invited her to visit again. The soon-to-be wall breacher was thrilled at the suggestion and made an appointment for three o'clock next Saturday afternoon, June 25th. Kayla Dixon's name was never referred to again and it was a good thing the woman was slightly forgetful. Hopefully, her hostess would remember their arrangement for the following Saturday!

As Ariella was about to go, Dora said, "Give me a hug!" Then she provided the greatest gift of all by saying, "I am looking forward to having tea with you again next Saturday, but on Thursday, June 30th at the end of this month, I will be going to visit my daughter in Florida for a week and returning the following Thursday."

The daring diva was almost speechless after hearing this place would be empty for seven days! Ariella knew she must somehow lay her hands on a keycard for the foyer and a key to the front door of this residence. There was to be not even a suggestion that she come in to water the plants. It would be best if a building maintenance person or a neighbor was the one showing up to take care of them. If Dora asked her next week to tend to the plants, the request would be turned down. Offering to check on the apartment would only be a last resort for Ariella if a foyer keycard and a door key could not be obtained another way.

She said goodbye and walked swiftly to the elevator. Her eyes scanned the hallway for cameras, and there were none to be seen. It was only in the entrance foyer that a single video box was pointing down primarily toward the front door. She would have to figure out a way to re-direct that spying lens or find another way to hardly be seen by it, at the time of the heist.

Ariella went out the entrance door, down the steps onto the Fourth Street sidewalk, and then turned left. This would take her away from the direction of the jewelry store and to the end of the block where the 125-Building terminated. She rounded the corner and strolled slowly along the edge of the property noticing that unlike the dressed-up façade in the front, the side wall was of plain red brick construction.

"Good." Her comment was a whisper. "That almost certainly means the other side, butting up against 101 Fourth Street will very likely be the same type of brickwork." She sauntered casually to where her Subaru was parked three blocks away. Once in her car, she perused the area and noticed again that although there were a few people out and about, no one was paying any attention to her.

Ariella pulled off the wig and shook her head, causing her blond trusses to fall to her shoulders. Looking in the mirror and after moistening a tissue with saliva, she slowly removed the beauty spot from her cheek. It was time to get going.

Now at home in the early afternoon, Ariella recalled how productive her day had been so far.

First, it was sitting in the coffee shop that morning and her noticing the height discrepancy between the two structures on Fourth Street. While downtown she bought a whole lot of useful disguises which would be essential for carrying out the heist. Later, it was getting into the 125-Building, having been let in through the locked foyer door by a kindly gentleman. Then there was Dora, so lonely and trusting, who invited a total stranger in for tea and asked her to visit again the following Saturday.

Ariella had effectuated a way to get a good look at the bathroom which could potentially be the best access point into the ceiling area above the store of the neighboring property. But most exciting of all was that the apartment would be empty, because Dora was going to Florida on Thursday, June 30th and would be returning a week later, on July 7th.

The pulchritudinous plotter reminded herself again, next week when visiting, she would need to find a way to get a duplicate keycard for the foyer door of the 125-Building and a key for the front door of the apartment. Maybe these items could be grabbed sometime on Saturday afternoon. If they were discovered to be missing, the old lady could easily get others from the building management. No doubt being somewhat absent-minded, these were misplaced by Dora more than once in the past.

It was now apparent that to undertake the rescue of nana's valuables or items of similar value, it would have to be soon, almost certainly during the time Dora was away in Florida.

CHAPTER 5

Sunday Morning, June 19th

T he gorgeous girl was lazily sprawled across her couch with the sun coming in from a large window on the south side of her house. Purdy was fast asleep alongside her.

Ariella thought about the availability of the apartment and realized the break-in could easily take place from Dora's bathroom. If there was ample time to work slowly and methodically, getting in from the ceiling above the store could work out well. Because she did not need to lease an adjacent space to use as a base from which to operate, there would be no record of her being a tenant anywhere close by. It was not her intent to physically get inside Barnwell's store, a drone would be used to snag, drag and grab the jewelry.

There was one thing the cool-contriver was not sure about regarding the brick construction of the two downtown buildings. The concern was, these might have double walls or thick cinderblocks or have been put together in a way that was too difficult to breach. She sat down at her computer and went online to research how the average four-story low-rise in New Jersey was built back in the early 1900s.

To her joy, she found many were made by using a basic steel frame structure, and within this steel, single-width brick walls were added as exterior integuments. Hopefully, this was the way these two were built. She decided that while breaking through from the apartment if a dual wall or some other type of obstacle was encountered, she would close it all up and abandon this approach for the heist. If there were any steel beams or columns in the exact spot of the opening, she would start again just to the side of that impediment or simply not go through with the venture.

In the double garage which adjoined the house, her car was parked on one side and of course, her workshop took up the rest of the space. This well-lit working area was where she tinkered with and built mechanical items including drones, robots, radio-controlled cars, and more.

Ariella knew that after slicing through the walls and robbing the store it would be imperative the bricks got restored to virtually what they were before. This way the authorities would be hard-pressed to find any point of entry or exit. She would also do her best to pin the heist on others to really confuse the police. For this, the gifted girl had some interesting ideas on how to plant misleading evidence.

In an upright steel cabinet, there were a variety of power tools including a rechargeable drill and a plug-in electric drill. For the heist, the plug-in one would be best because it would have the power to bore into the cement between the bricks to create a starting point for a mortar-raking blade. In addition, her kit would have a 4" diameter thin cutting wheel which could be installed to the electric drill. With this, the grout between the 8" square bathroom wall tiles could be cut away. She could grind out the grout first, crack the tiles with a hammer and then pull off the pieces.

Ariella understood, once the tiles and that section of the drywall were removed, she would likely encounter one or more 2" x 4" wooden studs. The 4" cutting wheel on her drill or even her reciprocating saw would be able to cut out any studs. But just in case, a small hand saw would also be brought with her. Various accessories including bits, routers, and more were stored in a drawer. She picked up a ¾" diameter, 6" long masonry bit and she tightened this into the chuck of her electric drill.

A long extension cord was plugged into an outlet in her garage, and unwinding it, she took this outside to the back yard together with two screwdrivers. Also taken out back was her electric reciprocating saw, a small face mask, and plastic goggles for eye protection. Ariella's house was built perhaps some 90 years before, and the garage was made of a single-course brick construction supported by vertical block columns, each about four feet apart. This presented an excellent testing site, allowing her to experiment with cutting into such a wall and carefully removing a given number of bricks, but still leaving these together as a set. Once behind the garage, she crouched down not far off the ground next to the wall.

The red bricks were of a standard size, being 8" long by 4" wide and 2¼" high. A segment of these needed to come out which would be three horizontally and four rows down. This would give her an opening approximately 24" across by 11" deep. To do this, four holes would first need to be made, one in each corner of the designated brick-set. She had already installed the masonry bit, and holding the drill with both hands, bored four holes into the mortar.

Ariella then disconnected the drill from the extension cord and plugged in her reciprocating saw which had in it a 6" long carbide cutting blade. She pushed it through the hole in the top right-hand corner. The saw made a scraping noise as it moved vertically downward, raking its way through the mortar as it went alongside the first brick. Thereafter she cut directly through the second one until the blade came to mortar again, which she sliced into, and the girl then cut through the middle of the next brick. Eventually, she had gone past four of these, for a vertical travel distance of about 11". The blade was forced into the top left-hand hole and the saw went vertically downward like before until it had cut through four rows.

It was now time for some horizontal action. She moved the reciprocating saw from left to right along the bottom of the brick-set and it abraded easily through the cement mixture, traveling a distance of three bricks which was about 24". Making the two vertical cuts and the horizontal one, took about four minutes to accomplish. The blade was then inserted into the top left-hand hole, and she cut through the mortar along the top of this group from left to right. As the saw finished traveling the 24" distance, the brick-set came loose, dropping down about ⅜" with a dull thud.

She picked up the two screwdrivers and maneuvered these under the assemblage which had just been separated from the wall. All twelve bricks still joined together, were lifted and jiggled out. They came away as one piece, and it felt to her that this weighed about forty-five pounds.

There was now a void about 11" deep by 24" wide. This size aperture would be cut out of both the jewelry store and apartment building walls.

When removing the two groups of bricks on the day of the robbery, Ariella would need to be careful not to drop these down into the space between the two structures, that is, if there was any kind of meaningful separation there. She would not know whether there would be a large or small clearance until the wall of the 125-building had been cut open.

While she did not intend to climb through the holes during the heist, she would want to look inside the main sales area. Ariella found her head and shoulders could fit through the 24" opening in her garage wall with ease. It paid to be of a slender build!

The test-cutting was over, so the extension cord, her drill, and the reciprocating saw were all taken back to the workshop. At this juncture, the wall had to be closed by putting the group of bricks back into place like she would have to do after the burglary was completed. It would need to be sealed up in an undetectable manner.

In her garage was a nearly full bag of granular mortar-cement left over from a prior project. She put a small amount of this into a bucket and added a little water, all the while mixing it to a thick consistency with a wooden paint stick. A few teaspoons of instant coffee powder were added to discolor it, so that it would take on an 'old look'. This way it would not look 'new' and too 'white' when it dried. Ariella took the bucket with its pulp-like contents outside, together with an empty plastic zip-seal bag, a pair of scissors, a trowel plus two ⅜" diameter x 4" long dowel stick pieces.

With her backyard garden hose, she wet the exposed bricks in the wall. Then lifting the heavy brick-set which had just been cut out, this was maneuvered into the opening. Using one of the screwdrivers, she pried up the left side of the group and slid one of the 4" dowel sticks into place. Then with the screwdriver, the right-hand side was raised, and the other short stick was inserted. The weight of it all was now resting on the two dowels.

Ariella filled the plastic zip-seal with some of the pre-mixed mortar, removed any excess air, and then closed the bag by pressing on the strip along the top. With a pair of scissors, she snipped off a small opening from one of the lower corners and squeezed the bag causing the pasty substance to eject out of the hole. Moving this along, while pushing the 'goop' into the spaces on the sides, along the bottom, and on top of the bricks, it reminded her somewhat of decorating a cake!

Because the mixture was of a thick consistency it did not run down the vertical openings but stayed in place quite well. Any of the excess compound was smoothed off with her trowel. The two dowel sticks prevented the segment from squashing down on the mush and forcing it out.

Ariella waited about fifteen minutes for it to partially dry, then she took a ½" diameter drill bit and wrapped a piece of thin cardboard around it. This was used as a 'pointing tool' to make grooves between the bricks before the cement hardened, and it provided a nice concave channel appearance to the new mortar, allowing it to match the rest of the wall. With this part now done, she gathered up her utensils.

Once back in the garage, it was under the workbench for her, and using the trowel, some of the thick mush which oozed out on that side was smoothed off, then furrowed to the 'pointing' finish. By cutting out the bricks and then cementing these back again, the testing phase of opening and closing a wall was successfully completed. Now the mortar-maestro felt ready to deal with the two old buildings downtown.

The bucket and trowel were washed with water, then left to air dry. Ariella went into the house and made her way to the bathroom to get a bottle of clear nail polish and a bottle of white nail polish. She took these into her workshop, poured a tiny amount of the white into the bottle of clear, and stirred this with a long toothpick. By mixing the two, a frosty-clear concoction was created. Using a small artist's brush, she painted a 1" square of this blend onto a piece of flat glass.

After ten minutes it was dry, and looking through the translucent mixture, light could be seen, but no definition of anything else. Great! This would help the heist be more successful. Ariella went back inside the house, got a large duffle bag, and took this into the garage.

The Heistess placed into the duffle most of the items she would require to pull off this caper.

- A trowel and some zip-seal bags. Two pairs of ladies' gardening gloves with rubber-grip coating. The bottle of frosty-clear nail polish. A Phillips screwdriver, two flat screwdrivers, a pair of pliers, a utility knife with spare blades, and a small pair of scissors.

- A large brown paper bag with powered mortar taped securely closed. A few squares of paper towel. An electric drill and her reciprocating saw for cutting through the mortar and bricks. A 6" long carbide cutting blade plus two spares. A variety of standard masonry drill bits of varying lengths and two 4" diameter cutting wheels.

- A 25' extension cord, a wire-framed work lamp with its long cord and 60-watt bulb, a spool of narrow, strong nylon rope, a roll of 2" masking tape. A few large sheets of thin, clear polyethylene plastic.

- A can of spray adhesive, a small hand saw with two spare blades, a box of different-sized nails, and assorted screws. Also included were some fishing hooks, a 5" long flashlight, a small jar of instant coffee, a tightly fitting white plastic shower cap, and some construction-grade face masks to protect against dust and dirt particles.

- A spare rechargeable battery for the aerial-robot as well as its plug-in charging unit. And then very important: She wrote a reminder note to pack a 13" x 26" thin plywood piece as soon as this was painted and ready.

After all these necessities were in the duffle, it was very heavy and quite bulky to lift, so she decided to remove a few of the items. Out came the electric drill, her reciprocating saw, the paper bag of powdered mortar, the pliers, the three screwdrivers, and the 25' extension cord. It would be best to take these items with her in a large over-the-shoulder tote bag this coming Saturday when visiting Dora, and maybe this could be hidden under a couch or elsewhere in the apartment while the old lady was not looking.

By transporting these implements ahead of time, on the night of the heist, the duffle bag and its contents would be easier to carry and a lot less cumbersome. There was now plenty of space in the duffle for the all-important drone and her FPV (First Person View) video headset which would show her where she was flying inside the store. Ariella also planned to bring a backpack with her to carry home some of the loot. A mixing container for the mortar would not need to be brought in, because Dora would no doubt have many large bowls in her kitchen which could be used for this purpose. Also, there would most certainly be a broom, a dustpan, and a vacuum cleaner in the apartment.

Ariella planned to install onto the aerial-thief two cameras allowing it 'see' forward and backward and to keep track of everything as it flew around the store on its multiple missions.

Next was to think about how to smash the glass on top of the display cases. This would require something heavy, and perhaps a small mallet could do the trick.

◆◆◆◆◆

Later that same day from a storage cabinet in her garage, Ariella took a four-rotor drone which was acquired a few months before. It was not very large, being about 10" square by 4" high. It would need to be fitted out with some special features if it was to be her 'accomplice' in this event.

Her plan was formulating fast, and she did not personally have to get into the store to rob the place. All that was needed was for her to skillfully guide the little quad-copter inside, after flying it through the two wall gaps and down past the opening in the ceiling where she would have removed one acoustic panel. Then with its sophisticated cameras, special hooks, and possibly other linkages, the craft would be able to pick up different types of jewelry.

Ariella changed the existing camera on the drone for two which had excellent night vision capability and good gimbals on them for steadiness. With this, she would be able to see in any light conditions. She wanted to execute the heist after nine o'clock when it was dark.

Any residual illumination coming in through the windows from the street outside would enhance the night observance images and this would be helpful.

Brightness inside the store could be increased, if necessary, by dangling into the main sales area her wire-framed work lamp with its long cord and 60-watt bulb.

Besides its special cameras, Ariella started working on equipping her brazen-buccaneer with some extra features comprising of retrieval accessories, which could be interchanged as and when these were needed. There would be various clip-on/clip-off attachments that fitted a special bracket made by her, and this would be affixed underneath the featherweight-flyer.

▪ The First of these extra features was a 6" length of thin wire which would dangle below. On the end of this wire, was a fishing hook, and this would allow her to snag and lift up various articles like gold chains, watches, rings, and bracelets.

▪ Ariella worked on making a 1" x 1" x 1" soft rubber cube. This unique piece would be held in place by the hook and located beneath the drone. On the underside of the rubber cube was some very sticky transfer tape with a protective release liner. This liner could be peeled off which would expose the adhesive, when necessary to gather up any difficult objects that could not be picked up by the hook.

▪ Taking a 12" long artist's brush, she sand-papered the stem just a little so that it would insert into a bracket under the drone. Now she could paint any messages or add color within the store onto small objects. A few other similar brushes were set aside to take with her on the all-important night.

Busying herself at the vice in her workshop she made a cleverly fashioned bracket to fit under the roving egg-beater. It was primarily a tiny clamping device to hold the wire with its hook and to also hold the artist's brush. This bracket was now attached to the machine's belly with four screws. The Klepto-Kopter was ready!

Ariella would be wearing her FPV video headset when guiding the avian-acrobat into the store, and all activities would be observed from right in front of her eyes because the two onboard cameras would show her exactly where the drone was going. Being as adept as she was at flying small rotorcraft in confined spaces, Ariella knew this could really work. But some practice was still needed.

CHAPTER 6

The Week of June 20th

During this week Ariella went to her job daily as usual. She was always on time and left her office well after five o'clock on most days, being conscientious to a fault.

On Tuesday, June 21st she took her car to work instead of commuting by bus as was normally the case. At the end of the workday, it took her about an hour to drive to a shopping center quite some distance from her home. This was just a precaution because she was paranoid that after the robbery the authorities would be looking in the immediate area for any clues as to who did it. Her objective was to visit a Home Depot and buy some tiles.

Turning down any help from eager store personnel, she found her way to the section where wall accessories and other similar items were kept. Upon opening a pack of twelve 8" square white ceramic tiles, they appeared to be identical to those on Dora's bathroom walls. Checking them against the pictures from her phone, there was no doubt these were the same as Dora's. Even though the apartment building was old it occurred to her, at some point in the recent past, a few upgrades were made to the 125-Building and its bathrooms.

Ariella knew a few pieces would likely be broken when she made the hole in the wall, but with these new tiles, any damaged ones could easily be replaced. A tube of tile adhesive and a small container of grout were next on the list, and easy to find. With the special coloring agent – her use of instant coffee – she could dirty up the grout with just a quick finger rub to make it match the rest of the wall.

Upon leaving the store it was the same long drive home, and once there, she packed the adhesive, the grout, and eight tiles into the duffle bag.

◆◆◆◆◆

It was now Wednesday evening, June 22nd and five days since Ariella first went into the 125-Building to meet with Dora. After spending many productive hours at work, she had just arrived home. Since the tiles were purchased the day before, she was now able to delete the pictures of Dora's bathroom from her phone.

The next order of business was to start practicing with the drone in her garage to see how well the hooks and other accessories would work. She put on the FPV video headset and placed some of her own jewelry onto the workbench. Sitting on a stool at the far end of the garage, the maneuvering of the hover-bird began. It was able to hook and lift up a necklace quite easily and transport it to her location.

Once Ariella broke the glass on top of the display cabinets in the store, the sparkling valuables would be lying out exposed, covered with broken glass, and ready to be picked up. So, to make it more realistic and to practice these moves, she took a piece of glass off a shelf in her workshop and wrapped it in several layers of newspaper. This was leaned against a wall by the floor, stamped on a couple of times, and then the paper was carefully opened. Some of the large and small broken pieces of glass were placed at random angles on top of her jewelry which was lying on the workbench.

She walked back to the other end of the garage and once again sat down on the stool. The craft was flown with its hook dangling below, over to the workbench, where the curved metal hitch was able to move the pieces of glass out of the way as it snagged a ring off the tabletop. To Ariella's delight, she discovered that two rings, a gold chain, and a pearl necklace could all be scooped up on the same hook. Awesome! She sent it back and was able to lift up four delicate wrist bracelets at one time. Her excitement was now building at how easily multiple items were able to be gathered at once. This type of efficiency would cut down on time, on battery usage and would make the heist go a lot quicker which would mean less exposure for her.

Within the assortment on the workbench, there were also three wristwatches, and these were able to be captured with ease. But because the hook was of the medium-sized fishing type, it could not get more than one timepiece per trip. She would have to remember on the night of the heist that getting watches would take longer than some of the other items, but a larger hook could be used if needed.

At that point, Ariella wanted to try to pick up a segment of broken glass. To do so one of the soft rubber cubes was attached to the hook on the end of the 6" wire. She peeled off the release liner leaving the adhesive exposed and then guided the fluttering-flyer over to the workbench. It landed on top of a piece of glass, but when raising up the little chopper, the sliver remained behind.

She dropped the drone down with a bit more force and then sped up the rotors to create an instant lift. This time the shard adhered to the rubber pad, staying on until the hovering-helo was flown over to where she was sitting on the opposite side of the garage. Great! Similar clear fragments were to be carried on the notable night, and this method of getting these into her possession seemed to work just fine.

Ariella needed to return the glass to the workbench, so she piloted the machine back with the crystalline component dangling off its rubber pad. After bumping the transparent piece a couple of times into the side of her workbench it dropped off, breaking apart a little more as it landed on the floor. Perfect! This important part of the robbery, 'transporting smooth thin objects back and forth' would work out well.

So far, all her practicing was done with the lights on. Now it was time to see how these procedures could function in a darkened room. She took some black paper and covered the window panels on the garage doors and the window on the side door. After mounting two small LEDs to the whirlybird's underside and activating these by way of a manually operated switch, she turned off the overhead lights in the garage.

Her operating skills could now be tested in this blacked-out area, using just the LEDs to help her find her way. This seemed to turn out well, and it provided much-added confidence she could pull off this caper even if it was necessary to work in tenebrous conditions.

For another forty minutes, the experimenting continued in the dark, with and without her FVP video headset being used. Jewelry was collected from many different angles using the 6" wire with its handy hook.

After turning the lights back on, she took the 12" long artist's brush and attached it horizontally so that it protruded well beyond the edge of the drone. Dipping the bristles into some white latex paint, the craft was flown to the other end of the garage where the aeronautical artist practiced painting a few tight circles and other shapes on the wall and onto parts of the ceiling joists. Ariella needed to make sure she could maneuver well enough to make coloring any small objects work out successfully. The results were good, and when this experiment was completed, she cleaned the brush with water. It was now ready to be put into the duffle bag.

After the rehearsing was all done in the garage, she packed everything away and removed the black paper from the windows. The bits of broken glass were gathered up and thrown away. She would break another piece if more training was necessary before the big day.

◆◆◆◆◆

It was eight o'clock on this same Wednesday evening, June 22nd and Ariella wanted to test her next change of appearance outfit. This one would be used when visiting the jewelry store on the upcoming Saturday morning, June 25th.

The retail operation needed to be evaluated as soon as possible but not too close to the date of the transgression. The night on which the heist would take place was now being dictated by the period during which Dora would be away in Florida. An exact date and time would have to be picked soon. When visiting the Fourth Street Jewelers and Gold Exchange in the very near future, a different look was required to the one for the 'Mandy Moore' persona. Now at home, the Heistess perused various disguises bought on the prior weekend and she took out the short, curly, charcoal-grey wig from the bag.

While at the party store, a face-putty makeup kit was one of the items purchased. The young beauty sat down in front of the mirror and started slightly changing the shape of her nose. From a perfectly straight sharp nose, she broadened it just a bit and gave it a slight hump in the middle, then put the brown contact lenses into her eyes.

Ariella wanted to look much older and to do so, two subtle but apparent forehead wrinkles were added. She put on some large oversized cheap earrings and darkened her eyebrows like before. When the charcoal-grey curly mop was pulled over her tied-up hair, the difference in her countenance was quite remarkable.

She managed to skillfully cover her eyebrows with the skin-colored putty so that only two thin dark lines were showing, a far cry from her normal look. Taking a selfie would make sure she remembered what to do with the makeup, to become 'Raquel Santos Gomez' in a few days' time. Ariella was fairly fluent in speaking Spanish and could put on an accent to sound like someone who was struggling to speak English. In her theater acting days, this type of speech-hesitation was used on countless occasions. It always sounded very convincing because a string of Spanish words could be thrown in by her while 'trying' to talk English.

On her computer, she created business cards for this new woman, and they were printed on a couple of sheets of white index board in the name of…

Raquel Santos Gomez
Wedding Planner / Planificador de la Boda

These were carefully cut apart using a utility knife and a metal ruler. By doing it this way and not using a pair of scissors, the edges came out straight and square. The cards featured a fake cell phone number, and if anyone dialed those digits it would not matter if it wasn't genuine. She just needed to visit the store, check it out, and leave. However, on the cards, there were two different addresses.

One was an authentic location in the USA belonging to a residential high-rise in a town an hour away, near to the recently visited Home Depot. But there was no suite designation. If law enforcement tried to track down that apartment building, they would find it but not be able to catch her, because this woman would not have been there anyway.

The second address on the business cards was in Ecuador. This too was real, but it was also inadequate. If asked by anyone why there were two locales, she would say (in her best English-Spanish accent) that her wedding planning undertakings were done in both countries, having clients in America and in Ecuador. There was a ring of international romanticism to it!

By the time someone would realize Raquel Santos Gomez was not an actual person, 'Raquel' would be long gone, and her face would not appear anywhere. And even if the authorities investigated whether she did or did not exist, it would not necessarily mean this individual was involved in the robbery.

Ariella felt the business cards were important to give away on Saturday, primarily to validate her being in the store. She wanted to hand out at least one, to confuse anyone following up leads in the days after the heist. A Wedding Planner would have many reasons to be visiting a jewelry retail establishment. These would include suggesting any special items for the bride and the groom, for any of the in-laws or for the wedding entourage.

Ariella had a pair of red narrow-framed glasses to wear with the 'Raquel' disguise if needed.

The business cards were carefully wiped clean of any fingerprints before these were put into her purse. She did not want to wear gloves when visiting the store because that might look suspicious. There was another way of not leaving a trace, in the event she inadvertently touched a surface.

At this stage, the face putty and other makeup was removed, and she was now confident with her good disguise which was ready to use in Barnwell's place on Saturday.

◆◆◆◆◆

At nine-fifteen on this same Wednesday night, Ariella was deep in thought going over the events of this past Saturday June 18th when she sat in the coffee shop checking out the area. It was very apparent how busy the Fourth Street Jewelers and Gold Exchange was on that day, and it would likely be just as crowded there on Saturday June 25th. Her intent was to videotape everything, utilizing a brooch-camera which would be pinned to the lapel of her jacket. A year before at a party, she worked with this hidden spy-device, and now it could be put to more serious use. She was not an electronics whiz-kid for nothing!

While going into Barnwell's business on Saturday morning, this would be in the 'Raquel' disguise. Following that she would go home and change to the 'Mandy' look for the afternoon when visiting Dora. Ariella understood a bit of running up and down would be required, but all this effort would be worth it.

There was certain to be some type of camcorder surveillance in the store, and after the break-in, the police would most assuredly be studying all DVDs covering many hours leading up to the date of the heist. Dora was going to Florida on Thursday, June 30th which was just over seven days from now. The Heistess wished there was more time between her visit to the *venue of valuables* on this coming Saturday, and the date of the robbery.

But that was not to be. With the old lady leaving so soon, this would only provide about a week and a half for her to be totally ready. In the back of her mind, she tentatively decided to execute the jewelry recovery expedition on Sunday night July 3rd.

There were two vital reasons why a disguise was necessary when casing the joint in a few days' time.

The first was that the owner Hunt Barnwell met her recently under very contentious circumstances. This was of course when she confronted him after her grandmother's heirlooms were unjustly taken. If he saw her in his store he would be riled up, and once the thievery happened, he would remember she was there.

Second, to further justify any suspicion being thrown on her (if she did not appear dressed in a misleading way), when the security tapes were reviewed, Hunt would recognize her. He would tell the police he saw her snooping around his place of business and now he could confirm this. One of the most obvious suspects to fit this crime would be her.

CHAPTER 7

Friday, June 24th

It was a week before the three-day weekend marking America's Independence Day.

Ariella asked to take the day off work and her supervisor agreed to her request. She was up and out of bed early and after showering, getting dressed, and feeding Purdy, it was time to head out in her Subaru. There were quite a few important things to put in place before the heist.

At just past seven in the morning, having driven from her home to the downtown area, she left her car at a meter and then walked to a community park. Only a handful of people were out at that time. Over her shoulder was a canvas tote in which were some kraft paper bags, poly gloves, a few zip-seals, and some personal items.

Two joggers were making their way across the grounds and there were three other people out walking their dogs. It was a surprisingly cool morning considering it was the middle of summer. There were a series of wire wastebaskets mounted onto short metal posts dotted around the area into which most responsible people deposited their garbage. Because it was still so early, none had been emptied from the day before and many were more than half filled with trash.

Ariella sat quietly on a bench, sipping a cup of coffee purchased from a food cart nearby. Having also bought a pretzel from that vendor, she was nibbling slowly on it. Her dark glasses were not only shielding her eyes from the morning sun, but they allowed her to glance around in many directions without anyone knowing what was being observed by her. An object of interest in one of the wastebaskets which was about twenty feet away, got her attention. She put her hand into the tote bag and very unobtrusively slipped a thin, clear poly-glove onto her right hand, gulped down the last of her beverage, and slowly stood up.

There was nobody to be seen in the immediate area, so Ariella casually walked over to the wastebasket with her empty coffee cup and deposited this into the receptacle. As her hand went in it came out with another Styrofoam cup which had been dropped there the day before and this was put into one of her paper bags.

After that, she walked out of the park and headed to a nearby bus station. The place was still a mess because no one was there yet to clean it up. Inside was a worker with headphones on, and he seemed to be dozing in his booth.

Making her way around the dirty area, she spotted a few cigarette stubs lying in a corner. Perfect! The sleeping attendant saw nothing as Ariella, still wearing the glove, bent down and picked up four cigarette butts, and placed these into one of the small zip-seal bags. It was eight-twenty when the strategizing scout wandered a couple of blocks down the road to a busy corner gas station, and going directly into the unisex bathroom, locked the door. She started looking for something special on the floor by crouching and shuffling along on her haunches. The last thing she wished to do was to put her hands and knees down, and crawl around!

While the bathroom was likely cleaned in the past day or two, Ariella was counting on the edges not being swept or mopped. With a pair of tweezers, she pinched a tiny clump of dust and dirt from a corner, and with it came a few human hairs. These were placed into a small zip-seal bag. Then it was time to examine the inside of the trash bin. Ugh! With a new plastic glove on her hand, she poked around moving many damp, crumpled, tan-colored paper towels out of the way until what she was looking for suddenly appeared. A white, used Kleenex tissue from someone who had blown their nose! Gross! But this was very important, and it was deposited into its own zip-top bag. She removed the glove, dumped it into the garbage bin, and then washed and dried her hands.

After leaving the gas station restroom, she bought a chocolate bar then went to her car and headed for home. Ariella took the paper bag which held the used coffee cup and taped it closed. This was placed into a small cardboard box together with the three zip-seal bags – one containing the human hairs, the other with the cigarette butts, and the third with the used Kleenex tissue.

Two more misleading pieces were needed and then she would be ready to proceed with her outrageous and nefarious deed! For one of these items, it would mean a visit to a wrecked car site. After that, it was about finding the last article with an unsuspecting person's fingerprints on it.

It was 2:00 p.m. and almost time for Ariella to go and visit the junkyard. However, to avoid the problem of showing her identification, she sat down at her computer and produced some new business cards…

Tiffany Crawford
Licensed Beautician
Tiffany's Hair Salon

On the cards was an address and phone number which related to nothing but looked genuine.

She tied her hair up, put on a long-hair brunette wig and this time did not add the beauty spot onto her cheek. The brown contact lenses were used again, and a baseball cap was put over the wig. The outfit worn was a casual shirt, a pair of torn jeans, and pink-framed sunglasses.

Ariella took a teaspoon from the kitchen, a small zip-seal bag, and a pair of thin gardening gloves. She emptied a small travel sized pump-bottle of hairspray and rinsed this out thoroughly, then filled it with water, screwed the spray-top back on, and put this bottle and the other items into her handbag. She got into the Subaru and drove for over an hour to a large auto scrapyard.

Upon arriving there, the only place to leave her car was in a dusty, sandy parking lot. "Good thing it is not raining," was her quiet comment, "or this would be a muddy mess!" She popped a stick of gum into her mouth and proceeded to the entrance gate where a grumpy, burly guard was checking a fuel pump that a customer just bought, and he was signing off on the receipt the man had in his hand.

The guard waved her in with a grunt, "The counter is through those doors and to the right."

Once inside, there was a dog-eared, dirty, records book to be filled out with her details. She wrote *Tiffany Crawford* together with the fake address and phone number appearing on her business cards.

"I.D. please," said the lady behind the counter in a raspy voice, crushing out a cigarette into an overflowing ashtray. Her face was blotchy and heavily lined.

Ariella rummaged in her bag and took out her wallet.

She made sure not to have any credit cards or her driver's license with her, these were locked in her car. In a convincing Southern accent and chewing her gum said, "Can y'all believe it, mah eye-deee and credi-cards are in mah other purse!" She searched in her bag again in an energetic way.

"Oh sheee-it!" Ariella exclaimed as if mad at herself. "Wait, ahh have right heeere a binness card for y'all," making sure to take out a stack of ten so that the lady would not think a card was being handed to her which might belong to someone else. "Heeere," she said, handing it over.

"How ya gonna pay?" asked Raspy Voice. "I cannot take a credit card without I.D."

"Ahh will pay cee-ash. Ahh only needs a tail-light assembly for a fo-y'old Wrangler."

Raspy looked at her and at the business card. "What's a pretty girl like you, a beautician, doing pulling parts off a car?"

"It's for maah boyfreee-end," she replied, chewing on her gum casually. "He wooodda done dis heees-seeeIf, but hee-ees ah-work t'day."

Satisfied, Raspy said, "Okay. Go ahead. You want to be in the third aisle over, turn left after you walk through that door." Then she yelled, "Hey Johnno! Take this gal and show her where she can find parts for Jeeps."

Ariella quietly said, "No wonder you speak with such a hoarse crackle. Between the smoking and the loud yelling, it is amazing you can talk at all!"

An overweight and awful specimen named Johnno came shuffling into the office from the car area outside. He wore scruffy, old denim jeans which were all but falling down, and a T-Shirt that had seen better days. As he flicked the ash off his cigarette he glanced up and saw this striking beauty. His pock-marked face lit up.

With her long brunette-hair disguise Ariella was lovely to look at due to her fine facial features, her full lips, and perfect nose. Johnno immediately straightened, pulled his pants up a bit, and beckoned her to follow him. He tried asking her mundane questions to strike up a conversation, but she would have none of this. It most times irritated her when handsome, wealthy men tried to hit on her. Certainly, no half-baked junkyard dog should be attempting to charm her!

"What color is your Jeep?" He was again trying to get a dialogue going between them.

"Theee-ats nunna ya'alls binness!" she snapped. "Just sho' me which row to look eeen and thee-en leee... me alone!"

"Hey, you Southern girls sure are snarky!" said the ungainly and maladroit oaf.

Suddenly out came her cell phone and she pretended to dial a quick number. "Hello, 911? Ahh want to report a sexual atteee-ack. Ahh am at the Long Whee-els Car Parts Yee-ard and I am bin' chased by a meee-ann named Johnno. Please hurry, hee-es attacked me, and I managed to git away but ahh am sure he wee-el fine' me any minna' neee-ow!" Ariella sounded breathless in a well-trained, on-stage, panicky tone.

Johnno seemed startled, hesitated for a couple of seconds, and then ran off as fast as he could, disappearing among the hundreds of wrecked cars, hoping he could hide long enough for the police to not find him.

Her ploy worked exactly as anticipated because a lout like this would certainly have a criminal record. He would likely have one or more outstanding warrants and did not need any kind of confrontation with the authorities.

The beautician-in-disguise smiled. *She* was the one here under an assumed name and was preparing for a major break-in, even though no crime had yet been committed. No one should be questioning *her!* But then again, she hadn't really dialed 911.

Ariella did not want to continue walking in the main lane from the front office, for there were quite a few people not too far away. It was best for her to go down the next aisle. Now in the second row, out of her handbag came a pair of thin gardening gloves. She slipped these on because leaving her fingerprints in any vehicle would not be a wise thing to do, and she also didn't want to cut or hurt her hands in any way.

Seeking out a suitable wreck was very important, and fortunately, almost in front of her, there was one which seemed promising. A badly damaged car would have something extremely valuable in it for her to use in the upcoming smash-n-grab event.

She glanced around to make sure no one was watching before pulling on the hatch of a red Mazda. The doors were too damaged to open. She slid inside from the rear, and crawled to the back seat, then studied the front section where the driver and possibly a passenger would have been sitting.

Looking everywhere including on the console and on the deployed airbags, there was no evidence of what was really needed.

Ariella exited the auto and continued walking down the second line of wrecks, occasionally peering in the dirty windows of one vehicle here and another one there. No smashed auto could be found which would be suitable for her. Moving along, she switched lanes again because two people were coming toward her, a man and his young son. Ariella did not want a discussion with anyone, and the fewer people who saw her there, the better.

Now in the third row, a badly ruined Ford Escort appeared a few yards ahead. The front doors were buckled but the posterns seemed to be intact. Yet she struggled to get either of them open even though the gardening gloves with their tiny rubber dots provided some extra grip.

Giving the left-hand rear door one more tug, it suddenly gave way and opened, nearly sending her tumbling to the ground. She got inside the back of the car and inspected the front seats. There it was, blood, and what a shame because the driver must have been injured or worse.

There were some red smears on the airbag which would not be helpful to her. But a dried, congealed, heavy trail had trickled down the side of the center console. Ariella opened her handbag, took out the water-filled spray bottle and lightly sprayed the blood area. After waiting for about a minute, then taking the teaspoon from her bag, she scraped it vertically up the side of the console from the floor mat to the top. By doing so, some of the now-moistened blood was able to be gathered up. This was repeated five times, and when done, the whole teaspoon was almost filled, and it represented an ample amount for her well-thought-out plan to work. The teaspoon was carefully placed in a zip-seal and this was put in her handbag. She got out, closed the door, and headed to the junkyard entrance.

At the front desk, she told Raspy Voice, "Ahh cou-nna fin' what I came hee-eer for."

The resourceful scavenger walked out of the office, and with a quick "goodbye" to the guard, got into her car.

After removing the wig it was time to go home. The drive there was uneventful.

Now in her house, Ariella sat down at the dining room table and made further notes about the heist, the date for which was rapidly approaching.

Part of her strategy for collecting the different items which contained other people's fingerprints and DNA, was that if at some point she got arrested and accused of this crime, there would be so much confusing evidence, they would have a hard time pinning this on her. She was hoping that in a court of law, this could all provide *reasonable doubt* in which case she might very likely get away with this act of larceny.

It was a little after six o'clock when hunger dictated it was time to put together a light dinner. Later in the evening, two drama shows on TV held her interest, and these were followed by a half-hour comedy. Purdy sat on her lap most of the time and at one point Ariella fell asleep on the couch. It was almost midnight when she wearily stumbled to bed. The next day would be an important one and it was now time to get some good rest.

CHAPTER 8

Saturday Morning, June 25th

Ariella knew that in a week and a day, she would be executing her break-in plan. Today she would be at the Fourth Street Jewelers and Gold Exchange in the morning and visiting Dora in the afternoon.

She needed to get into the jewelry shop soon, but doing so only a week before was not a good thing. By being in disguise and not drawing too much attention to herself, the hope was she would not become a suspect. But even if that were the case, would they ever find Raquel Santos Gomez?

The lovely lass sat in front of the mirror in her bedroom and started putting together the 'Raquel' look just like the rehearsal a few days before. Using her face-putty kit she changed the shape of her nose slightly, following the picture. Her nose was broadened a bit by adding a slight hump in the middle, following her prior practice.

She created subtle wrinkles on her forehead, darkened her eyebrows with a make-up pencil, and then with skin-colored putty, covered parts of her eyebrows and this had the effect of narrowing them. Ariella put on the large cheap earrings, perfect to use for this visit. She tied her hair up, donned the curly charcoal-grey wig, and added some bright red lipstick which created a totally different appearance to her normal quiet color. The brown contact lenses were once again put into her eyes.

If stopped by the Police for any remote reason, she could always say all this makeup was because she was rehearsing for a play. Not too convincing, but it could work. Her 'Raquel' cards were already in the business card holder in her purse, all carefully wiped beforehand so as to leave no trace of her ever having handled them. The 'Raquel' selfie was then deleted from her phone.

Ariella did not want to take the chance of her fingerprints being left anywhere in the store. It was essential there were only the prints of the dozens of customers who had been there. But with gloves on, even elegant dress gloves to match her outfit, it might still draw attention to her or make people suspicious. This would be especially so when the police were reviewing any videos pertaining to the days prior to the robbery. Even though every effort would be made by her to not touch anything, she came up with an ingenious way to not leave any trace evidence behind.

The brainy belle decided to apply clear New Skin, to the underside of the tips of her fingers. This is a medical paint-on bandage one can buy at any pharmacy. First, she painted the fingertips of one hand and dried this with her hair drier. Then she did the same to the other hand. Her prints were now non-existent, and if any of these showed, they would be muted. But more importantly, the New Skin creates a barrier that prevents natural oils from being transferred to flat surfaces, and it is mostly these oils or sweat which help the police when they are trying to identify criminals.

Ariella got dressed in an upscale pair of cream-colored slacks and a black shirt. She put on a dark tan jacket, carefully pinned her brooch camera to the lapel, and then slid her feet into a pair of shoes with heels of medium height, the type an 'older' woman would wear. She put on the narrow-style red-framed glasses which came out of her bag of disguises and was at this point ready to visit ground zero.

It was almost ten thirty when the would-be thief once again parked near the downtown area, this time on a different street to where her car had been before. It took her about twelve minutes to walk to the Fourth Street Jewelers and Gold Exchange. But just before getting there, she briefly went into a nearby alley and turned on the secret brooch camera.

Ariella strode confidently into the store, and as anticipated, it was crowded with the usual horde of Saturday customers. Some people were there to buy necklaces, rings, bracelets, and more, but many were there to sell their gold jewelry, coins, and watches. It was a pleasure for her to see the place was so full that day. There were only four helpers, including Barnwell, and they could barely keep up with the demand for attention.

At that moment a shop assistant, dressed in a business suit came out from the jewelry repair area. She was wearing the name tag, *Laura Kelly*. This clerk, emerging from the back, walked right into the retail raider and asked, "How may I help you?"

Peering at Laura through her red-framed glasses, the disguised Latina said, "Mi nombre es Raquel." She handed over one of her business cards and quickly added, "Habla usted Espanol?"

Laura looked at the business card, "Oh a Wedding Planner? That is great! I hardly speak any Spanish, do you speak English?"

The actress answered in her best English/Spanish accent, "Si, I can speek leetel Engleesh. I look for siete goll neckleeses for wedding brice-maice." She pointed in the direction of her neck with a sweeping motion of her hand.

"Yes. Si, I can help you. You want seven gold necklaces for bridesmaids?" asked the shop assistant, confirming she understood.

But before Laura could even show her anything Ariella asked, "Eees there un banyo… bathrooon I use?"

"Oh sure." She pointed to a door on the left of the entrance area. "Just look for me when you come out."

"Okk-kay. I weel fine' you. Gracias!" She headed to the bathroom watching the sales lady slip the 'Raquel' business card into her jacket pocket while walking to one of the counters to help the next impatient customer.

Once inside, Ariella locked the door, knowing there would be no cameras there. A business owner would never be so foolhardy as to risk getting sued for spying on people in so private a place as this! She took a flashlight out of her large handbag as well as a folding umbrella. Keeping it closed, she extended the handle to its full height, kicked off her shoes, and climbed on top of the toilet lid, pushing the umbrella against a ceiling tile located directly above her. It took a little effort to get the panel up due to there being fiber insulation above it and that was hampering her just a bit.

Ariella was able to raise it by at least fifteen inches and, because the insulation was laid in strips, the fiber material rose upward with the ceiling tile. She could see quite far into the empty space above, and shining her flashlight around was relieved to see SIX things that really pleased her.

First. There were no clips securing the acoustic panels. Not having to deal with any such hold-down anchors on the night of the heist would make it easier for her to lift a panel from the top. Also, when closing it all, no clips would have to be put back into place, especially considering she would be trying to reach down through a not-too-large hole in the wall.

Second. The space between the suspended ceiling and the concrete from the floor above appeared to be about 30". This would provide her with plenty of room in which to work.

Third. Although there were many wires holding up the metal grid, none were near the back wall, the likely entrance point.

Fourth. The drywall went all the way to the concrete floor and did not terminate where the suspended ceiling began. This was good because it would prevent mortar chips and dust from flying all over the dropped-ceiling panels when she cut through the outside bricks.

Fifth. The walls in the jewelry store had a plain white latex finish. This was a welcome sight because white paint would make patch-up so much easier!

Sixth. On the brown paper which was laminated to the fiber insulation strips above the ceiling tiles, there was a thin film of dust. She made a mental note to re-introduce some 'dust' onto any insulation pieces which were moved aside or cleaned off while carrying out the heist.

Ariella slipped the small flashlight into her pocket and then set her cell phone camera to 'flash' mode. While still holding the panel in its raised position with the umbrella in her left hand, she held her phone up as high as possible with her right hand and took a series of random pictures inside the open space, concentrating particularly on the rear wall area. She knew this would be the spot for breaking in from Dora's bathroom.

The crafty creature then brought down her hand which was holding the cell phone, and she lowered the umbrella. This allowed the ceiling tile to move back into its original position. Climbing down, she slid her feet into her shoes, retracted the handle of the umbrella, and put it in her handbag. Thereafter she flushed the toilet and washed her hands. Despite the New Skin on her fingers, any surfaces which might have been touched were wiped clean with a tissue, just as a precaution. After that, she unlocked the bathroom door and walked into the crowded store.

The place was of course still inundated with customers and the sales personnel were going insane. Besides being a Saturday, the key reason it was so busy was that the store bought and sold old rings, watches, gold chains, and so on. People were always seeking ways to pay off their debts, so they were constantly bringing in items of value and turning these into cash. If this was just a regular retail jewelry venue it would have been a more elegant and quieter place.

The logical lass had to keep up pretenses for just a bit longer, so she tried to get close to Laura Kelly who was now helping a lady with a bracelet while another patron was barking at her about how much a particular watch cost. With an exasperated look, the salesgirl told the man to hold on and that she would be with him shortly.

At that moment Ariella pushed her way nearer to the shop fixture behind which Ms. Kelly was standing and in a loud voice she said, "Por favor Señora, yo necesito… I need to buy the neckleeses!"

Laura looked up completely frustrated and all but shouted, "You will have to *wait!*"

Ariella turned toward the window allowing her brooch camera to photograph that part of the store: The display case which doubled as a serving counter was about seven feet from the Fourth Street window. This unit was immediately below the ceiling panel she hoped to remove after breaking through the wall above. She then made a slow, almost 360° rotation with her brooch camera, taking it all in but acting as if looking for another salesperson to help her. After swiveling around, she half threw her hands into the air much like a fed-up customer would do.

The no-assistance situation provided the perfect excuse for her to leave the shop and get out of there without being questioned about anything regarding the items for her clients. At some point soon when the police likely reviewed the videos, they would see this 'Raquel' person, and probably many others, exiting the crazy place because of bad service on that busy Saturday morning.

This was more of a low-level gold-buying business and so there were many large and small badly designed 'Sale' and 'Special Offer' posters taped up in the Fourth Street windows. These placards would act to block almost all the activity going on inside, on the night of the burglary. Only the closest observer with his or her face pressed up against the glass would even get an inkling of what was happening in the darkened store.

When leaving, she noticed for the first time a sign on the entrance door.

Open 6 Days a Week.
Tuesday - Friday 10:00 am to 6:00 pm
Sat & Sun 10:00 am to 4:00 pm. Closed Mondays.

Walking down Fourth Street she began getting many of her thoughts in order. Ariella understood that, since July 4th this year fell on a Monday, the establishment would be closed on the fourth, both for the holiday and because on the first business day of each week, it was always closed. That meant the break-in date could now be confirmed as Sunday night July 3rd.

With this being the Independence Day weekend, there would most certainly be all kinds of noise, fireworks, and people out and about being loud and unruly. That could be the perfect cover for whatever clatter she would be making cutting open the walls!

In her 'Raquel Santos Gomez' disguise she walked back in a roundabout way to where her Subaru was parked. She wanted to make sure any street videos would record her as being a regular Saturday shopper and not merely someone who went only into the Fourth Street Jewelers and Gold Exchange and then marched directly back to her car.

Ariella therefore stopped at an accessories boutique and went inside where she was able to turn off the brooch camera. She bought a scarf and wore this when exiting the store so that outdoor videos would show she went in and made a genuine purchase.

It was noon on Saturday when Ariella arrived back at her car. Sitting silently and seeing no one when looking up and down the quiet street, she pulled off the wig and untied her blond hair allowing it to drop to her shoulders. She yanked away the scarf, removed the red-framed glasses, and replaced these with her sunglasses before driving away. Raquel no longer existed.

Ariella, now at home, went directly to the bathroom to wipe away all remnants of her 'Raquel' appearance. She took off the face and eyebrow putty but retained the brown contact lenses. The curly charcoal-grey wig was placed into the bag with the other accessories. These items would be kept together and hidden after the heist in case the authorities ever came to search her house. The Raquel business cards were torn up and thrown into the garbage bin.

She then showered, dried her hair, and got dressed in a skirt and top in preparation for her meeting with Dora. At about one thirty Ariella put the kettle on to boil and made a cup of tea. In the microwave oven, she heated a small tub of macaroni and cheese, toasted two slices of bread, added some butter, and ate her light lunch.

Sitting on the couch, she continued thinking further about planning for the big event. Purdy arrived and lay down next to her. Every now and then he would get stroked by her and this would elicit an appreciative purr.

Soon it was time for the 'Mandy Moore' disguise and for her trip to the heist staging area. She tied up her hair, slipped on the short, black, straight-hair wig, darkened her eyebrows, and added the beauty spot to her left cheek.

Back on Sunday June 19th when the duffle was first packed, she chose to remove some items and take them to Dora's place ahead of time. These were her electric drill, the reciprocating saw, the paper bag of powdered mortar, the two screwdrivers, the pliers, and the 25' extension cord. All of this was now placed into a large over-the-shoulder tote bag. Although it was a bit heavy, she wanted to get these things to the apartment and hide them there.

It was about 2:40 p.m. when Ariella got into her Subaru, drove to the downtown area, and left her car in a totally different place from where it was parked that morning. Taking the tote bag containing the heist materials, she approached the 125-Building from a southerly direction, allowing her to avoid walking past the jewelry store. Once inside the vestibule, she pushed the button for number 1015. It took about half a minute before a voice came over the speaker.

"Who is it?" asked Dora.

"Mandy Moore." Her English accent sounded good.

"Who?"

"It's Mandy. Remember, I saw you last week and you invited me to come back again today."

"You were here? I asked you to visit again?" The dowager sounded puzzled.

Ariella was about to say something when the speaker crackled with, "Okay dearie, come on up."

A buzzer sounded by the locked foyer door. She speedily pushed it open, and it was just as well because the buzzing stopped almost as quickly as it began.

Walking up one flight she soon found herself at number 1015 on the first floor. After knocking loudly, slippers could be heard shuffling slowly inside the passageway and then the door opened.

"Oh, it's you! What is your name again?"

"I am Mandy. It is wonderful to see you!" Dora received a big hug.

"Please come in." The old lady did not question the large tote bag being carried in. They sat down in the living room for a few minutes and then Dora suddenly said, "I will make us some tea." She started to walk into the kitchen.

"Thank you." The friendly-fem stayed back spotting a handbag lying on a chair across the living room. She went over to it and popping it open found three magnetic-strip security cards for the foyer entrance door, and she took one. There was also a key ring with two identical keys on it and these had to be for the apartment door. Ariella removed one of these from the ring. Mission accomplished in the first two minutes, and she would not have to pick the lock to get into the residence. With both items now in her purse, it was time to go into the kitchen to see if any help was needed.

The two sat chatting for about half an hour while having tea and butter cookies. Even though her fingers still had New Skin on them, Ariella made a point of not touching any flat or shiny surfaces. After a while, she asked to go to the washroom and took the tote bag with her. Once inside she closed the door and looked around again, noticing the typical fluffy floor mats, and made a mental note to put these and the towels elsewhere in the residence before cutting open the wall. It would be unwise to allow any dirt or mortar dust to get on these items. Under the sink was a cabinet full of shampoo bottles, two large bags of hair curlers, and all kinds of assorted bits and pieces. The wily young woman quickly removed some of this junk and placed the tote bag with its all-important contents into the rear of the cabinet, then stuffed the other articles back in.

She made sure the large bags of hair curlers blocked the view of the canvas tote. After taking a few more snapshots she flushed the toilet, washed her hands, and went back to the living room to continue with their conversation. Dora did not notice her guest had no tote bag with her after returning from the bathroom.

Ariella was pleased with old Mrs. Jenkins' lapse in memory where at first, she did not quite remember having encountered her the week before. It could be by the time Dora got back from Florida, she might not recall ever having met 'Miss Mandy Moore' with her English accent.

After a further twenty minutes of small talk, it was time to leave. She gave Dora a hug. "Have a great trip to Florida and enjoy being with your daughter."

"Thank you, Mandy. I hope you will visit me again."

The old lady seemed to be extremely pleased about going to visit her daughter and two grandchildren. Her face glowed when she spoke about them. Ariella hoped Dora was really going away and would not suddenly change her mind or have the trip canceled for some reason!

◆◆◆◆◆

On this same Saturday evening, Barbara would be coming over soon for dinner and Ariella was busy setting the table. She prepared a salad as a starter, followed by a veggie lasagna, grilled shrimp, and green beans as the main course. For dessert, there was fruit salad. She also had cheese and crackers to have with wine before they sat down to eat.

Her adrenaline was still coursing through her veins and the excitement was building as she thought about what happened that day and how her plan for the heist was coming together. For now, her decision was not to say anything about her intention to break into the jewelry store. The sound of a car arriving prompted her to go to the front door. She opened it to greet her guest.

"Good to see you!" said Ariella.

"Well, hello!" Barbara gave her a light hug.

Five minutes later found the two of them sitting in the living room each sipping a glass of Chardonnay and munching on the cheese and crackers. Barbara started talking about the past week and how two containers, with products worth over $4 million, went missing. They speculated as to what they would do if they each had that amount of money.

"I would live on a yacht and endlessly sail the Caribbean," said Barbara. "I would have two Adonis-like men who would operate the vessel for me, keep it ship-shape, and do my every bidding."

They both laughed out loud at the idea. She went on, "Of course, you would be welcome at any time and my two deck hands would never know each night whether we wanted to make love to them or whether they were just there to do all the work!"

"I would spend a lot of time going around the globe," said Ariella with a smile on her face. "You would be my traveling companion and we could be meeting people from all over the world."

They moved off the subject of money and the two went into the kitchen to get their salads. Before too long they were at the dining room table eating. Barbara took the initiative and topped up their wine glasses while they gabbed about everyday things. She continued speaking about her week at work, referencing some new software programs which were installed to cover all the networked office computers.

Once they started on the main course Ariella broke up a shrimp into tiny pieces and put it on a saucer. This was of course for Purdy who arrived looking for his treat. He gobbled down the bits and then all but begged for more. After pulling apart another small shrimp, she gave this to him while saying, "Enough!"

The conversation between them inevitably drifted to Rachel's stolen jewelry, and what they felt could be done to get some form of restitution and retribution. The future filcher was careful not to breathe a word about the heist, the planning for which was so well underway.

Barbara said she knew of a private investigator who could look into Hunt, and it might be worth engaging him provided he did not charge too much. She said they should consider investing about $500 each for now. This would allow the undercover man to do some preliminary work and see if Barnwell had any real skeletons in his closet regarding people he cheated. Maybe he was involved in tax fraud or other financial shadiness. She said if enough pressure was put on Hunt, perhaps he would come up with some money for Ariella to make up for what was unjustly taken from her grandmother.

"Even if we can pin something on this crook, how much do you think we can really get out of him? Maybe $10,000 or perhaps $20,000?" Ariella's frustration was apparent. "That would be nothing compared to what he made off with. I do not see him giving up anything without a big and costly legal fight... and it would be his word against mine."

"You may be right, but I feel a private investigator could be worth considering."

"Okay. Just let me know when you want my cash contribution." She did not want to argue too much over this. The more the idea of a P.I. was considered to be a good one, the less her friend would think she was working on another plan or suspect her after the daring deed was carried out.

"Let me see if I can contact him and we will find out what he says about his costs."

"Good idea," said Ariella. "Now we should wash these dishes and then get our fruit salad."

Half an hour later found them watching a comedy show on TV. It was hilarious and enjoyable.

Just after eleven o'clock, Barbara said, "It's time for me to go home. We must get together again soon."

"Yes, perhaps we will go out for drinks and even get a light dinner at a decent restaurant."

"That is a good idea. Oh, there is something I meant to tell you." Barbara sounded enthusiastic. "A guy I know, Donnie Bolin, is having a big party and fireworks display on Sunday night July 3rd. I told him all about you, and I hope you will be able to come."

Ariella hesitated for just a moment with her answer because this was the night of her big break-in! "It sounds great, and I think it will work, but I will call to let you know."

They hugged each other and walked outside. Barbara got into her car, backed it out onto the street, then waved goodbye and began driving away.

CHAPTER 9

―――――

Sunday Morning, June 26th

After sleeping in that morning, Ariella eventually got up at nine-thirty because Purdy kept on mewing and reminding her about how hungry he was. She fed him, showered, and then got dressed into casual weekend clothes.

After having a light breakfast and spending a couple of hours tidying up the garage and her workshop area, she went back inside, ate a small snack, and then ventured into her living room. Sitting on the couch tickling Purdy's soft fur, the gifted gal was now reminiscing about the events of the day before. What a hectic experience!

First was her successful tour of the Fourth Street Jewelers and Gold Exchange in her get-up as Raquel Santos Gomez. Then it was having tea again with Dora and learning a lot more about the place and how it could work for the robbery. Some of the heist materials were able to be left there, and she also procured a keycard as well as a door key to the apartment.

While in the jewelry venue, she noticed two cameras in the main sales section. One was about 9" below the ceiling not far from the front door. The other was also 9" down but in the opposite corner, about thirty-five feet from the entrance. It was almost above one of the three large windows which faced onto Fourth Street. This second monitoring device was located fairly close to an important ceiling panel, the one which would be lifted up to give the drone access to the store.

In addition, no motion detectors were apparent in the large sales area – at least none could be seen. Whew! If there were any, she might have called the whole thing off. But there was an alarm system incorporating some magnetic contacts on the entrance door and a keypad nearby. Ariella chuckled, thinking about the police scratching their heads trying to figure out how the place got ransacked without the alarm being activated!

The artful artiste took her brooch camera, connected it with a USB cord to her computer, and downloaded the recording from inside the shop. There was some excellent video of everything, and all could be clearly seen including valuable necklaces, rings, watches, and more which were in the various display cases. There were good shots of staff behind the counters, and one could notice on two occasions salespeople opening the small horizontal doors at the back of the displays without unlocking anything. But Ariella knew the glass on all the merchandising units would have to be broken because the air-bot would be picking up the jewelry from above using its dangling hook.

At this juncture, she looked at the still pictures taken with her cell phone inside the 30" open space above the suspended ceiling tiles. One could gauge more-or-less where the area of the break-in should be. Although there were some heating and air-conditioning ducts as well as telephone and computer cables on parts of the fiber batting, there appeared to be none of these impediments resting on the insulation near her planned point of entry. There were of course support wires (which held up the metal grid) but again, none were near the all-important rear wall.

Ariella could tell, the spot where the bricks were to be cut out would give her access to the ceiling directly above the first display case. How convenient! She just needed to be careful not to let any dust, dirt, or bits of mortar drop down into the store. The paper lining on the insulation was to be thoroughly vacuumed after breaking through the wall, before lifting up the 2' x 4' ceiling panel.

The opening created once this panel was removed is the way her drone would enter the area. The slightest indication by way of debris that a break-in occurred from *above* would give the whole game away. Her intent was to keep the authorities as baffled as possible and confuse them with misleading evidence.

Once again Ariella re-played in her mind the sign indicating the operating hours of the store. It seemed that at some point on Sunday night July 3rd would be the most ideal time for the break-in. It might be best to begin just after nine o'clock because that is when the revelry would commence and the noise from the fireworks would be starting. It will certainly take her quite some time to get the job done, very likely going well into the early morning hours.

There were of course many implements for the heist in the tote bag, which was now in Dora's apartment, and soon Ariella would be taking in the duffle containing additional items needed to accomplish the daunting task. But what would she be coming out with and who might see her? Would this bag be heavy and cumbersome with the tools and all the loot inside? What about street cameras? This past Sunday she put a flat backpack into the duffle. Yes, the duffle, the backpack, and the tote should be able to hold all the jewelry and other break-in items she would be bringing back with her.

But three pieces of luggage will be a lot to carry, and it might look very suspicious. Maybe all goods taken could fit into two of the pieces, and the tote bag might not be needed. This decision would be evaluated when she was almost done perpetrating her fiendish feat.

Ariella was trying to come up with ideas to 'lighten the load' for her return trip home. Could a portion of what she brought in with her be dumped somewhere in Dora's building, perhaps in a trash-collecting area? No! The police may find such things, and this could indicate the robbery *had* taken place from number 125 Fourth Street.

Perhaps some articles could be dropped down the gap between the two buildings where they would never be found if there was a decent space between the two walls. She did, however, decide on one good idea: The drone could be pre-programmed with her home-address co-ordinates before she left her residence so it would be able to fly directly to her house afterward, meaning one less thing for her to carry.

The time was almost 1:30 p.m. on this Sunday, June 26th and one week before the break-in was to happen. Ariella knew there was another important project which required her dedication. Apart from cementing the bricks back after the robbery, the inside wall above the jewelry store ceiling would have to be closed. But she would be on the other side in another building and at the same time need to seamlessly patch the drywall! To most people without Ariella's smarts, they might think this would be impossible to do. But an ingenious idea came to her, to make the sheetrock appear to be to be untouched when looking at it from within the suspended ceiling area unless a close-up inspection was done.

And so, the *Patch-up-Piece* now got her attention.

▪ Cutting it to Size. From a sheet of ⅛" thick plywood which she had in her workshop, Ariella cut a 13" x 26" section.

Using a coarse-grain sandpaper wrapped around a small wooden block, all the edges of this layered wood were abraded in order to smooth them off. Then continuing with the process, a gently tapered bevel was added around the entire perimeter. After that, she took fine-grain sandpaper and worked on the top surface until it was completely glabrous.

▪ Boring the Holes. In the chuck of her drill press, a small ¹⁄₁₆" boring bit was secured, and with this, she created four holes in the plywood. Each was very near to a corner. Thereafter, four more were made, one in the center of each side. There were now eight tiny voids in the *Patch-up-Piece*, about ¾" from the edge around the perimeter.

■ Beveling the Cavities. She needed to slightly countersink the holes in order to recess the tops of the nail heads. To do this a ¼" diameter bit would do the trick, and the drill-press was set so the rotating action would barely penetrate the wood. Then, bringing the head of the press down each time, the board was moved from one hole to the next, creating a small countersink area above the round openings.

■ Adding the Nail-Hooks. Into every hole she gently hammered a 1½" nail, eight in total. Taking a standard pair of pliers and gripping one of the stems close to the laminated sheet, with smaller pliers she bent the rest of it over to form a 'hook'. One by one very carefully this was done to each nail.

When completed she had a piece of ⅛" plywood 13" x 26" with eight hooks sticking out the back. With these facing her, a few drops of epoxy glue were added to each, at the point where they emerged from their holes. This would ensure the nail-hooks would not move. Because of the countersinking, the heads did not protrude above the surface but lined up slightly below it.

Turning the sheet over so the hooks now faced downward, Ariella placed the *Patch-up-Piece* onto two 30" long 2" x 4" wood strips to keep the hooks away from the workbench. Then over the nail heads she added some wood putty with a small spackle blade. This took about an hour to dry. Once the putty hardened, she took fine-grain sandpaper and again moved this over the entire top surface which after a short while, gave it a sleek, planar uniformity.

■ The Painting Process. Ariella left this 13" x 26" panel atop the 30" long 2" x 4" wood strips and she proceeded to paint the face with a satin-finish white latex paint. This would match the same white color of the walls inside the jewelry store. It was left to dry for about twenty minutes and then it received another coat. Particular attention was given to the edges to make sure these were properly covered.

From a large bag of rubber bands that Ariella had in her study, she counted out twelve, (even though only eight would be needed) and these were put into a small poly bag ready to take on the night of the heist.

■ Spray Adhesive. The mechanically minded maiden already packed into the duffle, a can of very aggressive spray adhesive. When ready to close the wall in the ceiling area, she would apply this aerosol glue to the back of the plywood around its edges. This would help to hold it in place.

■ Thin Wire. From a coil of ⅛" stiff wire stored on a shelf in the workshop, a four-foot length was cut. This was curved to a diameter of 6" and then tied tightly with some string. She would need this to help her when closing the wall in the 101-Building.

There was another detail Ariella needed to prepare and take with her for the heist. After pulling down the retractable ladder which led into her attic and armed with a 2" paintbrush as well as a zip-seal bag, she climbed up these steps. There were large sheets of pressed board, located mostly down the middle of the attic, and these easily supported her weight. Adjacent to this board there was standard insulation. This was fiber batting with paper laminated to both sides – very similar to what was seen by her above the ceiling panels in the store.

She crawled along for a few feet and started 'sweeping' up some dust from what accumulated on the insulation paper over many years. Ariella moved around a large area gently gathering fine layers of dust and brushing this into the zip-seal until the particles collected were at least three inches high in the bag, and after that, went carefully down the attic steps. With a damp cloth, she wiped down her clothing to get rid of anything which clung to her and then washed her hands.

The polybag of dust went into the duffle together with the small box containing the misleading evidence. Each item was of course in its own zip-seal, and this included the human hairs, the cigarette butts, the 'snotty' tissue, and the dried blood. The coffee cup was in a taped-down paper bag. The sheet of 13" x 26" plywood together with the rubber bands and coil of wire were all placed in the duffle. She was ready with almost everything needed to effectuate the liberation of her family heirlooms.

Meticulously preparing the *Patch-up-Piece* was tedious, and the time was now a little past five o'clock. She poured a glass of wine and sipped slowly on this while warming up two Hot Pockets to eat.

Sitting on the couch watching TV with Purdy cuddled next to her, Ariella kept thinking that in one week and four hours from now she would be breaking the tiles in the wall of Dora's bathroom and the big deal would be underway! This thought both excited and terrified her.

But as soon as her mind went back to her grandmother being swindled out of a pile of jewelry worth hundreds of thousands of dollars, Ariella got re-focused and started working on her timeline chart. The robbery was to take no more than six or seven hours to execute. This would be from about 9:15 p.m. to perhaps 3:30 a.m. or a little after that depending on how it all went.

On her computer, she typed the following sequence of events which would give her a guide on how to proceed on the upcoming *night of notoriety*. Putting this into place was all part of her careful planning.

- Use the old Buick to get to and from the 125-Building when perpetrating the heist. The intent was to call Harry Woodward, her auto mechanic, and have him drop this vehicle off at her house on Saturday, July 2nd.

- Barbara was going to a party given by a friend of hers, Donnie Bolin, and Ariella decided to accept the invitation. It was scheduled to start at about six o'clock on Sunday evening July 3rd and would no doubt continue well into the wee hours of July 4th.

- To leave the party early, Ariella would let Barbara know during the afternoon about her pending migraine headache. This way Barbara and Donnie would be somewhat prepared for Ariella's early departure. They would understand she was leaving soon after arriving due to her not feeling well.

- Being at the party even for a short while should give her a partial alibi. In time to come if needed, Barbara, Donnie and others could attest to her being there and then going home early because of a bad migraine.

- Her goal was therefore to depart from Donnie's place at seven forty-five and head directly to her house, some twenty minutes away. Once there, she would put on her 'Mandy' disguise and place the duffle bag into the Buick. The Subaru would be conspicuously left sitting in her driveway. Around eight fifty she wanted to be on her way to the downtown area.

- After parking a block or two away from the 125-Building, it would be a short walk to Dora's apartment and the goal was to be there not too long after nine o'clock. At that point, her illicit activities could begin.

- Going home afterward, her objective would be to put the Buick into her garage, unload the bags full of jewelry and take them inside the house. The car would then be driven and parked one or two streets away and left there temporarily. During the following day, she would walk to the old vehicle and take it to Harry Woodward's garage. From there she would get an Uber ride back to her neighborhood Mall and then stroll casually home.

Ariella knew this was just an outline and that some of it could change, but at least it was a good idea of procedures on the night of July 3rd.

CHAPTER 10

The pretty plunderer stepped out of the shower and began to dry her hair. Before too long her makeup was on, and she was dressed and ready for work. Once in the kitchen, she started putting Purdy's food into his dish with him meowing in anticipation while he incessantly rubbed up against her legs. Her breakfast was a cup of coffee and two slices of whole-wheat toast, followed by a generous application of butter and marmalade.

The duffle bag was stashed in her bedroom closet, but for now, the drone was still in the garage. Her preparations were well ahead of schedule, and it was a good thing because during this week her plans could settle and gel in her head. In these few days, she would have time to think of any new refinements or ideas to execute it all in a better way. But now it was time to go and earn a living.

Ariella walked to the nearby bus stop and took the usual public transportation to her office. She kept thinking that by next Monday morning, the rip-off job would be over with enough grabbed to at least make up for what was stolen from her nana.

Sitting quietly on the moving bus, her mind wandered to a rather benevolent idea. If an inordinate number of items were able to be taken, where the value far exceeded what her grandma had lost, maybe she could try to locate other victims of Hunt's greed. Perhaps there would be a way to find some of these people and help them get a portion of their valuables back. Her new friend Barbara would also gain from some of the spoils because Barnwell had stolen from her too.

Things at work were normal but her mind was never far from the heist. She kept on smiling, thinking about the police being completely bewildered and confused as they tried to figure out how this robbery took place. Before leaving her office on that Monday afternoon, she called Harry Woodward with regard to him delivering the Buick to her residence.

"Hi Harry, this is Ariella Gerson."

"Well hello! It is so good to hear your voice!" As always, he sounded very pleased.

"I have a friend coming to stay with me for a couple of days. Could you please drop the Buick off at my house on this coming Saturday? Just leave the keys under the driver's side floor mat. I will return it to your garage again on July 4th or 5th. Oh, and Harry, I of course have Power of Attorney for my grandmother's estate, so I will sign the title, and before too long I will ask you to sell the car. At that point, we will split the money 50/50. Just keep the license plate for me as a memento."

"No Problem. I will be happy to drive it over to your home on Saturday sometime in the morning. I should be able to get it sold when you are ready for me to do so."

Harry had been to where she lived many times before to pick up her car when repairs were required. He was now thrilled to be in touch with her again. Of course, there was no friend coming to stay. Ariella simply needed to use different transportation for the burglary. She also wanted to make sure no one saw her Subaru leaving or arriving back at her house on the night of the break-in. It was often left parked on her driveway and not in the garage, thus leaving her car out after dark was not unusual. The neighbors would be able to see that on July 3rd she was 'home all night'.

◆◆◆◆◆

During that week all was uneventful at the office. Each day was the same calm duplication of the one before, and now, Friday July 1st was here. The firm gave everyone the afternoon off because it was right before the three-day weekend.

Ariella set up a three fifteen appointment with her hairdresser. The salon was not too far from where she worked, and it was a few months since her last hair trim.

Getting there exactly on time, the wait was only a couple of minutes before Melanie was ready for her. Melanie Rush had been her hairdresser for the past four years and the two of them got on really well. They always had a lot to talk about and the conversations were usually about fashion, hairstyles, places to vacation and sometimes they spoke about men.

"So glad you are here," said Melanie, hugging Ariella.

"I have not seen you since your grandmother's funeral. How are you feeling?" There was genuine concern in her voice.

"I am okay, but I miss her terribly."

"I am sure you do. Just remember I am always around if you need me."

"Oh, I know." Her usual dazzling smile appeared.

"What are we doing today? Just cutting off two inches as we did before?" Her fingers ran through the young beauty's long flowing tresses. Melanie was slightly jealous of this glamorous gal's fine features and her thick and lustrous naturally blond hair, and often thought this client was the most striking of all who frequented her salon.

"Yup, just trim off a little." She leaned back toward the sink so that the shampooing could begin.

The two chatted back and forth for the next hour, as the washing, cutting, and drying processes took place. The skilled stylist took a curling iron and added a couple of curls to the last few inches which immediately provided a softer and more girly appearance.

"There you go!" Melanie helped her stand up by taking her hand.

Ariella produced a credit card and left a generous tip. They gave each other a hug and then said their goodbyes.

◆◆◆◆◆

On this Friday evening, soon after leaving the salon, she was sipping a martini at Tyler's Tavern while waiting for her companion to arrive. The July 4th weekend was finally here, and this was it! Once again, her mind was filled with trepidation, knowing she either had to go ahead with the heist or drop the idea altogether. Should Barbara be told and at least get her input? It is always useful to bring in the opinions of others, especially for big life-altering decisions.

Perhaps it would be best not to, because of their friendship. If the police ever suspected Ariella and then questioned Barbara, she could spill the beans. No, it was far better to keep this wild idea under wraps. Lost in thought, everything about the impending burglary kept turning over and over in her head.

"Well, hi there!" Barbara startled Ariella who was far away in dreamland. "I see you got us our usual table!"

"Sure!" She signaled the waitress, for another martini.

"I love your hair! It looks like you had a trim. Those wavy curls are awesome!"

"Yes, I was at the salon this afternoon and Melanie did a great job. I needed to have a couple of inches taken off."

They each discussed their week at work and how they were eagerly awaiting this long weekend. Because Ariella decided to keep the upcoming thievery a secret and at this stage not say anything, she really wanted to steer her friend away from even thinking something rash would be done regarding Hunt and his jewelry store.

To this end, the blonde beauty encouraged the conversation again toward what 'legal action' could be taken against Barnwell. Their previous idea of advertising on social media to seek out others who might have been cheated by Hunt's unscrupulous tactics was again discussed. She also enquired as to whether any further thought had been given to the hiring of a private detective.

Barbara stated that she was still keen to do something about Hunt, and with her friend pushing the discussion along, the two of them continued mulling over various things they could be doing in this regard. Ariella was trying to make sure *no* suspicion would be cast on her once the robbery details came out. At nine-thirty, they left the bar. Barbara had her car there and Ariella took an Uber ride back home.

◆◆◆◆◆

It was Saturday morning, July 2nd at 9:00 a.m. The crime-planning researcher was busy on her computer seeking out yard sales in her area. Purdy was on her lap trying to sleep but he kept squirming around every time Ariella moved her position. She scoured through the local classifieds particularly wanting to find a sale regarding 'household tools' and other similar implements.

"Yes," she said out loud. "This advertisement is about the contents of a garage and workshop stuff one can buy." From the address, it appeared the location was in a town barely thirty minutes away. "Good. I hope they have what I am looking for."

Ariella wanted a mallet with a large metal head and a short wooden handle, but the intent was that her fingerprints not appear anywhere on this item. The prints which currently existed on it were to be left intact.

Getting up from her desk, she went into the bathroom where New Skin was once again painted to the underside of her fingertips. It dried rather quickly.

She then packed into her handbag some paper towel, a small roll of masking tape as well as an ace bandage, which would be wrapped around her hand upon arriving at her destination. Once again it was time for the 'Mandy' disguise comprising of brown contact lenses, a large beauty spot on her left cheek, and the short dark-haired wig. This time her words would carry the semblance of a New York accent. After giving Purdy a quick hug and kiss, Ariella hopped into her seven-year-old Subaru and drove to the yard sale.

It was a little past ten thirty when she got to the house where the sale was taking place. It took a minute for the ace bandage to be wrapped around her left hand. Because of this crepe swathe and the New Skin, no prints of hers would be left behind on the item she wanted to buy.

There were more than twenty autos out on the street as well as some motorcycles, and Ariella walked past five homes to get to the yard sale house. It was good to park a short distance away because she did not want the homeowners who were selling these goods to see her vehicle, just in case they were ever questioned by the police. There were a whole lot of household goods being displayed on either side of the long driveway, and at least three dozen people milling about. Ariella went directly to a section packed with tools.

There was a drill press, a grinding wheel, many screwdrivers, pairs of pliers, garden gadgets, boxes of nails, containers of nuts and bolts, paint brushes, rollers, paint pans, and much more. Aha! On a black metal table there was a collection of hammers and among these were three different-sized mallets. Two had large heads and long wooden handles, the kind a person would use for pounding posts into the ground or for demolishing walls. That was not the type she wanted. But there were also three smaller ones, and one of these would be perfect.

However, there were five men poking around, picking things up, looking at these items, then putting them down. Ariella hoped the fingerprints on the hammer selected would be from a stranger, and not from the people holding the sale.

Wriggling her way between two of the men, she was able to look closely at the mallets. The one most desirable had a hole near the end of its wooden handle and through this was a string showing a $5.00 price tag. With her wrapped hand she picked it up by its metal head and walked over to a table near the street. Here the homeowner and his wife were seated taking money from the packrats, collectors, and others who were there to purchase goods of value or things that were simply junk.

Ariella's right hand came out of the pocket of her jeans with a $20.00 bill. The woman took the money and glanced at the dangling tag which was clearly marked $5.00.

"Here is your $15.00 change. What happened to your hand?"

Ariella was expecting a question like this. "It is not as bad as it looks. I scraped the skin on the backka-mah hand when I was working in mah gawden yesterday. It should be healed soon." She spoke with a slight New York twang.

"Where are you from?"

"I am from Lawng-Guiland originally," said Ariella heavily pronouncing her G's, "But ah have lived in this area for about eight yeeears."

Fortunately, at that moment three people came to pay for the oddments they had found, which was a good thing because no long conversation was needed now!

"Havva good day." Ariella turned and walked away.

"Goodbye and thank you," said the woman, beginning to attend to her next customer.

Once back in her car, she carefully removed the price tag and gently wrapped a length of paper towel around the handle of the mallet. This was secured with pieces of masking tape to prevent any of the paper towel from unwrapping, and it was placed inside a shopping bag. She took off the ace bandage from her hand, started the engine, and drove off.

It was a tad after twelve when upon arriving home she was pleased to see her grandmother's old vehicle parked there. Great! Getting out of her car, she drove the Buick from the driveway, over the grass down the side of her house and into the backyard where it would not be visible from the street. The Subaru was then parked in her garage.

The paper bag containing the mallet was stowed in the duffle, and now one more piece of the puzzle was in place to help make this villainous venture a success.

At about one o'clock she poured a cup of tea and began munching on a peanut butter and jelly sandwich. All the necessary preparations to carry out the burgling of the eclectic emporium were now done unless some other idea came to mind.

Cuddled up on the couch next to her and sound asleep, was Purdy, and Ariella kept thinking about the break-in and how she was going to pull it off with no glitches.

At this point, she started worrying about the heist, as had happened before. Planning was not too difficult, and in fact, it was fun. Wearing the disguises, getting the implements lined up, finding the misleading evidence and collecting all the necessary items, many of which were in the duffle bag or were already at Dora's apartment. But now, being so close to the time of absolute commitment, she began feeling very uneasy.

"Am I crazy? Can this really succeed?"

Then the Heistess started to calm down, murmuring softly, "If I cut through the first wall and it proves to be too difficult, or if I encounter any steel beams or unforeseen obstacles, I will stop. I will simply patch it, vacuum the area and go home. No harm, no foul. In fact, if I breach both walls and get into the space above the jewelry store and then decide to back out, I will close it all and retreat. Dora will still be away until Thursday, so if I need to again make my way into her apartment for any further cleanup, I will easily be able to do so, and no one will be any the wiser."

Her articulation continued, "The real commitment will not be opening the walls. It will be smashing the glass on the displays and/or taking any of the jewelry. In any event, I know I can do this because I have it all figured out to the last detail. I will be able to commit *The Perfect Crime*, and nobody will ever be able to determine who did this or how they got in. I owe this to you, Grandma." Tears now started welling up in her eyes.

There existed compelling motivation to get back what was stolen. She spent the rest of the afternoon tidying her house, and this was excellent therapy because spotlessness indoors made her feel good.

◆◆◆◆◆

It was four o'clock on Saturday afternoon when Ariella called Barbara on her cell phone to make a dinner arrangement for that night. This was something the two discussed when they were together the previous evening.

Barbara was in her office this Saturday because she had a lot to do there but still felt she would be able to go out for a nice quiet meal that night.

She answered her phone, "Hello! I trust your day progressed well."

"Hi there, and yes, I was very active around the house. I know you were quite busy at your place of work, and I hope you got a lot done."

"For sure I did. I am really pleased I came in today because it will make things a lot easier for me on Tuesday."

"How about we meet at the Wild West Bar & Grill at seven o'clock?" Ariella had not been to this restaurant in a few months and was keen to go back.

"Great idea. See you there." Barbara sounded excited.

Later, while driving to the eatery, Ariella was one more time wrestling in her mind as to whether or not to divulge anything about the heist. Her plans and preparations were so ingenious, these really should be shared with another person. Perhaps she could get an enthusiastic endorsement and be complimented on her brilliance.

But then her thinking went to how serious-minded Barbara could be, and knowing there was no way her friend would let her go ahead with so dare-devil an escapade. Once again, she concluded the less anyone else knew, the lower the chance would be of someone opening their mouth and getting her into trouble.

And so, a pivotal decision evolved, not to disclose anything about her crazy idea, at least not at this stage. She wouldn't fully understand until well after her diabolical deed, how important it was that no one had any inkling in advance about the upcoming malfeasance.

Upon arriving at the Wild West Bar & Grill, Ariella got a small table in a corner. A minute later Barbara came into the restaurant, and in no time the two of them were hugging each other. They ordered a bottle of wine which came promptly, and the waitress poured the deep red Merlot into their glasses. They toasted each other "Happy July 4th Weekend," and then ordered their meals.

One thing the sly sorceress began to do, and then continued intermittently throughout the evening, was to feign that a cold or some type of bronchial condition was starting. Every so often she would reach for a tissue and blow her nose, or break into a coughing fit. This was all about setting the stage for the following night and an early exit from Donnie Bolin's party.

"I hope you do not have an impending illness like the flu."

"I do have a bit of a headache and I can feel a cold or such coming on. I will take something for this later at home."

Their food arrived and soon the two lovely ladies were relaxing and indulging in the tasty cuisine together. From the table where they were sitting, they noticed four men having drinks at the bar. Every now and again one or two of these guys would half turn to look at them.

"It is like we have said before," said Barbara. "I know exactly what they are talking about and for sure the discussion is how they would like to get intimate with us!"

"Perhaps we should flirt with them and wow their worlds!" Ariella had a wicked look and a half-smile on her face.

"Or we could disappoint them and let them know they have no chance."

"And how do you propose to do that?"

"Easy." Barbara got up, moved around the small table, and was now standing next to the opposite chair. Out of the corner of her eye, she could see the four studs at the bar looking attentively at her. Leaning down, the brunette gave her dinner companion a kiss on the cheek.

She returned to her seat. "That will get them talking!"

"I think we just burst their bubbles, or maybe we turned them on. Although I must confess, the guy in the blue shirt is certainly my type!"

"Oh yes!" exclaimed Barbara. "I can see why you want to get to know him. He appears to be tall, slim, and dapper!"

"I would love to somehow get my phone number into his hands," said Ariella. Suddenly, a slight frown came over Barbara's face and then it disappeared quickly.

When Molly their waitress came with their food, Ariella asked if she knew anything about Mister Blue Shirt.

"Yes, I do. You are talking about Roger Riley. He is divorced, has no kids, and is a lawyer. He is very full of himself However, an attractive and smart woman such as you should be able to tame him!"

"Here, after we leave, please give him my name and number. Let's see if he calls." She looked seriously at their waitress, handing over a white cocktail napkin with her handwritten details.

"For sure he will call you," said Molly. "Every time I walked past those dudes tonight, they were talking about the two of you. I think that kiss on the cheek really got them reeling... now they probably don't know what to think!"

"Can you believe he is a lawyer!" said Ariella jokingly. "That is all I need in my life!"

As Molly left the table Barbara seemed to have a sudden change of tone. "You surely do not want to hook up with that guy. He is divorced, conceited, and no doubt, trouble."

Ariella appeared quite taken aback by the comments. "Oh come on, you have to admit that he is cute! You even said so yourself."

Barbara just rolled her eyes. A slight iciness seemed to have come between them. From then on, they made small talk while eating. But after they were done and had consumed their coffee, Ariella peeked at her watch and felt it was time to go. They got up and gave each other a hug even though both were aware of the barrier which had suddenly sprung up. They half smiled at each other, and the guys were still staring.

"See you tomorrow night at Donnie Bolin's party. I have texted you his address and he is about twenty minutes from where you live, so you should easily be able to locate his house using your GPS."

"I am sure I can find my way there." Ariella suddenly broke out into a long noisy cough.

"I hope you will feel better by tomorrow. Take some lozenges and cold medicine tonight and make sure you will be ready to have fun!"

"I will be fine."

At that point, Barbara headed to the bathroom. Ariella said goodbye and walked to the door of the restaurant. Once outside she started making her way to her car, which was parked not too far away. Barbara came out of the powder room and went directly to Molly who was rushing around like crazy taking care of hordes of Saturday night, long weekend customers.

"Did you give my friend's information to that lawyer?"

"No, not yet," replied the waitress, appearing to be quite annoyed. "I haven't had a free moment to do so."

"No problem. Give it to me and I will take it to him."

"Okay, great. Thank you." She seemed relieved and put her hand into her pocket, retrieved the napkin, then handed it to Barbara. Molly watched her go over to the four guys at the bar and she saw a discussion take place. A minute later Barbara was on her way out of the restaurant.

Ariella walked almost to the spot where her Subaru was parked when she slackened the pace. There was something nagging in her mind which made her slow down and then stop completely. She turned around and proceeded to go back to the Wild West Bar & Grill, feeling very embarrassed and stupid for handing the waitress her personal facts that way, to give to the gorgeous stud.

"You're not in high school or college anymore." Her self-scolding was very apparent. "Putting that all on a napkin is childish. I will go back and make it right with him and introduce myself properly. If he wants to see me after that well then fine, and if not, so what!"

Not much had changed in the past few minutes, and the four horsemen were still sitting at the bar. Mister Blue Shirt was the first to see her rapidly moving in his direction. His face brightened as she approached, holding out her hand.

"Hi, I am Ariella Gerson,"

"Pleased to meet you. I am Roger Riley." The oh-so-handsome-Hollywood-actor-type was even better close-up!

"I must apologize for the napkin with my name and number. I should never have asked the waitress to give it to you. It was very immature of me to reach out to you that way."

Roger seemed baffled and then he smiled. "Oh no, Molly did not give me your details. But after you left, the tall chick with whom you were sitting, came over here waving a small paper with some writing on it. I assume that was the information you gave to the waitress. Well, your so-called friend told me and my buddies in no uncertain terms we should not be looking at you because you have a boyfriend."

Ariella was stunned. "She said that to you. Molly did not give you my name and cell phone number?"

"That's what happened. What is with you and her?"

"We are just friends, and I don't know why she told you I have a boyfriend when I do not. Please understand, I am unattached, and I happen to think that you are very attractive."

"Since you are putting your cards on the table so eloquently, I too will not play any games. I am always impressed with women who are open and honest. I find you to be lovely, hot, and sexy!" He was staring at her fine features while his three friends looked on jealously in amazement.

"I guess I will have to cool things with her in the future. I cannot believe you did not get my note." She reached to the bar counter, grabbed another white cocktail napkin, and once again scribbled down her particulars.

"Here. Please call me sometime."

"Thank you I will." He handed her a business card.

"A lawyer, eh? What's more, a corporate lawyer who also does some criminal defense work! Well, one never knows when I might need a knight on a white horse to save me!"

"With so lovely and innocent a face, you could *never* get into trouble! But don't worry, I will be there for you if you need to be rescued!" Roger had no clue at that moment how soon Ariella would be screaming out to him for help!

He introduced his friends, and they all shook hands with her. Then he and the demure damsel gave each other a goodbye hug. She left the restaurant and disappeared into the jostling crowd on the sidewalk, walking once again to her car.

While driving home Ariella was seething and reeling, and under her breath asked, "What is wrong with Barbara? I thought we were friends. She knew I had an interest in that guy and deliberately tried to ruin it for me. I would never have heard from him and spent months wondering why. I cannot trust her, so I must be very careful from now on. Thank goodness I did not let on about the big caper which is taking place tomorrow night!"

It was almost ten o'clock when the Subaru rolled into her garage. Ariella decided to get the duffle bag with the last of the heist implements over to Dora's apartment right away. She was concerned that on the following evening, Sunday, July 3rd there would be a lot of raucous people out and about. It might look suspicious if a woman on her own was seen carrying a big bag in the downtown area while others were partying and celebrating. Being on the sidewalk with bulky luggage could raise some eyebrows.

Ariella got into the 'Mandy Moore' disguise. Short dark wig and brown contact lenses. She left the beauty spot off, and this time wore the narrow style red-framed glasses. It was dark outside and raining, and that was a good thing. The worse the weather tonight, the fewer people would be around to see her taking something large into the 125-Building.

Besides what was already packed, she put into the duffle two old sweatshirts, knowing these could be used to help cushion the area over the bricks once the walls were opened. Ariella programmed into the drone the coordinates of the exact location of her house. With these, it would be able to fly itself home after completing its multiple missions in the store. She placed this into the duffle together with her FPV video headset. Everything was now ready. The bag was quite heavy, because among other things, the eight bathroom wall tiles already inside, added to its weight.

There was hardly any traffic, so it did not take long for her to drive to the downtown area. Parking not too far from her destination, she strode briskly with the duffle to number 125 Fourth Street. Ariella walked through the outside doors and into the entrance hallway. Holding the weighty bag close to the wall and out of sight of the camera, she kept her head down and went to the security door at the end of the foyer. In her hand was the plastic keycard, taken from Dora the previous week and using this, let herself in. There were no tenants or others to be seen.

Choosing to walk up the stairs rather than take the elevator, in no time she was putting the key into the lock and was relieved to find it opened the door! Once inside it was apparent that Dora was not there and had really gone to Florida. The start of the malevolent matter was getting closer!

Ariella put the duffle in the back of the closet in the spare room and taking a couple of blankets from the shelf above, dumped them over the duffle to hide it… just in case. Double checking on what was stashed away the week before, everything was still in the under-sink cabinet in the bathroom, and nothing had been touched. After looking around the residence one more time, she walked back to her car and drove home. It was time for bed and getting a lot of rest, because tomorrow night there was to be no sleeping!

CHAPTER 11

Sunday Morning, July 3rd

At eight o'clock Ariella woke up, and Purdy was mewing to let her know he was hungry. It suddenly occurred to her it was Sunday and her own exclamation all but startled her, "This is D-Day… it has finally arrived!"

After getting up, she took a shower and put on some old clothes. Thereafter it was into the kitchen, feeding Purdy and changing his litter box. She made a light breakfast being two fried eggs, toast, and a cup of coffee. Ariella walked over to the sunroom, plopped down onto the couch, and turned on the TV which was featuring a re-run of a cooking show. Leaving the TV on in the background, it was time to go over the procedures for that night.

Purdy wanted attention and kept trying to sit on her lap. He finally gave up because Ariella was constantly putting him down on the floor. He went to the corner of the room and curled up in the sun. She again studied her timeline, and it was essentially the same as before but with a few slight changes:

- Get to the party tonight early, perhaps at six twenty-five or thereabouts. Let the host and others know you have a migraine coming on and you do not feel well.

- Soon after seven thirty you must excuse yourself from the event and say you really need to go.

- Be back home by about eight fifteen at the latest. Leave the Subaru out on the driveway and lock it.

- Change into sneakers, dark-colored jeans, and a long-sleeved shirt. Put on the 'Mandy Moore' Disguise: Brown contact lenses, the short-hair dark wig, a beauty spot on the left cheek, and the large, black-framed glasses. Take the curly, charcoal-grey hairpiece for use later. Wear a Tan/Brown reversible lightweight jacket.

- Go out through the kitchen door to the Buick which is on the lawn in the backyard.

- Drive to the downtown area, and park on a side street about a block away from the 125-Building.

- Lock the car and go to the old lady's residence. Try to be there before nine fifteen.

- Get started opening the bathroom wall by nine thirty if possible. Try to have the heist done six or seven hours later. Be going home just before sunup.

Everything needed for the break-in was already stashed in Dora's apartment, and hopefully, this updated timetable would work out okay. Ariella at this stage felt fully prepared for the big night! She continued doing small tasks around the house for a while, and this included processing some paperwork in her study and paying a few bills from her computer. Every now and again she would stop and look at her timeline. At about two o'clock it was time for a long nap because understandably she would be up most of the night.

Her phone alarm woke her just before five o'clock and shortly after that, it was in the shower and then getting ready to go out. At a quarter after six, she got into her Subaru, and twenty minutes later arrived at Donnie Bolin's house. Many guests were already there, chatting, mixing and mingling. People were asked to show up early and have a good time! Barbara had just wandered in and greeted Ariella with a hug.

"Great that you are here, and how are you feeling?"

"I am not at all well," she said, breaking into a cough. "Besides a sore throat, I think I have a migraine coming on. I get these every now and again." It was of course not true, she never got headaches and was seldom sick. "If this does not subside soon, I may leave to go home."

Barbara introduced Donnie to Ariella, who handed him a bottle of wine as a party gift.

"Pleased to meet you," he beamed, looking at a face that belonged to an angel.

"Thank you for having me come to your party. Unfortunately, I have not been well all day and I feel a severe migraine starting. I hope I will not have to leave early."

"Have a glass of wine or something even stronger," said Donnie. "This might help you to perk up a bit."

"No thank you. I took some medication right before I left home and I cannot combine this with any liquor." She did not want to drink a thing because it was important to have all her wits about her for later that night. In any case, the last thing the Heistess needed was to be arrested by the police for driving under the influence.

"I will have a diet soda."

Donnie seemed to be disappointed Ariella would not be drinking wine or such to help liven up her demeanor.

"Come," said Donnie taking her by the hand and steering her toward the bar. "Meet my brother. He will give you the soft drink which you want. Max, this is Ariella."

The rugged co-host gave her a big smile. He stared at her baby blues, shiny blonde hair, and perfect teeth. His heart was melting. "It is a pleasure to meet you." He glanced away, busily trying to pour the soda because he did not want her to see he could hardly take his eyes off her.

"So, what brings you here?" He was trying to get chatty as he handed her the glass.

"I invited her." Barbara piped up with a feeling of jealousy rising inside. She had a thing for Max and all but pushed herself between him and the newcomer. "Before you get too excited," blabbed the brunette, trying to pour water on the flames of desire obviously growing in him, "My friend is not feeling well tonight, and may be going home soon."

"I am sorry to hear that. Maybe you will feel better later this evening."

At that point, Donnie gave Ariella an important opening. "Stay as long as you feel up to it," he said. "If you have to leave early, we will understand."

"I appreciate the concerns of everyone. Let me see how I manage for the next little while." After getting her soda she went and sat quietly on a couch, occasionally putting her head in her hands when any guest was in the area. This was all about setting the stage for an early exit.

During the time she was sitting down various people approached, to sort of pamper her. They were told about her sore throat and the beginnings of a bad migraine headache. She gave the same story to whomever tried to talk to her and in all cases, they expressed their good wishes.

At seven forty it was time to take off because of her important date with destiny. Donnie and Barbara were standing together talking to two other people. Ariella felt the host would give less of an argument about her leaving than Barbara would.

She walked slowly up to them. "I really need to go." Her voice sounded weak. "My head is pounding, and my throat is on fire. I must get home so I can lie down."

"You poor dear," said Donnie, and before Barbara could say anything he asked, "Would you like one of us to drive you to your place?"

At that moment Ariella made a split-second decision. No one knew of the Buick parked on the lawn in the back of her property. If someone drove her home that might be a good thing. All would know that she was 'stuck' there with no transportation. If anyone ever suspected her of the robbery this may serve her better. Yes, this could be more advantageous than leaving the Subaru parked outside on the driveway, so all could see her car there during the night. If everyone understood no car was at her house, that would be perfect.

"I was going to drive myself back, but maybe with this awful headache, your suggestion is a good one, Donnie. It would be better if someone took me."

Barbara immediately jumped in, "Let me take you."

Ariella didn't really want to be in the car with her. She did not want this now pesky woman to walk her inside when she got home and have her possibly notice the Buick in the back of the house.

"Thank you, but Donnie," said Ariella turning to him, "As I was walking past the bar area on my way over to you, I heard Max say that he did not have enough ice. I believe he is about to go out and get more. Maybe he can give me a ride and get the extra ice at the same time."

"Great idea. Hey!" Donnie yelled out to Max who was already on his way out the front door. "Ariella here needs to be driven to her place. Will you be able to take her?"

Barbara appeared to be a little miffed, not wanting to leave the dazzling damsel alone with Max, and now there was not much she could do about it. Barbara also wanted her friend to be dependent on her and be the one saying, "Look after yourself. Get some good sleep. Call me if you need me."

Max did not hesitate. "Of course I will!" In a few quick strides he was at Ariella's side and in a very forward manner took her hand so he could help her to his flashy SUV.

She had detached her car keys from her house bunch and now it was time to throw her gal pal a bone. "You can help me. Perhaps sometime tomorrow you and Donnie can get my car back to me. As you know it is the blue Subaru which is parked in front of the house next door. Here are my keys."

Barbara seemed a little relieved. At least she could be doing something useful for Ariella, and perhaps the next day, 'coddle' and 'mother' her a bit.

"No problem. I am sure we will be able to get your vehicle to you tomorrow."

It was almost eight o'clock when Max drove his sick-looking passenger to her residence, and he tried to talk to her. Ariella felt attracted to him and thought she would like to get to know him better, but not now. Tonight was all about acting weak and overwhelmed by an awful headache. The discussion going to her house was thus directional. "Turn right at the next corner. Go one mile then turn left," and so on. At eight-fifteen Max was waving goodbye to her. Home at last and 'stranded'... or so they would all believe!

Being spot-on regarding her timeline, she immediately began to change into dark clothing and the 'Mandy Moore' disguise being brown contact lenses, the short-hair wig, a beauty spot on her left cheek, and large, black-framed glasses.

Ariella took a reversible tan/brown lightweight jacket with her so that someone wearing a tan overgarment would be seen going into the 125-Building and many hours later, a person in brown would exit. She stuffed into a pocket the curly hair charcoal-grey wig. Ariella would be sporting the straight hair 'Mandy' look on her way in and the other hairpiece coming out, as well as having her outerwear color switched. Into another jacket pocket went a pair of thin gardening gloves, and there were also two pairs in the duffle.

Most important, she decided to leave her cell phone on the kitchen table because it should not be taken with her downtown. If someone called, it was essential there were no tower coordinates tracking it, GPS verification, or any other evidence she was not at home the entire night. There existed two remote-control garage door openers. Because her usual one was still in the Subaru, the spare would be the one to use in the old auto for returning home after the heist.

Her original timeline had her getting into the old vehicle at eight forty-five, and it was now five minutes earlier than that. Being a little ahead of schedule was a good thing, as she drove the Buick from the back of her house and onto the street. No neighbors could be seen. Awesome!

Fifteen minutes later found Ariella parking a block and a half away from the important downtown address. She locked the car and headed to the 125-Building. Although there were many people walking around, no one paid attention to her.

From not too far away she could hear 'Boom Boom Boom Boom' as the first of thousands of fireworks in the area started going off. What great background noise there would be to help with the heist!

It was a little after nine o'clock when Ariella arrived at her destination. Walking through the foyer and toward the locked door, she put her head down and stared at the floor to the right. Thus, what could be seen of her head by the camera in the vestibule was only the short, dark-haired wig and the black-framed glasses. By her not being too close to the wall, the recording would pick up the rest of her body but not her face. This way it would show a woman wearing a tan jacket entering the building carrying no bag, no implements, or anything else. If the police ever perused these videos and even thought the robbery was executed from this building, it could not have been done by this person!

The plastic keycard gave her access to the stairwell, and she walked up the steps to the first floor. Before utilizing the stolen key to open Dora's door, she took the gardening gloves from her pocket and put these on. Ariella wanted none of her fingerprints to be anywhere outside or in the apartment.

The gloves would also serve another purpose, which was to protect her hands and nails. If the police came to visit soon after the heist, her hands would not be rough or cut in any way from all the activity and her nails would still look good. Once inside she closed the door, locked it, and then went to the bathroom to pick up the two fluffy bathmats and the towels. These were placed in the spare bedroom, so they would not get covered in dust or dirt.

Her goal was to commence by nine-thirty, but it was now only nine-fifteen, a bit ahead of her timeline. She retrieved the duffle from the spare bedroom closet and took the tote bag full of tools from the cabinet under the sink. The reversible jacket was draped over a chair in the kitchen.

Ariella removed the 'Mandy' wig and placed it in the duffle. With her hair still clipped up she put on the tightly fitting vinyl shower cap to prevent her hair from becoming covered in fine dust and dirt particles. From the hall cupboard, out came a broom, a dustpan and brush, and Dora's vacuum cleaner.

Taking the plastic sheeting from the duffle, she cut two large 4' x 4' squares, taped one down on the bathroom floor close to the wall, and the other on the floor a few feet away.

Her eye protection goggles were now put on. She grabbed the 25' extension cord, plugged it into an outlet in the passageway, and then very carefully shut the bathroom door. The gap below was sufficient to allow the cord to not get pinched. Keeping the door closed would prevent brick-chip fragments and other debris from getting into the apartment. After connecting the extension cord to her electric drill, she installed a thin masonry cutting wheel into its chuck.

But before beginning to slice through the grout, Ariella cut a 3' x 3' section from the clear plastic sheeting, and with masking tape, this plastic was adhered to the wall about ten inches above the top row of tiles that were about to be removed. She added some tape to the sides of the sheet to further hold it in place but left it loose enough to work behind. This would stop the grout dust from going everywhere.

After donning her fabric facemask, she positioned herself on the floor to begin cutting the grout, so the six wall tiles could be pried away. This would start 8" off the floor, which was the height of one tile. Once these were removed, there would be a 16" x 24" area devoid of ceramic squares.

For a moment Ariella listened again to the din which had started before her arrival at 125-Building and this racket was now growing in intensity. The noise of July 4th celebrating by revelers out on the streets included a lot of yelling, and there were the sounds of car horns honking and people clanking garbage can lids. More loud booms in succession could be heard as fireworks were being set off everywhere.

Yes, this outdoor mayhem was providing a perfect smokescreen for the drilling, cutting, and possible banging which would take place as the walls were opened up.

Within five minutes the grout around and in-between the six tiles had been cut away. The clear plastic sheet did its job well, and most of the joint powder was on the floor close to the wall. Using Dora's small brush and pan this dirt was swept up and tipped into the paper shopping bag being used for trash. It was essential that constant cleanup took place after each process, so a huge mess did not accumulate.

She then placed a flat screwdriver close to the center where the six tiles met, poked it in, and began to jimmy one of these off. The tile on which the screwdriver was resting immediately chipped and cracked. It was understandable that one or more would break during this stage of the operation. Fortunately, the ceramic piece being pried away easily popped off the wall. It happened so effortlessly and quickly, Ariella had to grab it to stop it from dropping onto the bathroom floor.

"Huh," was her loud remark. "They are not well glued to the drywall and the adhesive is old. It seems detaching these white squares should be fairly simple to do!"

Now that the first was out of the way it was not difficult to get the screwdriver behind the second one. She rested it on a pair of pliers and levered up this next tile which all but fell off. It was the same with the other four. By nine thirty-five all six were removed.

Four screws were now apparent which showed the location of two vertical wooden studs positioned behind the gypsum board, and these were easy to undo with a screwdriver. She again reminded herself about how odd it was that drywall is also called gypsum board as well as sheetrock.

At this point, she lowered the clear plastic material to cover the same work area as before. Picking up her electric drill with its cutting wheel and using this, a 16" x 24" drywall section was cut out. It came away without any trouble and was carefully put aside on the bathroom floor.

Turning again to the wall, with her utility knife she gently sliced around the very old fiber insulation and then pulled it away. Ariella was concerned this old batting could have within it asbestos or other harmful content. She was glad her mask was on to protect her mouth, nose, and lungs.

With Dora's vacuum cleaner, the drywall powder which had fallen onto the linoleum floor was removed. The cutting wheel on the drill progressed through the two wooden studs by severing these top and bottom. Then using her small hand saw she separated the parts of the wood the wheel had not reached. Before too long the two pieces were freed from the wall and all sawdust was vacuumed up. No nails were holding these studs to the bricks behind them. The time was now nine forty-eight.

The masonry wall, which was technically the 'outside' of this building, now bared itself and her next challenge would be to create an opening here. Of course, the bricks to be removed would come out as a group joined together.

Crouching there on the floor, she noticed about seven inches above where a hole was about to be made in the mortar, there existed a horizontal steel beam. Yes, this building had been framed in steel with the bricks added afterward, and hopefully, there was just one course of these.

Ariella recalled her research online about 101 Fourth Street and the adjacent 125-address. Both were built in the early 1900s and were designed by the same architect. The construction of these four-story units was such that sturdy steel frames provided all the major support and therefore the bricks did not have to be load-bearing to any extent. The walls acted more as solid exterior dividers for the buildings.

Taking off her facemask, this was thrown into the paper trash bag and a new mask was put on. A 6" long ¾" diameter masonry bit was installed into the chuck of her electric drill. Once more she lowered the clear plastic sheet which was still taped to the tiled bathroom wall, to again stop the dirt from flying about.

Now it was time to get started on the big removal job. First, a hole was bored into the mortar at a corner point where two bricks met. This action was repeated at the other three corners of the section to be sliced out. Then she connected the extension cord to her reciprocating saw, installed its carbide blade, and poked this into one of the cavities. Ariella cut horizontally along the base of three bricks for a distance of about 24". Then starting at the top in one of the newly drilled holes, she began to incise downward through four rows, going into both mortar and bricks in a vertical sweep, like was done in the practice run in her garage. This allowed for a perpendicular cutting length of 11" from the top row to the end of the fourth brick. Going back to the other side, the saw again carved downward the same measurement of 11".

The shearing process made a loud rasping noise as it attacked the old joint compound in the wall, and even though it cut through everything quite easily, a lot of dust was created. Thank goodness for the clear plastic draped in front of her which kept most of the airborne dirt confined. Every now and again her plastic eye goggles were wiped clean by her gloved hand, because of the accumulating fine powder.

Three sides had now been cut through, two vertical and one along the bottom. This brick section was being held in place only by mortar along the top. Finally, going back up to the top, the blade raked out the cement composite horizontally, moving across the 24" width. This set of twelve bricks (including some partials) suddenly dropped down ⅜" as her reciprocating saw made it to the end of the row. The next task was to remove this detached group from the wall.

As was the case when experimenting on her garage wall at home, two flat screwdrivers were now inserted under the loose segment. Lifting the screwdrivers up and down she slowly jogged it all toward herself. When it was almost out, she held the clump along its base using both hands and with her arm muscles shaking, the wily weightlifter pulled this separated section away. Holding the heavy forty-five-pound load tightly she shuffled it onto the large square of plastic sheeting already on the floor near the back of the bathroom

With the vacuum cleaner and its wand, the dust and dirt were sucked from this group, and the bathroom floor was also cleaned in the same way.

Ariella studied the hole in the wall noting the outer façade was comprised of only one course of bricks! Elated, she stood up and stretched out, and then went into the kitchen, filled a glass with water from the sink faucet, and drank it. The glass was left there because it would be used again for sure.

The cutting process started at ten o'clock and it was now ten-twenty. So, creating this opening had not taken long. Being very old mortar, it was brittle, and it came away easily.

With the wall open, the noise outside could be heard even louder than ever. The crazy celebrating by so many people was non-stop and it made the lovely looter smile broadly! She was now also able to see the distance separating the two structures was about 5". The finish on the walls was very rough and no refinements or 'pointing' was ever done. That meant no time would need to be wasted doing any finishing on the 101 outer face when it was all closed later on.

Removing the canister from Dora's vacuum cleaner, she dumped the chips and other dirt out of it, into the void outside. The makeshift garbage bag was also emptied into the same narrow space. The clear flexible plastic which was attached to the bathroom tiles was again lowered by her, as part of getting ready to cut into the next-door structure.

Crouching down on the floor, Ariella put one of the two old sweatshirts which she brought from home, onto the exposed brick surface. This would allow her to rest her arms without tearing her long-sleeved shirt or chafing or scratching herself.

With her drill and its 6" long masonry bit at the ready, the next obstacle was about to be tackled. This wall was identical to the one cut through a few minutes before, and the same sequence would follow. She started by drilling the four important holes and then using her reciprocating saw, sliced the mortar horizontally for a distance of 24" along the bottom. Thereafter she made the two vertical passes 11" deep, and then cut along the top until this segment dropped down by ⅜".

Again, using two screwdrivers she pried the group up just a bit and jiggled this toward herself. Like before, Ariella removed the heavy brick assemblage, angling it through the first opening, and maneuvering it into the bathroom.

The demolition damsel vacuumed off the dirt and dust and then placed this group onto the clear plastic sheet alongside the first section. Taking her flashlight and observing the newly opened wall, Ariella was thrilled to see that here too, this was comprised of only one course of bricks. Somehow making the second aperture took only about twenty minutes, a bit quicker than when the first one was made in the 125-Building. The time was approaching ten thirty-five.

The insulation and one 2" x 4" wooden stud was now showing. Her utility knife sliced the fiber insulation with ease, and this was carefully removed and placed in the bathroom. She re-installed her cutting wheel, connected the extension cord to the electric drill, and then proceeded to cut the stud, again using her small hand saw to complete the job.

She pulled hard on the wooden stud because there was a screw holding it to the drywall inside the dropped-ceiling area of the jewelry store. When it came away, this was put alongside the other materials on the floor of the bathroom. The plastic dust-prevention sheet, previously taped to the tiles, was able to be removed because there was no longer a need for it. All residual dirt left on the floor emanating from this cutting procedure was swept into the dustpan and tipped out into the 5" space.

Ariella placed the other old sweatshirt across the exposed bricks of the second opening to protect her arms. There were now two large holes in the walls, and each was approximately 11" deep by 24" wide.

The back of the gypsum board could now be seen. This was in the suspended ceiling area above Barnwell's place of business, and it was the next barrier to be breached by the very motivated marauder. The cutting wheel was still in place in her drill and with this in hand, she reached across and got started. In about a minute the sheetrock was sliced on four sides and this 11" x 24" piece fell with a plop onto the fiber insulation which lay on the ceiling panels above the store.

Only a small amount of dust made its way into the apartment and the rest spilled down the gap.

It was almost ten-fifty when Ariella recovered this section of sheetrock by pulling it past the two wall openings and setting it down on the floor. She removed her eye protection goggles and shone her flashlight into the ceiling space, observing there were no support wires for the suspended metal grid close to the point of the break-in, nor were there any electric cables or ducting near this area. She took the vacuum cleaner and connected its extension wand and small brush attachment.

Stretching across into the ceiling area and using her flashlight, Ariella started suctioning drywall powder off the fiber insulation's paper lining near the wall opening.

When all the dust and granular bits were removed, she used the long handle of Dora's broom to lift up and push to one side the piece of fiber insulation closest to her. With that out the way, a 2' wide by 4' long acoustic ceiling piece was fully exposed. She now taped the small flashlight to her wrist, took two screws each 3" long, and grabbed a screwdriver. Being protected from the rough bricks by the sweatshirts, Ariella wriggled her arms, head, and shoulders through both openings.

Reaching down, she carefully turned the first screw partially into the ceiling tile and then secured the second one. By holding onto these screws, the panel was lifted off the metal grid and slid sideways, so that it rested on top of some adjoining insulation. She crawled forward a bit more and looked down. *She was in!*

The position was perfectly above two of the large, ten-foot display cases closest to this access wall. These merchandising units were parallel to each other with enough space between them for salespeople to walk. Adjacent to the ends of these, sat two more similar cabinets. Thus, two huge showcases filled with jewelry were right under her entry point with two more close by. Her calculations had been precise. There was also quite a bit of light coming in from the street even though the windows had so many 'Sale' and 'Discount' posters taped to them. But as she noted before, these posters would also provide excellent curtaining for the activities about to take place inside the store. Thus, the night-vision cameras on the drone would not need any additional help from its LEDs while it was operating in the main sales area.

In any event, more illumination could easily be provided by her wire-framed work lamp with its long cord and 60-watt light bulb.

The week before when in the bathroom, casing the joint, Ariella observed that in the dropped-ceiling space, there was a 30" distance between the concrete floor from the apartment above and the acoustic panels. Shining her flashlight around this open area she really began to appreciate how fortunate it was to have so much room in which to work, primarily for aviating and landing the tiny prop-transporter.

The tight-fitting shower cap could now be removed, and her hair was tied into a ponytail. The drilling and cutting actions were completed so there would be no more particles in the air.

It was almost eleven o'clock and time for her to smash open the display cases and get the actual heist underway!

CHAPTER 12

Ariella got the drone ready by installing into it one of the rechargeable batteries. She took the 12" long artist's brush and poured onto its bristles a small amount of the frosty-clear nail polish mixture, prepared at home two weeks before. This 12" long implement was then carefully clamped to the underside of the whirlybird.

Holding it in one hand, she worked her way through the two open walls into the 101-Building and then placed the little machine onto the insulation, which was atop a ceiling tile, next to the one just removed. Retreating into the bathroom and sitting on the floor, on went her FPV virtual reality headset. The turbo-troller could now be flown as if a person was seated right inside it! With both hands holding the remote control, the pretty pilot slowly activated the rotors and very carefully flew it into the jewelry store, keeping it high up.

Her visit there the weekend before allowed her to know where the two cameras were located in the main sales area, one in each corner about 9" below the ceiling. The orbiting offender was guided to the first surveillance unit, approaching exactly in the right position above the camera, so it could not be seen. She squashed the brush onto the lens, backed away, and then moved forward onto the same spot again. Within seconds that tiny piece of convex glass had been painted with the fast-drying, cloudy liquid.

Directing the micro-flyer back to its landing area on the insulation, Ariella reached in through the wall openings and poured a bit more of the frosty-clear nail polish onto the end of the brush. She repeated the maneuver by heading to the second spy-station and applying the coating in the same manner. Now that the lenses were glazed over, nothing regarding her burglary activities would be seen, except maybe some blurry images. Unless someone closely inspected the video modules from inches away, the translucent gel could not easily be detected. That would cause the police to not realize there were no valid recordings of the robbery for perhaps twenty-four hours or more after the break-in was discovered. They would likely glance up at the cameras and be unable to ascertain something was amiss.

At 11:09 p.m. Ariella brought the drone back past its original landing spot above the ceiling tiles, through both wall voids, and into the bathroom. The brush was removed and her main tool for the night was attached. This was the 6" length of wire with its fishing hook. It was almost time to start stealing jewelry but before doing so, the smash-and-grab girl had some glass to break!

She took Dora's broom and unscrewed its long handle from the brush part. Then using her electric drill created a ¼" diameter hole in the threaded plastic tip on the bottom of the handle. From the duffle bag, out came a spool of thin nylon cord, and this was cut off by her to a fifteen-foot length.

Passing a few inches of this through the hole in the plastic tip, she tied a knot and threaded the other end of the nylon cord through the hole in the handle of the mallet, then tied another knot there. The mallet's wooden handle still had paper towel taped to it, to preserve any prior fingerprints.

Ariella moved the broom pole, the mallet, and the cords through the gap in the walls and maneuvered her upper body into place. Looking down in the main sales area of the store and holding the broom handle tightly with it acting like a fishing rod, she dropped the maul down onto the glass of the display cabinet below her. It crashed loudly.

The top almost fell to pieces, but one large section remained intact. After grabbing the nylon cord and carefully lifting the hand tool upward, she hurled her battering ram down again onto the unbroken part of the first merchandise counter. It came apart as expected. She drew the heavy hammer up and aimed it at unit number two which paralleled the first retail fixture, dumped it down, and watched its entire glass surface disintegrate.

Ariella once again tugged her pile driver up into the ceiling area and got ready for more in-store wrecking. This time it had to be thrown a bit further so it could decimate the top of showcase number three. In her first throwing attempt, it missed and landed on the floor. But she was holding the broom handle tightly with her other hand, so the mallet was not lost, and pulling on the cord, she got it back. On the next try, the metal head found its mark and fell through the covering of the third display case shattering it like the others. After that, the pane on the fourth exhibit cabinet was fragmented in the same manner.

Ariella pulled the weighty implement up and, holding it, slid herself together with the broom pole back into the 125-Building. The demolition of the countertops was completed.

It was now time for the drone to earn its keep with its 6" wire and hook, both of which were already attached to its underside. All the practicing done two weeks before in her garage gave her confidence, because now it was 'show-time' and her piloting skills would be put to the real test!

And so it was that at 11:30 p.m. on this night of July 3rd the grabbing of the jewelry began! Moving her arms and shoulders past the gaps in the two walls, the rotor-robber was placed by her onto its landing spot on the fiber insulation. Then, retreating to the bathroom she sat on the floor, this time on the empty tote bag, not wanting to be sitting directly on the cold linoleum. Putting on her FPV headset and holding the remote control with both hands, she sent the multi-prop on its first fishing expedition.

As it descended quietly down, it went to the counter which was directly below the opening in the ceiling. Gliding past the broken glass, a series of gold chains were snagged, and the rear onboard camera showed how full the hook was becoming.

When it had scooped up six chains, the craft was brought up to its landing spot on the fiber batting. After letting it hesitate there for a few seconds, she shepherded it through the voids in the two walls into the bathroom and landed it on the floor. Removing her FPV headset Ariella took the gold-linked pieces and put them into a zip-seal bag, taken from a stack of these zip-seals which were inside the duffle. With her headset back on, the whispering-windmaker was carefully flown through the cut-out sections of the walls and back into the store.

From this first accessory display, she continued to pick up dozens of plain gold chains, countless necklaces with diamonds, and others with pendants attached. There were pearl and also emerald neck orna-mentations, and some were adorned with a variety of precious and semi-precious stones. It took about fifteen minutes for her to empty this first merchandising unit with the raiding-raptor going up and down, back and forth, each time delivering its catch to Ariella who was sitting cross-legged on the floor.

The next mission was cabinet number two and this one contained different types of rings. Some featured diamonds large and small, a whole host of them sported rubies, and a few incorporated emeralds. Others were magnificent gold bands with sapphires. The hook easily snagged these rings, many of which were lying loose under the broken shards. There were several in small open boxes which were difficult to get, but she still managed to hook and gather most of them.

Hunt Barnwell bought and stole in such volume that for the most part, the rings were not individually presented in mini snap-open containers or on any kind of stands. Instead, they simply lay loose in the clear-topped showcases for all to see. Presenting jewelry like this made customers think they were getting a 'deal' because there was such a wide array of items from which to choose.

And so, the battery-operated power-pillager went into the main sales area and back again, continuously. On each trip, it carried a payload worth hundreds, and sometimes thousands of dollars depending on the size of the single or multiple diamonds or other precious stones mounted onto engagement rings or wedding bands.

The third service counter featured watches. On certain occasions, the hook was able to grab many per trip, especially if these were ladies' timepieces with thin straps. But it could only ensnare one on each flight for the men's styles which generally had much wider bands.

Because of Ariella's quick mind and skillful hands, the quad-copter was going up and down every fifteen to twenty seconds. She soon moved from sitting on the bathroom floor to positioning herself through the breached walls where she could look down into the store. This way, the skilled operator could see what was going on below reasonably clearly and was able to work some of the time without her FPV headset. The aerial-abductor landed often on the ceiling insulation right next to her, where the haul was unloaded and simply dumped into a large paper shopping bag. The theft-machine was now able to pop up with its spoils and buzz back down a lot quicker than when it was made to fly through the openings.

As she finished emptying almost everything from this display case, there was noticeable laboring and slowing down of the shop-lifter. Therefore, this time when the perky pilot propelled it upward, she wriggled her way into the bathroom with it in her hand and also brought the bagful of sparkles with her. The drone's battery was replaced with a full-strength one. Then the fast-charge unit was plugged in to allow the run-down battery to regain its power. With another large, empty paper bag, she moved her upper torso and the little ornithopter back above the ceiling to continue with the heist.

The fourth fixture was filled with bejeweled bangles and more. The bracelets were easy to scoop up, but the earrings, most of which were mounted in twos on small velvet-surfaced cards, presented a bit of a challenge. However, with some good maneuvering, the drone was able to pick up many of these. Its hook would often find a way to snag some pairs when the earrings were mounted to their cards in a certain way. This took a bit of time, but that retail console was emptied in about twenty minutes.

At this juncture, the taking of items from the front part of the store had gone on for about an hour, and the time was twelve thirty-five on this July 4th early morning. Grasping the now-filled paper packet, Ariella slid back through the gaps and into the apartment. She stood up and stretched out, then sat down on the edge of the bathtub staring at all the jewelry, some of which was on the floor and much of it was in paper shopping bags.

The lovely larcenist decided to spend some time sorting the glitzy goods by category, (rings, necklaces, watches, and more) and placing these items into dozens of zip-seals. Before too long many of the polybags became stuffed to capacity. This packing procedure did not take too long, and the heist was certainly going extremely well.

It was about one o'clock when she activated the LED lights on the cruising-criminal and sent it to the rear of the store directly to the repair room. Once again, the navigator utilized her FPV headset. The night-vision cameras on the little-looter showed the Heistess a multitude of necklaces, chronometers, rings, and many other items. Most were there to be cleaned and a few were in various stages of repair.

Everything was lying out in the open on tabletops or on shelves. This smorgasbord of value was just waiting to be seized by the whirring bird-of-prey. Taking full advantage of these exposed spoils, almost half an hour later virtually all the better merchandise from this area was in her possession.

It all lay piled on the floor, and yes, this treasure had literally been lifted 'by hook and by crook'!

The time was 1:12 a.m. and Ariella felt she had taken enough of this treasure. It was true, more could be acquired, perhaps a few extra earring cards or even additional watches from the back, but this was sufficient. There was no point in being too greedy!

She removed her FVP headset and placed the last of the valuable articles into a bunch of re-sealables, then stuffed what she could into the backpack. But there was a vast amount of other clear plastic bags of jewelry lying there, and these were put into the duffle.

It was twenty-two minutes past one and time to plant the red-herring evidence. To this end, she picked up the small cardboard box containing the misdirecting markers. These were the vestiges gathered by her which would cause the police to look in the wrong direction when they went over the crime scene in a couple of days' time.

The polybag with the used Kleenex tissue was the first to be opened. There would be good DNA on this damp piece into which someone had blown their nose. Yuk! With her gloved hands, she pushed the hook through a tiny corner of the tissue, put on her FVP headset, then carefully flew the dangling, snotty, flimsy paper into the store.

It was transported to the floor between the first two sales counters until it touched the carpeting. The silent-skyjacker was made to slowly back away, trying to dislodge its delicate cargo as it dragged the tissue along. After it traveled for maybe eighteen inches, Ariella could see on the screen that the Kleenex suddenly freed itself. She reversed the drone very slowly at first and then returned it to the bathroom.

She attached one of the soft-rubber 1" cubes to the hook and removed the release liner exposing the very tacky adhesive which was on the underside of this cube. The flying-filcher was then directed down by her to the third display case. She caused it to make a hard landing, that is to rapidly fall onto a small piece of broken glass which was about 4" long by 2" wide with a sharp taper.

Her technique of dropping the rubber piece onto the glass worked well when experimenting in her garage at home and it was successful again this time. When the buzzing-burglar ascended, the jagged segment had adhered to the sticky cube, and this pointed payload was guided back into the bathroom. Once the transparent piece was in front of her, she opened the zip-seal which contained the dried blood scrapings, derived from the wrecked car in the junkyard. She stood at the sink, turned the faucet on ever so slowly, and let a few droplets of water fall into the bag, just enough to slightly liquefy its contents.

Ariella reached up into the mirrored mini-cupboard above the sink and found a small box of Q-Tips. Perfect! Using one of these she gently stirred the dried blood in the zip-top bag mixing it with the water drops. With the Q-Tip, she smeared some of this onto the sharp point of the glass and quite a lot more onto its flat surface. It was done in such a way it appeared someone had injured themselves on the acicular tip and the cut finger or lacerated hand deposited blood onto another part of the shard as well. It dried quite quickly.

She adhered the piece carefully to the edge of the sticky rubber block so that not too much of the tacky area was in contact with it, and then slowly steered the micro-marauder back to land in merchandise unit number three. Like with the Kleenex, she allowed the glass to drag along for a short distance. There was so much other sharp debris there, that in seconds the sliver with the blood on it got snagged by other pieces and it came free from the adhesive. The drone was brought back into the bathroom.

With her gloved hands, Ariella removed the foam coffee cup from its sealed bag. The residue of the beverage had long since dried out. The crafty chemist added a few drops of water, and with a clean Q-Tip agitated it very slightly so there was now a small amount of wet coffee at the bottom.

The rubber cube was re-positioned on the hook with the sticky part now sideways, and she attached the side of the Styrofoam to the adhesive. The lightweight load should, with luck, hang on long enough for her to deliver it exactly to where it needed to be. Hopefully, the blowing action from the propellers would not dislodge it too soon.

Holding her breath, Ariella slowly took this evidence down to the floor near the fourth showcase. Whew… it did not fall off! She allowed the hovering-helo to move close to the base of the cabinet. The cup started to drag on the carpet as it went lower and lower and then suddenly it popped off and came to rest lying on its side. Great! If any of the reconstituted coffee trickled out it would not matter too much.

There were of course the fingerprints and DNA of an unknown person on the Styrofoam. By leaving this lying there it would look like some careless thief dropped his hot-drink container at the scene of the robbery. How stupid!

As she maneuvered the controller to back away from what was just deposited onto the floor, the downdraft caused it to roll about slightly. Ariella could see this in her FPV headset, but because the rotors were moving somewhat slowly, the wind effect was not too bad. Once the birdlike-bandit was about three feet away and had risen up a bit, its speed increased, and it was directed back to the bathroom.

All along her intentions were to not put too many of the deceptive pieces close to the robbery ingress point. The deeper inside some of the objects were found, the more it would look like the thieves were active in the entire area.

With the airship now next to her, Ariella took a small piece of toilet tissue and folded it into a 1" square. A tiny bit of tape was used to prevent it from opening. This folded square was then adhered to the sticky cube, still hooked in place under the drone. She dipped the tissue into the zip-seal bag with the liquefied blood.

The LED lights were now activated for this special mission, and the greedy-grabber with its blood-soaked featherweight tissue, was sent by her down into the store. This time it flew through the main sales section and past the repair room until it arrived at a solid steel emergency exit door, located in the back of the shop.

Utilizing her FPV headset, Ariella expertly piloted the little crime-copter to slide the blood-soaked tissue onto the metal panic bar of the door. This red smudge made it look like someone found their way to that area, thus tricking the police into thinking this portal might have been opened or it was the exit point. The onboard cameras showed the door to be alarmed and bolted shut. Let the investigators try to figure out why the security system was not activated or how anyone got in or out of such a well-sealed barrier! This blood would also show that an injured thief walked to the furthest point inside.

On its return trip to the front of the shop, Ariella made the wandering-whirligig deposit another long rouge streak on the wooden frame of an open archway. After that, she brought it back and removed her headset.

It was time to plant the hairs found in the convenience store. Taking out the few hairs and holding them in her gloved hand she wormed her way through the brick wall openings of the two buildings. Peering down and with her hand outstretched, these were dropped into the display case directly below her. If the police found them among the shattered glass it would be good, but if not, it would be of little importance.

Ariella opened the polybag containing the four bus-station cigarette butts. Two were of one brand, and the others were a different kind, making it look like there were at least a couple of individuals committing this robbery. These were carefully thrown down, one pair at a time, to land somewhere on the carpeting quite far inside.

One last bit of evidence was the mallet, and once it was left in plain sight, it would be time to close the walls. She picked it up, undid the knot in the cord, and slipped this out of the holes in the broom and mallet handles.

Because paper was taped over the handle early on, and left there while using it for the heist, she hoped most if not all the original fingerprints survived. Carefully removing the paper and sliding on her stomach, she squeezed through the wall gaps. Holding the mallet by its metal head, of course with her gloves still on, she threw it with force, making it land on the floor near one of the service counters furthest away from her point of entry.

Ariella retreated into the bathroom, picked up a screwdriver, and once again taped the small flashlight to her wrist, before returning to the area above the jewelry store. She now grasped the edge of the ceiling tile, the one originally lifted out to create the access point. This was lying off to the side over some of the fiber padding.

By putting its far end into the metal frame, it was maneuvered into position, and holding onto the two screws which were attached earlier, she carefully lowered the panel, seating it firmly into the grid. She undid the screws with her screwdriver and then wiggled back into the bathroom where the screws were dropped into the duffle bag.

Taking the broom handle, Ariella pushed a 2" nail through the hole which she drilled into its threaded section before, and this nail was secured with some masking tape. Reaching into the ceiling area and clutching this long broom handle tightly, she snagged the fiber insulation. The nail grabbed hold of this, allowing her to slide it back into place above the ceiling tile. The Heistess pulled the wooden pole back, removed the tape and the nail from the threaded end, and took the flashlight off her wrist.

She wanted to make sure this thick batting looked like it had never been tampered with and that it did not appear too clean. To do this would require her eye protection goggles and the small bag of dust which was gleaned from the attic at her home.

Ariella once again crawled through the wall openings and placed some of the dust from the polybag into her hand. With her arm out-stretched above the suspended ceiling, she blew on the dust. It flew directionally, with much of it landing where it was supposed to, that is over the section of insulation which was originally removed, and also onto surrounding pieces. This action was repeated ten times.

Now the paper-laminated wadding was covered in fine particulates, with everything blending together as if none of it had been touched in years. It would certainly show signs of nothing having come into contact with it during the course of the robbery. Ariella had done a masterful job manipulating the appearance of the surface on the insulation. It was almost like retouching or repairing a painting, where once a competent artist had completed their work, it looked like the original.

Shining her flashlight into this open area she checked it again to make sure all was in order. Not one thing appeared to exist which would give the game away, and for sure this burglary didn't take place by thieves coming in from above.

The planting of the blood, the hairs, and the other items took about twenty-five minutes to complete. It was now just past one-fifty and time to close the hole in the drywall. Ariella took her carefully prepared *Patch-up-Piece*, the 13" x 26" painted plywood panel with its eight nails bent into small hooks. Holding this, with the back facing her, she took the can of spray adhesive from the duffle bag and applied this sticky glue to a 1" wide area all the way around its periphery.

The nimble nymph then crawled into the two wall cut-outs moving the panel ahead of her. By tilting it at an angle, it easily passed through to the open ceiling area.

Grabbing hold of two corner hooks she slowly and carefully pulled the thin wooden sheet toward herself keeping it as level as possible, and giving it one final yank, the board clung to the drywall. Tugging on each of the eight bent nails separately, this action made sure the wood stuck fast and evenly around its entire perimeter, adhering by about 1" all about its edges.

The plywood was now firmly in place, and it was time to secure it further with rubber bands. From the small coil of ⅛" diameter wire which was in the duffle, she used her pliers to cut off eight sections, each about 6" in length. To one of the hooks on the back of the closure piece, Ariella attached a rubber band and pulled it past the opening in the bricks.

She threaded the band over one of the 6" wire pieces and then by bending this slightly, was able to jam it in the 5" gap between the two buildings. The stiff filament held the elastic solidly in place. Rubber bands were then attached to the remaining seven hooks, with each being similarly secured by a wire piece wedged between the walls. The tension on the bands pulled the plywood evenly and firmly against the drywall, helping the adhesive to bond better. The large void in this section of sheetrock inside the jewelry store had now completely disappeared.

Ariella took a 3" wide paint brush and swept the loose dust off the exposed parts of the wall. Taking a plastic container from Dora's kitchen and filling this with water, she dipped the brush in and used it to wet down the bricks.

Now it was time to follow the same repair procedure which was done in the practice run at her house two weeks before. Mortar was first mixed with water to a fairly thick consistency, in one of Dora's glass bowls. From the duffle, out came the zip-seal bag filled with instant coffee powder. She added a small amount of this to the cement mixture to discolor it so that it would not appear too 'white' relative to the rest of the joint compound on the outside of the structure. This was stirred and set aside.

Ariella lifted the rather heavy section of bricks, cut away by her just a few hours before. Tilting it, and with difficulty, she moved this through the opening in Dora's building, and with her arms once again shaking from the forty-five-pound weight, this group of bricks was slowly shuffled into place in the wall of the 101-Building. She was extremely careful not to let this segment get anywhere near the plywood piece which had just been adhered to the drywall. What a nightmare it would be if it crashed past and plunged down through the ceiling panel into the store below!

From inside the duffle came the two ⅜" diameter 4" long dowel stick pieces to make space for the mortar. Again, using a screwdriver, the now experienced masonry expert leveraged up the brick-set and slid one of the dowels into position about six inches from one end. Then at an identical distance from the other end, did the same with the second dowel so that it was all now raised up by ⅜".

Following her home experiments, the piping method could now be used to fill in the spaces around the brick-set. Taking one of the large zip-seals and her trowel, this bag was loaded up with mortar mixture. Using her scissors to snip a small hole in one corner of the bag, she started squeezing out the cement along the base of the group of bricks while dodging the two dowels. The same process was done to the remaining three sides of the replaced section, using moderate pressure as it all moved along. Like the test run in her garage at home, the two dowel stick pieces again adequately supported the assemblage and prevented it from squashing down on the mortar and pushing this out.

Sufficient material had now been applied in between these bricks, so she simply left this with its rough look, matching the rest of the wall, and only smoothed it off a little here and there with her trowel. Ariella surmised that when these structures were built so close to each other years before, no one cared about finishing the appearance on the outside.

The aperture which was earlier made in the side of the 101-Building was now sealed closed. It was time to remove the wires jammed between the two walls, used for holding tension on the thin plywood. These wire pieces were pulled off and allowed to drop away, and the parts of the rubber bands sticking out were snipped off with her scissors. The repair was now done, and it all looked much like it always had. The time was two thirty-six.

The Heistess breathed a sigh of relief, stood up to stretch her legs, then went into the kitchen, took off her gloves, and again had a drink of water. The glass was washed and dried with a piece of paper towel which removed any possible fingerprints, and it was placed back on the shelf. At that point, she returned to the bathroom and stood quietly for a few minutes while munching on a granola bar.

Donning a new pair of gardening gloves, she was ready to replace the next chunk of bricks, but first she had to decide what things should be kept and which could be disposed of in the narrow 5" gap.

Ariella selected several implements to throw away. It was more important the duffle and the backpack be used to carry home the Carat-Collection rather than things of low priority. While there were some items brought in which would go home, others could be sacrificed.

Even though her hands were shielded the whole time, the tools and accessories were wiped with paper towel before being abandoned. First, the extension cord was unplugged and with the utility knife, this was cut into six segments. The nylon rope was also shredded, and these pieces were thrown down between the outer walls. Her wire-framed work lamp with its 60-watt light bulb was ditched after slicing apart its cord.

She took one of the two old sweatshirts as well as the discarded gloves and using her scissors, snipped these into small scraps and let them drop down into the abyss. The cleanup specialist grabbed the insulation chunks which were gathered from behind the sheetrock in both buildings and these were sliced apart and dumped. She then disposed of the scissors, the pair of pliers, the trowel, the can of spray adhesive, her flashlight, and the small handsaw.

She did not simply let these fall in one place, but they were hurled some distance from the break-in spot, so they landed randomly on the ground in the narrow chasm. There were already many years of accumulation of paper, plastic, and other trash which had piled up there, so heavy items such as the pliers, the scissors and the handsaw simply sank beneath the garbage never to be seen again. Although it was an expensive item, Ariella flung her valuable reciprocating saw down the middle of the interstice because it was too bulky to take home. She also disposed of the electric plug-in drill. Her rechargeable drill was at home to use for any projects there. Three wooden 2" x 4" studs had been gleaned from the walls and only two were still needed, so one was let go into the gap.

She took the paper trash bag and tipped it out, with the dust, dirt, and debris disappearing down below. However, she retained this garbage packet for further use. Taking the piece of drywall cut from above the ceiling in the 101-Building, she held this outside and broke it into small portions. These chunks were tossed far from the opening. But the 16" x 24" section of gypsum board which came from Dora's bathroom, was kept. There was a specific need for that.

Ariella had brought with her eight replacement wall tiles, knowing only six were required. She decided not to re-use any of the originals, because of the dried-out adhesive on them and they would not lie flat when glued back into place. She took the six old tiles (one of which was already broken), snapped these into small fragments, and threw them away. Of course, all eight new ones were kept. Two of these would be used as spares if any cracked during installation.

At this time, Ariella was ready to seal up the hole in the masonry wall of the 125-Building, and her same closure method would be used. She once again brushed away all the dust and dirt from the exposed bricks and these were wet down with water using the 3" paintbrush. As was done for the structure next door, she lifted the brick section from the bathroom floor and with her muscles straining, jiggled this into place. Like before, with the screwdriver, she pried up the left-hand side of the group and slid one of the short dowel-stick pieces into position about 6" from the edge. The other side was then raised up and the second dowel was inserted.

Ariella mixed another batch of mortar with water and again added a little instant coffee powder. After stirring it well and following her usual pattern, the zip-seal bag was topped up, and its contents were piped into all gaps and spaces. On the brick surface, which was facing her, the excess joint amalgam was smoothed down with her gloved fingertips, so it more-or-less matched the rest of the interior wall. Taking both 2" x 4" wooden studs which were removed earlier from the 125-Building, she applied a thick coating of the quick-setting tile adhesive to the short side of each. These were gently pushed up against the newly installed brick section so the 4" length protruded out toward her. They were positioned about fourteen inches apart from each other.

Ariella took the 16" x 24" piece of sheetrock originally derived from Dora's bathroom wall and adhered this to the studs using some of the tile glue. This was held in place with her hands for a little while and then left to dry for a further fifteen minutes. In the meantime, she tidied up by gathering the few remaining items and packing these into the duffle bag together with her FVP video headset.

Soon the adhesive had hardened and the 16" x 24" piece was now secured to the studs. Taking six of the new white tiles, she stuck these to the freshly installed gypsum board. Then opening the plastic container of grout and using a putty knife, the gaps around the edges of the new tiles were filled in by her, and the excess material was wiped off with a piece of damp paper towel.

Ariella knew the color of the new compound needed to match the old. To do this she removed her gloves and put a little of the grout into the palm of her hand. With a few pinches of instant coffee powder, she changed this until its hue corresponded with the old look between the ceramic squares in the rest of the bathroom. Using her finger, this was rubbed over the new and old grout so that it all blended to achieve the same off-white appearance.

Again, a piece of damp paper towel was used to wipe away bits left behind on the tiles and any possible fingerprints of hers. The job of closing the wall was now complete. The skillful scoundrel stood back, admired her handiwork, and whispered, "You are quite the artiste!" It was 3:17 a.m.

She washed out the mortar mixing bowl in the bathroom sink, took this to the kitchen, then wiped it thoroughly with paper towel and returned it to the cabinet where it belonged. The small plastic container which was used to hold the water when wetting down the bricks was rinsed out. This was dried and placed onto its original shelf, with her holding only the paper, and being careful not to touch the item. Then she put her gloves back on. Back in the bathroom, everything was tidied including taking the clear plastic sheets off the floor, one of which had remained taped down where all the work was done, and another was where the brick-segments were temporarily stored. All this garbage was put into the paper trash bag.

Into the duffle went the small grout container and the tube of adhesive, followed by the screwdrivers and a few other items including the drill bits and the drone's charger. The two leftover 8" square white wall tiles were placed into the rear of the under-sink cabinet, to lighten her carry-out load. If these were ever found, one could surmise they were extra pieces from a prior renovation.

Taking Dora's vacuum cleaner with the brush attached to its wand, she went around the entire staging area, picking up the last bits of dirt, and then used it all over herself, most especially removing any grit or powder from her clothing.

The Heistess vacuumed the bathtub, the sink, the windowsill, the toilet, the towel racks, and every other surface as well as the walls, to make sure all residual dust was removed. These areas were cleaned one more time with a large piece of slightly moistened paper towel.

Ariella rolled off some toilet paper to be certain it had no particulates left on it. She emptied all debris and dirt from the vacuum cleaner canister into the paper trash bag. Again, damp paper towel was used to virtually sanitize the canister and the vacuum cleaner, to prevent any traces of drywall granules, sawdust, or brick chips from being found anywhere in or on this machine. These cleanup sheets all went into the trash bag, and she sealed it by folding over the top, squashing it down to compress it all, and taping it closed. This was stuffed deep into the duffle together with the tote bag which would not be used. Other than the drone's remote control, the last to go in would be the remaining sweatshirt.

The bathroom was now spotless. She had already put the jewelry into various zip-seal bags and these items were either in the large backpack or in the duffle. At that point, she put the fluffy bathmats back onto the bathroom floor, and the towels were returned to their racks. The broom's handle was reattached to its brush, and this immediately hid the hole which she had drilled into the threaded part to secure the cord for tossing and retrieving the mallet.

Ariella used the vacuum cleaner to go over a section of the hallway carpet so the canister would not be too spotless, in case anyone studied it closely. It now had a small amount of normal fuzz and dirt in it. Then it was a case of walking back and forth over that part of the carpet, so it did not look like it was recently done. The vacuum cleaner, the broom, and the dustpan were returned to Dora's utility closet, and each placed in the exact position in which she had found them.

She took the drone and moved the small switch which instructed it 'Return to Launch'. Since it already knew its home coordinates it was ready to fly there. The fully charged battery was installed, and then kicking off her sneakers, Ariella climbed up onto the bathtub and opened the window just a crack. It was three thirty-five as she glanced down and noticed there were no people out on the street, other than a young couple walking hand-in-hand, kissing and hugging. It seemed they were about to enter the foyer of the 125-Building.

Waiting for them to go inside, Ariella opened the bathroom window as wide as it would go, then jumped down, grabbed the remote control, and started up the drone. She skillfully flew it out of the window and in seconds it was up and gone on its way to its special destination which was the front lawn of her house. This was one less thing for her to carry! With her gloves still on, she closed the window, climbed down, and slid her feet into her sneakers. The remote was placed in the duffle followed by the sweatshirt, and then the zipper was pulled closed.

She used the toilet in the bathroom, washed her hands, tied her hair up, and donned the curly-hair, charcoal-grey wig. It would of course be best to leave the 125-Building wearing this hairpiece just to fool whoever would be reviewing the foyer camera recording, or if anyone saw her on the street and they were called to testify one day. She was finally ready to exit Dora's apartment and head home with her spoils!

While feeling very relieved at what was accomplished in just a few hours, a nagging fear began to haunt her. Ariella had just committed a criminal act, and even though her motive was justifiable, she had broken the law. But then a smile came over her face realizing that she got back what was taken from her nana. Perhaps no one other than her could have executed this mission so well.

Ariella came into the 125-Building wearing a dark shirt and jeans with a tan lightweight jacket. She turned the reversible garment inside-out, so it was now brown. The foyer surveillance camera would have recorded a female with short, straight dark hair wearing tan outerwear coming in and a lady with greyish curly hair dressed in a brown wind-breaker going out. This way they would be hard-pressed to match the incoming with the outgoing person.

It was 3:42 a.m. One more time she checked around the staging area, took the over-stuffed backpack and put it on then lifted the bulky duffle, pleased the extra tote bag was not needed. Leaving the bathroom, and making her way to the entrance, Ariella felt gratified because all her objectives were accomplished: Opening the walls, taking back a fortune in jewelry, closing it all up, and then planting incriminating evidence. What an eventful night… victory was in the air!

◆◆◆◆◆

Walking down the passage and approaching the door, she stopped. What was that noise? Were there voices in the hallway outside? She hesitated for a moment, not wishing to run into any other tenants in the building and certainly not at this early hour of the morning. It was essential no potential witnesses should see her emerging from this apartment carrying a large bag and a backpack.

Suddenly there was the sound of a key being put into the lock and the door began to open! Ariella froze.

"Oh no! Dora is back early from Florida!" The barely audible words tumbled out of her mouth. Spinning around and fleeing into the darkened living room, she dumped the duffle, removed the backpack, and dropped to the carpet behind the couch.

Voices could be heard of a man and a woman… who was not Dora! They were talking in a half-drunken state as they staggered together into the room where Ariella was lying on the floor. Horrified, she mouthed quietly, "This must be the couple who entered the building, the people I saw just a few minutes ago from the bathroom window!"

The two now stood within feet of her, but fortunately, they did not switch on the lights. There was, however, some illumination coming in from the passageway. The couple turned to face each other, then hugged, kissed, and laughed.

They flopped down onto the couch, close to where the panicked purloiner was hiding right behind them. Her mind was racing, and she could not believe it, "Just *five* more minutes and I would have been out of here!"

Ariella was breathing as quietly as possible while the man and the woman on the couch were really getting into it. The panting was becoming intense, and the woman began to moan rather loudly.

Suddenly the petting between them slowed down and the male's voice said, "Hey Sarah, whose place is this and how did you get a key?"

Sarah replied, "I told you earlier! It belongs to my great-aunt Dora. I was so pleased to hear she was going to be away until Thursday visiting her daughter Linda in Florida. I have a key because I was asked to come in, to water the plants, and to check on the place. I haven't tended to the plants yet so maybe I will do so while I am here, and Jerry I am keeping an eye on her apartment and an eye on you!"

"You are so funny," he replied as his hands started wandering all over her body again.

She gasped quietly and said, "To imagine my husband thinks I am at work all night!" Sarah told him the hospital where she was employed as a nurse needed people on standby because of accidents and other serious events which could happen over the July 4th weekend. He did not seem to mind. Sarah was convinced he was having an affair of his own.

Jerry added, "Well I am glad my wife and I are separated, and I am so pleased you and I have a chance to be alone. This has worked out perfectly. Good thinking, Sarah!"

The kissing and petting resumed, becoming very hot and heavy. Ariella was mortified, lying sprawled out on the carpet directly behind the lovers. To think she successfully robbed the place next door, to consider how much meticulous planning went into this heist, how her drone expertise and other creativity really paid off, and now to get found out literally at the last second!

Racing through her mind were thoughts of going to prison. The consequences of her actions were never really considered because she had worked out all the details. Virtually every eventuality was considered except something unforeseen like what was taking place now.

This situation was most unfortunate, but at least the couple did not walk in on her while the wall was open! There was still a slim chance of her sneaking out of there. If they found her, could she kill them? That would be impossible because she was not a murderer!

But how else do you silence witnesses? Ariella began to understand why law enforcement many times will say that perpetrators make mistakes. Often it is not stupidity, but it is because unexpected things happen, or witnesses suddenly show up during a crime when least expected. That is when criminals panic and start leaving evidence behind. If these two lovebirds discovered her, perhaps she could offer them some of the loot to keep them quiet. But what if they chose not to be involved and instead called the police?

She gingerly peeked around the edge of the couch and saw a cabinet across the room which had glass doors. In the semi-darkness and not-too-clear reflection, the duo could be seen moving around on the couch half-clothed.

"Oh, give me a break," was her quiet mumble. "Just get on with it then go home!" It concerned her the two could be all over the floor of the living room in moments. Where else could she hide? What a pity they had not put on any loud music, because if she got up now, they would almost certainly hear something or see her. What if any of the jewelry began to clink a bit when she tried to leave? Ariella began sweating and feelings of fear and foreboding were beginning to set in.

"Let me get us something to lie down on," said Sarah suddenly as she rolled off the couch.

"Okay," Jerry muttered. "I will go to the bathroom in the meantime."

As they stumbled out of the living room Ariella decided to make a dash for it. She got up quickly, picked up the backpack and the duffle bag, and carefully strode through the doorway. Sarah, who obviously knew her way around Dora's apartment, went into the spare bedroom, grabbed some bedding from the closet, and in a few seconds was on her way back. Ariella whirled around, once again dropping down in the exact spot where she was before. Sarah walked into the living room, and even in the half-light if she had looked down and to her right, she would have seen a woman with two bags on the carpet behind the couch. Fortunately, her glazed-over eyes were simply watching where she was going, trying not to step onto the blankets which were dangling around her feet.

Then Jerry reappeared and he headed straight for her. Sarah was standing up, gyrating her partially clothed body around for him, and he was not taking his eyes off her, which was Ariella's saving grace!

In no time they were both completely naked and were lying on the floor on one blanket, and half-covered by the other one. Then they started making love together. It was a wild and noisy event and the jewelry pirate lay there silently, hoping it would soon be over and the two of them would leave without seeing her. Before too long they cried out in ecstasy together and then suddenly all was quiet. Ariella could hear her own heart pounding as her anxiety level began to rise again. What if they found her now?

But neither got up. All she could hear was rhythmic breathing as they cuddled together, and then both fell into a deep sleep.

The time was 4:04 a.m. and once again she peered around the side of the couch to look at the cabinet's glass doors. The reflection showed the two lovers exhausted and entwined in each other's arms. Ariella rose gingerly, lifting the backpack and then the duffle. Something inside jingled a little causing Sarah to stir slightly and move about just a bit.

The Heistess was now standing up, and very slowly and soundlessly went out of the living room, being careful not to let either bag touch a wall or the small table which stood in the hallway near the entrance.

Putting the duffle onto the carpet and carefully unlocking the deadbolt, Ariella slipped out of the apartment after opening the door. She closed it softly behind her deciding not to use her key to secure it.

Her thinking was, "Let them imagine they forgot to lock it when they came in." After putting on the backpack and lifting the heavy duffle, she walked along the hallway and down the flight of stairs to the ground floor. There were no neighbors or other residents to be seen anywhere in the corridor or in the stairwell. Arriving at the interior door which led to the foyer of the building, she cautiously opened it, keeping the duffle bag close to the floor and to the wall, out of the purview of the camera. With her head down and looking to the left, Ariella walked through the vestibule and onto Fourth Street. Only then did she remove the gloves from her now sweaty hands and stuff these into her jeans pocket.

The time was almost ten after four. The escapade with the two uninvited guests delayed her by about half an hour, but at least she was now outside. There were only a few people on the sidewalk, and she went along as unobtrusively as possible, praying no one would start any trouble with her or try to mug her. Ariella was hoping there would be no officers on foot patrol or even driving by in their vehicles, especially since she was wearing a backpack and carrying a bulky bag.

Walking with determination back to her car, it was her understanding this would be another tricky part of the heist, to not get robbed or assaulted. It was important there were no troublemakers or rioters out and about who could cause the police to think Ariella was a looter from a store where windows may have been broken by other people.

These were possibilities barely thought of before, but it was a chance she had to take.

Now away from the heart of the downtown area and on the semi-dark road where the Buick was parked, she pressed the remote which unlocked the car. The backpack was dumped on the driver's side rear floor, and the duffle bag was thrown onto the back seat, and then she slid in securing the doors.

Panting, out of breath, and with her heart pounding, Ariella realized the worst was now over. The jewelry store had been robbed... through the ceiling, and then the breach was patched up as if nothing ever happened. She broke in without breaking in! Her feeling was that the authorities would remain confused for days, perhaps even for many weeks, and this case might never be solved. The Heistess put her head into her hands, let out a huge sigh, and then started sobbing. The relief of making it to the old Buick despite almost being caught by the lustful couple, as well as so many other things which could have gone wrong, was quite overwhelming.

After a short while Ariella dried her eyes knowing it was time to get out of this neighborhood and go home. Her makeup was all smudged and when looking in the visor mirror, she was quite startled at how pale and awful her face appeared. The charcoal-grey wig still covered her hair and she now put on the large, black-framed glasses, wanting to remain in disguise until safely at home in case of street monitoring or being seen by any pedestrians or other motorists.

It was four seventeen when Ariella started the engine and began to drive away carefully, neither too fast nor too slow, not wishing to attract any attention to the Buick. Her thinking was, on a long weekend like this, traffic patrols would most certainly be out there on the lookout for any bad drivers. While relieved to be in the car and finally on her way, she had no idea her troubles were about to get even worse.

◆◆◆◆◆

It was 4:25 a.m. when Ariella rounded a corner not too far from her house. In front of her, in the middle of the road was a sobriety checkpoint! They were most certainly looking for July 4th drunk drivers and there wasn't a way out. The police positioned themselves where they could see any automobiles which tried to turn away or take a different route and such cars could easily be pursued.

With only twenty yards to go, there were no vehicles in front of her and the Buick was rapidly approaching the checkpoint. Relieved she had not been drinking, they would not be able to arrest her for that infraction. But then it dawned on her the disguise would not match her driver's license picture!

With her car barely fifteen yards away she grabbed the wig, yanked it off, and threw it onto the passenger-side floor mat. With one hand on the wheel, she tossed the large, black-framed glasses onto the seat next to her, pulled on the clips holding her hair, and shook her head causing her ample but now crinkled blond mop to tumble to her shoulders. The beauty spot on her cheek remained. The auto came to a stop.

"License, registration, and insurance cards please," said the officer as he peered in at her. Ariella was terrified and stared at his name tag, J.T. Taylor. The car was still in her deceased grandmother's name and that would take some explaining. Was the insurance up to date or not? At least she remembered to bring her driver's license and retrieving it from her jeans pocket handed it to the stern authority figure.

She dared not reach into the center console for the registration or the possibly expired insurance card. He glanced at her license and seemed to somehow forget about the other two items. He was more intent on his next question.

"Have you consumed any liquor tonight, ma'am?"

"No. Absolutely not." Her voice was a whisper.

"What did you say?"

"No, I haven't."

Looking at her smudged makeup and disheveled hair, he was not convinced. "Please step out of the vehicle."

She did so, and he made her walk in a straight line, one foot in front of the other. That small task was accomplished without a problem, and then she breathed into the proffered breathalyzer tube. He appeared astonished when it showed no signs of her having even one alcoholic beverage that night.

"Well, you spoke the truth. You have not been drinking." Sounding surprised and perhaps a bit disappointed, he handed back her driver's license.

The officer shone his flashlight into the car and at the same time, opening the rear door, immediately noticed the over-stuffed duffle and the bulky backpack on the floor.

"What's in this luggage?" he growled. His hand went onto the duffle and his thumb and forefinger closed on the zipper-pull. She was horrified as he started sliding the zipper open. This was technically an illegal search, but she did not say a word, not wanting to arouse any suspicion.

The game was now up because he was seconds away from discovering some of the implements used for carrying out the robbery and seeing all the rings, watches, gold chains, necklaces, and other stolen jewelry.

Fortunately, the drone was sent to fly home on its own, but all the other evidence was right there. She suddenly broke down and started sobbing again. He stared at her strangely and said, "Obviously you have been involved in a bad situation. This is not good for you!"

Ariella was half choking with fear, her breathing now came in short gasps of desperation, and she wiped her nose with the sleeve of her jacket. As her right hand came down from her nose, she started lifting her left hand to meet it, to hold both wrists out in front so he could handcuff her. She was giving herself up because it was all over.

The patrolman began sliding the zipper on the duffle even further along, opening the top of the bag. Now he was staring at it as he moved his flashlight about. "It is a real crime when this type of thing happens." Her heart sank even further and she almost fainted.

"Yes, as I said, it is a real crime when this happens." He was repeating his words while looking down at the partially unzipped flap. The dirty and gritty sweatshirt used for cushioning her arms on the bricks was right on top. He pulled on a portion of the sleeve, and it came out. As he did so, part of a polybag containing gold chains with diamond studded pendants started to show.

Ariella almost collapsed from feelings of dread, understanding she was caught red-handed, and thinking that after coming this far with a plan so ingenious and perfectly executed, she was done for and would be spending many years in prison.

The policeman seemed to not notice the jewelry, and began babbling, "My daughter also recently broke up with her boyfriend, in fact it was just last week. I can see that must be what is going on with you. Moved your stuff out, eh?" He gestured toward the sweatshirt sleeve which was protruding and the backpack lying on the floor.

She brought her hands down rapidly, still trying to absorb where this was all going. Was he not going to arrest her?

"Best you be on your way young lady. Drive carefully and do not be concerned. I am sure without smudged makeup from your heartbreak tears, you can be quite attractive. I know you will find another love before too long. That is what I told my daughter."

"Thank you." Moving back into the car, Ariella could hardly get the words out. The rear door was still open, and she should have closed it before getting inside. Once again, her heart almost stopped as he reached onto the seat and took hold of the duffle. He pushed the sweatshirt sleeve back in and at the same time, the partially showing bag of gold chains disappeared. Then he pulled the zipper closed, shut the rear door, and properly closed her front door as well.

"Have a good July 4th holiday," he said.

It was a little after four-forty when she started driving away. Another car arrived behind her, and the patrolman turned to confront that driver.

With her hands shaking on the steering wheel, her mind was racing over the two harrowing encounters of the past hour.

A couple of lovebirds out of nowhere suddenly show up at Dora's apartment! How could that happen so early in the morning on the very night of the break-in? Again thinking, if they arrived just five minutes later, she would not have gone through all that worrying.

And then it was running into a sobriety checkpoint. The cops were of course out scouring for any inebriated July 4th revelers. Ariella understood this was something she should have anticipated, and perhaps taken back roads for the drive home. Here too it seemed like the game was up and yet somehow, she skated past this one as well. The officer asked for the registration and insurance cards and then seemed to forget about those two items which alone could have unraveled everything.

"Grandma," her utterance could hardly be heard, "Thank you for protecting me while I was trying to right the wrong done to you."

Arriving at her house about ten minutes later and opening the garage door with the remote, she drove directly inside. Ariella turned off the engine, closed the garage door, and then sat in the Buick for a short time, decompressing. Stealing a fortune from a secure retail outlet was no easy feat, but at this juncture, it was home sweet home.

However, the perturbed pillager could not know there would be a lot more drama yet to come because of this heist!

Out of curiosity, she opened the center console to see if the car's registration and insurance cards were there. They were, but the insurance had expired. Thank goodness he did not insist on seeing these, and of course, the car was still registered to her grandmother.

How could Harry Woodward, who was holding the Buick at his repair shop, give her the car without looking at the status of its insurance? All he had to do was ask and she would have paid for the renewal. This was a huge oversight on his part which could have put her freedom in jeopardy. But then she realized it was really her responsibility to have checked it.

She went indoors and placed the duffle and backpack into the closet in her bedroom. The two wigs and the black-framed glasses were put into the disguise outfit bag, and this also went into the bedroom closet. Ariella came back into the garage, drove the Buick a block and a half away, and parked it on the side of the road. The spare garage door opener was taken and put in her pocket because this old car would no longer be visiting her house. There was not a soul to be seen anywhere in her neighborhood, and it was just starting to get light outside as she walked back home.

Her heist clothes were thrown into the laundry basket, she slipped into pajamas, removed the brown contact lenses, and then wiped the beauty spot off her cheek.

Although hungry, she did not feel like eating so after brushing her teeth and cleaning the makeup off her face, she looked at her phone and listened to four messages from Barbara. Ariella thought to call back later in the morning because there was no point waking her friend at this crazy hour!

Purdy was being a pest by constantly rubbing against her legs, so he was given a little food and told he would get more in the afternoon. It was 5:35 a.m. when the fatigued female finally got into bed and fell sound asleep. But not for long!

CHAPTER 13

Monday, July 4th at about 4:00 a.m.

Al night at the party and even when Barbara arrived home at this early morning hour, her concern for Ariella was very real. Every time she dialed, the call went to voicemail, because Ariella did not have her phone with her and was not answering. Barbara remembered her friend left the party just before eight o'clock because of a cough and a migraine headache. Although she understood Ariella would be at home and asleep, she was still feeling troubled. At four fifty-five the party girl had not yet gone to bed, and calling for the fourth time, again heard the *leave a message* recording.

At this point, although somewhat drunk from over-indulging, Barbara decided to have a snack and then go to check out what was going on. It was about half an hour later when she got into her car and set out on her quest. Something did not feel right.

She arrived there just after six o'clock and Ariella, who was already in bed and in a deep sleep, woke up startled upon hearing the doorbell ringing.

"Oh no!" was her panicked thought, "They have come to arrest me! How could they know so quickly?"

The frazzled female got up, threw on her bathrobe, walked to the spare bedroom, and looked out the window, expecting to see flashing lights. Instead, what a relief, there was a white Toyota parked in her driveway. She went downstairs to the front door and opened it.

"Are you okay?" asked Barbara looking anxious.

Ariella was still shaking from the sudden noise of the doorbell and waves of guilt and distress were washing over her. "I told you I was not feeling well. I have been asleep most of the time since I got home from the party last night." To be courteous, she invited inside the inebriated Barbara, whose words were not slurring quite as much as they were on the voicemail messages.

"I called you many times and asked you to phone me back," said Barbara walking through the front door wobbling a bit, now staring at how pale and sickly Ariella appeared.

"I needed to rest, and you knew I was suffering from a terrible migraine. I put my phone on 'silent' so I would not be woken up."

"Oh, I am so sorry to have disturbed you. Can I make you a cup of tea?"

All the blond burglar wanted to do now was to sleep and get past the incredible strain of the past few hours. "I would really like to get back into bed. Why don't you come by later today? We can throw something on the grill, or do you want to bring some take-outs? That is if I am up to eating."

"Okay. I will bring some to-go Chinese food. I am glad to see you are safe at home. I don't know why but I had a strange feeling of deep angst about you all night."

"I am sure I will be okay by this afternoon," said Ariella smiling, trying to look a bit relaxed and normal.

"Fine. Donnie and I need to bring your Subaru to you anyway. I will see you around say, three o'clock?"

"Great. I need my car because I don't like being stranded at home." The point was made, there was no going anywhere without a means of transportation. She leaned forward, gave her uninvited guest a light kiss on the cheek, and then opened the door to let her visitor out.

At that moment Ariella froze in fear, hoping and praying that Barbara would not glance to the left and see what was lying there. On the edge of her lawn slightly hidden by a large clump of geraniums was the 'accomplice' which found its way home like it was programmed to do. Ariella forgot it would be there, and still in her slippers, ran out after Barbara to distract her from seeing the drone.

"Just one more thing!" She hugged the departing guest.

"Wow! I will see you later." Barbara was pleased for this sign of affection once again.

Ariella stood on the side of the car waving and blocking the view of the four-rotor craft. The Toyota reversed onto the street and a few moments later it was gone. Walking in her slippers over the lawn, which was damp with dew, she picked up the four-prop and kissed it while going back into the house, thinking about how drunk Barbara was, murmuring, "I hope the police don't stop *you* in a sobriety test!"

The Heistess was pleased for her early morning visitor dropping by, because if the drone had been left outside a neighbor might have spotted it on the edge of the lawn. Heaven knows, this levitating-looter may have been stolen from her garden while she was asleep during this July 4th morning. Down the road, it could have been used as evidence to her detriment if the person who found it reported what they discovered in Ariella's yard.

What if her invitees noticed it in the afternoon when they returned her car? There would be no good explanation from her as to why she was recovering from a bad migraine but was well enough to be playing with a small flying toy. If she ever became a suspect, the two could have been witnesses against her because of this. Ariella shuddered at the thought.

Walking back to her room, she said out loud, "Thank goodness I did not leave the duffle bag and the backpack on the living room floor! I would not have been able to rationalize *that* to Barbara a few minutes ago!"

Her phone alarm was set for noon, then she got back into bed and once again fell sound asleep. A few hours later the wake-up beeping sounded. Ariella had been in a deep slumber dreaming of sparkling diamonds floating in rivers of molten gold. She got out of bed, showered, dried her hair quickly, and then pinned it up. After putting on her usual minimal makeup, feeding Purdy and changing his litter box, it was time to get the Buick off the street. As a sort-of disguise, she simply wore a baseball cap and sunglasses.

Once at the parked getaway car, she started it up and noted on the dashboard clock the time was one-sixteen. Driving off she figured it would take about twenty minutes to be at her destination. Five minutes before getting there, she stopped and used the Uber app to summon a ride to pick her up at the Woodward's Auto Center address.

Of course, upon her arrival, there was not a soul to be seen. Being Monday July 4th Ariella did not expect anyone to be working because most businesses would be closed on Independence Day. The Buick was driven past the side of the building into the back parking lot. The keys were left under the driver's side floor mat with a thank-you note to Harry for leaving the car at her house.

Ariella walked to the front of the property and waited for only two minutes before the Uber vehicle appeared. She was thankful it showed up so quickly because standing alone outside in an industrial area on a day like this when there was no one else around, was not a good idea for any woman. The driver seemed puzzled to see her there on her own, and she asked him to please take her to the Pebblestone Mall.

"What are you doing here since it seems this garage is closed now?" he quite rightly asked.

A question like this was anticipated. "My car has been running very erratically lately. Since I must be at work early tomorrow, it was best I dropped it off today, so they can fix it in the morning."

"Oh, I see." He said nothing more, and they arrived at the large shopping plaza before too long. Ariella exited the vehicle and went inside but just for a minute. As soon as the Uber operator was out of sight, she left the mall and began to walk home, getting there shortly after two o'clock.

It was time to unpin her hair, wet it in the sink and brush it straight, because her hair needed to be somewhat damp when the guests arrived. That would make it look like she was sleeping until well into the afternoon and had just emerged from the shower.

Opening the door to the closet in her bedroom, Ariella stared at the duffle and the backpack, then her mouth slowly broke into a smile. There had not yet been a minute for her to savor the victory, and a distinct sigh of relief could be heard as she picked up a couple of zip-seal bags and looked through the clear plastic at dozens of sparkling diamond rings. It was hard to believe this impossible heist had been pulled off. But now it was back to reality. The two were due here shortly to drop off her auto and they would have take-out Chinese food with them. Ariella returned the jewelry to the backpack and this time, locked the closet door in her bedroom, hiding the key in an almost-empty jar of face cream in her bathroom.

It was not necessary to lock the goods away, because it was highly unlikely either of her visitors would go wandering around her house, but it would be best if that door could not be opened. She went to the kitchen and took a large bottle of chilled Chardonnay from the refrigerator and put out three wine glasses. She got some plastic knives and forks as well as some paper plates and napkins from a cupboard, knowing that the food would be there shortly.

Ariella heard a vehicle door closing and then heard another thump, and thought, "Good! They have brought my Subaru back." As expected, the next thing to happen was the ringing of the doorbell, and it was time to greet them.

"We're here!" said Barbara giving her a hug.

"Hello guys, and thank you for bringing my car."

"We told you we would," said Donnie. "How are you feeling?"

"I am a lot better. My throat is not quite on fire like it was, but more importantly, the migraine is now just a dull ache. I am sorry to have left your party early, but it was just as well because I was feeling so sick last night including throwing up quite a bit before going to bed."

"Well, I am glad you got a good night's rest." Barbara turned to Donnie, "I was worried about her, especially when there was no answer every time I called. But now I know her phone was muted so she could sleep undisturbed."

"Yes. I was finally able to drop off at about ten-thirty and I slept soundly until you woke me up early this morning! At least I was able to get some shut-eye again after that for a few more hours."

"As long as you are recovering well." Barbara looked somewhat embarrassed for dropping in at the crack of dawn.

"I appreciate you guys buying Chinese take-outs." Ariella began pouring wine into the glasses. "I am only giving myself a little. I should not really be drinking until this migraine is completely gone."

She started to dish up some food for each of them onto the paper plates. Soon they were all eating and chatting, taking their time devouring the tasty Chinese cuisine and laughing over their fortune cookies. Ariella was pleased to have a decent meal, not realizing until then how hungry she was.

At about five o'clock Donnie said he had to go home. Being in one car they would have to leave together, and that was a good thing. Barbara would be gone and not be trying to stick around. Ariella was still very annoyed with her after what happened this past Saturday night with Roger Riley at the Wild West Bar & Grill.

"I will touch base with you during the week," said Barbara smiling.

Ariella kissed her and Donnie goodbye and closed the front door. Whew! She could now sit down, gather her thoughts, and decide what to do going forward.

◆◆◆◆◆

It was 5:10 p.m. and time to look over and sort through all which was seized. With the drapes tightly closed, her front door secure and the alarm on, she set up a folding table in her spare bedroom then went and got the duffle bag and the backpack from the closet. She put on a pair of thin, white cotton gloves, not wanting her fingerprints to be on anything, especially the larger items such as watches and lockets.

The Heistess began to unpack it all. Some of the jewelry was put onto the table and other items were laid out on the spare-room bed.

At this stage, there was no dollar value to the haul, and it was unknown as to whether it would be greater or lesser than what was stolen from her grandmother. It sure appeared to be worth a lot! She kept thinking, "How I am going to dispose of part of this without raising the suspicions of anyone?" It was understandable the police would very likely be watching all nearby pawnshops and gold-buying stores and looking for 'fences' from the area or from out of town. Ariella started to classify the items into various categories.

First, there were the wedding bands: She grouped together all the plain ones. They were mostly gold although some were silver, and others appeared to be made from platinum. A number of these were quite ornate.

Thereafter her attention went to the more than ninety-five engagement rings with one or more large diamonds on them. Wow, even to an amateur many looked like they were three carats or more. While the clarity and color of each were yet to be determined, these multi-faceted 'rocks' must be very valuable. Besides the rings with large gems, there were about three dozen with smaller stones mounted to them. For sure these were all worth a lot of money.

Then to her surprise, she identified one of her grandmother's pieces, a large three-carat diamond in a patterned gold band. On the inside was the engraving, DG–RG (David Gerson to Rachel Gerson). Yes, it was the engagement gift her grandfather David had given to her grandmother Rachel! She clutched it in both hands and began sobbing. It took her a while to calm down.

She whispered, "I need to keep this separate from all the others." Ariella was anxious to find more of what belonged to her nana if these articles were still here and had not been sold. Hopefully, those pieces could be recognized. After gathering herself together, she continued sorting through all the other rings which incorporated stones such as sapphires, opals, rubies, and emeralds. Many were quite breathtaking.

Necklaces were next: Here too, sparkling gems adorned pendants on a lot of the items. There were at least forty made of gold with very large diamond settings of three or four carats. In addition, there were seven with lockets attached and many strings of pearls, of which some were made up of pearls together with precious stones.

One specific gold chain featuring a distinctive locket caught her attention. Staring at it, she asked out loud, "Did this belong to my grandma?" Opening it up, there was a tiny photograph inside of her grandparents together. "Oh, my dear Rachel!" she cried. "I have found you… again!"

For the second time, it was a case of being lost for words and clinging to the piece, recalling memories of many good times experienced with her grandmother.

Ariella regained her composure and after a further ten minutes had all the necklaces neatly laid out on a section of the table. These were packed into zip-seals averaging ten per bag, but the two Gerson heirlooms were kept aside.

Now it was over to the timepieces: There were twenty-seven with the Rolex trademark, seventeen Patek Philippe, nine Piaget, fourteen Bulgari, some Tag-Heuser, and another nineteen of lesser value. These were categorized by brand name and placed in various medium-sized clear bags.

And so, this sorting continued until well after eleven o'clock on this very different July 4th night, separating each set of valuables onto the bed or the table and putting many of the same types into poly bags. Thereafter each group was placed into its own larger bag. In the end, there were several master-packs representing rings, necklaces, watches, earrings, bracelets, and brooches.

Ariella wrote on these packages with a black marker pen what was contained inside. A record was also kept of what was in every zip-seal bag, and each one was numbered. By the time it was all done, a good inventory of the spoils existed. On her list were written certain details such as, 'Ring with two diamonds,' or 'Bracelet with small rubies,' or 'Brooch with one large diamond, three medium-sized emeralds, and a few tiny sapphires.' Everything was now itemized and classified. The jewelry was put into two large cartons each about 18" wide by 24" long and 16" high.

She took the robbery drone as well as two others which were in her garage and placed these into their own corrugated container, together with some spare propellers and other related parts, batteries, chargers, and the like. She did not want to leave any flying machines or their accessories lying about the house in case one day the police came calling!

But first, she detached the bracket from under the craft and took the 6" wire and hook and the long lens-altering paintbrush. These were to go in the trash. A plain drone with no accessories would not mean it had been used to rob a store.

Ariella mused… "The police *will not leave one drone unturned* as they look for the perpetrators!" Into another cardboard box, she put the two paper shopping bags containing the disguises including the wigs and various pairs of plain-lens glasses.

It was twelve-fifteen in the early morning of July 5th. Everything was packed into four strong cartons and for now, these were left in the spare room with the door locked until a decision was made on where to stow it. Should the spoils be concealed in the attic? Another idea would be to open a wall in one of the spare bedrooms and jam the small bags in between the studs behind the sheetrock. She could leave it closed for a year or two until the hue and cry died down, and thereafter slowly start to sell some of the items.

Ariella began thinking seriously about using the basement in which to hide the goods, remembering that when fixing the leaking PVC pipe, she noticed a gap of about twelve inches from the gypsum board to the actual block wall. Yes, this could be the most ideal secret place. Perhaps open it again, take the master bags out of their cartons, and put it all into that large area. Thereafter, close it, spackle, sandpaper and paint it. No one would ever know a vast amount of valuable jewelry was lying there. Everything from the heist could simply disappear into a hidden space in the basement.

She quietly said, "This spot makes the most sense. There certainly is ample room here for stashing the loot from the break-in." Besides boxing all the spoils, she put her nana's two heirloom items into her personal jewelry box.

Ariella felt that time was of the essence because the authorities might suspect her and come pounding on her door soon. What would happen if Dora discovered something suspicious in her home or if there were camouflaged cameras in the apartment or in the outside hallway? She was jumbling her mind with crazy thoughts about the possibility of getting caught.

Since all the sparkly-stuff was now sorted, the empty backpack and duffle were taken to the garage and placed high up on a wooden shelf on which some folding canvas chairs were stored. She put away the few implements brought back from the heist. Ariella dumped her paper bag of trash and the very dusty sweatshirt, into an almost-full large black garbage bag and tied it closed. This was dragged outside and left at the end of her driveway for the usual Tuesday municipal pickup.

It was 12:40 a.m. when the weary warrior finally made her way to her room and went to bed. At just after three o'clock she woke up suddenly. Various concealment options were swirling through her head while she was sleeping, and a great idea came to her for the best location in which all could be kept out of sight. Ariella felt that without delay the boxes containing the valuables, the disguises, and the drones must be stashed away.

She crept downstairs, went into the workshop to get the necessary tools, and then did what was needed. It was all hidden in a place that would be very safe no matter how well the police or anyone else searched her house. Her feeling was it would be highly unlikely her treasure trove would be found once everything was confined in this obscure compartment.

Thirty-five minutes later Ariella was back in bed, and immediately fell sound asleep. It was a good thing all was now in its own invisible hideout, because little did she know how soon law enforcement would be showing up at her home! She slept until just after six thirty when her phone alarm jolted her into reality. It was time to rise and shine!

CHAPTER 14

Tuesday Morning, July 5th

It was time for Ariella to get ready for work. She showered, applied her makeup, fed Purdy, had a quick breakfast, and walked to the commuter bus stop two blocks away. When leaving the house, her feelings were of both relief and anxiety. The long weekend was over and any minute now the wrongdoing would be discovered. Panic again set in as she thought about the cops swarming all over the jewelry store. Were any clues left behind which could incriminate her? Will they notice the point of entry in the ceiling? She began to doubt her own thoroughness.

At the office, it was all about trying to focus on the job, but her mind was preoccupied. At lunchtime, while sitting in the break room, the TV was on, and tuned to the local news. There it was, a brief clip about a theft at the Fourth Street Jewelers and Gold Exchange. "The police are pursuing many leads," said the serious-faced announcer.

"Many leads," Ariella said. "Really?" Then she smiled remembering the DNA, the fingerprint evidence, and more left there by her. Oh yes, they will be running down a lot of confusing rabbit holes!

Just after two o'clock her cell phone rang, and she answered it right away. "Hello, Barbara. I am so glad we got together for Chinese food yesterday and thank you for bringing back my car!" Nervously trying to make small talk, she knew instinctively what this call was about.

"Hi there! Did you know the Fourth Street Jewelers and Gold Exchange was broken into over the weekend?"

"No! You have got to be kidding! When did you hear about that?"

"It came in a news update on my phone and then I saw it on a TV set here where I work."

"Do they know who did this? Have they caught the guys yet?" Ariella specifically used the word 'guys' because one would assume men would more likely have done this.

"No. It only just happened. I understand the authorities are combing through the store right now."

"Well, it serves that bastard Barnwell right. It is about time someone took something from him since he defrauded so many of his customers in the past." To act as any normal person would, Ariella added, "Anyone who steals from that crook is a hero to me."

Barbara said, "Yes. I agree. It is time Mr. Barnwell lost some of his fraudulently obtained goods."

"I guess he is probably well-insured, and this will hardly cost him anything. In fact, for him, it is a quick cash sale. Listen, I have a project to finish here in my office and I need to get back to it. But thanks for letting me know, and please, call me again if you hear anything else. Thieves usually leave some type of evidence behind so I am sure they will catch them soon."

"Okay. We can talk later."

Ariella kept busy throughout the rest of the afternoon and got a lot done. At the end of her workday, it was time to leave the office and walk to the bus station. By just before six o'clock it was home at last.

She decided the best thing to do was to lie low, leave all where it was hidden, and hope if the police ever came, they would never find anything. It took over forty minutes for her to walk around the house again, check out the garage, and make sure nothing was left out in the open which could connect her to the robbery.

Now it was up to her to lead a normal quiet life. Sell nothing, flash no money around, and *never* wear any of the jewelry items.

The TV was on in her kitchen, and shortly after six o'clock a local reporter began giving details about the break-in. Staring at the screen, she vaguely recognized Detective Wakefield from her visit to the precinct. He was addressing various news organizations, and while talking about the incident he was saying "… we have positively identified two male suspects…" He babbled on for a bit and ended with "… we have patrol cars on their way to the homes of these alleged perpetrators and we expect arrests to be made imminently." Ariella chuckled. The planted evidence was doing its job!

Soon after listening to the TV update, it was time for her to take the initiative and call Barbara. Ariella wished to stay engaged because she had no desire to appear as if shying away, especially now that the burglary was all over the local airwaves. No suspicion should be pointed in her direction.

"I am glad you called," said Barbara. "We really must get together. I would like to discuss the downtown theft with you and how that horrible man who swindled so many people got his just desserts."

"Good idea, we should definitely do so," said Ariella. "By the way, according to the TV news, the police have already identified two men and they are about to arrest them!"

"I heard about that too. It sounds like this crime will be solved very quickly." Barbara was pleased to hear two males were being pursued. For a moment earlier, the thought crossed her mind that her gal-pal was involved, especially since she left the party early. But now with these individuals under suspicion, this ruled her out as being a participant.

The young ladies arranged to meet at Ariella's house for coffee the following night.

After hanging up the phone, Ariella decided to confide in her friend the next evening. It would perhaps be time to relay that she was the one who gave Barnwell what was coming to him. Ariella wanted a 'pat-on-the-back' from someone who would appreciate how smart she was in being able to execute this heist.

Her opinion would be stated that the quiet, legal path which Barbara wanted to follow was not the way to go. Ariella was now ready to grant forgiveness regarding the Roger Riley incident.

♦♦♦♦♦

Earlier that same Tuesday morning, July 5th, Detective Leyland Wakefield was sitting behind his desk at the Averton police precinct getting caught up on paperwork after being out of his office during the three-day holiday weekend. A lot happened over the past few days, and everyone here had their hands full. There were many incidents of unruly activities and even vandalism when people over-indulged on Sunday night and also on Independence Day.

Leyland was briefed on all new matters and the files for a few of these were now on his desk. Someone smashed the windows at a house in one of the nearby neighborhoods, but nothing was taken. There were also three cars stolen the day before. He was getting ready to start working on these minor cases when at nine fifteen they notified him the Fourth Street Jewelers and Gold Exchange had been ransacked!

He grabbed his jacket and jumped into to his car. He got there in short order and saw a police officer standing at the door. It was Patrolman Fred Smythe.

"G'mornin' sir," said Smythe. "I was driving by not too long ago when this man came running out of the store yelling his place was robbed. I stopped and told him to stay outside and then I called it in. I put up yellow crime tape immediately. No one else other than this man, who is the owner, has been inside."

"Good morning, Fred, and well done," said Leyland. He noticed the 'Do Not Cross' banding and walked toward the store's entrance door.

Huntington Barnwell, pacing around on the sidewalk, had just finished babbling to Officer Smythe about how he arrived at work just after nine o'clock and found his display cases shattered. He said a vast amount of diamond rings, gold chains, watches, necklaces, and other items were missing.

Barnwell, standing behind the yellow tape saw Leyland and asked, "Will you be in charge of this case?"

"Yes, I am Detective Wakefield. What is your name? I take it you are the proprietor?"

"I am Huntington Barnwell and I own this shop! What took you so long? Can't you see some people have looted my place? With each minute we cannot let customers in I am losing money!" Hunt continued yelling, "And with every moment you delay searching for the thieves the less likely will you be able to catch them!"

"Please calm down. I need you to answer a few questions." Leyland was trying hard to be respectful.

"You say calm down! I have been ripped off! What are you going to do about it?" His arrogance and impatience were apparent in a dramatic way.

"Who opened up this morning?"

"I did!" He continued in a loud voice. "As soon as I noticed my store had been burglarized, I ran outside and was about to call 911 when I saw this squad car approaching. I flagged him down. That officer," said the irate man, jabbing a finger in Smythe's direction, "He put up the yellow tape."

"Has anyone other than you been inside since you got here?" The detective glanced around. He saw no one else there other than Barnwell and Smythe.

"No," said Hunt in a much quieter voice. "I am the only one here. My staff does not get in until ten o'clock."

Leyland noted it was a little past nine-thirty. "Well, don't touch anything. In fact, I want you to remain outside the door and you may not enter again until I say so. By the way, when your people get here, I will need to question them and until I instruct you otherwise, they too may not go in. Tell me, when you arrived here earlier, was this entrance door locked?"

"Yes, my keys fitted just fine and I do not think the two locks on the door have been tampered with. The alarm was still set and not deactivated." Hunt was now trying to play investigator.

"Wait here." Wakefield walked out to his car and came back with what appeared to be a toolbox. At that moment Charles Weston from the crime lab showed up.

"Glad you got here so quickly," said Leyland. "This appears to be a major break-in. I guess you can start by fingerprinting the outside of the door. Then go around the whole interior and let us see what you come up with."

Wakefield asked Hunt for his keys and then took a look at the two locks. He tried the keys, and each one slid in and turned without a problem. From his toolbox, he got out a magnifying glass and studied the mechanisms. There were no obvious signs of a pick or other implement having been used on either of them.

Then he went inside a little way and surveyed the scene. "I see you have security monitors in your store," said Leyland to Hunt who was standing at the door but not daring to come in. "Do they work?"

"Absolutely. The equipment holds its recordings for four weeks. I will give you the DVDs to take with you and you can look over the data."

Leyland glanced at the camera nearest to the door which was mounted about 8' from the floor and about 9" below the dropped-ceiling tiles. He walked over and looked up at the other one. "Well, they may have broken the glass on your merchandise cabinets but at least the video units look fine to me. We will get good information regarding what went on inside here from these." Leyland sounded confident. He proceeded to make his way around the store with Weston.

They noted that the windows were heavy-duty and did not open. The heating and air conditioning ducts all ended in 9" square grates coming out of the dropped ceiling so there was no way anyone could have crawled in through this ducting. In any case, the grates were firmly screwed into place, so they absolutely were not touched.

While Charles was dusting for fingerprints, Wakefield asked Hunt to get a ladder from the building's maintenance person, and Hunt returned with it after a few minutes.

Leyland took a small flashlight out of his toolbox, opened the ladder, and placed it in the center of the store. He very carefully thrust one of the ceiling tiles up, and it rose somewhat easily because there were no clips holding it down. However, he had to push it up with a bit of effort because there was fiber batting insulation above it.

He moved the light beam slowly around the entire suspended ceiling space. The gap between the concrete floor above and the metal grid appeared to be about 30". Besides the heat and air conditioning ducting, there was MC-Cable electrical wiring for the lights, cords for computers, internet connections, and also phone lines. In addition, there were a number of vertical wires holding the suspended ceiling grid in place. As he gazed around, Leyland noticed that nothing seemed to have been disturbed there.

He slowly shone the flashlight around the walls in this 30" expanse and observed there weren't any signs of tampering. Because his flashlight was small, it did not pick up the micro-detail of the slightly raised *Patch-up-Piece* on the drywall, and thus he could not see an indication of a breach anywhere. When he looked up toward the concrete from the floor above, there was no apparent hole or opening. It was obvious no one had bored through thick solid concrete.

He took the ladder and moved it to various points on the jewelry store floor, each time ascending, poking up a ceiling tile together with its insulation, and glancing around in every direction. Some of the tiles were a little tricky to lift because they had wires running on top of the fiber insulation. A few would not rise at all because of the ducting which was resting on them. But overall, he was able to look around the entire open ceiling space. Everything appeared to be normal and intact. However, he was not able to position the ladder by any of the large display cases, so this prevented him from getting physically near the wall closest to the 101-Building, again precluding him from identifying the point of ingress.

From his observations, he was able to conclude there were no signs of forced entry or disruptions anywhere in this 30" void. He studied each section looking for a hint of something having been moved or a flaw in the fine layer of dust which had settled over a period of time on the insulation. There was no evidence even a mouse had scurried across the surface, or any tiles had budged.

Wakefield left the main sales section and went to check the ceilings above the bathroom, the accounting office, and the jewelry repair area. He could not see any indication that the panels or the fiber batting had been touched, and it all seemed to be okay, which left him rather puzzled.

Leyland wanted to speak to the four full-time store workers. Two of these just arrived and the other two were expected to show up at any minute. There were also three part-timers and they tended to work mostly on Friday afternoons and on weekends. The detective would need to find out which employees had keys. It was starting to look like it could be an inside job.

Weston beckoned his associate over to where he was standing behind one of the display cabinets. The glass on top had been shattered and there were shards inside the unit and on the floor.

"I found this disposable cup on the carpet near a corner here," said Charles. "There is some wet coffee in the bottom, so this was for sure left here in the past day or two. As you can see it is made of plain white Styrofoam and thus there is no indication from where it was purchased. We will have to canvas the area to see which nearby restaurants or coffee shops sell their drinks in containers like this. I did not find a lid anywhere. However, I managed to get two fingerprints off the cup. Maybe it will also yield some DNA."

"Well, that is promising," said Leyland.

"I have more. These thieves must be stupid because I found four cigarette butts behind the counter on the floor. Two are of one type and the others are of a different brand. That means there were at least two people here committing this robbery. I just asked Mr. Barnwell about his crew, and which might be smokers. He tells me none of his people smoke and not one of their clients has ever come inside holding a cigarette. This is a non-smoking building."

Leyland turned to his sidekick and said, "For one or more perpetrators to break in here might not be too difficult. It was either someone who usually has keys to the entrance door or a former salesperson who had duplicates made. Maybe it was a relative of a current or past worker. Perhaps it was an outsider who figured out a way to get a set of keys. But if so, how would a stranger know the alarm code?"

"We will look into *everyone* who works here and see if any have a family member or a close friend who may be a drug addict or who might have a motive," said Charles. He went on, "We should find out if there were break-ins at Barnwell's residence, or at the homes of any of the personnel. In such a circumstance a thief could steal keys temporarily, get copies made and return them, with the homeowner not knowing such a thing ever happened."

"I think this could have been done by a person associated with the store," said Leyland. "There is a security system here so one would not only have to get through the door, but the alarm code would be needed as well. Also, for anyone robbing the place, it was likely done at night, so they must know their way around. Thieves may not have turned on the lights, because of the risk of being seen by people walking past or driving by, or maybe they used muted flashlights."

"How many motorists are in this section of the city past say nine or ten o'clock?" asked Charles. He was assuming the crime happened after darkness set in.

"I guess there are not many individuals out and about. Hardly anyone is downtown past ten on any normal day."

"I will tell you one thing," said Charles in an animated way, "This malfeasance was not committed on Sunday night. That is the one night in the summer when there are countless revelers celebrating the July 4th holiday. Remember we had fire trucks, police vehicles, and hundreds of people out here on Fourth Street until well after midnight. With so many potential witnesses, if this robbery took place late on Sunday into early Monday morning, someone would have noticed. No one could be foolhardy enough to do this dastardly deed at that time."

"Hmm, good point, and I tend to agree with you. We can rule out the evening of July 3rd. Anyone breaking in must enter from Fourth Street and if so, they would have easily been observed opening the door, whether they turned the lights on or not. But what I do not understand is the doors on two of the merchandising cabinets were unlocked and the other two were locked, yet the glass was broken on all four displays."

"It seems to me someone was angry and wanted to not only steal stuff but also intended to make a real mess or create more harm for the business proprietor." Weston was shaking his head as he noted all the damage done.

Leyland moved to the door and began questioning the owner again. He found out there are time and date recordings of the alarm when it is turned on and off, and he asked Hunt to give him a printout of these as soon as possible. He also discovered there were no motion detectors in the store as part of the security system. Barnwell told Leyland two of the four full-time employees had keys and they were the only ones who knew the alarm code.

Both were older people. One was Hunt's aunt, a seventy-year-old woman who did the bookkeeping. The other was a seventy-eight-year-old man who made watch and jewelry repairs on the premises, and he did not drive. Each had worked there for over thirty years, and they were very trustworthy. Neither seemed to fit the profile of a thief and both were visibly upset when they arrived a few minutes earlier. The two appeared eager to help in any way they could.

The detective walked over to a chair in the main sales area and sat there for a while, thinking. If the only other people with keys besides Barnwell were the bookkeeper and the repair man, it may rule them out as individuals, but it does not mean this atrocity did not come from their direction. Older people could perhaps have a grandson or granddaughter, or even a niece or nephew who knew where they worked, and such an employee could be an unwitting conduit to the devilish action. They might not be so cognizant as to notice their keys missing for just a few hours on a Sunday afternoon after four o'clock or on a Monday when the store is closed. They would not know if duplicate keys were made.

Leyland told Hunt and all his staff members that everyone's fingerprints would be taken to rule them out as suspects. But the police also needed to deal with dozens of prints from customers on the broken glass and on the cabinet frames. This was going to make things very difficult for doing the necessary analysis work.

"Hey! I've got something!" Charles shouted. "I found some dried blood on a small piece of glass lying here in this display case. One of the crooks must have cut himself. We can get some DNA from this. I also came across a mallet on the floor which was no doubt used to smash the countertops. There is bound to be trace evidence on its handle."

Leyland came over and was becoming a bit more encouraged. "Yes," he said. "With this small amount of blood, we will certainly be able to make great headway."

After ten minutes Charles suddenly cried out, "I have discovered a human hair in the corner of this cabinet. Wait, here is another one! These two hairs are each about two inches long and are dark in color."

Leyland chimed in, "They likely belong to a male."

"Oh my goodness, look here! Someone left behind a used Kleenex tissue! There will unequivocally be DNA we can use from this. Ugh!"

"I know you are always meticulous but please be even more so today. Carefully bag separately, everything you have found so far." Leyland sounded like a father. "You have a coffee cup, a piece of broken glass with blood on it, those human hairs, the four cigarette butts, the used tissue and the mallet. These perpetrators are fools not only to break in but to leave behind a trail. This case will be wrapped up quickly."

"We have so much to go on here." Charles was busy bagging all the significant objects which he found. "Once we analyze this and get the results, I agree with you we will be arresting some folks before too long."

"These low-level artists are too smart for themselves!"

Leyland now began to make his way into the rooms in the rear. At the first double-doorway, he called out to Weston, "I have found some blood here on the doorframe. It appears these idiots were running wild all over the store!"

"Okay, I will be right there."

The detective walked into the watch repair and jewelry cleaning area, and he was startled at the mess. While it seemed a lot was taken, there was still quite a bit of stuff left behind. Could one of these perpetrators be a young, hasty teenager? This all appeared to have been carried out either in a real hurry or with much stupidity. Why would they not take everything in plain sight and within easy reach? Why did they leave so many of the diamond earrings in this area as well as some out in front amongst the broken glass?

He did not know a drone with a hook underneath had its limitations, especially for picking up those types of items!

Leyland finally got to the back door. It was made of steel, and it had a panic bar with a spring latch to hold it closed. There was also a deadbolt secured in place. With his gloved hands, he carefully slid the bolt and opened the door. Behind it was a large atrium in the 101-Building. He glanced around. There were various stores including a mini pizza place, a beauty parlor, a nail salon, and a sandwich shop.

He looked at the outside face of the steel portal, and it was totally plain. There was no lock or typical handle, just a small metal plate with a lip on it as a sort-of haft so that a person could pull it open if it was not bolted from within.

One therefore could not unlock this from the outside. There was a sign above the frame in the store which read EMERGENCY EXIT ONLY.

He again called out to Charles, "There is smeared blood here on the panic bar in this back room. It could be where they tried to leave from, but they could not have exited here because I found the deadbolt in its closed position."

Charles came running over. "If this rear door provided no way in or out, then I believe they must have come in and also made off through the front of the shop."

"Perhaps on Sunday, in the late afternoon, someone left this door unbolted and hooked open very slightly and that is how they got inside. Maybe they managed to tape or jam the spring-clip so this would not lock. Thereafter they might have gone out from here." Leyland was hypothesizing.

He peered at the latch and saw no signs of it having been tampered with in any way, nor was there any adhesive residue from duct tape or such on the frame. But if they departed from here how come the deadbolt was secured? No one, not even Barnwell, was in this part of the store since the break-in was discovered earlier.

Charles proceeded to take samples of the smeared blood on the panic bar using a special DNA gathering kit. He also began dusting the door for fingerprints on both sides.

After poking around everywhere for over five hours, it was three o'clock and time for them to return to the station.

They now had DVD discs for the past month of recorded video from the security system which monitored all indoor activity. Both men were anxious to see who was inside when it was being robbed. They also wanted to try to identify every customer or vendor who was there recently. It was their feeling this turpitude could not have taken place without one or more people studying the lay of the land ahead of time.

Hunt was instructed earlier in the day to hand over all keys, provide the alarm code, and keep the store closed until further notice. He understood no one was allowed back in, and an officer would be posted outside the front door for a day or more until the police decided the place could re-open. Barnwell expressed his extreme displeasure about this. He was also told he would be required to come to the precinct at a moment's notice when summoned, to be questioned further. The police would start going over the DVD history the next morning to see what they could find regarding all who were there lately either buying or selling and they would need Hunt to provide names of customers where possible.

There were very likely going to be outdoor videos from up and down Fourth Street. With these, they could see who came in and went out of the jewelry store or identify people loitering outside.

Now back in his office, Leyland commented to Charles, "Someone had keys to the front door, or they taped open the latch on the back door. These burglars must have an intimate knowledge of the entire place and they no doubt knew the alarm code, or they figured out a way to hack into it. We will see what the security cameras tell us as well as what we can glean from any digital recordings on the street."

Charles added, "Yes, and we have several items with DNA and/or fingerprints on them. I do not think it will take us long to apprehend those who did this."

Leyland commented, "The thing that baffles me is it appears the alarm was not turned off or on, from Sunday afternoon when all the employees went home, to this morning when we got the call of the break-in at about nine-fifteen from Smythe. I checked out the memory setting on the alarm and it showed no activity. I cannot imagine how that can be possible and I wonder if Barnwell broke into his own establishment for the insurance money. Maybe he hired a hacker to disable the outgoing signals so his own personal code and in-out times would not be noted."

"The red-alert system was turned on from Sunday afternoon at about four twenty when the owner left until this morning when he arrived. I just called the monitoring company and they confirmed this. How can thieves come in through either door if the electronic sentry was never shut off? And if it was de-activated, there is no record of it being put on again. Once we have the video data, I think we will get some answers." Charles sounded quite serious.

"Strangely enough," remarked Leyland, "Barnwell seemed very willing to give the DVDs to us. Again, the only way perpetrators could come in was via the front door or the back door and they somehow by-passed the monitoring."

"I asked patrolman Fred Smythe to canvass all nearby businesses to see if any have external cameras. Hopefully, we will get additional information from this street footage."

"Thank you. Obtaining outside recordings will be very important," said the detective. He went on, "I raised a few ceiling tiles in the main sales section, and I looked carefully into that open space, shining my flashlight everywhere and especially around the wall perimeters. I also lifted additional panels over the back office, the watch repair area, the bathroom, and the kitchen, examining for anything unusual above those rooms. I searched for any disturbance to the dust on the insulation and found none. I know I am repeating myself, Charles, but no one came in from the top. Nothing has been moved or touched in the ceiling space for years."

"What if one or more people hid in the store after closing on Sunday, robbed the establishment, and then somehow got out? But if the deadbolt was in place, it could not have been out the rear door." Charles was trying to come up with a rational explanation but so far could not.

"Both you and I studied the steel door emergency exit with its panic bar, located in the back. We now know this goes into an atrium where there are a few small retail businesses and there are also some cameras there. As we noted this door is normally locked and cannot be opened from the outside because there is no key lock on it. We may well have to look at it again and we need to see what those atrium video recorders show us."

"I agree we should go and review the whole place," said Charles. "Maybe the thieves did get in through the rear door, or perhaps they tunneled in from under the floor! We did not inspect the carpeting."

"You are right. We must get back soon. I am so pleased we have posted an officer there and prevented Barnwell or any of his employees from going inside for now."

Charles retreated to his lab. It was now three forty-seven and he intended to stay there until five o'clock or later so he could study some of the items left in the store. He sent out the used Kleenex tissue for DNA analysis and the four cigarette butts, the two human hairs, and a sample of the blood found on the broken glass and the metal door. He was hoping to have preliminary results back soon.

At ten minutes after four, Charles came running into his cohort's office excited and breathless. "We got a hit on two of the fingerprints! We have identified who we believe was holding the mallet and we know for certain who was drinking from the foam cup."

"That was quick!" Leyland seemed pleased. He was delighted his compadre jumped onto analyzing the evidence so quickly. "Tell me!"

"On the coffee cup are the prints of someone already in our system, Jake Rawson. He is twenty-eight years old, and he has a rap sheet for mostly petty theft and car break-ins."

"That sounds like one of our guys for sure," said Leyland. "He appears to be changing his game! We should pick him up right away before he has a chance to fence any of the jewelry or to skip town."

"Already on it," said Charles. I have a unit with two men on their way to his house as we speak.

"Good! And what about the mallet?"

"Well, there are a few different prints on it, some are smudged, and they have me puzzled. Whoever owned this mallet may have lent it to friends or maybe they work for a building contractor or such because it appears various people were handling it. Anyway, I did manage to lift one good thumbprint and that belongs to a Marcus Valla."

"I have heard of Valla!" exclaimed the detective. "I think he is out on probation for being involved with a major drug ring, and that was all over the newspapers recently. Let us haul him in too."

"I have two officers going to his residence." Charles added, "Oh, before I forget, there are reporters from our local TV station downstairs, and they are asking to interview someone about this case. They want a statement for the evening news before we leave for the day."

"It will be my pleasure to give them some details, especially since it seems we are already making such rapid progress." He grabbed his jacket and walked down, with his colleague trailing not far behind. There was quite a hubbub going on in the lobby. A TV news crew was present and also two newspaper journalists, a few bloggers, and a radio station host. In addition, there were some curious onlookers.

"Quiet please!" His voice sounded loud and authoritative as he held up his hand. "Good afternoon, ladies and gentlemen. I am Detective Wakefield. As most of you know the Fourth Street Jewelers and Gold Exchange was broken into over the weekend. We have been on the case since early this morning."

He paused, took a deep breath, and then continued. "I am going to keep this very brief, but I do want to give you an update. Our people have been working non-stop for the past few hours gathering and analyzing evidence. I am pleased to announce we have positively identified two males who were in the store at the time of the robbery, and they are very likely part of a larger gang."

He knew he was getting a little ahead of his skis because nobody was in custody at this point and no person had yet been questioned. But solid fingerprint evidence is very hard to refute. Based on experience, prints found on objects at a crime scene will almost always relate back to the offenders. He wanted to show the public how efficient the police department was. It would also be good for a possible future promotion if his higher-ups saw this on the evening news, the same day as the break-in.

Wakefield beamed at the crowd. It had now grown to over twenty-five as some police officers and a few more civilians added to the group. "As we speak, we have patrol cars on their way to the homes of the two men we believe were involved and we expect arrests to be made today."

A wild babble arose from the reporters, all barking questions at him. He rebuffed them with, "That's it for now ladies and gentlemen. Tomorrow morning at eleven o'clock here in the precinct lobby we will make more information available. We will also be able to give you the names of those in custody. Thank you."

And with that, he walked back up to his office. It was time for him to go home and for Weston to do the same. He tidied his desk, turned off his computer, and took the elevator down.

On his way out he said to the night duty officer, "As soon as they bring in the bad boys, please let me know. You have my cell phone number. I might even come back later to start questioning them. But if they are brought in after nine o'clock, do not disturb me. I will find them here tomorrow morning when I get in."

Leyland drove away feeling very motivated and pleased, even though at the back of his mind he felt a slight twinge of nervousness. Perhaps he should not have been so bold as to tell those present about the two suspects.

But then he tried to convince himself he did the right thing, and he recited his thoughts out loud, "After we have questioned these perps and once the DNA evidence comes back it will for sure confirm these guys were involved in this banditry. As soon as they understand how much time they will spend in prison they might give up the other members of their group. This will be an easy open-and-shut case." Leyland's ramblings continued, "Both Charles and I will be well-recognized and appreciated for the speedy way we handled the aftermath of this crime."

CHAPTER 15

Wednesday Morning, July 6th

Wakefield marched boldly into the precinct, ready to start his day on this sunny Wednesday morning. He was looking forward to grilling the thieves who no doubt were brought in the night before and this would give him some important new information for his scheduled eleven o'clock meeting with the Media. He ascended the stairs to his office. Charles was already there and seemed to be concerned.

"What is going on?"

"Well," said Charles, "We were unable to take into custody either of those two men. Both have airtight alibis for the entire weekend during which time the theft took place!"

"What?!" Leyland looked stunned. The first thing racing through his mind was the news conference that was to take place shortly.

"Yes," Charles continued. "Marcus Valla, whose fingerprints were on the mallet, has been in hospital since Saturday early afternoon according to his wife. She told the officers who went to arrest him, that he was on his motorcycle riding back from a yard sale when a car turned in front of him. It did not hit him, but he braked so hard, he lost control. He will be okay but has a few broken bones and some serious abrasions. As I said, he has been in hospital for the past five days."

"So how did his fingerprints get on the mallet?"

"I am not sure, but it is possible someone purchased it at the yard sale on Saturday morning. Valla may have picked it up, decided not to take it, and then another man bought it."

"Find out where that yard sale was and get whatever information you can from the homeowners as to who paid for the mallet. What about the other guy, Jake Rawson?"

Charles was almost afraid to speak. "Those were Rawson's prints on the coffee cup for sure, but he was arrested late last week for assault when he attacked a co-worker at the warehouse where he is employed. He really hurt the other guy. He has been in jail since Friday unable to post bail."

Leyland put his head in his hands and asked, "How can this be… we found irrefutable proof at the place of the crime? Tell me, when will we have the DNA back for the human hairs, the cigarettes, the Kleenex tissue, and the blood?"

"Maybe some of these other items are also a plant, sir, to mislead us," said Charles softly, "But the blood for sure happened on-site due to the broken glass. Why, we even found blood elsewhere in the shop and smudged on the panic-bar at the back door from where they perhaps tried to make their getaway! I did request priority processing on the DNA so we could have some results by this afternoon."

"Well, I hope you are right. Since we cannot rely entirely on what we discovered at the scene at least we will have DVD videos showing all the activity which went on inside the store. When can we see this?"

"Sir, our tech-expert Steven Parker said he will be ready at about ten o'clock to show us what he has found. I guess we should make our way over to his area right now because it is almost that time. I will postpone the news conference and tell them it is because of 'new developments' which we are working on."

"Good," said Wakefield. "Fortunately, as of now no one knows we were misled, or we would have egg on our faces. If possible, we must not let them find out our first two supposed suspects had nothing to do with the break-in. Hopefully, the DNA and the videos will put us back on track. When this happens, the Media will be none-the-wiser about us falling prey to the two pieces of false evidence."

Wakefield and Weston walked over to Parker's office. He was about to start viewing the DVDs.

"While I have the video of Saturday July 2nd ready, I want to first look at the recordings of Sunday and Monday," said Parker. "This occurrence took place sometime after four o'clock, the close of business on Sunday, and Tuesday morning when the owner came in and discovered the smashed display cases. If we can clearly see the gangsters committing the crime, then we will have no need to look back at Saturday or even a week before to see who was snooping around."

"I would say that makes sense," said Leyland. "Let's get the information for those two days, now."

"I am starting the DVD from Sunday afternoon at four o'clock. That is shortly before the monitoring system was activated by the owner as he was leaving."

All three were looking keenly at the two screens which Steven Parker set up, one for each camera covering the main sales area. At 4:18 p.m. they could see a woman employee exiting and they saw Barnwell on his cell phone as he moved toward the door. He was the last one to leave. They watched him hang up on the call and walk to the control unit. The keypad was deliberately obscured as his code was punched in, and then he walked out. Leyland, Charles, and Steve could see Hunt securing both locks from the outside of the glass door. After he left, the image showed no activity taking place inside.

Steve immediately said, "Nothing of course will change until the intrusion occurs. But do not be concerned… we will not have to sit here for forty hours or so. I can fly through this time period in about fifteen minutes. If we see anything suspicious, I can slow my equipment down to its normal speed to see how they were committing the assault on Barnwell's business. I can also freeze any frame when we get a good view of someone's face. With one click I can send it to the Facial Recognition Database. I am sure I will have the name or names of these bandits for you in less than half an hour if they are in the system. At the very least you will have photographs of the thieves."

"We really need these pictures and if possible, who they are," said Charles. "Even though I have managed to delay the Media, they are waiting for an update, and we have nothing to give them at this moment. By later today I should have DNA results, but having solid information in the next half hour would provide us with a significant leap forward."

"Don't you worry," said Steve. "The recording of Barnwell leaving is crisp and sharp. I am sure the rest will be just as good, even in fairly dark circumstances at nighttime because if the store's fluorescents were not turned on, the large windows look like they can easily let in a lot of light from the streetlamps outside. You will have this all soon."

"I will get us each a cup of coffee," said Leyland.

Steve and Charles were watching as the video was run at a fast-forward pace, knowing it could all be slowed down when they needed to look closely at any aspects of the crime. They could see the conditions getting dimmer as the sun was setting and the digital clock on the equipment showed it to be 9:02 p.m. on Sunday night July 3rd. The light coming in from the well-lit street was still sufficient for the cameras to monitor any activity in a reasonable way as Steve predicted. He continued operating the recording at super speed.

"I cannot wait to see when and how they got in." His voice was a whisper of eager anticipation. "I wonder if this took place on Sunday night or on Monday night?"

"Maybe it was Monday in the day," said Charles.

Suddenly the tech expert slowed the pace and pointed to the screen on the left. "That's odd. I know the illumination in the store is low because the time-indicator is now showing 11:10 p.m. But this screen suddenly looks blurred."

He stopped the playback and started working with various keys on his keyboard. "I am not sure if the security camera malfunctioned or if my apparatus is not picking up the image off the DVD properly."

Wakefield returned carrying three cups of coffee, one for each of them.

"The computer needs adjusting," said Charles taking his hot beverage and sipping slowly on it.

All three were now looking at the two video screens. One showed the semi-darkened jewelry store quite clearly but the other was fuzzy. Parker now clicked his mouse and moved it in various directions. Wakefield and Weston watched as the whiz-kid worked away. They saw the images get enlarged, then reduced, and go back to normal size.

"Hey guys, give me a few minutes. I will have this problem fixed shortly, but I cannot do it with both of you standing here breathing down my neck!"

"Okay, okay," said Leyland understanding that sometimes complicated technical issues require tight concentration. "Give us a shout when you have it resolved."

It was ten-fifteen when he got back to his office. Charles retreated to the crime lab in the basement of the precinct building. Both had plenty of work to do regarding this situation as well as other cases they were handling.

◆◆◆◆◆

Earlier that same Wednesday morning, July 6th, Ariella woke up at six forty-five, slid out of bed, took a shower, got dressed and put on her usual exiguous amount of makeup. She didn't sleep well the night before because of a few bad dreams about being caught red-handed committing the break-in.

After feeding Purdy, and having some toast with marmalade and a cup of coffee, it was time to walk the two blocks to the bus stop. She arrived at her office punctually as usual, and immediately got engrossed in her work. The previous evening there was a brief report on TV and Ariella smiled when they stated, "two male suspects were about to be arrested." What will they say at eleven this morning when the names of these guys are revealed?

Using her computer, she found the website of the local TV station, curious to hear about the break-in. At 10:50 a.m. the anchor came on to say the police were postponing the scheduled communique, because of "rapidly changing circumstances and new developments." He went on to say the authorities would be providing more details later that day in the form of a press release or as a live TV news update.

Ariella was becoming very worried. What could this mean? Surely, they have identified two people from the planted fingerprints and DNA. The case ought to be going in that direction, with them pursuing three or four people. By now at least one must appear to be extremely suspicious, and they should be focusing their attention on that man or woman.

For the rest of the day at work, the thespian thief could hardly concentrate. She simply wished there would be a good announcement about a couple of people being taken into custody. Arrests like this should keep the Police distracted and cause them to be looking in many directions at once. The hours dragged on until finally, it was time to leave for the day.

Once at home, she was too nervous to eat anything. Barbara was due to come over soon for coffee and to talk. Ariella put out a plate of chocolate chip cookies and covered these with plastic wrap to keep them from drying out.

Along the lines of what was under consideration the day before, she would confide in her friend tonight. Ariella wanted someone strong to lean on and maybe her visitor could help with some ideas on how to sell a portion of what was taken or advise her about other ways in which to dispose of the spoils. Guidance is what was needed regarding how to proceed from here. The enormity of this break-in was now dawning on her and it was all becoming a huge weight on her shoulders. She put her head into her hands and sighed, "Why did I even do this? What was I thinking?" But then remembering how her grandmother was cheated, made her feel the robbery was justified.

◆◆◆◆◆

It was that same Wednesday afternoon at three o'clock, and Barbara was in the process of leaving her place of work for the day, having been at it diligently since arriving there in the morning. Various bills of lading were being reviewed by her for a large shipment of toys about to come in from the Far East. At lunchtime she asked her supervisor for time off, to get out a couple of hours early, and he agreed.

She was looking forward to seeing Ariella that night and having coffee and dessert with her, but primarily, it was to talk further about the whole rip-off scenario. There was something still bothering her, and she could not quite put her finger on it, feeling somehow her blonde buddy was connected to the insidious incident.

And then on the other hand she doubted her own suspicions. Ariella left the party early with a bad cough and a migraine headache… or was this faked? The Subaru was at Donnie's place until Monday afternoon, and Barbara recalled when she showed up at the house in the early morning of July 4th, Ariella looked terrible, an indication her illness was real.

The distrustful damsel continued asking questions in her mind. Did her friend rent a car and carry out this theft on Sunday night? If so, could such an automobile be tracked, and were the cops checking with car rental agencies? Dubious of her own craziness, she wondered how her lady pal could have made her way inside and then got out again. Ariella certainly did not have keys or know the alarm code.

Barbara long ago noticed there were cameras in the store, so whoever committed this crime would be showing up on video recordings. The police would certainly be nailing down the perpetrators very soon even though their morning news conference was postponed. Barbara sincerely hoped Ariella was not involved.

After leaving her office, Barbara got into her car and drove to a Holiday Inn Suites Hotel about half an hour away, because of an important rendezvous at this location scheduled for three thirty. She smiled at the greeter behind the counter as she walked to the elevator. Her male friend would be waiting for her in their usual room. The receptionist didn't know this long-haired brunette by name, only by sight, but knew the lover, and he was very generous with his money. The room was unofficially 'rented out' for the afternoon. The bribe money the desk clerk received was well worth the expense. She would certainly keep her mouth shut for $150 each time.

Barbara knocked gently on the door of number 224. The code was two knocks, then another two. He opened the door wearing his hotel bathrobe and holding a bottle of wine in his hand. His free arm curled around her followed by a long welcoming kiss.

"I have been eagerly looking forward to this," he began. "It has been three weeks since we last got together."

"Something like that. But we should not talk about our days apart. Let us enjoy our time with each other now."

After a few sips of wine, she put down her glass and he did the same. The sheets and blankets were pulled back and both scampered onto the bed. Before too long they were all over each other with their hands and their mouths. Taking turns back and forth, the foreplay went on for some twenty-five minutes until they could hold off no longer.

He plunged into her. She tried to muffle her cries of passion because this was a hotel, and the walls might not be too soundproof. He was not great in bed, but she was quite the sex goddess. Before too long, both cried out, each in their own height of ecstasy and then cuddled together falling into a deep sleep.

They slept for about an hour, and at about five o'clock Barbara sat up and woke him. With pillows propped behind them and pulling the sheets and blankets up to their shoulders, they lay quietly together. Then a conversation started.

"Everyone is talking about the jewelry store situation," she said.

"Yes, that has been the chit-chat these past two days."

"I wonder who did it?" She stared inquisitively at him.

"So far from what I understand the police are being very tight-lipped, but it seems they have a couple of people in mind." He spoke quite softly. "But although two suspects were mentioned, they suddenly canceled their meeting with the press this morning. I wonder why?"

"There is one person who I think might have done it because they spoke about potentially breaking into that place recently." Barbara was still mulling this idea.

"Is he a seasoned professional thief?" asked her lover.

"No. Just a regular girl who works at a normal job."

"A woman, you say? How can that be?"

"Well, there are a few individuals who feel they were cheated out of their valuables. She is one of them. Perhaps these people should be identified, tracked down and their names given to the police. Any one of these very upset customers could be possible culprits."

"Huh. Interesting idea. That could be a strong angle to consider."

"I think so, but there are of course videos, so arrests will be made soon, for sure."

And then it was back to fondling and kissing each other. After a little while she picked up her phone and saw the time was five twenty. "I must go home and get ready because I am visiting a friend tonight. Don't stress out, just a female!"

He was about to ask her to leave and was relieved she took the initiative. "Oh, I worry anyway. For all I know, you could be attracted to women."

Barbara jumped out of the bed and got dressed. "Don't be concerned, my love. I am just getting together with her for coffee and dessert."

"Okay, well enjoy yourself." He stood up, put on his bathrobe, then kissed her goodbye and closed the door. He turned around, quickly straightened up the bed until it appeared as if no one had been in it, then washed out the two wine glasses and dried them.

The seductress took the stairs down and was soon getting into her Toyota, headed for her apartment to take a quick shower before going to visit Ariella. Driving out of the parking lot, she did not notice a small green car coming in. An attractive thirty-something got out and strode into the hotel lobby. Cindy winked at the receptionist and walked to the elevator. Minutes later she was knocking on the door of room 224. The code was different this time, being two knocks then three.

Huntington Barnwell opened the door. He had a bottle of wine in one hand and put his arm around her, followed by a passionate kiss. He was not only unfaithful to his wife, but he was unfaithful to his girlfriends. He liked the one he had just been with, but he preferred Cindy.

◆◆◆◆◆

It was the same Wednesday morning back at the precinct, and Wakefield was busy in his office after being with Weston and Parker when they noticed the DVD image on one of the screens became blurry. He was trying to figure out how the thieves broke in. Could it be the entrance point was the Emergency Exit, unobtrusively left very slightly open by a customer or by a member of staff? Leyland felt he and Charles needed to return there to thoroughly inspect the front and back doors.

It was shortly after eleven o'clock when his desk phone buzzed. It was Steve Parker. "You have *got* to come back here and see what is going on with these recordings."

"Be right there," said Leyland.

He quickly called down to the crime lab on the internal line. "Parker has the video figured out," he said breathlessly. "We're gonna catch these bastards now!"

"I have good news too!" Charles also sounded lively. "The DNA on the blood came back. It belongs to a Ryan Barron. This guy was involved in three bank holdups sometime back. I believe he served a long stint in prison. He got out two years ago and has not been heard from in a while. It appears he is lying low. However, he has always been close to his mother, Thelma Barron, and she lives not far from here. He also has a brother who lives in Virginia. I am sure through his mother we will be able to track him down or we can check to see if he had moved in with his sibling."

"Find out where Mrs. Barron lives, so I can visit her right after we look at the security tapes. Parker should be able to give me his picture off the video and I will have her tell me where her son is."

"I already have her address, which I can give to you when we meet in Steve's office in a minute."

"Great, see you there!" said Leyland enthusiastically. Suddenly his cell phone rang, and it was Colleen Stafford from the local TV station.

"Detective Wakefield, when will we have information on the pillaging of the jewelry place?" She sounded quite frustrated.

He spoke to her, walking and talking while on his way to Parker's office. "Miss Stafford, we are pursuing multiple leads and we will have details for you soon."

"Soon? What does that mean? We thought we were getting an update from you this morning and then you canceled the news conference. Are you and your people bungling this case?"

"New facts are coming in rapidly. Call me tomorrow morning at ten o'clock and I *will* give you at least one name. We have plenty of evidence and we are about to make one or more arrests." He knew once again he was getting ahead of the facts, but he understood from experience that DNA evidence, especially from blood found in multiple places at a crime scene, was irrefutable.

"Well okay. I will call you tomorrow. But if you cannot tell the public what is happening, we will be broadcasting a piece depicting your incompetence!" Colleen hung up.

Leyland and Charles arrived simultaneously in the technology office.

"Show us the recordings! We really need to see these!" Wakefield was rubbing his hands with glee.

Steve turned on his machine and they looked at both screens. Let me explain in detail what is going on. "We saw this video earlier when we all observed the light changing as the sun went down around nine o'clock on the night of July 3rd. The place at that point was illuminated only from outside streetlamps, but it was still enough for the surveillance instruments to pick up the 'no activity' inside the store. However, one can note it is quite dark nearly nine feet up where the cameras are located."

"Go on," said Leyland, sounding a bit frustrated.

"Now look at the digital time numbers in the corner of the picture. It shows that at exactly 11:10 p.m. on Sunday night something happens to the recording device above the entrance door because our screen here, while still lit up, suddenly goes hazy. In an almost imperceptible way, a translucent cover goes over the lens. We cannot see what caused this because it is dark just below the ceiling. About a minute later the other lens gets tampered with." They all noticed an instant frosty appearance in the output from the DVD.

"Look at both screens now. We can see there is sort-of light in the area, but the cameras are no longer able to pick up any details of what is going on there."

"Okay, so when do the images, the pictures, become clear again?" The detective was almost screaming.

"They don't, sir," said Steve cautiously. "They do not even show Mr. Barnwell arriving at his place of business this morning nor patrolman Fred Smythe being there on the scene. In fact, the recording does not show you sir, or Charles starting your work after you got there. I believe if you go to the jewelry store now, you will find some kind of sophisticated covers on both the lenses."

"But if there were people placing something translucent over the first piece of optical glass, why do we not see them tampering with the other one?" Leyland's voice was once again a loud shout.

"Sir," said Steve, "This has me totally baffled. We are dealing with a well-seasoned group of gangsters who know exactly what they are doing. These thieves have deep experience at a very sophisticated level having come from a background perhaps in the NSA, the CIA, or the FBI. Instantly covering the lenses on the camcorders without being seen takes the greatest degree of skill and ingenuity. These people are experts in disabling monitoring equipment, deactivating security systems, and in larceny. That could also explain the alarm being hacked. This crime, in my opinion, was committed by two or more highly trained ex-CIA operatives."

"Charles," said Leyland, "Get all the exterior videos from up and down Fourth Street. Steve, I want you to study these and look for groups of two or more men for a month before the break-in who were repeatedly in the vicinity. Go over the past few weeks, showing what was taking place inside the store. Once again look for two, three, or more guys who are surveilling the area together. If you find any people who look suspicious run their pictures through the Facial Recognition Database and haul them in. You all focus on that while I go to visit our DNA suspect's mother."

Wakefield was now getting very worried. The Media were breathing down his neck and he knew he needed to come up with answers, fast. He regretted offering to hold a news conference. It was now eleven forty-five on Wednesday, just over twenty-four hours since he was first called to the site of the break-in. He went to see Captain Brian Morley.

"Sir," he began. I am going to call on the mother of a possible culprit, Ryan Barron, who absolutely was in the store committing the robbery. His blood was found there in a few places. I may need to provide money to encourage her to reveal where he is. Could I please have $10,000 in cash to take with me as an incentive payment?"

"Wakefield," said Morley, "You scheduled a meeting with the press based on hope. Our police department has already been embarrassed once. I will sign off only on $5,000 and I will rely on you to spend very little of it. Hopefully, just $1,000 will help nab this alleged thief. But do not let us down." His voice was cold and definite.

"I will make sure I get him, and we will have this case back on track by this afternoon. I am positive I will return either with this man in handcuffs or at the very least, with his exact location."

"Okay, go downstairs and get the money," said Morley handing over a signed authorization order.

It was twelve-twenty when the detective got into his car and drove to the residence of Mrs. Thelma Barron.

He soon arrived at his destination. It was a small home in a low-income area but was one of the best-kept dwellings on the block, with its neat front garden and a brightly painted porch.

Leyland rang the bell, and he heard footsteps inside. A rather old woman with dyed reddish hair opened the door just a crack, leaving the security chain in place.

He showed his badge as he said, "Mrs. Barron, I am Detective Wakefield. May I have a word with you?"

She cautiously let him in. "Please come inside. How can I help you?"

"It is about your son, Ryan," he began.

"Oh yes, always trouble that one," she said wistfully.

"Do you know where I can find him? It is very important." He spoke as civilly as he could. He desperately needed her cooperation.

A look of slight puzzlement came over her face and she hesitated for a moment.

"Please Mrs. Barron, I require your help."

Suddenly she spoke more boldly. "I know where he is and I can lead you to him, but it will cost money for me to tell you."

"It will cost me, did you say?" He tried to sound intimidating.

"Yes. I will not give up his location for nothing."

"Okay," said Leyland putting his hand into his right-side pants pocket. "Here is $1,000 for you and we appreciate your help." Before leaving the precinct, he measured out the money into groups of $1,000 and placed these in various pockets in his trousers and his jacket.

"I cannot give up my son's whereabouts for a measly $1,000," she said loudly. "$10,000 and I will tell you where he is, or you can leave now!"

"I can give you $3,000 and that is it."

"$5,000 and not a penny less or go!" Walking to the door, she opened it.

"All right, I will give you $5,000 but I assure you if he is not in the location where you say and if I cannot find him today, I will return here to get this money back."

"Deal! I will tell you where he is. Let me get something to write on in the kitchen."

He followed her as she picked up a piece of paper, and with a pencil, scribbled down the location, 1055 Powers Street. She handed it over. "I believe you will find him here with no problem." Glancing at her watch, added, "Huh! It is just after one o'clock and I know he is not up. He never wanted to work for a living! He will for sure be at this address."

"I won't tell him you told me where he is," said Leyland trying to be gracious. "Are you certain he will be there?" Fishing around in his various pockets for the money, he gave her the $5,000.

She nodded and said, "If you leave now, you can be there in about twenty minutes. If you hurry, he should still be around when you arrive. By the way, I will not call ahead and give him a heads-up you are coming. I got into serious trouble with the police in the past for doing so, and I definitely want no more problems. Besides, I want to hang onto this money."

"I am glad you volunteered not to give him any warning. I was about to ask that of you." He took a gander at the note. "This is just a street number, is there a specific apartment or such?"

"Oh yes, I forgot." Taking back the paper, the suspect's mother wrote down 646-B. "That is where you will find Ryan."

He thanked her one more time and got into his car, then putting the address and zip code into his GPS navigation system he called for two officers to meet him there. Wakefield did not want this individual to escape out a rear door, thus getting some backup would be a good idea. He sped off in the direction his GPS map was indicating, and twenty minutes later stopped in front of two brick entrance pillars. A squad car was already there, and two of Averton's finest were waiting outside their vehicle. The sign above the brick pillars read, The Powers Street Cemetery - 1055 Powers Street.

Leyland stared at the street number then banged his hand on the steering wheel, screaming a string of profanities! The two female officers trying not to laugh, were having a hard time controlling themselves. He grabbed hold of his cell phone and called his compadre at the precinct.

"Hi, are you bringing him in?" Weston asked innocently.

Infuriated, Leyland vociferated, "He is buried in a grave! Please do some research and find out when Ryan Barron died."

"Is he dead? How is this possible? He just robbed the jewelry store!"

"I am sitting outside a cemetery which is where his mother sent me!" roared the detective.

"Hold on." Charles went immediately to his computer. "It says here he died in a car crash about four months ago."

Wakefield yelled out loud, "Then how on earth was his blood at the scene of the robbery?"

"I don't understand, but we will do some intense work to find out what is going on here."

"You know," Leyland said to Charles as he drove away, "This is the most brilliant gang of thieves we have ever encountered. Please start delving into other crimes with similar patterns. We will get to the bottom of this! I am headed back to Mrs. Barron's place now to get our money back."

"Oh, sir, one other thing, Captain Morley wants to see you imme-diately when you return. The mayor just left here and both he and the captain want an update from you. I am afraid they are expecting you to have Ryan Barron in custody."

He banged on the steering wheel again and bellowed,

"When are we going to get a break?" Upon arriving at Thelma Barron's home, he pulled up, scurried from his car to the front porch, and rang the bell. Nothing. He knocked loudly on the door. No answer.

"Is anybody there?" he shouted. Still not a sound. A couple of neighbors came out of their homes and stared at him. They could not tell he was a police detective and one of them dialed 911. Leyland went to the rear of the house and pounded on that door. He *had* to get the money back. He came around to the front and walked to the entrance again, and moving to his left, peered in a window, shading the reflection with his hands. There was no one inside. She was not there.

"Hands up and turn around slowly!" A policeman barked out the order.

"What the…" He turned, now staring at an officer whose gun was drawn, and it was pointed directly at him. This was no doubt a newbie, someone who did not know Leyland. Behind him was a vehicle with its lights flashing. Curious onlookers were now crowding closer, recording the scene with their cell phones.

"SHOW ME YOUR HANDS and GET DOWN ON THE GROUND!" The rookie looked deadly serious.

Leyland immediately raised his hands and started to explain "I am Detective Wakefield from the Averton Police Department. I am here to interview the mother of a suspect. My badge is in my wallet in my trouser pocket."

"Keep your hands where I can see them." He started calling for backup on his shoulder radio.

"You do not need help! I am Detective Wakefield!" He was beginning to lose his cool.

"A gumshoe huh? Yeah right! What were you doing hammering on doors around this house and looking in the windows? That is not what any of us are trained to do!"

Leyland's phone suddenly rang. It was in the top outside pocket of his jacket. "May I take this?" He was hoping it would be Charles.

"Okay but keep your other hand in the air!"

He reached down, slid the phone out of his pocket, and answered. It was the captain.

"Where the hell are you?" Morley hollered.

"I returned to Mrs. Barron's house, and right now I have a policeman with his gun drawn and it is pointed at me!"

"What?" Morley was furious. "Let me talk to him!"

Leyland held out the phone. "The captain, for you."

The rookie seemed confused for a second and still aiming his gun, took the phone.

Two minutes later Wakefield was in his car and on his way to the precinct. Realization set in. The $5,000 was gone for good. How was he going to explain *that?* Feeling somewhat dejected he drove back in a roundabout way. This was certainly not his day.

It was three forty-five when upon arriving back, he went directly to the captain's office where a loud screaming match took place. Not only was there no suspect but the department had been duped out of a lot of cash.

Both Leyland and Morley realized that Thelma Barron gave him exactly what he asked for. She told him where her son was and in fact, even provided the assurance her son "would not be up at this time." They knew no court of law would uphold their argument and it would not be worth dragging the department through a costly lawsuit, negative publicity and ridicule, over a financial mistake such as this.

"All you needed to do was ask her if her son was still alive before you gave her the money!" snarled Morley. "Listen, I want you and Weston to get back to the scene of the crime *now* and find out what went wrong with those cameras! Inspect the steel door again, for that could be the way they got in and out." He was getting frustrated with the lack of progress. Every lead was producing no results and this Barron incident was literally a 'dead-end'.

Shortly before they left to return to the jewelry store, Wakefield was told some more disappointing news.

"I just got off the phone with the couple who had the yard sale where the mallet was purchased," said Charles. "I was told over one hundred and twenty people attended their sale and they had dozens of tools which were sold, including a number of mallets. All transactions were done with cash. They simply do not remember who bought that piece. Valla's fingerprints were on it because he handled it that day."

Upon hearing this, the detective shook his head and walked to his office to see if there was anything urgent to take care of before going out again.

♦♦♦♦♦

It was that same Wednesday afternoon July 6th. Leyland had the alarm code and keys given to him by Hunt the day before when the theft was discovered. He was still permitting no one inside much to the ire of Barnwell. Wakefield and Weston arrived back at the store close to four fifty. Their sole mission was to check out the cameras and to look again very carefully at the emergency door.

The ladder was left there the previous day. Charles used it to look at the camera nearest to the entrance door, and then at the other one. He gave a soft shout, "It seems the lenses have been covered in some kind of frosty-clear emulsion. How on earth were these painted separately and yet neither of the cameras recorded anyone walking through the store to apply this coating, first to one lens and then to the other? This situation is insane!"

Both men checked the rear door again, this time with a magnifying glass. There was absolutely no sign of anything amiss there.

Wakefield turned to his associate, "I think one of the thieves left something like a thin piece of cardboard or even a pencil to hold this door open just enough so it would not lock, but still allowing the alarm to be armed. Then somehow the security system was hacked or overridden on Sunday after closing time. We must go over the videos from July 3rd and look at all the people who were here that day."

Weston walked around inspecting the carpeted floors and the tiled areas to make sure no one had tunneled in from below. He took the ladder and climbed up. Like Leyland did the previous day, he lifted a few ceiling tiles in the main sales area and in the back of the store. He took a small flashlight from his pocket, and shone this everywhere within the open spaces, glancing at the insulation and all the perimeter walls. He could see no sign of anything having been disturbed.

"I agree with you. Not a soul came in from above and we both took time to inspect this area. The accumulation of fine dust on the insulation paper shows nothing has been touched up there for years. There is zero evidence anyone broke in through a wall. I have checked the floors and no people came in from below. I concur with your thought, perhaps they came in from the back door, which was somehow hooked open, then bolted it closed from the inside. They left with all the jewelry through the front door."

"But we know for certain the alarm was never disabled, and it is very carefully monitored with in-out time recordings." Leyland continued, "The only other thing I can think of is since it appears neither the front door nor the back door was used for entry or exit, the burglars must have cut a large hole in one of the windows on the street. Then once done with the robbery they broke the glass completely and replaced it with a new pane." Even though he knew this theory was implausible, the detective was now looking carefully at the carpeting near the front of the store. He found no sign of any window being smashed.

"The break-in did not happen through one of the windows," Charles commented. "Steve Parker has studied all security footage of the nearby exterior cameras and there are *no* signs of one or more men or women doing something so brazen out in the open. And in any case, look at the size of these panes. They are easily six feet high by eight feet across. It takes experts with the proper equipment to deliver, unload and then install this kind of plate glass. No, this break-in definitely did not happen from out here on the street."

"I know you are right, but I can think of no other way thieves could have got in and out of the store."

"Steve also told me," said Charles, "That all cameras belonging to businesses on Fourth Street showed no indication anyone entered or left this jewelry store through the front door between Sunday afternoon and Tuesday morning. So, what the hell happened here?"

"This case gets more incredulous by the minute." Leyland sighed.

It was a bit past five thirty as the two began driving back to the precinct when the detective's phone rang. It was Hunt, who was in between Barbara leaving his hotel room and Cindy arriving. He wanted to talk briefly about Barbara's idea.

"It's Barnwell here," he began. "I thought of something. There have been a few people in recent months who claim they were treated, should I say, unjustly by me... but they were not. These individuals thought I did not pay them enough for their jewelry. In this business that kind of erroneous thinking happens a lot."

"Go on." Wakefield was now listening in earnest.

"I would like to give you the names of a few clients who I believe are very much upset with me. They all have a motive and each one has been in my place of business one or more times, so they know the layout."

"That is an interesting angle," said Leyland. "We are going to comb through recent in-store video activity tomorrow so maybe you can identify on-screen some of these disgruntled customers plus give us any additional names you feel might be relevant. However, we believe we are dealing with thieves possessing the highest level of experience, expertise and ingenuity. The average person who sells their family gold, or who purchases sparkly stuff from you, will very likely not fit that mold."

They spoke for another minute and Hunt promised he would be at the police station early the next morning. The detective told him he could open his store again the following day because the police were done with the crime scene. "When you come to see us tomorrow, I will give you your keys."

They were almost back at the precinct when Weston took his cell phone out of his pocket. "It seems I missed a call from Parker."

He called the number to retrieve the message and relayed what he heard to Leyland. "Steve left me a voicemail saying that beyond doubt, there was no activity in the atrium area of the 101-Building on either Sunday or Monday. All the small shops there were closed on both days. He says these cameras do not lie and he thus has irrefutable proof no one came in or left through the steel door at the back of the jewelry store."

Wakefield took his eyes off the road for just a moment as he glanced at Charles, and then gave a groan of frustration.

◆◆◆◆◆

On this warm and muggy Wednesday evening, at 7:30 p.m. Barbara had just arrived. Ariella opened the front door inviting her inside, and they hugged briefly.

"You appear a lot brighter than you did on Monday... when I saw you in the morning and also when I was with you that afternoon."

"I am feeling so much better," said Ariella. It was most particularly because she was a bit more rested and was now also very motivated to talk about the biggest secret of her life. "I know you are here for us to chat, but first we will get some wine and raise our glasses to an amazing event. After that we can have our coffee and cookies."

"Why the wine?" her visitor asked, seeming a bit puzzled. "What are we celebrating?"

"You will see in a minute." Her blue eyes were sparkling. Before too long her friend would know what a genius she was and how *The Perfect Crime* was committed.

They sat down on the couch in the living room. Ariella put two wine glasses onto the small table in front of them and filled each with Chardonnay.

"Cheers!" said Barbara.

"To good health! I have something really exciting to tell you. You know all the talk that is going on right now about the…" she did not get a chance to finish.

Purdy, who was sitting on the windowsill suddenly jumped down onto a table which was under the window. He knocked over a small potted plant and it crashed to the floor. The earthenware container broke into a dozen pieces and there was soil scattered all over.

"Purdy!" Ariella yelled. This was more of a reaction because they both got a big fright. The feline fled in terror. Ariella's wine glass jerked into the air and splashed her. She grabbed some napkins and started mopping her sleeve, a bit on the side table, and whatever spilled onto the carpet.

"Let me help you clean up the mess," said Barbara.

With a brush and pan, they swept the potting soil from the floor. Ariella got her vacuum cleaner and removed what dirt the dustpan did not get. It was almost twenty minutes before both returned to the couch and then Ariella refilled her glass.

"Now where were we?" This was her absentminded question, knowing she wanted to talk about the break-in and get back to the conversation.

At that moment her cell phone rang, and the number was one she did not recognize. "Let me get this, it could be someone from work and I am into a huge project right now. Why don't you go and pour the coffee and get the chocolate chip cookies?"

"Sure, no problem." Barbara got up and went into the kitchen.

"Hello, who is this?"

"Greetings to you! It's Roger Riley. Remember me?"

She gasped. It was the hot lawyer, the guy she really liked, and wanted to learn more about.

"Of course, I know who you are! I am about to have dinner. May I call you back later, say around ten o'clock?"

"Yes, sure. Talk to you then, gorgeous." He hung up.

Gorgeous! Her heart fluttered. Then her thoughts went back to Barbara who intercepted the information which was supposed to be given to Roger by the waitress. No, I will not confide in her about the heist right now. I really need to think this through.

Her company came back into the living room carrying a plate of cookies and returned with the two coffee cups.

"Work?" she asked, sitting down again.

Ariella thought quickly. "Yes. That was about the new important project I am in the middle of, and I am doing very well with it. The reason for the wine is to recognize an upcoming promotion I am about to get!" It was the quickest lie that came to mind, but for now, nothing would be said about the ingenious way she got into Hunt's hideout and how expertly her tracks were covered.

They raised their glasses and drank to the soon-to-be promotion. Ariella had no clue how close she came to being caught. Purdy saved her as did the phone call from Roger. She did not know this vixen was suspicious of her and was of course, unaware of the affair with Barnwell. If Ariella told her supposed gal pal about the heist, there is no doubt Hunt would have reported her in a heartbeat.

After finishing the wine, they drank their coffee and indulged in the crunchy chocolate chip cookies. They made small talk for a short while and then the subject of the jewelry store came up.

"I wish they would quickly catch the thieves who robbed that place," said Ariella. "It makes me nervous to think burglars could be wandering around town, and I hope they do not start stealing from homes in this neighborhood."

"I don't think you have to worry." Barbara tried to sound reassuring. "With the police really digging into this, the perpetrators are probably long gone from this area by now. If they haven't left, I am sure they are about to be arrested."

"I guess you are right."

They continued talking about who might have done it, and after almost an hour of interesting discussion, Ariella said she had to be up early for work. Her guest decided she also did not want to get to bed too late and it was time to go home. The two agreed to connect again soon for drinks or for dinner but made no definite arrangement.

Right after Barbara drove away Ariella was on her cell phone.

"Hi Roger! It was so good to hear from you earlier. Sorry I could not talk."

"Thank you for returning my call so quickly." He sounded very enthusiastic. "I just wanted to say hello. I would like to get together with you in the near future, but I need to sort out my travel schedule first. I have been running up and down to Philadelphia lately handling a large transaction for one of my clients."

"Not to worry. You let me know when you have time to meet and then we can make plans."

"Okay. I will reach out to you in the next day or two. Have a good night."

"You too, sleep well and we will talk soon."

Ariella was thrilled about him contacting her and that he sounded so upbeat on her call back to him. His number was now added to the contacts in her phone. She thought this could be the start of a great relationship.

After tidying the kitchen and washing the cups and wine glasses, she went to bed.

CHAPTER 16

Weston and Wakefield were at the precinct discussing the case and each knew they had no suspects and barely any leads to help move things along. The crime lab expert was unable to get any DNA or fingerprints off the cigarettes, but he was still waiting for information from the Kleenex tissue. While knowing this evidence could be a plant, they would follow up on the result once it was received.

Barnwell arrived at the precinct where he gave Leyland the names of five people whom he felt really detested him. Two were very old ladies and there were repercussions from these clients because Hunt received lawyer's letters from each. He explained, to make the problem go away, he paid almost the full amount their lawyers demanded, and he also took care of their legal costs. But the other three names were those of people who might still be bearing a grudge.

As he sat in the interview room with Leyland and Charles, Hunt told them about a particular female whose name was on this list who threatened him.

"There was one lady who was very belligerent. She felt I swindled her grandmother out of a lot of money, but I did not. Hers was mostly fake and costume jewelry, but this Ariella Gerson did not believe me."

"Do you know how to contact her?" asked Leyland.

"Oh yes, she came into my place of business and demanded I return everything to her granny, and that is when she left me with her name and phone number. I have her home address as well." Hunt was lying as to how he got her details. The day Ariella went into the store he only knew she was old Mrs. Gerson's granddaughter. He did not know anything more about her and she stormed out in tears.

He certainly did not disclose, it was he who sent his girlfriend running after her. He hurriedly said to Barbara who happened to be in the store at that moment, "*Befriend her and find out what she is up to. I do not want another surprise lawsuit on my hands.*" The femme fatale followed his instructions and since then, gave her lover whatever relevant details she could, even providing Ariella's full name, address, and phone number.

Hunt produced a slip of paper with the information. Leyland glanced at Charles and said in almost a whisper, "I believe this Ms.

Gerson is the same woman who came to see us here about a month ago complaining that a family member of hers was robbed by Mr. Barnwell. She is certainly worth investigating."

"I think you are right, sir. Although the desk sergeant introduced her to us at that time, I did not remember her name."

Barnwell was given his keys and told he could conduct business again. Charles then took him to Steve's office so they could begin to review the in-store activities of the past two weeks. At that moment Laura Kelly, the store's top salesperson, arrived to help with consumer identification. She brought with her a box of cash slips, credit card receipts, and other paperwork which could be useful.

It was nine-thirty when Steve, Hunt and Laura began to peruse the videos. They were looking for suspicious customers or even those known to be dissatisfied clients. First, they went over the most recent recordings which were of Saturday, July 2nd and Sunday, July 3rd. Every now and again Steve would stop the playback as he listened to comments from the store owner or from his assistant. Occasionally she would point to a person and provide their name because she knew it. Often to find that client's details, Laura would look through her well-organized box of information and produce either a cash sale record or a credit-card receipt. Sometimes there was a voucher for something purchased from a client. This salesclerk really understood the way the business operated.

Based on details from Laura and Hunt, Steve made notes about some long-established patrons and a few new ones, printing a photograph of the person when they all agreed it might be needed. The three discussed various names and then whittled these down to just four people of interest. Going through the two days of security tapes took about an hour and a half. After that, they studied the recordings from the past week, the previous weekend, and a few days prior. All of this took a couple more hours, but when they were done, they had two more names of suspicious people each with a reason to be very angry at the owner of the store.

Together with the three names Barnwell provided when he first arrived, they now held a list of nine malcontented or questionable customers, some from the recent past and a few from quite a while back.

Watching the videos of Saturday morning June 25th, a week before the robbery, Laura noticed one person she clearly remembered.

"There," said Laura pointing to the screen which Steve had just frozen. "That woman came in the front door and immediately started talking to me. I cannot quite recall her name, but she spoke with a heavy Spanish accent and gave me her card. I know it is here somewhere."

Delving through her box of records Laura came up with the business card. "Oh yes, here it is! Now I remember. Her name is Raquel Santos Gomez, a Wedding Planner working both in the USA and in Ecuador. As we can all see on the screen, she went into the bathroom moments after introducing herself and was there for maybe four or five minutes which now is of concern to me."

"Well five minutes is not really a long time if you have 'big business' to do," said Hunt in a sarcastic voice.

"Yes, but Laura may be right, to me she appears to be shady," said Steve. "We should follow up on this one. Her name now brings the total on our list to ten. We have the information so it should be easy to find her."

"Look now," said Laura. "This Gomez woman comes out of the bathroom and tries to get served, but we were all very busy. Then you can see her body language is showing total frustration and before too long she walks out."

"I guess we cannot blame her for not buying anything," said Hunt, "But since we have her business card which shows her address, it is worth chasing her down. Maybe her presence there was to look around the place for a criminal coterie to which she belongs, who rob stores like these."

At two o'clock Steve called Charles over to his office and handed him the details of nine customers and in addition a person named Raquel Santos Gomez. "Please follow up on these ten people," said Parker. "We have provided addresses and phone numbers for all of them. I have also printed some pictures of what a few of these folks look like, where I was able to get a decent image. I have noted the date and time each one was in the store and also an idea of what they may have sold or purchased. Most of these are disgruntled customers."

"This is awesome, and I will get right onto it," said Charles, desperate for new avenues to pursue.

He took the list and made a photocopy of it on his way to Leyland's office. "I have some good information here," he said handing over a copy of the names. "Steve says these are *ten definite suspects* and he also said, in the opinion of both Barnwell and Laura, many of these people would love to get back at the illustrious store proprietor. Besides this hard copy, Steve is also emailing these details to you in case you wish to make any modifications as the investigation progresses."

"Good." Wakefield hoped that these leads would bear some fruit.

"I do have some bad news though," said Charles. "I just got back the preliminary results for the DNA on the Kleenex tissue. I will spare you the minutia, but of course it is also fake evidence. It belongs to a man in his seventies who is confined to a wheelchair. He lives in a retirement community and does not own a car. A caregiver or family member probably took him to a park or such, and that could be where the perpetrators picked up his discarded tissue."

"We have not much to go on," said Leyland. "I guess I will follow up with this Ariella woman. I see her name is on this *List of Ten Suspects* but frankly Charles, it looks like a very complex operation done by people with a lot of experience, or it or it was done by someone from this store. I believe there is no way this was carried out by a simple suburbanite like Ms. Gerson, even if she was very upset."

"I agree. This woman sounds like a highly emotional person as Barnwell has described, and being so volatile, she could not have pulled this off. Leyland, you go and see her, and I will start to look at the other possible perpetrators."

"If we get nowhere after this, we must really start digging into the proprietor and pursuing the possibility he did it. The back door may or may not be part of this whole thing, but the front door is unquestionably the exit point. However, we still have the mystery of the disabling of the cameras and the turning off of the alarm system with no record of when or how these were tampered with."

◆◆◆◆◆

At about four o'clock Leyland arrived at Ariella's address, parked across the road from her double-story dwelling, and sat there for a few minutes. This was a nice neighborhood and the residence, although quite old, seemed to be well-maintained.

He got out of his car and ambled across the street to the front gate. After opening it, proceeded up the pathway to the small porch by the front door and rang the bell. There was no one home so he decided to look around the property.

Going from the pathway onto the green turf he suddenly stopped. Something caught his eye in one of the flower beds close to the house.

While there were plants and shrubs filling most of the area, this garden spot had a large void in it. The earth looked like it was dug up not too long ago and then filled in. Was there something buried underground, perhaps spoils from the theft of the downtown store?

He walked on the lawn alongside the structure looking at the siding and other aspects of the house and stopped again. Close to the ground was a small window which provided some natural light into the basement below. Carefully stepping over the cultivated patch, he crouched down and peered inside.

The lights were on, and he noticed on the wall opposite, the sheetrock appeared to have recently been opened and then closed in. The fresh spackle around a large area was clearly visible. Could this Ariella woman possibly have robbed the downtown diamond depot, buried the haul in her garden, or maybe hid it in her basement?

The detective made his way around the property and was now standing in the backyard. He observed another area where dirt had been disturbed. The earth was cleared from that spot, leaving behind a slight depression.

He phoned Captain Morley. "Sir, I am at the home of a person whom I believe to be a very disgruntled jewelry store customer. She was the one Barnwell referred to as being extremely agitated with him and her name is on our *List of Ten Suspects*. In my opinion, she had a strong motive to commit this felony. There appears to be something suspicious here so I would like to get a warrant to have this place searched."

"Wakefield, I will get you the warrant from Judge Shafer immediately because we need progress on this case, and quickly!"

"Sir, our crime lab specialist Weston, is still at the precinct and I will need him and a couple of officers to come here now. I will call and tell him to stop by Judge Shafer's office on his way."

"Okay. Just wrap this up as soon as you can!"

Using his cell phone Leyland reached out to Charles who agreed to pick up the warrant and arrange for two policemen to come to Ariella's address. He went back to his car and waited. Looking at his *List of Ten Suspects*, he carefully observed each name and put lines through the ones which were not relevant. His thinking was, maybe they would get lucky with this first search and the case would be solved before too long.

At about five o'clock Ariella arrived home, having left her office earlier than usual to take the bus which dropped her off two blocks away like always. When approaching her house, she did not pay attention to a sedan parked across the street or the man sitting in it.

Barely inside for ten minutes, she happened to look out the living room window and noticed a squad car pulling up to her front gate. It stopped and two men in uniform got out as well as a third man who was dressed in a business suit. Another individual exited a nearby vehicle and they were now gathering at the entrance to her driveway. One of the men held a paper in his hand and he kept pointing to the house and talking loudly.

Ariella was terrified! How could they know in merely a few days about the crime she just committed? Understanding speed was essential, she grabbed her phone and called Roger Riley. He was supposed to be this super lawyer... or so she had been told.

He picked up his phone as it rang and saw who it was.

"Hi beautiful," were the first words out of his mouth. "I am pleased you called. I enjoyed our little chat last night."

In a stressed voice she stammered, "Roger, I need your help now! Immediately! Where are you? Can you come to where I live right away?"

Suddenly he sounded all lawyerly and serious. "Ariella, what is going on? Are you okay?"

"I cannot explain too much at this moment but there are four policemen about to approach my front door. I believe one has a warrant in his hand. You know the jewelry store that was broken into this past weekend? Well, I am sure they think I did it. I never stole anything from anyone, and I certainly would not know how to ransack a retail shop!"

"Slow down! Why would the police suspect you?"

"I had a big argument with the owner of this place recently after he cheated my grandma out of a fortune. They are probably looking into every restive customer with a reason to break in. I am so scared! Please come quickly!" She rattled off her address to him.

"I am downtown and just leaving my office. I can be at you in about twenty minutes."

"Please hurry!"

At that moment the doorbell rang. With her heart beating rapidly she opened the door, trying to stay calm.

Leyland was standing in front of the others. "I am Detective Wakefield from the local police department. Are you Ms. Ariella Gerson?" While flashing his badge, he immediately recognized as her as the woman who visited the precinct about four weeks before.

"Yes. What is it you want?" She stared at him. Was he in the meeting down at the police station? That event was now just a blur in her mind.

"We have reason to believe you may have been involved in a burglary at the Fourth Street Jewelers and Gold Exchange and we have a warrant to search your premises."

"This is outrageous! You have no business being here. What makes you think I had anything to do with this?"

"You had strong words with the owner not too long ago and you made menacing remarks to him. You even came to see me to complain about Mr. Barnwell, remember?"

"I never threatened anyone. What I can tell you again is that he swindled my grandmother out of a lot of jewelry, and I am glad he got ripped off. He can now get a taste of his own medicine, but I had *nothing* to do with this!"

"Ms. Gerson, we can see you have rage against the proprietor of this establishment. Please step aside. We need to search your residence."

There was about $1,500,000 in stolen goods stashed away close by, and the police were about to come inside and tear the place apart!

Wakefield, Weston, and the two officers pushed their way past her, and first started looking in the kitchen. They took their time, even though there were no obvious hiding places. The freezer door was opened, and various foodstuffs were removed. They studied these carefully and put most of the items back. But there was a large box of frozen peas and another oversized pack of broccoli.

Leyland took the box of peas and put it into the microwave. "I need to defrost these to make sure that you have no gold chains, or other such articles concealed inside."

As he spoke, he was watching for a reaction from Ariella. If there was any metal hidden in the box, she might have yelled out for him to stop, not wanting to damage the jewelry or her microwave oven.

"Go ahead," she said. "I haven't done anything illegal, and you will not find any stolen items here."

"We'll see about that," said Leyland, setting the microwave on 'high' and pressing the start button. There was no burning or exploding. He ran it for fifteen seconds, hit the 'stop' button, and then did the same with the broccoli. As he returned both packages to the freezer, he somehow kicked Purdy's water bowl causing it to splash into the dry food.

"Look at the mess you are making!" she shrieked at him. There was no apology, even though he glanced about to see where the cat was.

After a few more minutes in the kitchen, they moved into the next room, her study. One of the officers took out three drawers from the left side of her desk, crouched down, and with his flashlight stared into the open area. He tapped on the wood trying to find any false panels. The others were opening her steel filing cabinet and pulling out the individual drawers as far as they would go. They looked in the shell of the unit to make sure that nothing was hidden in there.

A loud knocking was suddenly heard, and Ariella ran to the front door. It was of course Roger, and after coming inside, he signaled with a finger on his lips for her to not say a word. They went to the study where books were being taken out of her bookcase and strewn across the floor.

"Okay stop!" He walked into the room. "My name is Roger Riley, and I am Ms. Gerson's lawyer." He gave the detective his business card.

"Oh, so you've lawyered up! That tells us a lot!" said Leyland sarcastically as he introduced himself, Charles, and the two officers. "We have a warrant to go through this house. I gave it to Ms. Gerson,"

Ariella retrieved it from the kitchen and showed it to the tall and confident new arrival.

"Why is she a suspect in this break-in?" he asked. "From what I can gather from the TV news and online, the case has you all in a tizzy and it seems this was done by a very high-level and experienced crew."

"We are exploring all possibilities to find the perpetrators," commented Wakefield. "Ms. Gerson feels her grandmother was taken advantage of by the owner and Ms. Gerson threatened him. We have many people who despise the man, and their properties will all be searched."

To let the lawyer know Ariella was not being singled out, Leyland took the *List of Ten Suspects* from his jacket pocket, sort of waved it about, and then placed it on the desk.

Roger checked over the warrant. "This is valid. You must allow them to look everywhere throughout your home."

"I did not do this! I am not capable of breaking windows or smashing down doors to get into a place selling valuables. Why would I do it? I have a good job and I am able to pay my bills on time every month." She purposefully referred to breaking windows and smashing down doors, making everyone think she assumed the store was ripped off by forceful means. This was to further throw any suspicion away from her and from the actual point of entry.

Leyland hesitated for a moment after this statement was made, briefly thinking that maybe she played no part in this. But then his group continued tearing the room apart. More books were taken from the bookshelves as the police sought out secret compartments or panels. They even tapped on the walls searching for the slightest clue of a possible hollow area or hiding place. Ariella was really upset when one of the men started pulling up the carpeting from a corner of the room, trying to find a trapdoor, in case items were stored under the floor.

"Is there a basement in this house?" asked Charles.

"Yes, there is."

"We will get to that in a little while," he said, as he lifted a big picture off the wall. Behind it was a large wall safe.

"Well, well! What have we here?" Leyland's gloating voice made them all look at him. "Please open this right now!"

"No, I will not!" She was now yelling at them, and Roger became very worried at her defiance.

He thought, this is it, there must be evidence inside. He glanced at Ariella, "Because of the warrant, you must show them what is in there."

"I will *not!* I will *not!*" she screamed.

The detective seemed to be happy. Victory was within his grasp! There were certainly going to be incriminating items right behind the door and that must be why she was refusing to cooperate. "We have an order signed by a judge. Now unlock it!"

"It is nobody's business what is in here!"

"Yes, it is. A jewelry store was broken into, you threatened the owner, and we demand right now to see what is in this safe!" Leyland sounded menacing.

"Okay. I will open it, but please all look away while I work the combination." Within ten seconds they heard the handle click and the secure door swung away from the wall.

Leyland quietly said, "You are finished, Ms. Gerson!" He moved forward quickly and stared inside. The disappointment showed on his face because it was empty except for $120 in $20.00 bills and Ariella's passport. There were no gold coins, no diamonds, nothing of value. The others appeared disheartened. Roger breathed a little easier.

"I think we are done in this room," said Wakefield.

"Wait a minute, aren't you going to put back all these books?" Ariella was almost shouting. "You have made a huge mess in here. Look at everything scattered on the floor! What about the pulled-away carpet? You must clean up right now!"

"We do not put things away. We search, you tidy."

"This is outrageous! Roger, can I sue the police department?" A very irate Ariella was on the verge of hysteria about what they were doing to her house. "I am blameless!" She was also becoming extremely worried these men who were very thorough, would find the hidden treasure trove before they were done.

"Calm down and let them finish, then we will see what actions we can take." He was trying to be reassuring.

Leyland suddenly turned to her and asked, "Where were you on Sunday night, the night of July 3rd?"

"Ariella, you do not have to tell them." Roger was trying to do his lawyer-like duty.

"It's okay. I have nothing to hide. It was the Roman Orator, Horace who said, 'Innocence is its own Defense'. I am 100% innocent so I will answer the question. At about six thirty in the evening, I went to a party at Donnie Bolin's house. I met up with my friend Barbara McKenna and there were dozens of people who can verify that I was present."

"Oh, so you were at a party with many others who can provide an alibi for you. That is a good thing which will help you," said the detective.

"It's not that simple because I was not feeling well. I had a bad cough and an unbearable migraine coming on, so at about eight o'clock I came home. I got into bed half an hour later and did not wake up until perhaps six the next morning when Barbara came knocking on my door to see if I was okay. She had been calling me on my cell phone during the night, but I did not answer because the sound was turned off."

"Oh, so after eight o'clock you were on your own alone at home?" asked Leyland.

"Yes. That is what I said."

"Well then, there is no one who can verify where you were between eight that night and six the next morning?"

"So what? No one needs to confirm where I was. I told you I was here, sleeping."

"How very convenient for you to leave the party early, feigning illness!"

Ariella raised her voice, "I told you I was not well! Have you ever experienced a migraine headache?"

"It seems from the time you came home at eight o'clock until daybreak the next morning you had plenty of time to drive to the downtown area, somehow break into the Fourth Street Jewelers and Gold Exchange, rob the place, and come home again." Leyland was crowing at her. He had made these types of assumptions countless times before when interrogating suspects. Many, if they were guilty, would eventually crumble and also give up their accomplices.

Roger was not happy with the idea there was no one to confirm her being at home on Sunday night. But on the other hand, he was thankful her words were not 'in bed with my boyfriend.' That would have disturbed him on a personal level to know there was a man in her life.

Leyland said, "You are our top suspect, Ms. Gerson."

"Why? You have found no evidence here that I stole anything from anyone. I heard on TV you are about to arrest some men for this crime. Tell you what," said Ariella taking her cell phone out of her pocket, "Here, you call Donnie, and he will tell you about Sunday night. You just accused me of driving downtown to break into some stupid bling boutique. How could I go anywhere when I did not have a method of transportation?"

Leyland spoke directly to Ariella. "Of course, you have a car! I walked around your house before you came home, and through the garage window I saw one parked there."

"I was too sick to drive home from the party on Sunday night, so Donnie's brother Max brought me here at eight o'clock. My Subaru was parked all night outside Donnie's place. I left him with my keys. He and Barbara brought it back to me on Monday afternoon. I only have one vehicle, so you call my friends and ask them." She again held out her phone to the detective. Upon hearing this Roger suddenly felt a bit more encouraged. He did not like Ariella's 'no alibi' position.

Leyland was caught a bit off-guard by what she said. He ignored her offer and tried to keep control of the situation. "Good excuse about the auto but I think that was just a cover-ploy on your part. No doubt your accomplices picked you up and took you downtown to help them commit this felony. In the meantime, we will need to check on a few things outdoors before it gets dark." He looked at his watch, understanding they still had more than two hours of daylight left.

He wanted to find out why a hole was dug in the garden, then filled with earth. He really felt the spoils of the theft were likely concealed there. One of the officers got a shovel from the garage and they all went outside.

Wakefield pointed to the depression in the flower bed. "We believe something is buried in this area," he began. "We will be digging it up to see what is here." He was not asking permission, just stating a fact of what they would be doing and why. Then he turned to Charles and said, "Take the metal detector which is in my car and go around the yard, look closely at places where any ground has been disturbed." Charles ran off to do so.

In the meanwhile, the two policemen took turns excavating the area where the tree was just a few weeks before. The ground was still soft, and the soil came out fairly easily. Leyland was validating the fact there was a hole here not so long ago. After digging and sweating and going down to a depth of almost three feet, they were told to stop.

"It appears there is nothing here," he grumbled. "Why was there a filled-in hole at this spot?" He addressed this question to Ariella.

Roger immediately said, "Don't answer that!"

"No, it is quite okay. Detective, if you asked me prior to going to all this trouble and before your men threw that huge pile of dirt onto my beautiful shrubs and colorful plants, I would have told you what took place."

"Well, what did happen?"

"There was a tree here and it died this past winter. I removed it not too long ago by pulling it out of the ground with a tow-rope using my car. Come with me and I will show it to you. But before we go behind the house, please have your men put all the soil back into this void they just created."

"I told you, we search, and you clean up. You will have to fill it yourself." He then added snidely, "You did it before, so you have the experience to do the same job over again." Ariella cursed him from under her breath. But one of his men took the shovel and began to fill the hole with the earth which was piled up, off to the side.

Leyland said, "After we are done out here, we will continue indoors."

They all followed her to the backyard, where in the corner of the property they saw the cut-up dead tree. Then she took them to another suspicious-looking spot. "I dug some soil from there," she said waving her hand toward a scooped-out area. "I put it into my wheelbarrow and filled in what was needed where you just dug that hole."

Wakefield was satisfied because it answered the question of the disturbed earth in the front and back of her property. Roger seemed relieved at the plausible explanations.

Charles, at that point told everyone he had been around most of the property, and besides a few old nails, the metal detector found nothing buried anywhere.

They walked back inside the house to go on with their search. As they continued dissecting room after room, one of them noticed the pull-down steps for access to the attic. He climbed up, but after a minute came down and said there were no valuables to be found there.

Ariella was very upset when they got to her bedroom and started taking apart her underwear bureau. They made a point of scattering her panties all over the floor. She felt particularly ashamed because Roger was standing there. Leyland looked at the small nightstand next to her bed hoping he might find some evidence there. He yanked out the top drawer and tipped it over. Some books, hand cream jars, and a bottle of eye drops fell onto the floor. In the next one, there were some crepe bandages, a pair of scissors, and an elastic wrist guard. He was more than disappointed.

Charles crouched down and tried to see if anything was hidden in the back of the bed or under it. There was nothing. When he found a small wooden jewelry box on a side table, he opened it. Inside were standard girly items such as earrings, bracelets and necklaces. The two heirloom pieces from Ariella's nana were also there, but Charles ignored what he considered to be usual everyday adornments.

It was hard to believe they were turning over everything in her bedroom. This was her personal space and how could they do this to her? She ran out virtually in tears and went down to the study.

There on her desk lay Wakefield's *List of Ten Suspects*. While everyone was still upstairs, this was the perfect time for her to snap a picture of it with her phone. Ariella did not know why she photographed it, but something compelled her to do so. A few minutes later they all came down from the second floor, and as they got to the bottom of the stairs she joined them, still embarrassed about everything being thrown about in her bedroom.

"I left something in the study which I need to retrieve," said Leyland, and then we need to check the area below." He walked into the study, picked up his *List of Ten Suspects* and together with the others headed into the basement.

He had noticed some spackle on part of the drywall when looking through the narrow ground-level window earlier and was frustrated they found nothing in the hole in the front of the garden. There was also not an iota of evidence in the backyard and no stolen items in the wall safe. Leyland thought, "This will be it... here we will find the cache of treasure!"

The two policemen led the way downstairs, and as everyone got to the bottom, Ariella's had thoughts of anguish racing through her mind. "Oh no! They are going to see the patch-up job which I did. I really meant to sandpaper the spackle and paint it a week ago. It will be torn open by them, and I cannot have that happen. If they keep going, the jewelry will be found!"

When all were in the basement, Wakefield walked directly to the repaired section of the back wall. The size of the cut-out area was easy to identify. It was about 2' x 3' and the unfinished plaster paste provided a clear indication this was opened at some point recently, and then closed again.

"Well, look at what we have here!" He appeared to be crowing. "We will need to see what is behind this patchwork."

A look of grave concern came over Roger's face.

"Ariella, you do not have to say anything, nor are you obligated to let them proceed."

"You are wrong," said Leyland. "Attorney Riley, I think you are forgetting we have the properly signed authority to do so. We can dissect this place any way we wish."

Ariella knew, by ripping out the spackled area, they would create a big hole and they must be stopped. She was concerned that with them keeping up this thorough search, the police would soon find what they came here for.

"You leave this wall alone! Go away now!" Her house had been ruined enough and there was one major secret none of these unwelcome visitors should ever discover.

Roger was worried and wished she wouldn't antagonize them. He was also unsure as to whether Leyland was right or not about the warrant allowing him to do as he pleased. But then he knew if this one did not cover it, within half an hour they would have another which would permit them to see what was hidden behind the newly repaired section.

"We are going to remove this wall segment and find what you took illegally. You will be leaving here in handcuffs tonight!" Wakefield spoke in his sternest voice. He was looking forward to getting back to the precinct and telling Captain Morley the case was now solved.

He sent the two officers to the garage to look for any tools including a crowbar, a hammer, and whatever else could get the job done. They returned a few minutes later with various implements to accomplish the task at hand.

Ariella was at her wits end with the way these buffoons invaded her privacy and ravaged her house. They had already done plenty of damage, so she jumped up with her arms outstretched. "You must get out! Immediately!" She was all but shrieking at them. "You have no right to open this up and to destroy my home any further!"

"Move her out of the way!" said Leyland firmly. One of his men grabbed hold of her and dragged her kicking and screaming to the other end of the room.

Roger ran to her side. He felt bad because he now completely doubted her innocence. The police were likely right about accomplices. Her excuse regarding not having a car with which to get around on the night of the robbery did not seem to be holding water.

"Ariella," he said quietly, "If you are part of a group that did this, don't worry. I am here for you. I will come up with whatever bail money you need." He was careful to use the word 'group' and not 'gang' like the Media did.

This is what she wanted to hear from him. Her charade was partly about testing Roger, trying to figure out how supportive he would really be. The clever young actress cried into his shoulder but was also petrified they would discover her secret. "I had no hand in this! I do not like them accusing me and breaking everything apart!"

"Let them do their job. By getting in their way you will only make it worse for yourself." He left off the bit about 'when they take you into custody' or 'when the judge is deciding on bail.'

The two officers started hammering on the drywall, prying off chunks with a crowbar. There were gypsum bits, chips, and dust flying everywhere. Leyland took a few steps back while the assault proceeded. Then his phone rang.

"Hold up," he shouted, raising his hand. They momentarily stopped their actions. "Oh, hello Captain Morley. Yes, we are still at Ms. Gerson's place, and we have found the wall in which she buried the spoils from this reprobate act." He hesitated for a moment as Morley spoke to him, then continued, "No, not yet sir, but I am certain we will have some or all the hot property in our hands within minutes. We will be arresting her and bringing her in. I will call you shortly."

Standing back smugly with his arms folded, he kept glancing at the pale, sniffling Ariella and at her attorney whose facial frown lines were getting deeper. The two policemen went back to banging and ripping as they created a big opening.

"Got you!" Wakefield whispered.

Charles spoke quietly back, "Good call to obtain a search warrant, sir! I am sure we will find out in due course who her co-conspirators are."

Leyland felt sorry for Ariella, thinking, "What a gorgeous young woman." He began to soften his tone. "Ms. Gerson, after we retrieve it all, if you provide us with the names of the others who assisted you with this grand theft, that will go a long way to help you get your jail time reduced." He was trying to be conciliatory.

Because of this sudden change in attitude, Roger began to feel a bit better. Maybe now he *could* help her, especially if Wakefield was prepared to work with him.

But then to Roger's horror, Ariella, who had been standing quietly at his side, uncontrollably flew at the detective and got right in his face!

She screamed, "You are not listening to me! I didn't participate in this or any other crimes. I am blameless! There is no jewelry here! Get out this instant!"

Roger grabbed her hand and pulled her back. Now he was getting annoyed. How could she provoke the person who had just offered an olive branch? All the plunder was about to be found.

"Calm down!" he urged. "This man is trying to help you."

"He is not helping me! He is attempting to pin this thievery on me, a heinous act in which I was not involved! It's a good thing you are here to witness their aggression because if you were not present, they would be planting evidence!"

Suddenly there was an announcement, and everyone became quiet.

"Sir!" exclaimed one of the officers. "We have this wall open and there is just a plumbing pipe in this area. A twelve-inch-wide space exists behind the studs which would make an excellent hiding place but there isn't anything here. No valuables, not a thing!" He shone his flashlight into the gaping hole. It was very large and spacious, but empty for all to see.

His comments shocked Wakefield who was momentarily lost for words. Weston was staring into the opening and saw it was devoid of any stolen goods. He too could not speak. Roger felt a burden lifting off his shoulders.

Leyland tried to grasp for an explanation and sheepishly asked, "Why was there patchwork by this section?"

"If you inquired before you ripped it apart, I would have told you! I had a leaking plumbing pipe about four weeks ago," said Ariella. "I removed some sheetrock, made the repair, and closed it again. I have not had time to sandpaper and to repaint this area." She walked over to the open wall, remembering at that moment she forgot to take the 6" long piece of cracked PVC pipe which was cut away.

Ariella reached in and got hold of it. "Here," she said handing it to Leyland, "See, it is split halfway down. The leak in this pipe damaged the drywall so I replaced it. The water stain is still visible on the carpet if you clear away the dust and debris which *your* individuals just generated! This plumbing problem was easy to remedy."

"Oh, I see." He did not know what else to say. Every suspicious-looking scenario at this residence had been nullified with perfectly reasonable explanations.

"Each one of you must listen to me," Ariella said loudly, realizing she was now in full control. "You have pulled this place apart and damaged my garden and my house. I have been unjustly accused of a crime that had zilch to do with me. There is a police vehicle parked out in front, and the neighbors are believing who-knows-what because of you people! Do I look like a felon?" She pulled her cell phone from her pocket and snapped some pictures of everyone standing there and the pile of drywall rubble on the floor.

The detective gazed at her. She was right, how he could have been so blind! That awesome long blond hair, those vibrant blue eyes, that perfect nose, that slim sexy body and the face of an angel. She was no criminal!

"We are so very sorry," he said quietly. "We will be leaving now." What was he going to tell Captain Morley who was expecting a phone call at any minute informing him the stolen items were found?

"Roger," she said boldly, "Will I be able to sue the police? You saw all they did both inside and outside. I would like to hold my own news conference tomorrow. Please make sure you get the exact spelling of everyone's names."

It was Wakefield's turn to look troubled. "No need to talk to the Media. I will find out quickly what we can do to pay for what happened here today." How was he going to ask his superiors to compensate Ariella when he threw away $5,000 the day before chasing down a dead man? He shuddered at the thought of going before Morley with this debacle.

"I still need the full spelling of all of your names," said Roger jumping on Ariella's idea. Suing the police department or having them provide a meaningful settlement could generate some good money for his law firm. He took out a pen, and on the back of two of his business cards, wrote down their details. He could not believe how the tables were turned in just a few minutes.

At that moment the gem-fem had a great idea and decided to direct the bunch of bullies to walk where she wanted them to. "You all have drywall powder and dust on your shoes. When we get upstairs, I will not allow any of you to tramp that dirt through my house and most especially on my entrance-hall carpeting. You will have to leave by way of the kitchen."

"Yes Ma'am," said Weston on behalf of the others.

Ariella led the way upstairs and they all followed her into the kitchen, which was still a jumble from their prior antics. Then she held the back door open as the men went outside. It was 7:43 p.m. and not yet dark.

Each said, "Goodnight," and she heard, "I am sorry Ms. Gerson," from one of them. They all walked over the newly tightened 4' x 4' wooden landing which was only recently secured in place. Their boots and shoes created a loud clopping sound as they made their way over the platform and down the wooden steps: "Clunk, clop... clunk, clop... clunk, clop...!"

She was secretly smiling as they marched on top of the plywood piece and into her back yard.

The artful Ariella forced them to walk directly over the secret repository containing the evidence they were looking for. Little did the policemen know, right under their noisy feet, hidden below the landing was over $1,500,000 in jewelry as well as the disguises, the robbery drone, and other airborne-assault components. Everything was safely out of sight in zip-seal bags and boxed up neatly. All the goods from the heist would hopefully remain hidden right there, waiting for the brilliant beauty's next move.

Nothing was locked away. It was all outdoors where anyone with just a screwdriver could show up and take it. But first, one would need to know it was there.

Ariella stood watching how these men who represented The Long Arm of the Law, stomped over the spoils, plodded over the plunder, lumbered over the loot, then walked around the back of her house to the front garden, and ultimately to their vehicles.

Roger was waiting in the kitchen and talking on his cell phone, sorting out a client's business problem. A minute later he was done.

"Would you like something hot to drink?"

"I would love that." He wanted to get closer to this amazingly beautiful young woman. All he could think of now was getting Ariella into bed. Her fury downstairs made her sexier than ever to him!

Within a couple of minutes, they were sitting on the couch eating oatmeal cookies and having a well-deserved cup of coffee.

He was the first to speak. "About two and a half hours ago I was getting ready to leave my office, with no idea my evening would turn out like this! I must admit, Ariella, there were times I thought you might have been in on it. When I saw how interested the police were in the void of earth in your front garden, I was worried. As the digging proceeded and the hole was getting deeper and deeper, I was convinced they would find a box or a crate or such. I apologize for my erroneous thinking."

"I know," said Ariella, "And they were just as certain. All I did was pull a tree out of the ground a couple of weeks back and it was turned into a whole big drama."

"I was so relieved to see there was nothing in the safe in your study, but when I saw the patched-up wall in the basement and especially when you stood in front of it shouting at them to back off, I once again imagined there would be all kinds of incriminating stuff hidden there." Roger had a twinkle in his eye as he smiled. "I was so happy when nothing was found… and then you showed Wakefield the small section of damaged pipe!"

"His spirits were as broken as that piece of PVC! They really wanted to pin this on me. I wonder why they did not already find the real perpetrators. Surely, they must have better leads than a few people such as me who at one point had an argument with that Barnwell character?"

All along with every denial, Ariella understood she was not 'lying' to the police. From her vantage point, nothing was ever stolen. She merely took back jewelry, which was unjustly wrenched from her grandmother. What she recovered in the heist, irrefutably belonged to her.

Roger put down his coffee, reached over, and put her cup on the table as well. Drawing her close, he hugged her tightly on the couch.

Without saying a word, she stood up, then taking his hand led him upstairs to her bedroom. They stepped over the underwear and other items which lay strewn all over the floor. Within seconds they were tearing off each other's clothes.

They kissed passionately as they rolled around naked on the bed. They made wild love together for the longest time. Roger did not go home that night.

◆◆◆◆◆

Still on Thursday night July 7th at 7:50 p.m., after leaving Ariella's residence, Wakefield drove to where he lived. His compadre, Weston was headed to his apartment and the two police officers who helped with the search went back to their regular patrolling.

On his way Leyland called Captain Morley and gave him an update.

"Do you mean to tell me after three days of non-stop investigative work you have no results?" Morley was infuriated. "You wasted $5,000 on a lead that went nowhere and now you have wrecked a woman's house who will likely sue us!"

"We have other disgruntled customers of the Fourth Street Jewelers and Gold Exchange which we will be pursuing tomorrow," he said, still trying to remain positive even though it was very difficult.

Technically, there were no solid leads or direction. He hung up on the call and continued driving home, all the while in a very somber mood. The more he thought about it, the more he decided it was time to really delve into the activities of Hunt Barnwell.

The detective could not believe that after thoroughly searching Ariella's place they found nothing. He and his team did a very good job looking diligently into every room and in all possible hiding places.

Charles even used a metal detector out in the garden and apart from a few rusty nails, came up empty-handed.

Wakefield felt convinced that Ms. Gerson was somehow connected to the unlawful entry into the store, but he could not prove it. Or was the owner the real perpetrator, or perhaps someone else?

CHAPTER 17

The divine-looking lawyer waved goodbye to the sexy siren as he drove away from her house. He needed to go home and get ready for work. Right after he left, Ariella jumped into the shower, then dressed and prepared for her busy day. By eight o'clock she was walking to the bus stop two blocks away while thinking about the night before, as well as what needed to get done at her desk in the hours ahead.

Roger got to his office a little after ten thirty and did some research online. After a few minutes, he discovered the business organization he was trying to find. It was based in New York. He made a phone call, got connected to a Mr. Renfrew Hillman, and made a proposal offering his services.

In less than an hour he received an email which was a Letter of Engagement from Renfrew Hillman. Roger printed it, signed, scanned, and emailed it back. He felt good about the potential money he could make from this deal.

◆◆◆◆◆

And now on this Friday morning at eleven forty-five, Leyland was back on the case and had just visited the jewelry store where he questioned Barnwell again. After that, he walked across the road to a small coffee shop, ordered a latté and settled down at the counter in the window where he could watch the people and cars going by.

Sitting there needing a new course of action, he tried to gather his thoughts. It was then he noticed, directly next door to the 101-Building where Barnwell's business was located, there was another low-rise structure. This was number 125 with commercial spaces at street level and three floors of residences above. Wakefield observed that Fourth Street was at an incline, and the retail stores in this 125-Building were about four feet lower than those at number 101.

His eyes went to the apartments above. "Huh," he articulated softly, "The floor of the dwelling closest to the place which was just burgled could well be on the same level as this store's ceiling. It appears these two structures are virtually butting up to each other." He got up, left a tip on the counter, and exited the coffee shop.

Walking across the road to 125 Fourth Street, Leyland found a man in the foyer standing on a ladder fixing a light bulb.

"Are you the Superintendent?"

"Yes siree, that's me, Mr. Fixit!" said the man in a sing-song voice.

"I am Detective Wakefield from the Averton Police Department." Showing his badge he asked, "What is your real name?"

"I am Freddie Doyle. How may I help you, sir?"

"Can you please take me to a particular suite, one flight up on the first floor?"

"For sure I will do that!" There was an eagerness to cooperate.

"I need to look at a couple of things there. It could be some suspicious activity may have taken place from this location."

Doyle opened the locked door at the end of the foyer with his keycard and the men walked through. They went up the stairs and when they got to the top, Leyland stopped to get his bearings, then pointing to the left said, "Take me to the end of this corridor." Soon they were in front of a paneled door.

"Who lives here?"

"Ah, that would be Mrs. Dora Jenkins."

"I will need an introduction and you must wait with me while I look around. But please do not touch anything."

"Well sure, I am always pleased to help out those who are here to protect me!"

Freddie rang the bell. After a short period, they heard the shuffling of slippers on the floor. "Who is there?"

"It is Mr. Doyle."

"Oh, okay! Wait a minute!"

The sound of a security chain slowly sliding could be heard. A deadbolt was turned and then the door opened. Looking out at them was the face of a sweet old lady.

"This is Detective Wakefield from the police," said Doyle.

"Oh my! What is the matter?"

"He just needs to look around to make sure everything is okay."

"Well, all right then." Dora seemed willing to oblige. She invited them in, and they went into the living room and sat down, Leyland on an upright chair and the others sat on one of the couches. "I hope nothing happened while I was in Florida."

"You were in Florida?" The detective became even more interested in being here. "When did you return?"

"Umm, let me see... Yesterday, that was Thursday, right? Yes Thursday."

"How long were you away?" His curiosity was piqued.

"I was gone for one week visiting my daughter." Then Dora proudly added, "She is a doctor, you know."

"Let me ask you something, Mrs. Jenkins, and I want you to think very carefully about this. Did anything look out of place when you arrived back?"

"I would say all was normal. No, wait a minute, there were two blankets piled up on this couch. I found them like that when I got home, and it was not so when I left. Everything was tidy then. I keep it that way and I have been wondering why they were out and not where they should be."

"May I see these?"

"Yes. I folded them up and I put them where they belong, in the spare room closet."

They followed her there. Leyland carefully opened one blanket at a time onto the bed. He saw nothing on the first one but the second had on it a tiny area of what appeared to be dried semen as well as three long, dark female hairs and a few short male hairs. He immediately asked Doyle for two large, black plastic garbage bags. When the superintendent brought these, Wakefield bagged the blankets for evidence, telling Dora he must take these with him, but they would be returned.

He got on his phone, called his colleague, asked him to come to the apartment, and provided the address. Not too long after the call, Doyle went downstairs to escort Charles into Dora's place. Leyland immediately updated him regarding the Florida trip and how the robbery could have taken place from this venue.

He instructed his teammate to take fingerprints in the kitchen, in the living room, and everywhere else. But before doing so they made their way to the bathroom. After putting on latex gloves, Leyland climbed up on the side of the bathtub, opened the window, and surveyed the street below. The 125-Building was quite close to the adjacent structure like he saw from the coffee shop across the road. No doubt this floor lined up approximately with the ceiling of the jewelry store.

They got onto their hands and knees and studied the area. Leyland surmised this room was not too far from the outside wall of the 101-Building. Then he asked Charles, "I wonder if someone would be able to break into the ceiling next door from here?"

They peered at the tiles noting the grout appeared to be old and discolored throughout, and in fact it all looked the same. Charles ran his fingers along the linoleum and past the base of the bathtub.

"I cannot imagine anyone trying to breach this wall to get into the neighboring space. I am certain no one cut their way through because there is not the slightest trace of dust or grit from grout, cement, or anything else here."

"In a way that is a problem," said Leyland. "It is almost too clean." Walking over to the kitchen and taking a piece of damp paper towel, he wiped it around the edge of the kitchen floor. It came up very dirty. Then he did the same thing in the bathroom.

"You see," continued Wakefield, "I am telling you this area is spotless... too much so. Someone has cleaned it very thoroughly."

Weston proceeded to lift some fingerprints from various areas in the apartment. Also, they did not have to put Dora or Freddie through a wet ink process. A portable scanner was used, and this machine easily got their prints for purposes of elimination.

Wakefield and Weston went over the entire residence and when they got to the utility closet, Charles took the broom and the vacuum cleaner and dusted these for prints. He found faint fingerprints which belonged to Dora, but most of these appeared to be smudged or all but wiped away.

That really bothered the detective. "I think these items may have been used by someone wearing gloves,"

He checked out the vacuum cleaner to see if there was any dirt in it relating to a wall being broken open. There was nothing other than a small amount of normal carpet fuzz.

Upon taking fingerprints around the apartment, Charles found some of two unknown persons and he ran these through his laptop computer.

"Both of these people are in our system for minor offenses, namely public drunkenness." He was now getting a bit more enthusiastic, and turning to Dora asked her, "Do you know a Sarah Durand or a Jerry Brassky?"

"I have never heard of Jerry Brassky, but Sarah Durand is my great-niece. I asked her to come and water my plants while I was away. Has she done something wrong?"

"We don't know yet. How can we contact her?"

The old lady went into the kitchen and from one of the drawers took out an old spiral-bound notebook. After wading through dozens of scribbled notes she finally found Sarah's name and phone number, and showed this to Charles, who told her he needed to ask Ms. Durand about a few things.

They all went into the living room, sat down on the couch, and told Freddie he was no longer needed. But they asked him to please get the DVDs from the foyer camera so they could see the recordings for the past month. He eagerly agreed to provide these.

Leyland now had a series of questions for Dora, while Charles sat there taking notes and interjecting occasionally.

"Before you went to Florida, was there anyone who came to visit you, most particularly a person you have never met before?"

She answered slowly, "Definitely not. No one came here to see me."

Wakefield appeared disappointed. "Are you sure?"

"Wait a minute! I remember now… there was a young woman from England."

"Someone from England? Can you describe her?"

"This lady was very well-mannered with a lovely accent and short dark hair. I believe she came from London and was calling on someone in this building, I think it was her cousin. She knocked on my door by mistake, and I invited her in for a cup of tea."

"What was her name?"

"Let me think, now. I am not sure. It might have been Marcy or Mandy or something like that."

"Did you get her last name?"

"I do not really know what it could be."

"How long before you went to Florida, was this woman visiting you?" Leyland was trying not to intimidate her. "How many times did she stop by?"

"I am not certain. Maybe it was a week or two before I went away. I think she only dropped in once and did not stay long. We had a cup of tea together."

"What is the name of this relative?"

"I don't know. She did not tell me."

Weston in the meantime brought up Ariella's picture on his computer screen. "Is this the person from England who came to see you?"

Dora replied, "Oh no! The lady who came here was older with dark, straight hair and brown eyes. She was not anything like the beauty you are showing me. Look at those bright blue eyes and long blonde hair. Is that girl a model?"

Both men stared at Dora who must have been quite lovely in her youth. She too had blue eyes and it did not surprise them that the old lady would recognize exquisiteness in a person as attractive as Ariella.

"We would like to ask you another question. Are you sure there was not a man who came to visit you here, either on his own or with this English woman?"

"No, I am certain. If a man knocked on my door, I would not let him in. Freddie is the only man I know."

Leyland felt that if somehow the robbery was staged from this apartment, one or more men as part of a theft ring must have done it. "Let me ask you something else. Who tidies up and takes care of this apartment for you?"

"Sometimes I do a little vacuuming, but there is a cleaning service which comes in monthly. I think they came before I went to Florida. Wait a minute… yes, they were here. The toilet did not shut off properly and flooded just a little onto the bathroom floor. Mr. Doyle fixed the toilet and the cleaning people arrived to mop up the bathroom. You can check with Freddie for the date when those people were here."

Damn! The detective's theory about the all-too-spotless floor in the bathroom was just blown it away!

"That is all for now." He sounded subdued. "We want to thank you for helping us, Mrs. Jenkins. If we have any more questions, we will contact you."

They left the apartment with Charles carrying the two black bags which contained the blankets. These needed to be tested for DNA and any other possible evidence. On their way down they stopped at Doyle's office, which was located near the front foyer. He handed them two DVDs and said these were copies covering the past month of who came into the building and who left. He told them dates and times would show on the screen. They thanked him for his efforts.

It was two-thirty when they got into their respective vehicles and headed back to the precinct. While driving, Leyland recalled his observations from the coffee shop regarding the 101-Building. He lamented, after two hours at the Jenkins' apartment, there was nothing to show for it. Once again, his suspicions were high, but results were low. This was yet another roadblock.

◆◆◆◆◆

Dora had given Charles Weston the telephone number for her great-niece, and from his car he phoned Sarah, but it went to voicemail.

He left a not-too-detailed message and a short while later she returned the call. He asked her to please come to see him soon because there were a few questions regarding her great-aunt's place of residence.

Sarah was extremely worried. Why were the police summoned to where Dora lived? Did this have something to do with the affair with Jerry, or was this a matter concerning her elderly family member?

Weston and Wakefield arrived back at the precinct at two fifty-two. Leyland walked to his office while Charles went to the crime lab, hoping to get DNA off the semen and the hairs found on the blankets. But even if the break-in took place from the apartment, would this evidence really matter?

After a short while, Leyland gave Steve Parker the DVDs which Doyle provided, and Charles was summoned to join them. They told Steve they first wanted to see who came in and went out of the 125-Building starting Saturday night July 2nd and into Sunday July 3rd. The tech guru sped up the playback until people of interest showed up, and in these cases, he slowed it down so they could all look carefully. It was essentially a boring video, with residents and perhaps a few guests entering and exiting intermittently throughout the weekend.

When going over the recording of Saturday night, they noticed at about 10:30 p.m. a lady with short dark hair came into the building. She seemed to be carrying a large bag, the handles of which were barely visible because she walked close to the wall, and her face could not be properly seen. But her presence was nothing untoward, and in any event, Saturday night was not when the break-in occurred. As they perused the video for Sunday night July 3rd they paid little attention to what might have been the same woman with short dark hair in a tan jacket, and who came into the building just after nine o'clock. She was carrying no bag or purse or anything to arouse suspicion, and like all the others who entered and exited the vestibule, there was nothing about her to cause a second look. This woman appeared to simply glide through the secure foyer door, so she was most certainly a tenant with a keycard.

Once the time got past one thirty, most of the July 4th celebrating was over and the DVD showed individuals coming into the building only sporadically. Hardly any were leaving, so these people were, for the most part, residents returning home. At 3:36 a.m. on Monday July 4th the recording showed a male and a female walking into the foyer hugging and kissing. It appeared the female had a keycard because she let herself through the locked inside door quite easily.

There was no further activity on the video until about 4:10 a.m. when they saw an older lady with short, curly charcoal-grey hair wearing a brown jacket and large dark-framed glasses departing the building. Because her face was turned away, the DVD showed mostly the back of her head. They could not quite see what she was carrying, but they could observe her hands and the handles of what may have been a large bag. They also noticed she was wearing an over-stuffed backpack. Had this person just breached the wall and somehow got into the retail shop next door?

"I think I recognize that mop of curly hair even though I cannot see her face," said Steve. "It could be this person is on one of the previous recordings depicting customers in Barnwell's place of business. I will go over a few of the other videos again and let you know what I find."

The three continued watching the sped-up scenes and around seven o'clock in the morning, the 'hugging and kissing' guy and girl were seen leaving the building. The female was carrying a large black plastic garbage bag which appeared to be very bulky.

"How long were these two there? I wonder if by some chance they were in the Jenkins' apartment?" asked Leyland.

Steve reversed the DVD and perused a portion of it again. "It seems from the time they arrived until when they left, they were there for three and a half hours."

"That is enough time to figure out a way to break through from one structure to the other, to get into the ceiling of the dazzling depot and drop down to where everything is displayed."

"Yes, but how could anyone bust through like that?" asked Charles. "The walls are no doubt built from bricks or block and even the big bad wolf could not blow these down!"

"I don't know yet," said Leyland, "but we will need to determine if that is what took place. I agree with you, it would be extremely difficult for someone to cut through solid walls without heavy equipment of some sort. Thereafter they would have to reconstruct and close it all up again leaving no trace of such a break-in. Perhaps this theory is simply too far-fetched."

They watched the DVD for a little while longer and told Steve to call them if he saw anything else of interest. Wakefield and Weston thanked their video expert and returned to their work areas in the precinct.

Just after four o'clock Weston got a call from the desk sergeant telling him Sarah Durand was there asking for him.

Charles took her to an interview room and notified Leyland. They immediately recognized her as being one of the two people who entered the foyer of the 125-Building in the wee hours of July 4th. In the room were the two black garbage bags containing Dora's blankets. The men introduced themselves and got straight down to business.

The young woman was very worried and agitated as she sat down for the interview. The two told her they had just left her great-aunt's home and there were some questions to be answered.

"When were you last in that apartment?" asked Charles.

"As you probably know my great-aunt Dora was away in Florida for a week. I went there sometime on the morning of July 4th to water her plants."

"When you say, 'on the morning of July 4th' exactly what time were you there to take care of the plants?"

There was no way Sarah was going to tell them about her intimate encounter with Jerry Brassky. If her husband found out, things could go very badly for her. She married him for money, and he controlled it all. Even though he was having an affair of his own, Sarah knew he was looking for any excuse to extricate himself from their union. If he threw her out, she would be destitute.

"I believe I went there around ten o'clock on Monday morning." Her blatant lie sounded convincing.

"Was that the only time you were there while your great-aunt was away?" Leyland leaned forward as he asked.

"Yes. Aunt Dora was gone for just a week, so the plants only needed to be watered once while she was out of town."

Then came the bombshell. Wakefield felt sorry for her as he asked the next question. "Do you know a man named Jerry Brassky?"

Ms. Durand went pale. Her mouth opened but no words came out. Then the sobbing began.

"Do you want to change your answer to me from earlier? When exactly were you in the apartment?

Sarah started babbling and the truth emerged, with her telling them how she and Jerry got to the building just after 3:30 a.m. and admitted they were having an affair. She begged them not to tell her husband.

"What time did both of you leave there?"

The teary-eyed Sarah grabbed a tissue from the box, which was on the table, and blew her nose. "I am not sure, maybe we left there around seven o'clock."

"I need to ask you something very important," said Leyland. "Was anyone else there when you arrived?"

"No, just me and Jerry."

"Are you sure? Did either of you use the bathroom?"

"There was no one besides us. It is only a two-bedroom and if someone else was there, we would have seen them. And yes, we both used the bathroom. We also each took a shower."

"Why were you carrying a large black garbage bag when you left and what was in it?"

"How do you know I had a garbage bag? We showered and I took home with me the two wet towels to wash and dry them. I was going to return these soon."

"Apart from the fact you and this Jerry person were having an affair, how did you manage to break into the jewelry place next door?"

"*What?*" Sarah was shocked. "That never happened!"

"We did some research and found out your boyfriend Jerry is a building contractor. If anyone understands how to get through brick walls and patch these up in a professional manner, he would. We believe what was in that black garbage bag were not towels, but the spoils from a burglary."

"He is *not* my boyfriend... I am married! We are just having a fling together, that's all. We did not steal anything from any shop!" Sarah was most indignant. "Ask Jerry. All we did was make love, sleep, and take a shower."

"Oh, we will ask him. He will be interviewed soon."

"Am I under arrest? I want a lawyer!"

"No, you are not under arrest, but don't leave town." The detective sounded quite firm.

At that point they allowed her to go home. She did not intend to tell her husband anything. Maybe this would all blow over and he would never find out.

It was the end of a long workday for Leyland and his crime-lab associate, and it was time for them to head on out.

As they were leaving Wakefield said, "It is crazy to think someone could have got from Dora's apartment into the ceiling of the jewelry store. But when one looks at how the two buildings line up and how close together they are, it appears to be quite feasible."

"Yes, but don't forget, we also strongly believe this could have been done by way of entry from the back, then securely locking this door with its deadbolt and the perpetrators exiting out the main sales area. We have spoken about this theory a lot. In any event, perhaps we should now start investigating Barnwell."

"You are right," said Leyland. "We can pick this up on Monday."

"Since at this stage we know it was Sarah and Jerry there making out, I do not need to waste any time and money testing the two blankets for DNA. We should return these to the old lady soon."

"Agreed. But there is one other thing troubling me. The DVD shows Sarah and this Jerry character arrived there at 3:36 a.m. We also have video of a woman with curly dark hair leaving the building carrying some type of bag and a backpack at 4:10 a.m. Right?"

"That is correct," said Charles.

"If the ransacking of the store did take place from the Jenkins' bathroom and into the building at 101 Fourth Street next door, was this curly-haired woman hiding somewhere in the apartment unbeknownst to the two lovers? Sarah said she and her guy were the only people there. Or, maybe this woman was visiting someone else in the building on a totally different floor and should not even be considered as a suspect."

"What if this crime was from one structure to the other but from a different residence? Maybe there is another potential access point?" Charles was trying a novel idea.

"I am not sure. We both noted the closeness of these two low-rises to each other and the steepness of Fourth Street. Thus, the most probable pathway for a break-in would be from Dora's place. In any case, we have no evidence this infiltration happened like we are discussing."

"You make a good point," said Weston. "We carefully went through the apartment, and we studied the area above the ceiling in the store. Neither of us found any trace of a breach taking place in this manner. If the burglary occurred from the bathroom of the 125-Building, I could understand patching up the apartment wall, but how could a thief repair a hole in the sheetrock above the ceiling if they already exited the store? How do you fix something when you are not there to do so?"

"Yes," remarked Leyland. "To seal up an opening in sheetrock when you are no longer on that side of the wall is impossible. Also, if thieves dropped down from above, how did they climb back up a nine-foot distance? There was no ladder to be found anywhere in the store, and the metal ceiling grid is too flimsy to hold onto, in order to pull oneself up. As we both know, we needed to bring in a ladder to look around in the high-up areas. I believe we should get started on scrutinizing what Barnwell has been doing in the recent past and how he stole from his own enterprise. I will tell Captain Morley that is our current supposition."

The detective picked up his car keys, and then he and his sidekick walked to the elevator to go home for the day.

◆◆◆◆◆

It was 6:30 p.m. on that same Friday evening. Ariella had a dinner arrangement planned with Roger and was waiting in her living room for him to arrive. When the doorbell rang she opened the door, he came inside, gave her a long, lingering kiss and hugged her tightly.

The night before, they made wild, passionate love together and could not wait to see each other again. He was pleased to be taking her out on a date and was very much looking forward to coming back to her house after that.

"Are you ready to eat?" His eyes were sparkling.

"Oh yes! I hardly ate anything today."

"We are going to The Esplanade. The food is excellent, and I know you will like it."

Ariella knew of The Esplanade and heard it was very elegant and upscale. Twenty minutes later they arrived, and Roger managed to find a parking spot close to the entrance.

The maître d' greeted him saying, "Good evening Mr. Riley. I have a table reserved for you by the window."

"Thank you, Bruce."

When they got to their table the maître d' helped the ravishing beauty into her chair. Their waiter soon arrived with an extensive, four-page Wine List. Her date began perusing it carefully and proceeded to ask a few questions.

She was impressed by his knowledge of different wines, and gazing at him lovingly, did not notice Barbara walking in and standing in the front of the restaurant. After a minute Hunt joined her. Ariella didn't see them talking rapidly together and then they whirled around and left. Roger saw nothing because he was not facing that way.

A few seconds later Ariella happened to glance downward out the window through the slatted blinds at the very moment Barbara and Hunt were walking by holding hands, on their way to where his Mercedes was parked. Although they flashed by quickly, and she saw them for just a brief moment there was no doubt the two were a couple. She stared in horror as they disappeared into the throng of people on the sidewalk.

Roger did not notice her gasp of disbelief, nor see the look on her face. He was still busy figuring out what wine to order.

Ariella regained her composure and tried to put out of her mind, what she just witnessed. Not wanting to ruin the evening with her new guy, she said nothing. On her own at home at some point, there would be plenty of time to process this and decide what to do.

The two enjoyed a delightful meal and found they really liked each other's company. When they were done eating, they agreed to go back to Ariella's house for 'dessert'. It looked like another wild evening was in store for them.

Once again, they made love passionately and fell asleep at midnight, not waking up until about seven thirty the following morning. Although it was Saturday, Roger said he had work to do in his office preparing for an upcoming transaction involving one of his clients, and later he would be driving to Philadelphia for a meeting. They had a quick breakfast together and then he left to get on with his day.

◆◆◆◆◆

On the previous night, Friday July 8th, Barbara had a dinner arrangement planned with Hunt Barnwell. He dropped her at the entrance to The Esplanade restaurant and went to park his car. Standing in front and talking to the maître d' she suddenly noticed Roger Riley sitting at a table by the window accompanied by his date. She was totally taken aback and was furious with Ariella for being there with him.

Although this minx was having an affair with Hunt, she did not want the blonde belle to be out with the lawyer. Barbara of course tried to head off a relationship between the two previously, but now seeing them together, she knew her recent plot with the waitress at the Wild West Bar & Grill did not work out as planned.

When Hunt arrived, Barbara immediately told him Ariella was there with a man and pointed to where they were seated.

"I don't want her to find out we know each other," she said under her breath. "I still believe Ariella had something to do with what happened at your store and I need to spy on her a bit more to see what I can uncover."

"Good idea," said Hunt. "Let's go." They left the maître d' gaping and quickly exited The Esplanade to make their way to another restaurant.

Walking briskly to Hunt's vehicle, they were unaware Ariella was looking out the window above them through the slatted blinds and that she saw them holding hands.

The two lovebirds drove to a bistro some eighteen minutes away and got a small table in a corner where they could have a little privacy. Hunt again began to confide in Barbara about his daily activities and how the burglary affected him.

"I have very good coverage for theft," he said, "But the insurance company is somewhat hesitant about paying me anything until the police zero in on the actual perpetrators."

"I am sure the bandits will soon be found."

"The problem I have is, the cops are starting to suspect me! But I assure you, I had no hand in this."

"Then you don't have anything to worry about."

"Well not as far as the robbery goes, but if they start delving into my finances, my buying and selling of gold, silver and diamonds, and the loads of cash which I siphon out every month, I could run into huge tax issues and other problems. Then there is the money and jewelry which I constantly give to you."

Barbara was quiet. Over the past two years, she benefitted greatly from the mountains of cash he showered upon her, and never complained about some of the amazing pieces received from him. All along she knew, not only was he stealing from his clients, but a lot of his transactions skirted around paying taxes properly. Barbara also surmised Hunt was embezzling from his father who, now retired, still owned a part of the business and derived income from the profits. She did not want the authorities to start targeting Hunt, because part of his illicit dealings could very likely lead back to her.

"I have a thought," she said suddenly. "We know the police suspect some of your disgruntled customers including Ariella Gerson. They even searched her house, so they certainly distrust her. Maybe we can plant some jewelry on her property and notify them. This will lead to her being arrested, and it will confirm the suspicions which they already have."

Hunt said, "From my conversations with Wakefield and his crew, they already went over her place thoroughly and found nothing. While they did suspect her, she had no means of transportation on the night of the robbery, and it appears she did not leave her home because of illness."

"Yes, I know. As I told you before, we were both at Donnie Bolin's party and she exited early because of a cough and a migraine headache. Ariella was in no condition to drive and thus her auto was left there. Someone else drove her home and it was me and Donnie who brought her car back the next afternoon. While it appears she did not commit this crime, I still have a strange feeling she was involved."

"The police even speculated she might belong to a theft ring and therefore did not need her own vehicle to get to my shop on the night of July 3rd. But so far from what they told me, no evidence has emerged regarding her, or a known gang perpetrating this break-in." Hunt sounded a bit frustrated.

"Well, what about my suggestion of leaving some incriminating items at her residence?"

"I must say it's an interesting idea. Heaven knows I can come up with some stuff to drop there! Since there is no definitive record of what was stolen, any precious-pile will look like it came from the actual burglary."

"We must give this some serious thought. I have been inside her house, so I know a bit about it. Maybe we can place some sparkling finery in her garage or such. It should not be difficult to do and then we can call in a tip and they can go after her." Barbara was still angry with Ariella for hooking up with Roger and resolutely wanted to protect Hunt from being accused of this larceny.

"How will you get inside without her knowing?" He had a curious look on his face.

"You make a good point. I could situate the evidence out in the yard somewhere. Wait a minute! There is a large flowerpot on her porch. I could dig down a bit and push a bag of jewelry into this pot. Then you can contact Wakefield and give him a vague indication of where to look. Let his guys find the goods on their own."

"I like the idea, and this way you will not need to gain access inside. You can do this at night when she is out or asleep."

Barbara again thought that incriminating Ariella could cause her and Roger to break up. In any event, the bewitcher wanted to hold onto the cash and gifts which ceaselessly flowed from Hunt to her. She most times reviled having sex with him and in fact, hated it. But for the money and more, she kept it all going, not knowing how long he would keep her as his 'girlfriend on the side'. At any moment he could find another woman with whom to have an affair. Barbara was unaware he already had a second romantic interest. At some point his wife might stop him from carrying on with others. Yes, Ariella must be sacrificed so Hunt and his business dealings do not get investigated.

Before they were done eating dinner, he told her to stop by his store the following day, saying he would give her a *bag of bijouterie* to plant at Ariella's house. They decided Barbara would put the stuff there in the early morning of Sunday, July 10th, and by then her gullible friend should be deep in dreamland. Hunt would call Leyland at about midnight to inform him.

"By the time the police change shifts and get a warrant, it will be after 12:30 a.m." Hunt sounded quite pleased with this idea, but he did not want to call it in later than about 11:45 p.m. "Try to set this up as soon after midnight tomorrow as you can."

Both felt that at some point on Sunday, Ariella should be in handcuffs… and not part of any kinky sexual exploits! They left the restaurant shortly after ten o'clock and drove to Barbara's apartment. They romped around in her bed for an hour and then he left to go home to his unhappy wife.

CHAPTER 18

Roger left his new girl's place after the two gulped down a light breakfast, and she was now alone at home. Ariella thought about her observations from the window at the restaurant the night before and could not believe Barbara was involved with Hunt. Now Ariella remembered, on the day she first stormed out of the store, on May 24th, this woman came running out after her and claimed that she too was cheated by the owner. Ariella understood this so-called 'friend' getting close to her was all a ploy, and a way for Hunt to keep tabs on her. She exclaimed out loud, "Thank goodness I never told her anything about the heist!"

From now on she would be extremely careful, but felt cutting off all contact with the hellcat was not a good idea because that might look too suspicious. Going forward, her cards must be played very cautiously.

❖❖❖❖❖

It was shortly after eleven on this same Saturday morning July 9th when Barbara arrived at the Fourth Street Jewelers and Gold Exchange. Walking inside, she saw Hunt concluding a transaction on one of the newly-repaired display cases. In front of him was an assortment of pearl necklaces, gold antique timepieces, and a few diamond rings. He was counting $400 in cash which was handed to the customer.

The woman took the money and stuffed it into her handbag. She looked pale and drawn and was obviously in a financially stressed situation. With tears in her eyes, she left the store. The unscrupulous Barnwell had grossly underpaid another desperate victim for her valuables.

Hunt scooped up the items and placed these into a small box retrieved from under the countertop. He then signaled for his chick-on-the-side to follow him as he headed to the repair area.

The store was of course very busy, being a Saturday morning. The people buying or selling seemed oblivious to the deal that took place or the very low amount which was paid to the tearful client.

When they got to the office in the back, Hunt opened his huge walk-in vault. Barbara's eyes went wide when she saw piles of paper money stacked up on shelves as well as many rows of assorted jewelry. Her lover selected a variety of necklaces, pendants, earrings, and watches, as well as a few diamond rings and some gold coins. He put these into a plastic shopping bag, folded it over, and taped it closed.

"Here, take this," he said quietly. "What I am giving you is worth at least $30,000 but it is a small price to pay for us to have the bitch thrown in jail and to get any suspicions diverted away from me. By her being arrested this will speed up my insurance claim so I can be paid out soon."

Barbara smiled at him and said, "I am anxious to hide this on her property and then send the cops after her! I will put it there just after midnight tonight when she will of course be asleep. The police should come by soon afterward and before too long they'll be well on their way to solving this case."

"Okay. I shall call Wakefield around 11:45 p.m."

They gave each other a brief hug and then she left.

Once in her apartment, she opened the shopping bag and softly said, "Before this ends up in the evidence room at the precinct, I must see what items I would like for myself!" In her own way, Barbara was as crooked as Hunt.

Helping herself to two diamond rings, four gold chains, and a Rolex watch, the dishonest diva looked at the rings and felt these alone were worth over $2,500 each.

"I need to be paid more than the scraps that awful man throws my way and for me putting up with his overweight, sweaty body in bed! This bag will be left at Ariella's house tonight and then the fun will begin."

Barbara decided, before too long she would be done with Hunt, and she would be able to work on getting her claws into Roger Riley. How easy will that be once the blonde bobblehead is locked up?

◆◆◆◆◆

Ariella was home alone this Saturday night, with only Purdy for company. Roger had of course left early in the morning, and he spent most of the day at his place of work. He could not see her that night because of a meeting commitment in Philadelphia.

Having time alone was important, and although she was falling head over heels for him, it was perhaps best to take it just a bit slower until they got to know each other better. A lot of her day was spent cleaning and tidying the house. There was much to do after the mess Wakefield and his merry men made, both inside and out.

That night, after having a small dinner, a Netflix movie was next on the menu. However, by ten thirty it was time to get some shut-eye, and Purdy dutifully followed her to the bedroom. Before too long she was out like a light.

It was just after midnight in the early hours of Sunday, July 10th when Purdy, who was sleeping near Ariella's feet, suddenly sat up. He heard the faintest noise, and it disturbed him. With the curiosity of a cat, he jumped off the bed. The thump awakened the slumbering beauty, and in the almost-darkened room, she was able to see Purdy standing in her bedroom doorway staring down the passage.

Putting on her bathrobe and slippers, she walked to the spare room which faced the front of her residence, and moving the drapes aside ever so slightly peered down to her right. At first, it looked like nothing was going on in the garden. Perhaps there was something in the back of the house. She was about to go and look out another window when, to her surprise, there was movement below. Someone was on her porch! This character seemed to be digging into the very large flowerpot, located near her front door. She could make out a figure dressed in black, and this person appeared to be very active in the corner.

It was dark outside and only a small amount of light from a streetlamp located about two houses down the road allowed her to discern something was amiss. The pajama-clad lass could vaguely see this individual slide a large item into the flowerpot, then he or she started pushing down on the soil to cover up what they did. Ariella moved quickly to the hall closet, grabbed her binoculars, and ran back to the window. Looking down onto the porch again she could now see the person's face quite clearly: It was Barbara!

At that point, the trespasser stood up and began to take off quietly but rapidly, down the walkway to the gate. She turned right and proceeded in a southerly direction, no doubt going to where her car was parked.

"There is something strange going on here," Ariella vocalized softly. "Thank goodness for Purdy. My watch cat was able to wake me with a thump which is better than having a watchdog. A canine would have barked and sent the perpetrator running and they might have returned to make mischief another time."

She bounded back to the bedroom and turned on the small lamp next to her bed. Quickly getting dressed in a T-Shirt, jeans, and sneakers, Ariella rushed downstairs, not turning on any lights in the house. Armed with a flashlight she ran into the garage and found a pair of thin work gloves, picked up a small hand-held garden spade, and an old newspaper from the recycling pile. She went back into the house, opened the front door, and slipped outside.

Ariella shone the flashlight at the earthenware container noticing the soil on one side was disturbed just a bit. Barbara had buried something there and did a masterful job disguising her work.

After balancing the flashlight on the wide railing, with her gloved hands Ariella very carefully began removing some of the potting mixture from around two geraniums, putting each handful carefully onto the newspaper. Using the spade, she gently pried these flowers up and placed them on the paper as well. Her hand groped around in the soft earth and found something containing lumpy items.

She slowly pulled out a standard supermarket shopping bag which was folded over and taped closed with masking tape. After opening it and shining her flashlight inside, its contents startled her. The bag was packed with an assortment of jewelry, similar to what she grabbed from the Fourth Street Jewelers and Gold Exchange.

It suddenly occurred to her, Barbara put this here as a frame-up! What was going on, and why would her close acquaintance be trying to implicate her? She was definitely in cahoots with Hunt Barnwell.

Ariella put back some of the dirt to fill the hole created when the package was removed and re-planted the geraniums. She slowly lifted the newspaper and tipped in the remainder of the earth around the two shrubs. But they were now sitting lower than the rest of the flowers in the pot. Using the flashlight, she could see a small pile of soil in the garden and this was most certainly dug out to make space for what was left behind in the pot. Cupping her hands, Ariella scooped some of this loose fill and added it around the geraniums. She raised them up a bit more, then pressed down with her gloved hands to seat these plants properly.

Ariella knew this bag with its precious contents must be concealed immediately, perhaps in the same place where the other loot was stashed. The brainy beauty understood, since this evidence was now on her property, someone would be calling the police soon. For sure they would be searching her house again, and hopefully, they would not find the original haul as well as this new batch of valuables. She stood up and gazed around, then something caught her eye. There were flashing lights far up the road and they seemed to be headed in her direction.

"Oh no!" she yelled, "They are already on their way!"

She thought frantically about what to do with the goods from the flowerpot. There was no time to hide the items indoors or with the rest of the spoils from the heist. Whirling around, Ariella raced down the long walkway toward the front gate. She stuffed the shopping bag into her mailbox, then rapidly closed its small metal door. Running back to the porch, she picked up the spade, the newspaper, and her flashlight, then flew into the house, slamming and locking the front door behind her. She barreled into the garage and dumped the gloves, the newspaper, and the small garden spade.

Back inside and with her flashlight in hand, the sprinter charged up the stairs two at a time. Off came the T-Shirt, sneakers, and jeans, and then it was back into pajamas. At that moment a loud banging could be heard, coming from her front door. She picked up her cell phone and called Roger. It was twelve-fifty, very early on Sunday morning July 10th.

"Ariella!" He sounded both annoyed and concerned. "Why are you calling me at this time of night?"

"The police just arrived at my house and are hammering on the door. Please get here as fast as you can! Hurry, please!"

"They are there *again?* I just got in from Philadelphia, but I can be there soon. Don't let them in. Tell them I am on my way."

She put on her bathrobe and began to slowly turn on a few of the lights, giving the impression of someone just waking up from a sound sleep. Ariella took her time walking down to the front door, trying to go as tentatively as possible. The longer these oafs could be delayed, the more she would not be on her own with them before her savior got there.

The frightened female turned on the outside porch light. "Who is it?" she asked.

"It's the police. We have a warrant. Open the door!"

"Well, I need to call my lawyer first. I cannot let you in until he tells me what to do."

"We have a warrant! Open the door!"

"Hold on. Let me hear what he has to say." She made out as if talking to someone. "Okay, I will tell them they must wait until you get here."

Ariella said through the door to them what they already heard, "My lawyer says he will be here in fifteen minutes and told me not to let you in until he is on the scene."

"Open the door or we will break it down!"

The Heistess was petrified to be on her own in the house with these aggressive men. She did not want them marching around and wrecking the place as they had done before. What if they brought other evidence to leave there because they wanted to incriminate her? Could they be in on it? Two deterrents that would buy her a little time quickly came to mind.

"I am on my own here in my pajamas. My attorney said that you cannot come in unless you are accompanied by a female officer. He also instructed me to video and voice-record everything using my cell phone, so since I hung up with him, I have been recording everything you have been saying including your loud and menacing tone."

There was a momentary silence on the other side of the door. "Okay. We do not have a policewoman here with us so we will wait for your council. You said fifteen minutes, right?"

Asking for a female and stating it was all being recorded, caused them to temporarily stand down, to back off.

Before too long, Roger arrived, and he could be heard talking to the officers on her front porch. Then he knocked on the door.

"It's okay, you can open up."

She disengaged the deadbolt and let them in. Then a car pulled up in front of her house and a familiar figure got out. It was Wakefield. He was angered about getting a tip-off at almost midnight from Barnwell and certainly did not want to be out at one o'clock on a Sunday morning.

Ariella spoke earnestly to her lawyer lover. "They already went through my house a few days ago and made a huge mess as you saw. Why would they want to come back again? What can be so urgent in the middle of the night?"

Leyland came walking in, overhearing the last bit of their conversation. "We received a tip that evidence from the downtown break-in is at this location. We are going to search here again, and most particularly around the garden. We believe the stolen items could be in the yard and not necessarily in the house."

Ariella hugged Roger and sobbed on his shoulder. It was not put-on, it was real. She was petrified they would find something because the big stash *was* outside and not indoors! "What has this got to do with me? I told Mr. Barnwell he swindled my grandmother, but lots of people felt he took advantage of them. How can the police even *think* a girl like me could steal from his place?"

"It is important they prove you did not do it, and the sooner the better, so they can focus on the real thieves."

At that point, Ariella went upstairs to get dressed. Roger said he would accompany the policemen around the house, and they would start on the lower level first. This time the group was a bit more respectful and did not simply fling cupboards open or pour out the contents of drawers onto the floor. They went again down to the broken basement wall which was still open, and that was a good thing.

An hour later they were done inside the house, and the time was a little after 2:00 a.m. It was very dark, but the men used their flashlights to go over the outside again, scouring her back yard and then migrating to the front garden. Ariella and Roger followed them around, but only she knew how close they came to the actual cache which was so well tucked away… under the wooden landing outside the kitchen door!

She kept thinking, "You dumb idiots! You have been walking right over the spoils of the robbery time after time while going in and out of my house and you have no clue!"

Wakefield and four policemen were doing the searching. Two began removing earth from the same spot which they originally dug up where the dead tree had been.

Roger was not concerned, but his anxious angel started panicking a bit. What if Barbara got there earlier than when Ariella saw her and placed something in this spot as well before going onto the porch? She stood there watching the men dig, very worried something would turn up in that patch of soil. But within a few minutes, her fears were unfounded because nothing was discovered there.

Then Ariella glanced toward the front gate and terror set in again for her. Two of the policemen were taking a break and were hanging out by the front entrance to her property, each drinking from a plastic water bottle. One had lit up a cigarette and he was now leaning against her mailbox! Suddenly the small metal door popped open and staring at this from about thirty feet away, she nearly fainted. The officer who was standing on the sidewalk reached over and promptly closed the mailbox door without looking inside. The Heistess was softly gasping, for this was another narrow escape!

It was at that moment the detective walked over to the large flowerpot on her front porch. "We need to look inside here," he said in a loud voice, shining his flashlight at the intended target.

Ariella thought, "So the best is saved for last! He wanted to search inside the house again, look more thoroughly around the garden, and then once done with that, it would be all about heading to where the tipster told him the evidence was hidden. The bastard... he knew all along the earthenware container would be his *coup de grace!*"

"Well! Would you look at this!" His pompous words filled the air.

"What is it?" asked Roger sounding genuinely anxious, secretly petrified Ariella would be caught and go to jail if she was in any way involved. He did not want to lose his sexy, gorgeous new girlfriend.

"I would say the soil in here appears to have been recently disturbed." The bright police-issue flashlight lit up the freshly moved dirt on the surface.

Roger responded, "You have got to be kidding! This looks normal to me and in any case, I do not think all which was reported stolen can fit into that pot full of flowers! I really believe you are now being ridiculous!"

Leyland unceremoniously pulled out the two geraniums and threw them aside. "Well, look how easily these shrubs came out!" He plunged his fingers into the sizeable clay planter.

"Aha! Soft soil under which no doubt we will find what we came here for!" He rapidly started taking out handfuls of earth and throwing this down around his feet while his compadres were watching somewhat gleefully. Ariella understood, these brutes who had just invaded her house, knew all along some jewelry was supposed to be right here on her porch. Barbara and Hunt absolutely notified them!

Wakefield's hands were going deeper inside, and the potting mix was now dirtying his white shirt. In his eagerness to find the loot, he didn't care to roll up his sleeves. The further in he got the more frenzied became his digging. Suddenly he tipped over the large pot destroying the rest of the flowers. When it was almost upside down, he pulled the pot away completely, then scrabbled with his hands to break apart the clumps of sand and roots frantically searching for what he believed would be jewelry from the recent break-in.

"It's got to be here! It's got to be here!" He was yelling out loudly to himself and to everyone else standing there.

"What's *wrong* with you!" Ariella shrieked, causing the officers to look at Leyland. "What have you done to my lovely buds and blooms? I specifically asked you not to trash my house like you did before!" Her loud voice was all put on and she was deliberately trying to be dramatic, holding up her phone as she recorded the crazy scene.

Wakefield turned around angrily, still crouched on the ground, the knees of his good trousers now resting in the damp dirt. Then he realized all of this was being videoed.

"Get that damn phone out of my face!" His frustration and anger were now very apparent.

"This is the second time you and your... your goons... have come in here with the sole intention of damaging my home! I think you have all lost your minds! I agree with my lawyer, how can you even remotely think a large amount of stolen jewelry can be hidden in a flowerpot? I am flattered you would even imagine a stupid blonde like me, can smash my way in and steal stuff from a well-secured store."

Leyland stood up sheepishly and looking at his associates said, "Let's go." He was glaring at Ariella who was still recording everything on her cell phone.

"Excuse me!" Roger sounded annoyed. "You cannot leave the place a mess like this! Who is going to tidy up now? I again need everyone's names." Like before, he started getting details from them, much to Leyland's chagrin.

"I am sorry to have inconvenienced you... ma'am," said the detective to Ariella. He felt he should show some contrition, especially because of the recordings. He knew that trying to put all the potting mixture back into the terra-cotta container would be futile. The plants were already ruined, and he dared not ask if he could go inside to wash his hands!

Within a couple of minutes, they were gone. Ariella went into the garage and got a garden shovel and a broom. Roger stood the vessel upright and he held the spade while she swept some of the earth into it whereupon he tipped the contents into the pot. They did this a few times until the porch was clean. She picked up all the damaged and broken plants, and in the almost darkness, took these to the backyard and piled them onto her compost heap.

With the cleanup completed, he said, "Let's go inside."

"Sure, you go in and get some coffee ready. Just give me a second.

A neighbor left in my mailbox some tools which I lent him, and I need to get these."

"Okay, I will see you in a minute."

Ariella walked to the front gate and made sure there were no squad cars in sight. She pulled a Kleenex tissue out of her jeans pocket to avoid getting her prints on the plastic shopping bag. With the tissue shielding her fingers, she grabbed the bag and pulled it out of the mailbox, then came into the house with it tucked under her arm. It was mostly hidden by her body as she walked nonchalantly past Roger directly from the kitchen into the garage.

Her lover did not even look up because he was busy filling the mugs. The bag was placed into the recycling bin marked 'Plastics', then she closed the lid, went back into the kitchen, and washed her hands. They sat down at the counter and began drinking their coffee, staring lustfully at each other.

"The nerve of them," Ariella said. "Why can't they leave me alone? It is the middle of the night, for goodness' sake! I was fast asleep when I heard this banging on my door, and thankfully you were already back from your trip to Philadelphia. The real thieves must have alerted them to try and throw suspicion onto me. How could I have plundered that place? What is their problem?"

"From what I hear, they have no real leads to pursue, and even Wakefield said they are looking into all disgruntled customers so don't feel like they are targeting you." Roger really felt there was no way Ariella could ever have been involved. "They appear to be totally bamboozled, and I agree with one strong theory, this is the work of a seasoned, experienced burglary ring, or Barnwell is behind it."

"That's what I think!" She confirmed his suspicions. "They must really be at a loss for suspects if they are coming after a simple chick like me. I believe this band of bad ones which you speak of, is sending misleading tips to the police about many possible 'who-dunnits' just to confuse them."

It was almost three o'clock on that warm, July Sunday morning. They stood up and then holding hands his lips found hers. The two made their way upstairs to her bedroom and once again they were all over each other engaging in more intense lovemaking. The third time in as many days!

◆◆◆◆◆

"What am I doing at my place of work before dawn on a Sunday morning?" Wakefield, speaking in an agitated manner, sounded really frustrated. "Every stone we have turned over so far has had nothing underneath it!"

He was back at the precinct at 3:20 a.m. and called his confrere after leaving Ariella's home. Weston said despite the early hour he would come in for the latest update, and after arriving there, Leyland described what happened.

"Four police officers got to Ms. Gerson's residence at about twelve forty, and I showed up around one o'clock. We looked everywhere and turned up nothing. This was all because Barnwell telephoned me at home last night at eleven forty-five."

"Wow, that is late at night," said Charles.

"Yes, it is, let me continue. Hunt said it was his understanding there was evidence at Ms. Gerson's house and he was very specific: She hid some stolen jewelry in a large flowerpot on her front porch. I asked him how he knew, and he said a customer of his, Barbara McKenna told him firsthand. This customer is a friend of Ms. Gerson."

"We suspected Ms. Gerson from early on," said Charles, sipping on a cup of coffee. "We were simply unable to find anything when we searched there initially and now you tell me once again, not a thing was found this time either. It seems we are being fed with bad information."

The detective nodded. "As I said, Barnwell called me quite late, and since we were about to have the midnight shift change, I could not get anyone there until half an hour later. I also needed to obtain a search warrant and that was not easy, but I got it! Judge Beckwith was unimpressed with a phone call from me at that hour."

"The judge will not be happy when he finds out it was all futile." Weston was stating the obvious.

Leyland sighed, "Yes, this pretty blond is still a person of interest in my eyes and that's why when Barnwell called me, I really believed him. Apparently, Ms. McKenna, who Hunt claims to know vaguely, was going to surprise Ms. Gerson with a visit around nine o'clock. But when arriving there, saw her friend placing a plastic bag supposedly packed with a lot of the stolen items, into a large earthenware planter on her front porch."

"How did she know there was jewelry in it?"

"I asked Barnwell the same question. He said it was almost dark and Ms. McKenna was about to walk through her friend's front gate when she stopped after seeing Ms. Gerson looking at some gold necklaces and watches before putting these into an already bulky plastic shopping bag. The light on the porch was quite bright and Ms. Gerson didn't know she was being watched. It was at that point the witness saw the bag being buried in the flowerpot. Upon observing this, she slipped away unnoticed, and called Barnwell to let him know."

"Wow! Lots of hearsay! But why if this took place at nine o'clock, did Barnwell only contact you close to midnight?"

"He volunteered to me Ms. McKenna called him earlier, but he did not hear his phone ring. He only got her voicemail much later, which was just before he reached out to me."

"Perhaps this Barbara woman was lying for some reason," said Charles thoughtfully.

"Yes, but there might be something to this story. When I checked out the pot, the soil down one side had definitely been dug up recently. Maybe the homeowner placed the jewelry there and noticed Ms. McKenna, then removed it and hid the bag somewhere else."

"I guess we should call Barnwell," said Charles. "We could tell him his information was wrong."

"Not so fast. It is very possible he might be involved in planting evidence at the Gerson house to throw us off track. It could be time we took a deep dive into his business dealings to see how this theft could have been perpetrated by him. You and I have spoken about this, many times."

"Okay we will hold off calling him." Weston sounded cautious. "Let us leave him thinking we found some of the hot goods there and that Ms. Gerson is our prime suspect. This will keep him off guard while we thoroughly investigate his activities.

◆◆◆◆◆

It was 9:37 a.m. on this bright Sunday morning and Purdy's loud mewing woke Ariella and Roger from a deep sleep. The cat was hungry and wanted to be fed. The gorgeous girl got up and put on her bathrobe. "I need to go downstairs and feed Purdy." She smiled at her handsome lover. He too began to get out of bed.

"I better be going," he said. "I was in Philadelphia yesterday afternoon and well into the night. I have so much going on in my office so I will spend the rest of today there, even though I do not like working on Sundays."

"I would rather you stayed here with me, but I understand." Ariella was quite relieved. She had a lot more to do regarding the heist and needed to make plans about what should be done with the bag of booty found on her porch.

She went downstairs followed by Purdy, while her beau got dressed. In the bathroom, he washed his face, brushed his teeth by putting toothpaste on his finger, then combed his hair with a comb he found in a cabinet.

Roger appeared in the kitchen as Ariella finished giving Purdy his food. She poured a cup of coffee for them, he took a few gulps and then told her he needed to leave. With a quick kiss goodbye, he got into his car and drove away.

Ariella took her cup, topped it up, then walked into her sunroom and curled up on the couch. "Okay, what happened over the past two days?" were her softly spoken words.

She thought back to Friday night when Roger took her to dinner at The Esplanade restaurant. That was where Hunt and his date were spotted by her walking under the window, and it became apparent Barbara could not be trusted. Ariella smiled, remembering how after leaving The Esplanade, she and her suitor came back to the house and the two of them indulged in passionate lovemaking.

After sunup on Saturday, he left to go to his office and worked there all morning, followed by a meeting in Philadelphia in the afternoon, which went on into the night.

She took another sip of her coffee and continued thinking back. So, I spent most of Saturday cleaning, I was home last night and went to bed early. Purdy woke me up just after midnight and I saw someone, who turned out to be Barbara, hiding jewelry in the flowerpot near my front door.

Ariella mulled over how she found the shopping bag with its valuable contents and hid it in her mailbox of all places! She thought about the police showing up and Roger coming to her house to help her out. After searching everywhere including the garden now for the second time, they departed once again empty handed.

She chuckled when thinking about Wakefield and his henchmen walking over the spoils of the robbery, time and again, and all of them being none the wiser! Ariella had a warm feeling recalling how she and Roger repeated their lovemaking in the early morning hours. What a wild session we had! And now he just left, and I am on my own.

What to do at this stage? "Well, Mr. Barnwell and your no-good friend… you do not know who you are dealing with! You want to leave incriminating evidence? Let me show you how it's done!"

◆◆◆◆◆

It was one o'clock on Sunday afternoon and Hunt was at Barbara's apartment. While he enjoyed being with his attractive girlfriend-on-the-side, she was barely tolerating the relationship.

"I buried the bag just after midnight like we agreed because the patsy more than likely would be sleeping at this hour of the night. No one saw me, her house was in darkness when I arrived, and it was the same when I left. I did the deed in less than five minutes, and I know neither she nor anyone else knew I was there."

"Well, I called Detective Wakefield around 11:45 p.m. on his private cell phone as you and I planned." Hunt stared into her eyes. "I told him I heard a rumor that Ms. Ariella Gerson, one of my disgruntled customers was involved in the break-in and that she hid some of the stolen jewelry in a large flowerpot on her front porch. I figured with a precinct shift-change and needing to get a warrant, they would not immediately go and search the house which would give you time to leave the bag there and get away."

Barbara nodded, "After I was done, I drove and waited in an empty commercial parking lot which was not too far from Ariella's house. I thought I would hang around for an hour or two to see if the police would come. As I told you on the phone earlier, they came within fifteen minutes of me leaving there. I made it out just in time!"

Hunt checked his watch. "I guess they have arrested her by now!"

"I think so. I tried contacting her three times today and it keeps going to her voicemail. She is not returning my calls. It could be they have not allowed her to keep a phone in her cell! It seems that she does not have a 'cell' phone with her!"

CHAPTER 19

Ariella was back at her place of work. For the first part of the day, things were uneventful and she focused on getting a lot done. Her mind was very preoccupied the week before, but now she was able to concentrate a lot better.

At about two thirty Roger called. Her face lit up when his number appeared on her phone.

"Hello sweetheart!" she cooed. "How are you? When will I see you again?"

"Hi my darling. We will get together in the near future socially, but I just got a call from Detective Wakefield, and he wants to see you at the precinct this afternoon at four o'clock. As your lawyer I will be there for you."

"Are you kidding! What do they want *now?* You and the police know I did not participate in this piracy! They searched my house twice for stolen jewelry and found *nothing!* It is time I was left alone!"

"I understand, but Wakefield says some different facts have come to light and they want to interview you again."

"Interview? You mean interrogate!" She was really upset. "There is no new evidence unless someone planted something to incriminate me!"

He tried to calm her. "Will you be able to leave work early enough to meet me at the police station by four o'clock?"

"I am behind on some important projects and my boss is not going to like this. But okay, I can be there at that time."

"All right my love. I will see you soon." He hung up with Ariella, then called a number in New York City.

Roger heard it ringing and Renfrew Hillman's secretary answered and asked who was on the phone. When the lawyer gave his name, she put the call through to her boss.

"Attorney Riley, old chap!" said Renfrew in an ever-so-British accent. His company, the Atlantic Consolidated Insurance Corporation had some vague affiliation with the 'mutualized marketplace' of Lloyds of London. "What news do you have for me about the Fourth Street Jewelers and Gold Exchange over there in your town?"

"Hello Renfrew," he said politely. "As you heard, besides Hunt Barnwell the store owner, the police also suspected Ms. Ariella Gerson, a querulous customer."

"From what you and they told me, I believe there are a few such disgruntled clients. What is with Ms. Gerson?"

"Well, as I reported to you previously, she is a person of interest, and they searched her house last week on Thursday July 7th. That was when she asked me to help her out. As you will recall, during that raid they found no stolen watches, rings, or other items. It was of course after this on Friday morning July 8th when I reached out to Atlantic Consolidated, and you engaged me to help find the perpetrators."

"Okay, I know about all of that, so go on."

"Well, very early yesterday morning, Sunday, they went through Ms. Gerson's residence one more time. She again called me to be there with her, which was a good thing because I could see for myself what was going on. Apparently, the police were told some of the stolen items were hidden in a large flowerpot on her porch. They found nothing this time either, even though they combed through her house, both inside and outside."

"So why are you calling if yesterday again naught was found? Was this tip-off a misdirection hoax?"

"I am talking to you because the police just contacted me and said some new evidence came to light. They want me and Ms. Gerson to be at the precinct by four o'clock today. I will get there earlier so I can find out more before she arrives."

Renfrew asked, "Really? What is this information?"

"I am not sure, but it is about one of their sobriety checkpoint patrolmen stopping a car in the early morning hours of July 4th. A woman possibly matching Ms. Gerson's description was in the vehicle and was questioned at about 4:30 a.m. I don't know any other details or how certain they are about it all, but I will call you this evening once I find out."

"You still seem to suspect Ms. Gerson, don't you?"

"At times during both raids on her house, I really thought it was her. I was convinced at any moment they would find some or all the robbery spoils stashed away. But on each occasion, there were plausible explanations for what seemed to be ideal hiding places. And yet when I look at her, she is beautiful, hard-working, and very indignant about not having been complicit in this theft. I go back and forth as to whether she did or did not partake in it."

"You are not getting romantically involved with her by any chance, are you?"

"Oh no!" He immediately veered from the truth. "She called me for help both times when the cops showed up. I am keeping things on a very professional basis with her."

The slick-tongued liar gave his convincing answer. He went on, "I have looked into her background, and she is not in debt, she has a good job and makes ends meet. I have very surreptitiously scrolled through her cell phone to see if there is any connection to other likely co-conspirators, or if she is part of a gang or such. There are no strange calls, she appears to be a loner and has hardly any friends from what I can tell."

"It seems to me you may be wasting your time with this person, especially if the police came up empty handed twice after searching her house."

"There is one other suspicious thing, and I need to dig deeper into it. Barnwell has a girlfriend named Barbara McKenna. It seems Ms. Gerson and Ms. McKenna have recently become acquainted. I have seen them hang out socially, they could be in league with each other, and maybe together figured out a way to steal from Barnwell."

"You should investigate that theory. There might be something in it and of course see what happens at the precinct later today. We are paying you a good retainer plus there is a substantial reward if you can help us solve this mystery. If today's interview goes nowhere, I suggest you start concentrating elsewhere for suspects. We need to get this matter concluded quickly before we must pay out $1.5 million or more in an insurance claim. We have little faith in your local law enforcement people, so we are counting on you."

"Don't worry, Renfrew. I am sure I will have good news for you soon… maybe even by tonight."

◆◆◆◆◆

Roger sat back in his chair thinking over recent events. After he left Ariella's house on Friday morning July 8th, which was the day following the first Police search, he felt even though no 'baubles, bangles and beads' were found, this beauty may still in some way be connected to the crime. Because of this, he did some research and found out with which company Barnwell was insured. He then called the Atlantic Consolidated Insurance Corporation and offered his services to help find the perpetrators.

He explained his law office was in Averton New Jersey where the jewelry store was located, and he also stated that he recently met and got close to this woman who was considered a suspect. Roger thus spoke to Renfrew Hillman over the phone and Renfrew immediately sent out a Letter of Engagement. Atlantic Consolidated understood, with a pending large insurance claim, it would not be a bad idea to have a 'Man on the Ground' in Averton and especially one who appeared to be quite intelligent. The opportunistic lawyer asked to be put on a retainer fee and this was agreed to.

So, the good-looking, suave, Mr. Riley was really a sleazy, money-grubber. Representing the insurance company and at the same time acting as if he was defending and helping his lady friend, was completely unethical. Little did Ariella know this guy, like Barbara, could not be counted on.

◆◆◆◆◆

Advocating for Ariella when she was being grilled at the station would allow Roger the opportunity to gain valuable insights into where this whole situation was going. Any data gleaned could be useful in helping him solve the case and allow him to cash in on a big reward. The avaricious man felt no guilt continuing down this path.

He got to the precinct at about three fifteen, because he wanted to get a head-start on what the new development was before Ariella arrived. Wakefield immediately sat down with him and gave a brief synopsis of what they would be discussing. He also shared snippets of relevant parts of videos and pointed out certain things. The shifty lawyer made notes about some details and told Wakefield he would like to confer with his client for a few minutes after she got there before they all sat down together.

Ariella, who did not have her car at work, used an Uber ride to get to the police station. She walked in just before four o'clock and was shown into the interview room where her lover was waiting. He spoke to her for a short while and wrote down some additional points. Then he let Leyland know they were ready to meet. Although secretly working for Hillman's company, he still intended to fight for his girl, to the best of his ability.

When Wakefield and Weston walked in, they sat down across the table from Ariella and Roger, who was furious with Leyland for his accusations in their preliminary discussions.

"I heard what you told me, and I spoke to Ms. Gerson. You realize you have nothing!" Roger was quite resolute in his statement. "You explained to me your officer, who is currently away on vacation in Mexico, said he stopped a woman in an older model tan-colored Buick just after 4:25 a.m. early on Monday July 4th. Well, my client owns and drives a blue Subaru. But as you know she did not have her car with her that night and I will state again it is because she left early from a party due to a bad cough and a severe migraine headache."

Roger went on, "You were told by her when going through her house on Thursday evening, July 7th, her vehicle was left at that July 3rd party venue and Max Bolin drove her home. Only by the following afternoon did she get it back, so she was thus stranded at home. How could Ms. Gerson break into a store downtown without transportation?"

"Well, somehow she got her hands on that older model Buick," said Wakefield, trying to make an argument which was already starting to sound quite feeble.

"According to our discussion moments ago, you spoke with three auto-rental places in the immediate area, and you talked to her neighbors. Not only did Ms. Gerson not rent anything that night, but none of the neighbors lent her a car to use. In any case, you checked the location of where her phone was all night. It was in 'silent' mode while she slept, and Barbara McKenna called her throughout the night. Local Tower activity shows her phone was at her house from the moment she got home at about eight fifteen on Sunday night until Tuesday morning July 5th when leaving to go to work."

"Well okay, but Ms. Gerson matched the description which my man gave." Leyland tried to sound very stern.

"No, she does *not* match this!" Roger was now raising his voice. "When you met with me about half an hour ago you showed me the report from Officer J.T. Taylor, and you have it right there in front of you. In it, Taylor notes the lady had scraggly, wavy blond hair and dark eyebrows. When you look at my client you will see that she has straight, naturally fair hair and light blonde eyebrows!"

The two policemen glanced at the beauty queen.

Roger continued, "Your man reported, the person he stopped had brown eyes and Ariella has blue eyes, quite striking blue eyes which most people never forget. He made a note of a large beauty spot on her left cheek. In fact, he wrote down that he clearly remembers thinking, 'A pity this young lady has this glaring blemish'. My client has no such mark on her face. She has flawless skin as you can see."

Leyland then said, "When we watched the video of the foyer in the 125-Building, we saw someone exiting this vestibule at 4:08 a.m. holding a large bag and wearing a backpack. We surmise these held the spoils from the break-in. My officer reported Ms. Gerson was the lady he stopped in the Buick. She had a duffle bag and backpack in her vehicle."

"I have of course seen the DVD recordings just moments ago when you showed these to me," said Roger. "The person you are referring to leaving the 125-Building at that time had short, curly, charcoal-grey hair but my client is blonde. Yes, the individual was wearing a backpack and it is clearly visible, but besides that, all one can see in the video are handles from another bag being carried. How do you know it was a duffle? Your man could not provide a color or a description of the bags he saw in the Buick. You searched Ms. Gerson's house twice and you didn't find either of these."

"Well, we were not after bags, just valuables, and lots of them. Perhaps we should go back to her home and look again. There is much we cannot prove right now, but we know your client had something to do with this." Leyland was again grasping at straws.

Roger said with a smirk on his face, "What has someone exiting the 125-Building so early in the morning of July 4th got to do with a robbery next door? If your incomprehensible supposition is correct that thieves broke in from the first floor of one building and dropped down through the ceiling into the adjacent one, where are the holes in both walls that would have allowed bandits to crawl through and then get out again? Did you find a stepladder which the perps used so they could climb in and out of the ceiling? You did not find a ladder, did you?"

"It is our belief this infiltration did take place by entry from one complex to the other because neither the front door nor the back door appears to have been opened. The alarm did not even go off."

"Detective Wakefield, it is time to get real!" He was now talking like a scolding father. "Only some kind of masonry expert could make large holes in two walls and brick these up again with no trace of either opening ever having been there. But then which side would this expert patch up?"

Roger took a breath and continued, "Assume a hole was made into each wall of the two structures and one or more people got in, then crawled back out. I can understand them occluding and carefully finishing the side they were now on. But how would they close the other side when they were not there to seal it up, to patch it, spackle it and paint it? If a person is not in the store but has now moved through to the building next door, how would they repair the breach in the drywall and the brickwork on Barnwell's side? How can anyone accomplish that? Your theory is preposterous, to say the least! It simply does not make sense."

"We still believe something like that happened," said Leyland. But he and Charles discussed this riddle: Patching a wall when you are not there to do so. "Sooner or later, we will figure it out. Meanwhile, my patrolman picked out Ms. Gerson from photographs. He said she was the person he stopped at four twenty-five on the morning of July 4th."

"No, he did not!" said Roger angrily. "In his report, he admits the lighting was very bad on the street and conditions were dark at the time. He said he was 'somewhat certain'. Well, 'somewhat certain' is not a positive identification. In any event in his written report, he describes a totally different female with brown eyes, a mole on her cheek, and dark eyebrows. That does not match Ms. Gerson's appearance."

"We presume it was she who was driving the Buick, and her Subaru was purposely left at the party the night before as part of her alibi." Wakefield continued to pursue his wild theory. He knew these were crazy presumptions, but he was hoping to find something which would stick.

"That is just nonsense. Now, let me ask you a question. At this sobriety check, a woman was stopped who was driving an older-model Buick. Your man could easily have seen to whom this car belonged by looking at the registration and insurance cards. So, with the information which he noted from these cards, you must know who owns this Buick. Have you tracked down the owner and found out who was driving it?"

It was interesting Roger asked this question and Ariella who was sitting quietly alongside him was pleased he did. Roger did not know the policeman requested these items when he stopped her but forgot to follow up about getting this driver to produce her insurance and registration details.

The detective was silent for a moment, not wanting to admit J.T. Taylor had not seen these two cards. Although he looked at her driver's license, he reported that he didn't clearly remember her name, being more intent on seeing if she was drunk, and getting her to walk in a straight line.

Leyland understood this officer made many stops since the early evening of July 3rd and was working overtime past his shift change. He dealt with seven very drunk and aggressive drivers and said, by just before dawn, his mind was 'scrambled eggs'. He was tired from working so many hours and did not even want to be there on that July 4th early-morning inebriation patrol.

"Well, what information did the registration and insurance cards provide? Did they match the name on the driver's license?"

"We are not sure at this stage. I am waiting for more details." Wakefield was lying and Roger could sense it. He realized the police had little or nothing to go on and their vacationing enforcer was an unreliable witness.

The lawyer sighed and then spoke further. "Your man states in his report he opened the duffle bag on the back seat and there was clothing inside. He understood the woman had just broken up with her boyfriend, she packed up her stuff and was headed somewhere else. If this was just normal luggage, why would the driver of that old Buick even be a suspect? Your man stated, 'Just broken up with her boyfriend', not 'Just broken into a jewelry store' Surely you know the difference between *broken up* and *broken into?*"

"Well, my officer said he didn't look very deeply into the bag." Wakefield was trying to create the impression there might have been stolen goods below the clothing.

"Your man had *no right* looking into a duffle bag on someone's car seat. He violated the rights of that poor distressed woman whose boyfriend just left her. I wish I knew who she was, I would love to represent her!"

Leyland stared glumly.

Roger continued now in a somewhat demeaning manner, "Your cop said all he saw was a sweatshirt in that duffle. So, which is it, stolen jewelry or simply wearables found during an illegal search? None of this will ever stand up in a court of law and you know it. Why don't you go and pursue the real perpetrators and look properly into the inside job which this obviously is instead of blaming all kinds of people everywhere? We understand from news reports that so far you have accused a dead man, a man currently in prison, someone who is in hospital, and an old man in a wheelchair. You have also tried to lay this on my client whose home has been searched twice, and where no evidence was found! When will this ridiculousness end?"

"We still feel Ms. Gerson is somehow culpable."

"You have no fingerprints or DNA, she was at home all night sick with a migraine and no auto to drive. By your own admission, her phone did not move from her house. Your officer saw a totally different woman in a car that my client does not own, nor did she borrow or rent such a vehicle. Do any of the auto-rental places have older model Buicks? No! They only provide new or almost-new cars."

"We will be back in touch," said Leyland sheepishly. Every time he approached a situation to do with this larceny, his case evaporated.

"Let's go," said Roger. Ariella stood up with him. She hadn't said a word the whole time because he asked her not to. Roger's arguments were perfect, and the police were knocked down at every turn.

"I will need a ride home. Will you take me?"

"Of course, my love." He held her hand as they walked out to where his BMW was parked. They got in and drove off in the direction of her house.

The Heistess now felt Roger was someone to confide in. She would tell him soon, maybe even tonight when they got back to her house. Her break-in was impeccable, yes it was *The Perfect Crime*. The way her beau stood up for her at the precinct caused the entire police department's suspicions about her to crumble. Roger will be awestruck when he hears the details of her ingenious plan and how well it was executed, right down to closing the hole in the wall above the store's ceiling, to how she hid everything away.

Ariella thought about how ideal they were together. Her face was glowing, and she was extremely relieved because Wakefield could not pin this on her. She would work out how to plant evidence to incriminate Barbara and would give some of the stolen valuables to others who were wronged by Hunt. Ariella had photographed Leyland's *List of Ten Suspects* the night he inadvertently left it in her study. Some or most of the people on the list were cheated by Barnwell. Once this was all over, she would be able to get on with her life and have a great future with her new boyfriend!

On the way home they chatted about what just took place, and both chuckled when referring to Leyland's case being simply a house of cards.

The two arrived at Ariella's place at 5:48 p.m. and were now standing in the kitchen. For a moment they simply stared at one

another and then were once again kissing with fervor. She felt happy
because life was finally going her way and the days ahead now looked
very promising.

"Honey, I can only stay for a few minutes, but then I should go.
Like you, I left my office early today after Wakefield called, so I must
get back there and work for a few hours to get some big contracts done
because I need to be in Philadelphia again from tomorrow."

"I understand." Even though he wanted to leave soon, she could
still inform him all about the heist. He will be so impressed, and he
will learn how smart she really is.

"We will have a cup of coffee and at the same time there is
something I must tell you." With a broad smile on her face she waited
for her Keurig machine to do its thing. Although Barbara was not to be
trusted, at least Roger could be made aware of the caper.

"While you get the cups ready, I really need to go to the bathroom,"
Roger said, heading in that direction. He left his key fob and cell
phone on the kitchen counter.

As she heard the door close to the nearby powder room, his
phone which was still set on 'vibrate' mode since being at the police
station, suddenly buzzed as a text came through. The message popped
up on the home screen for a moment like it normally does, before
residing in the text-message app.

The curious cutie glanced down at the phone when it vibrated.
She was able to see the text for several seconds before it disappeared. It
was from a 212 New York number, and she was horrified at what she
read: *It's Renfrew. How did the interrogation go today? Did the little
bitch do it? You must help us resolve this robbery quickly or we will have
to pay the $1.5 million insurance claim. Let me know, buddy!*

And just as quickly as the message came up on the screen, it faded.
A minute or so later Roger emerged from the bathroom. Ariella was
now on a chair at the kitchen table waiting for him and was looking
straight ahead. He walked over, picked up his cup, and drank a few sips.

"Sweetheart, I know you want to talk to me, but I need to leave. We
can chat about your news when we next get together." His tone was
cold, and it made her realize that deep down he had little or no feelings
for her. She was a business opportunity for him and a sexual plaything.

"Okay," was her quiet response, relieved he no longer wanted to
discuss her happenings. At least no made-up lie would be needed.

Ariella now understood Roger was not on her side and that he too was against her.

"I hope to see you sometime this weekend," he said gulping down a bit more of the coffee. On his face was a put-on smile. "Sorry it cannot be sooner but as I just mentioned, it's essential for me to be back in Philadelphia for the next few days and nights."

"That's okay. You should be on your way because I know you have a lot to do. And Roger, thank you very much for your help today."

Ariella stood up next to him. He left his half-full cup on the table and gave her a hug and a kiss, not detecting Ariella's sudden aloofness as she merely went through the motions. They said their goodbyes and he scooped up his key fob and cell phone. Once in his car he looked at his phone and saw that a text had come in. When clicking on it, up came Renfrew's message.

Whew! The fact that the message indicator was still showing meant she had not opened and read it while his phone lay unattended in the kitchen. "Good thing," he said out loud, "It would be disastrous if this chick knew I was working for Atlantic Consolidated." Driving away, his idea was to contact Renfrew when he got home.

It was a bit past six fifteen when Ariella flopped down onto the couch. She tried to cry but no tears came out. At first, it was Barbara spying on her while they were supposed to be friends, and now her lover was betraying her. Is he really a lawyer for the jewelry store's insurance company? What the hell kind of a name is 'Renfrew' anyway?

After a few minutes, she stood up and still shaking a bit, walked into her study, and turned on her computer. She did a search for a few words, 'Renfrew… Insurance Company… New York'. Immediately it came up. *Renfrew Hillman, Executive Director. Atlantic Consolidated Insurance Corporation, New York, NY.* Ariella suddenly appreciated the man having such an unusual first name. It made finding him easy and gave her an instant answer. So, Roger was involved with an insurer, and he was reporting back to them!

She poured another cup of comfort, sat down again on the couch, and then the tears began to flow. Ariella sat there for a good half hour dazed and confused. Then she went to her computer and deleted the internet search which was just done. Thank goodness for that text because Roger was about to be told all about the heist. She closed her eyes and quietly thanked her grandmother for saving her from spilling the beans to Barbara during the prior week, and now for preventing her from divulging this important secret to another person who was not on her side.

She thought, "If he is getting paid by Hillman's group and I told him where everything was hidden, he would have turned me in, accepted a fee from them, and probably received a huge reward as well."

Ariella understood it was up to her to carefully begin to distance herself from him without raising any suspicion and to not get intimate with this guy again unless she could turn such intimacy to her own advantage.

Her guard was now up and that would be vital for her own safety. She was disturbed for letting the two of them get so close to her. Sitting there, a plot began to formulate in her mind about getting even with Barbara.

It was a little after eight o'clock on that same Monday evening July 11th when the motivated maiden was now ready to begin her next move. It was time to pick up her cell phone and call her 'frenemy'.

"Good evening to you!" Ariella sounded upbeat hoping to make things appear all was normal between them.

Upon answering her phone Barbara said, "I am just in the middle of something, let me get back to you in a couple of minutes."

"Okay, talk soon."

Barbara needed to buy a little time to think things through. She heard from Barnwell earlier in the day that he enquired as to whether any persons of interest were taken into custody. Leyland said nothing to him about an arrest or anything being found on Ariella's property. But Hunt understood the police were to be questioning this female suspect in the afternoon because of some 'New Evidence'.

The vixen figured this interrogation must be because of what she placed in the flowerpot just after midnight the day before. But what her lover did not know was that Ariella was being called to the precinct to be grilled about an officer's report from a traffic stop, in the early morning of July 4th.

Hunt told her the Police had 'New Evidence'. In Barbara's mind, this meant the bagful of high-ticket items on the porch was now safely under lock and key. Ariella would not be able to wriggle out of being found guilty when she was soon put on trial. Barbara surmised Ariella was contacting her now because she must be out on bail or such.

"Sorry about that," said Barbara when calling back. "It is good to hear from you." Her voice sounded endearing because she was curious to learn first-hand what was going on. "We have not been together since last week on Wednesday night when I visited you at your home and your cat knocked over that potted plant! I am glad you called because I would love to chat for a bit."

"Well, I wanted to speak on the phone, but if you would rather get together in person, perhaps we can do so." Ariella really wanted to find her way into this she-devil's apartment for her plan of action to work. But she did not want to be the one to suggest meeting there.

"Yes! We must see each other. Come over to my place tomorrow night for dinner and we can chat for a while." Barbara had played right into Ariella's hands.

"I do not want you to go to any trouble." The Heistess was trying to be coy.

"It's not a problem. It will be easy for me to make a salad for us, and I can pick up a cooked chicken on my way home from work." Barbara was primarily thinking about prying as much additional information out of her friend as she could. By getting together, her goal would be to learn a lot more than simply gabbing on the phone.

"Well okay, if you insist," said Ariella. How about I bring a bottle of wine with me? I will take an Uber ride from my place of work to you, and I can get home the same way. Thank you for the invitation."

"Great. Tomorrow night it is, at about six o'clock?"

"That will be fine. See you then." The conversation went exactly as Ariella wanted it to. But for this to work she would need to have a five-second window of opportunity to make the visit worthwhile.

"You poor, stupid girl!" said Barbara out loud after she clicked off her cell phone. "You are in trouble with the police because of what I stowed at your house and at this moment it is all in their possession."

Barbara thought she would be able to glean many new details the following night. With the authorities now strongly suspecting this blonde bimbo, they had very likely charged her but let her out temporarily. This would serve to keep Hunt in the clear. However, she continued to consider the possibility that her lover perhaps robbed his own store, because he was dishonest at the best of times.

But in any event, Barbara needed Ariella to be found guilty of this crime to prevent anyone from ever coming along and investigating *her!*

Hunt gave her so much by way of cash and jewelry over the past couple of years, worth perhaps $45,000 or more, and she did not want to run into problems and be fined or even arrested for tax evasion or such.

She immediately called Hunt to let him know about the dinner arrangement at her apartment the following night.

◆◆◆◆◆

After finishing her phone conversation with Barbara, Ariella sat quietly for a short while, going over some ideas in her mind. Then she began to get ready to go out later that same night to temporarily hide the plastic shopping bag, filled with jewelry. She went into her garage and wearing gloves, retrieved the bag from the recycling bin, being careful not to smudge or wipe away any possible fingerprints which may have been left by Barbara. Using a soft 2" paint brush, Ariella gently removed any residual dirt and then placed the bag onto a large piece of cloth. She proceeded to roll this fabric around it and fold over the ends, then closed this large fabric tube securely with two rubber bands.

Ariella did not think a disguise was needed when visiting the parking lot adjacent to the apartment building where Barbara lived. Black jeans, a black shirt, and a tight-fitting dark baseball cap to cover her hair would allow her to get around unnoticed. She packed a few garden implements, a flashlight, and the bulky fabric tube into a canvas tote bag and was now ready to go on the first stage of a two-night mission.

Being July, the sun did not set until around nine o'clock, so she waited some twenty minutes before driving to where the devious diva resided. Before too long Ariella arrived in the area, and it was now quite dark. She pulled her car over about half a block away, grabbed the tote bag, then headed to where Barbara's Toyota was parked.

There was no fence around the parking lot, just an entrance and exit gate with booms to control incoming and outgoing cars. All residents in the apartment building who used this next-door lot were provided with a magnetic card for access. While there were some flood lights to prevent thefts and break-ins, the place was not well-lit.

She gazed around and there was no one there except for one small pickup truck at the exit gate in the process of driving out. Having been to the apartment and the parking lot previously, she knew exactly where the white Toyota would be. Glancing at the building, it was easy to tell where Barbara's kitchen was located. It was in the middle section of the 6th floor, and it overlooked the parked cars.

Ariella scouted around to find a suitable place to provisionally hide the jewelry. In the far corner was a twenty-cubic-yard dumpster, and like all large scrap receptacles, below it were several 4" high steel skids. She knelt down, and using her flashlight, tried to look under these rails. There was a lot of debris all around including bits of concrete, bricks, metal chunks and more. After clearing some of this away from the end of the trash container, a perfect hollow area between two of the rails appeared. But first, this space had to be made larger. Using her small garden trowel, she dug out some of the earth and thereby increased what was a 4" void and turned it into a 9" deep channel.

The fabric tube was now able to be carefully pushed into this scooped-out section. She replaced some of the debris along the base, thereby closing and disguising the hole. The stealthy strategist was about to leave the area when she suddenly heard a few loud voices. Two men and two women were walking into the parking lot from the apartment building and were heading in her direction. She 'hit the dirt' and lay close to the dumpster. The four people made their way to a burgundy Honda SUV which was less than fifteen feet away.

Ariella was keeping very still in the dimly lit area and being dressed in black served her well. One of them unlocked the doors to the vehicle and they got inside. She suddenly realized the front of the car was facing her and as soon as the engine started this would put her directly in the spotlight! There was no time to hide, and Ariella had only a few seconds to react. She grabbed a small chunk of concrete which was roughly the size of a golf ball. From her sitting position, she lobbed it as accurately as possible into the air aiming for the back of the car, then immediately lay flat to the ground.

As the driver was reaching for the starter button there was a loud thud on the trunk. He whirled his head around as did all his passengers. "What was that?" he exclaimed.

The instant the gallant gal saw them looking away, she grabbed the tote bag, jumped up, and darted behind the dumpster out of their line of sight. The doors opened and a verbal commotion ensued as all four people scrambled out and moved to the rear of the auto. They were anxious to see what was going on and what caused the loud noise.

At that moment Ariella began to run quickly to the apartment complex and went all the way around the back of it. She sprinted along the far side, getting almost to the main thoroughfare in front of the building. Right before reaching the road there was a narrow-landscaped area comprising of some small trees, flower beds and a few shrubs. It had not been attended to lately, so it was a bit overgrown.

Ducking down between the trees and lying on the ground, this was her temporary area of refuge, and concealed by the vegetation she was able to see the exit gate of the parking lot and the street in front of her.

Not thirty seconds later a man came by with his small pup. The animal detected someone was there, lying just a few feet from the sidewalk but not noticeable because of the shrubbery. The dog started yapping away and pulling on his leash. The owner seemed frustrated to be walking his pet in the first place and angrily scolded the mutt.

Even when they passed where she lay hidden, the dog kept on yelping and trying to pull them back to where Ariella was. The man glanced toward the shrubbery and trees as she remained motionless. Then he turned to continue walking and said loudly, "Stop trying to find stray cats at night!" After a bit more noise the barker gave up and the two moved on.

Ariella exhaled a sigh of relief and was now focused on watching the gate of the parking area. Sure enough, a moment later the boom began lifting and the Honda with its four passengers exited the lot. It made a right-hand turn and headed straight to her hiding place. Lying on the ground she was able to observe the occupants of the car who were scouring the sidewalks as they looked in the direction of the apartment building and elsewhere. They were trying to see if they could spot a lone individual out and about, a person who might have tossed something onto their trunk.

After the burgundy SUV passed by, the hidden heroine figured it was best to stay there a bit longer, making sure the four people had left the neighborhood. It was now almost ten thirty, and there was not much traffic at that time. Only a few other automobiles drove by during the next two or three minutes. And then, sure enough, the same vehicle came slowly back down the street from the other direction. She lay there quietly until it disappeared down the road.

After five more minutes, it was safe enough for her to get up and go to her car. She arrived home just after eleven o'clock. Once out of the dusty clothes, Ariella showered and went to bed. Tonight's ordeal was over, and all was set for the next phase at Barbara's apartment the following evening.

CHAPTER 20

Tuesday Morning, July 12th

It was six-thirty when Ariella woke up, and after her early morning getting-ready routine, she went downstairs to give Purdy his food for the day. All the while the TV was on, but there was not much happening about local news except when the announcer referred to the break-in from the week before and again stated the police were pursuing several leads.

"Ha!" Ariella remarked out loud. "You dummies have nothing! But don't worry, within a few days you will have a suspect in custody… one you will catch red-handed with a bagful of stolen stuff!"

After having a fried egg on toast and a cup of coffee, she left the house and walked to catch the bus to her office.

Ariella was extremely busy all day and worked non-stop other than taking a short fifteen-minute lunch break. The afternoon flew by, and suddenly her watch showed it was already past five. She quickly finished a report in her computer and tidied her desk. Taking the elevator down to the ground floor she walked out of the building to the corner where a small liquor store was located.

Selecting a bottle of fine Merlot, Ariella thought this would be an excellent wine with which to secretly celebrate getting even with the spying witch! The Uber app was easy to find on her cell phone and eight minutes later in rush-hour traffic, the car arrived to pick her up. Shortly after six o'clock, she was ringing the doorbell.

Tonight, her goal was to be very sweet, not wanting her so-called friend to suspect there was an ulterior motive for her being there. But in any case, Barbara was the one who invited *her* over for dinner. Ariella also made a point of carrying a small clutch purse and not a big pocketbook, making it obvious she had no large handbag containing a lot of jewelry that could be planted somewhere.

Barbara opened the apartment door and welcomed her guest inside. She of course had no inkling Ariella knew about the affair with Hunt or that she was seen stashing incriminating articles into the flowerpot. As far as Barbara knew, the authorities found new physical evidence, and standing in front of her was the prime culprit.

"Hello and welcome!" This was her friendly greeting, but deep down she was hoping the police would file charges against this individual soon, if they had not already done so.

"Thank you for asking me over." Ariella wanted to emphasize the point that she was invited here, even though it was her initial phone call the night before.

"I am happy to have you, and thanks for bringing the wine. This looks like a really fancy Merlot."

"It should be… it wasn't cheap!"

A few minutes later the two were standing on the verandah drinking wine and nibbling on crackers and veggie dip. This porch overlooked the parking lot, and the white Toyota could clearly be seen. Ariella thought, "I hope my plan works. I believe the car is not too far away."

For a while, they chatted and neither one broached the subject of the break-in just yet. Ariella spoke about how busy things were at work lately and her counterpart referred to some interesting electronic components one of her clients was exporting to Europe. The banter went on for a bit.

Barbara then said, "Let's go inside and eat."

"Good idea, we should do that."

They went into the kitchen where Ariella refilled their wine glasses and took these to the table. Barbara began dishing up the salad and the pre-cooked chicken onto plates.

Ariella came back into the kitchen, gazed around, and at first was very concerned because the keys belonging to her hostess were nowhere to be seen. Then she spotted them on the counter in the far corner, and the car-key-fob appeared to be part of the regular bunch. Good. Finding the keys will allow her to unlock the car doors without being seen. Well, now was not the time, there will hopefully be a chance later.

Within a couple of minutes, they were sitting down enjoying their food. They clinked their glasses to "Good Health." Barbara was first to talk about the heist.

"So how about The Pearly Plaza getting broken into? We spoke about this a bit when we got together at your house last week on Wednesday. Neither of us liked the owner… what was his name again… oh yes, Mr. Barnwell."

Ariella thought, "You liar! You know the jerk's name. You are sleeping with him!"

"The Pearly Plaza… that's cute! I guess the thieves stole a lot from that place." Trying not to hide or cover up anything Ariella brazenly kept speaking, "As we discussed before, this Barnwell character swindled my grandmother out of many family heirlooms, and he also took you for a ride."

Ariella purposefully used the words 'for a ride' and this was quite effective. She noticed a slight blush coming over Barbara's face who was now thinking, "He sure takes me for a ride, and continues to do so!"

The brunette added, "Yes, he stole from me as well. From what I see on TV they are considering a few suspects but there is nothing definite happening as of now." She was trying to elicit something from her guest and was testing to see how forthcoming she would be.

"Can you believe it? They imagine I had something to do with this!" Ariella sounded indignant.

"No! Surely, they are not considering such a thing?" Barbara was pleased with these details, not knowing the young beauty had been rehearsing most of this in her mind for the past few hours.

"Yes, those bastards! They are speculating that because my grandma got cheated by Barnwell, I would invade his store and take some of his goods! Do you know they searched my home… not just once, but twice!"

"Oh, my goodness! What would make them decide to go through your house?" Barbara was told by Hunt that Ariella's property was turned upside down the week before by the police, and they must have done this again right after the bulky shopping bag appeared on her porch. She wanted to hear more and find out why this woman here in front of her, was roaming free right now and not behind bars.

"Yup! They came last week on Thursday and again just two days ago on Sunday at one o'clock in the morning! I went to bed early and I was sound asleep. They woke me up and waved around a warrant! I *had* to let them in."

"Did they find anything?"

"Well, I don't really know. There were a few cops, and they removed some items from my place. I called my lawyer, and he came over at that ungodly hour and dealt with them." Ariella wanted to be a bit vague and to talk in generalities. She was succeeding. "However, I did appear at the precinct yesterday afternoon."

"No! You went there?" Barbara could not believe this gal was being so candid with her. "How did it go? Surely, they do not suppose you did this?"

"I am not certain what they are surmising. My lawyer is handling it all, but I am very scared. You know, I had zero to do with this and now I believe the real perpetrators are trying to pin this on me!" She stopped talking and went back to eating her salad.

Barbara was quiet and thoughtful for a moment. *Okay so a gang from somewhere robbed Hunt's store and the police rationalized this to be the case. Maybe they found the jewelry in the flowerpot but concluded that Ariella did not or could not have done it. So, they kept the evidence and are perhaps hoping before too long, the real ring of thieves will be found.*

She continued with her thoughts. *In a way that is a relief for me, I guess I was in over my head trying to frame her.* Barbara felt a twinge of guilt for what she did, but then the feeling quickly left her. She was jealous of Ariella being with Roger and wanted to make sure nothing regarding this crime ever came back to incriminate Hunt or even land in her lap. No, best to let them theorize Ariella was somehow involved.

"I have ice cream for dessert." Barbara smiled as they finished their dinner. "We can add slices of banana."

"Great, I would love that. Let me help you take these plates off the table." She was becoming a little anxious about getting the five-second opportunity needed to unlock the car doors without being seen.

They walked into the kitchen and Barbara took a small tub out of the freezer and cut up a banana, putting half the pieces into one bowl and the other half into another, followed by a generous scoop of ice cream for each. She picked up the two dessert dishes and carried these to the dining room.

Ariella saw her chance and said out loud, "I will get cups down for coffee." This was the moment for her to stay back briefly, and now on her own in the kitchen, she went to the corner and grabbed the bunch of keys trying not to let them jingle. Finding the 'unlock' icon she moved quickly to the window and pushed the button… twice. The Toyota's headlights went on and off. Great! The vehicle received the signal, and its doors were now unlocked.

The keys were put back in their original place and Ariella immediately opened the door of an eye-level cupboard just as Barbara returned.

"Where do you keep the mugs?" she asked casually, pretending to look in the cupboard, which had in it baking trays and glass dishes.

"You are in the wrong place. They are on this shelf."

"Oh thanks. Now I remember from before. Sometimes I think my mind is going!"

They sat down to have their coffee and dessert and continued talking about various matters. Neither referred to the break-in at the store again. The Heistess got what she came for and was now anxious to leave, however, not to be rude she stayed for a while longer.

Barbara struck up a new angle of conversation and began speaking about a vacation being planned for later in the year. Ariella said she had no immediate ideas to go anywhere right now. They went back and forth for a while with their discussions.

It was almost ten o'clock when Ariella decided it was time to go. Barbara was also ready for this to happen so there was no argument from her.

Ariella's intention was to go downstairs, walk over to the parking lot, retrieve the precious fabric tube and put it into the parked vehicle. After that she would get an Uber driver to take her home.

"Well, thank you for dinner and for inviting me over." She was doing her best to convey that all was still perfect between them. "I just texted for an Uber car to meet me, so I need to get down to the front of the building right away."

"Don't take an Uber ride, let me take you home. We had such a great evening together and I don't want you going with a stranger."

"No, stay here. If you take me, it will be at least another forty minutes before you are back at your apartment. Besides you already consumed two glasses of wine, and being behind the wheel is not a good idea!" Ariella didn't want Barbara driving her because then the evidence could not be left in the Toyota without her coming all the way back. Also, if she was driven home, the Toyota would be locked upon her return! The opening of the vehicle's doors was well planned, and she could not afford to have her efforts ruined. Fortunately, Barbara relented.

"Okay, you are right. Let me go with you downstairs."

Ariella who lied about already calling for an Uber car said suddenly, "Oh, it looks like the app did not work properly. Let me try again." She clicked on the app and then on her pre-set address. Done! "We are good to go. My ride will be here momentarily."

Once on her way, she would have to think of an excuse to get the driver to return to the building. Oh well, that could work.

The two of them got into the elevator making small talk again. As they reached the foyer her driver was already there. They hugged and wished each other a good night.

Ariella got into the auto and as it pulled away Barbara blew her a kiss before going inside. The dinner evening was over, and so far, the first stage of the important mission for this night was successful. Part two was to follow now.

The bold beauty decided on a change of plan, in that she would let the driver take her directly to her house. At first, she wanted him to get her back to the apartment building when they were part of the way home, but then felt no one should know about the return trip. Also, it would be more advantageous if she came better equipped for the task, rather than trying to dig out the wrapped-up evidence with her bare hands while wearing dressy office attire.

Once they got to her residence, she exited the vehicle, went to the bathroom, and gave Purdy a little more food. Like the previous night, Ariella put on a pair of black jeans, switched her beige blouse to a long-sleeved black shirt, and with her hair tied up, put on the black cap. She again took with her the small tote bag with its tools and implements and her thin gardening gloves.

It was a bit past ten thirty when she arrived again at the apartment building. Her new plan was clearly a more desirable one than having the Uber driver turn around and wait for her.

Barbara would no doubt be asleep by now and in any case if she did happen to look outside, it was highly unlikely she would see anything untoward going on considering Ariella was once again dressed in black and the lighting where the cars were was so bad.

Ariella stopped her vehicle a little way down the road like before. Grabbing the tote bag, it was a quick walk to the apartment building, and once there, she slipped around the back and scurried to the rear of the parking lot. In moments she was crouched down alongside the dumpster where the treasure was hidden.

With her gloved hands, the few concrete chunks were removed, then using the small garden trowel, she scooped away the earth from the channel hideout. Sliding her hand into the open space, out came the fabric tube.

The concrete bits were put back into the hollow area to close it so the hole could no longer be seen. Taking a small 2" wide paint brush, she brushed the residual sand from her gloves and from the fabric tube and then put these implements back into the tote bag. Ariella stood up and surveyed the area. There was not a soul to be seen anywhere. Glancing above to where she gauged Barbara's apartment was located, it appeared to be in darkness as was most of the building. Hopefully, her spurious friend was asleep in bed at this point.

The Heistess went slowly to where the white Toyota was parked. She put one of her gloved hands on the driver's side handle and gently pulled it. The door opened quietly. Whew! Using the remote from upstairs a couple of hours earlier certainly worked! Not wanting the car's interior light to remain on any longer than necessary, she quickly looked for the latch and popped the trunk open, then carefully closed the door.

Walking to the rear of the vehicle, Ariella raised the lid, and the light came on allowing her to take a good look inside. There was a T-Shirt lying on top of a few large envelopes filled with papers, and one could assume these were work-related.

Removing the rubber bands from around the fabric tube, she gently took the plastic shopping bag filled with the valuable goods, and lifting the wooden carpeted base, placed the bag into the space by the spare wheel.

Ariella hoped Barbara was not smart enough to wear gloves the other night. If that were the case, then the shopping bag would still have her fingerprints on it, but if there were none, it would not really matter. To get it to fit alongside the spare wheel, the bag had to be jiggled around just a bit. She lowered the wooden base, put the T-Shirt and the envelopes into their prior positions, and quietly shut the trunk.

Studying the area once again, it was apparent no one else was there, so she walked to the driver's side door and opened it. Pushing down the lock button, a distinctive click could be heard as the car was secured. The door was then softly closed.

Ariella pulled off her gloves, placed them in the tote bag, then took out her cell phone and snapped a picture of the back of the Toyota. This was to record its license plate number, needed for when alerting the police to look inside the car. She left the parking area by walking along the same route taken before, around the back of the apartment building and up to the street, going past the small garden patch where she lay hidden the prior evening.

A few minutes later Ariella got to her vehicle, slipped inside, and in no time was on her way home. The evidence was now in place and the crime at the jewelry store had been directed toward Barbara who would soon be *Hoist with Her Own Petard*. The Heistess felt she would never have planted actual jewelry on the property of another person, except the bitchy brunette had done exactly that to her.

Once at home, Ariella wrote down the letters and numbers from the license plate on a piece of paper and then deleted the picture. She did not want any record of the Toyota in her phone if the police ever scoured through it.

CHAPTER 21

Wednesday, July 13th

Once again in her office, Ariella was trying to stay focused on the various tasks at hand. But her mind kept on going back to how and when law enforcement could be alerted by her to look in Barbara's car.

A burner phone would certainly be used, and her voice disguised when making this call. Maybe she could send an anonymous letter to Detective Wakefield and mail it from another town. A few lines could be typed on her work computer with gloves on her hands to leave no fingerprints on the paper or the envelope. She pondered over this, and by mid-afternoon figured out how to get someone else to provide the tip-off so nothing about it could get back to her.

At this stage, her hope was that the Toyota would not get a flat tire before the warrant was issued, and trust all would remain hidden until the important message was sent.

Ariella was a very productive and smart worker, and she got well ahead on her major project in the office. By the following afternoon, Thursday, her desk work was completely caught up. Upon asking her supervisor if she could take some personal time and have the next day off, he agreed.

Before leaving the office, Ariella checked the weather on her cell phone and this showed it would be cloudy and dry all day tomorrow but then early on Saturday morning, it was supposed to start raining. Good, the weather would be clear on Friday night, and that was important. Using the telephone on her desk she called her mechanic at Woodward's Auto Center.

"Hi Harry, its Ariella."

As was always the case he felt a flutter of excitement in his stomach when he heard her voice. How he loved this beautiful customer of his and wished repeatedly that he was thirty years younger and a million dollars richer!

"Well, hello!" Harry expressed the usual enthusiasm.

"I want to bring my Subaru in for service tomorrow and I require a loaner from you. I need to borrow something small from one of the used cars you have for sale on your lot."

"What about the Buick? You used it recently."

"I do not wish to take that big clunker! I need a compact to drive around for the day while you change the oil and rotate the tires on my Subaru."

"Sure, whatever you want. I have an eight-year-old silver two-door Chevy Cruze available. Will that do?"

"That's good. I have one other request. Because I have Power of Attorney for my grandmother's estate, I will sign the title for the Buick so you can sell it at any time. It is probably worth only a few thousand dollars and I will split 50/50 with you whatever you get for it, like we recently discussed."

"As I said before, that works for me! I will go ahead and try to get it sold in the next week or two."

"Oh Harry, remember I mentioned I would like to keep the license plates from my nana's car as a memento? Please give these to me tomorrow and then go ahead and have the numbers taken out of service with the DMV."

"Okay, consider it done! I shall have the Chevy ready for you early in the morning and my dealer's plates will be on it. What time will you be stopping by?"

"I would say around eight-thirty."

"Great. See you then." He was beaming. Tomorrow he would be able to stare into those awesome blue eyes again!

She hung up the phone. Ariella had been thinking for the past few days about how perfect the old license plates would be for what she needed to do. The letters and numbers were C31 FPO and these could be temporarily altered then changed back again or disguised in some other way.

It would be good to get this silver Chevy from Harry. With it, she would be able to set the stage for the next steps to be taken. He would not get the car back from her until Friday night or on Saturday morning sometime, but he wouldn't be upset if the car was returned a little later than scheduled.

She stated, "I guess I belong to a group titled the LTA: What I would call the *Liberty Takers Association*."

And so, on this Thursday afternoon July 14th, Ariella waved goodbye to her supervisor, and leaving the office, took the bus home, arriving there a bit past six o'clock. After giving Purdy more food and making a quick sandwich to eat, it was time to start preparing for the following day.

She got into the Subaru and drove to a Lowes Home Improvement Center, and once there, bought two big empty plastic buckets with lids. They gave her, at no charge, several wooden paint-stirring sticks. She purchased six large 16-oz bottles of clear dishwashing soap.

The clever cutie left the Lowes location and walked to an art store nearby. There she got two 1-lb bottles of red and one bottle of black Tempera Paint. After that, it was into a supermarket to get a bottle of liquid starch. Ariella got home at eight o'clock that night and went to her workshop with the ingredients to make her 'Witches Brew'.

- The two 1-lb bottles of red Tempera Paint Powder were dumped into one of the plastic buckets.
- Then four 16-oz bottles of clear dishwashing soap were emptied into the same bucket.
- After that she poured in half the bottle of liquid starch.
- Finally, one cup of water was added.

These components were all mixed together, and after three minutes of stirring, it had the consistency of ketchup. This could be thinned down by adding more water. The lid was put securely on the bucket to make sure the compound would not dry out. Now it was time to create the specially formulated black paint. She needed a smaller volume than the red, but the proportions and procedures were the same.

- The 1-lb bottle of black Tempera Paint Powder was poured into the other plastic bucket.
- Then she added the two 16-oz bottles of clear dishwashing soap.
- After that came half the balance of the liquid starch.
- Finally, half a cup of water was tipped in.

Using a clean wooden paint stick she combined these ingredients together like before. When it was all thoroughly integrated, the lid was placed on the bucket and both mixtures were now ready for the next day.

Ariella went back into the house in time to watch a nine o'clock TV show. Purdy curled up on her lap and they fell asleep in the living room. It was almost eleven o'clock when she woke up, turned off all the lights, and dragged herself to bed.

Tomorrow was going to be another exciting day!

CHAPTER 22

After arriving at Woodward's Auto Center and before getting out of the Subaru, Ariella took her garage door remote control off the visor and put this into her handbag. Then, exiting her car, proceeded to the front office.

"Good morning," said Harry warmly.

"Hello, Harry!" Ariella genuinely liked him and knew he would have the compact car ready. Any male would do whatever she wanted because virtually every normal man was instantly taken by her beauty. "I appreciate you making a loaner available to me while you service my vehicle."

He got straight down to business. "Let's talk about the Buick first. You requested I sell it and I managed to do so with just one phone call this morning! I was surprised to find someone willing to pay me $3,800 plus the sales tax. This is a good price considering it is quite old. As discussed, we were to split the proceeds 50/50 and while I will not have the buyer's money until Monday, I can give you a check for $1,900 right now. I also have the license plates for you."

"Well, thank you. I could sure do with these funds." Ariella was careful with her finances now and would be just as cautious in the future to never let on there was a fortune in jewelry hidden away at her house. She really understood, one major mistake thieves make is to start flashing their greenbacks around. They buy fancy cars, clothes, appliances, boats, and so on, and tend to live high on the hog.

"I have the Chevy ready for you to use today and I had my guys wash it. I have filled the tank with gas, and you do not have to worry about topping it up when you return it."

"I will try to put gas in it before I give it back to you, but if I cannot, I will leave you some cash. Here are the keys to the Subaru. You of course know it needs an oil change, the tires must be rotated, and it requires its annual inspection. Like before, just mail me an invoice and I will send a check."

"Okay, I will do that." He handed her the keys to the Chevy and gave her the Buick's old license plates C31 FPO. "I will have the loaner back to you by tonight or by early tomorrow. If I am not here at five o'clock today, leave the Subaru in the back with the keys under the front floor mat.

She left the office and walked directly to the silver two-door which was out in front. Driving slowly from the parking lot, she got acclimated to this coupe, which had a somewhat different feel to her car. At a small electronics shop near her home, she purchased a burner phone, then stopped by a parcel shipping store and bought seven small cartons each 8" deep x 10" inches across and 16" wide.

It was almost nine twenty when she approached her house and turned into her driveway, opened the garage door with the remote control, and driving right in, shut off the engine and closed the door.

Ariella went inside the house for a quick look around and found Purdy fast asleep lying on a windowsill in the living room. Oh, to live the life of a cat!

The young lady went back into the garage and took a roll of 2" blue painter's tape off one of the shelves. She perused the Chevy, and then starting on the left-hand side from the bottom of the front plastic bumper, ran a length of tape past the two radiator vents and over the hood all the way to the windshield. With a ruler, she measured a distance of 4" from the first strip and lightly marked this with a pencil in a few places on the hood, then took another section of tape and placed this 4" away, parallel to the first band. The outside edges of both strips were thus 8" apart.

Climbing up on a small ladder she proceeded to run additional parallel lengths of painter's tape over the roof and then across the trunk and down to the end of the rear plastic bumper. The car now looked like it had two blue 2" racing stripes on it. But the blue ribbons were only there temporarily, that is until the color-changing task was completed.

Ariella put some old newspapers on the floor next to the sedan and partially under it. Then she got the bucket with the red tincture, prepared the night before, and using a 2" wide brush and starting at the back right-hand bumper, proceeded to hand-paint the Chevy. She went around the entire car focusing only on painting the extremities, next to the windows, outlining the lights, around the license plates, and so on.

By the areas with the blue tape, she slowly made her way along the outer limits of this. After about fifty minutes of deliberate work, the initial edging was all done and the 2" brush was washed in the small garage sink.

Ariella went inside the house for a brief rest and to grab a soda to drink. About ten minutes later it was time to go back into the garage to continue with the important task. Now a 4" wide brush was used to colorize the large open areas. Being the middle of summer, the air was very warm, and the sweat was dripping off her brow, even though the two garage windows were open. At one point a floor fan was turned on by her, and that helped to make things a bit cooler.

Two hours later she was done altering the silver to red. The brush was rinsed off with water and Ariella went inside for something to eat, and to drink another ice-cold soda. The talented tigress knew the color coat would dry rather quickly in this hot weather. Getting a small compact car from Harry was a good idea, it was certainly better than trying to change up the larger old Buick.

It was 1:25 p.m. and the process continued. The red was already dry, so she was able to carefully peel up the blue painter's tape. The Chevy was now red all over but sporting an 8" wide silver stripe from front to back. Of course, the red finish was dull and lifeless, and even slightly streaky in places. But this was not important for the way in which this automobile was going to be used later.

To alter the last of the silver color, it was time to use the black composite, made the previous night. Again, using a 2" brush, she started very carefully working along the edge where the silver ended, and the new red emulsion began. Because Ariella's mixture would only adhere temporarily to metal and plastic, she could not mask the red in any way or it would have lifted upon removal of the tape. So instead, the black Tempera concoction was applied in a free-hand manner.

It would not matter if this 8" wide portion was not perfect or a bit wavy in places, and she slowly proceeded to paint the edges in black from the front to the back. Then using the 4" brush and being very careful not to drip any over the red areas, more of the black was added to the middle section.

Almost an hour later it was 2:30 p.m. and the task was done. What now existed was a red car with an 8" wide black racing stripe. The last thing to do would be to work on the license plates.

Sitting on a high stool at the workbench in her garage, the Buick's C31 FPO license plates were now in front of her.

Using a fine artist's brush and a small amount of the black solution, she proceeded to alter the letters and numbers on the plates where C31 FPO was transformed to become O84 EBC. The "C31" easily became "O" "8" and "4". The "F" was turned into an "E" and the "P" became a "B".

For the "O" to become the "C" a tiny part of the letter needed to be blocked out in white. To create this white color, she made some thick paste out of flour and water and thus evolved the letter "C" from the "O". With this white paste, the tiny tail on the top of the #1 was covered so the #4 would have a cleaner look. The changeover was done, O84 EBC.

At that point using a screwdriver, the dealer plates were removed from the front and back of the Chevy and these were replaced with the now-altered plates from the Buick. The loaner car was ready for its Friday night adventure! Ariella took both buckets and poured their water-soluble contents down the drain and thereafter washed them out with water. No trace of the liquid Tempera mixture existed anymore.

The brainy beauty walked into her backyard with a garden trowel and a plastic food bowl. She dug up some soil, put this into the container, and came back inside. Using a stainless-steel strainer from her kitchen, the soil was sifted onto some newspaper until it was a little pile, then lifting the newspaper, this fine material was dropped into the bowl.

She added four heaped teaspoons of instant coffee powder to the earth in the small tub and then mixed this with water until there was a wet, muddy, thick slurry.

Ariella got an almost empty window-cleaning spray bottle, tipped out the liquid, and rinsed this with water. Then she poured in the brown solution, added some water to further dilute it, and shook it vigorously for ten seconds. This was tested by her spritzing some of its contents onto white paper. In seconds the paper had a grimy, mucky appearance.

"Awesome," was her enthusiastic comment. "The dirtier the better!" She put the spray bottle and a 4" paintbrush into the trunk of the car. This would all be very important for her to use in the evening.

◆◆◆◆◆

It was 3:40 p.m. and much of Ariella's preparation for her upcoming expedition was completed, but there was still a bit more to do. She tidied the garage and went inside to make a cheese and tomato sandwich and have a cup of tea. After that, Purdy was given a little more food. It was still overcast outside like it had been all day. At that point, the weather forecast on TV showed it would remain cloudy, with rain starting around 11:00 p.m.

"That should be okay. Now I need to begin getting the packages ready." Her words were barely audible.

This was delivery night when some of the spoils would be given to customers who were cheated out of major amounts of jewelry by Barnwell. It was great that Leyland briefly left on Ariella's desk his *List of Ten Suspects* the night of Thursday, July 7th. It showed the names, addresses, and phone numbers of these people. How fortuitous that she took a picture of this list with her phone before Leyland grabbed it back. Now the *List of Ten Suspects* could be put to good use.

There were written notes next to each name, and three including that of Raquel Santos Gomez had lines through them, meaning Wakefield did not consider these to be people of interest or perhaps they couldn't be found.

But next to seven names was written 'Very Upset Customer'. Ariella's name was one of these seven so that left six people who could be helped. The addresses by each name showed they all lived not too far away and in the general geographic area. After forwarding the list to her computer it was printed onto paper. She now had a hard copy of details regarding the individuals to be visited. The picture on her phone was then deleted as was the email on her computer.

It was ten-past-four when Ariella went into her garage and came out with a five-foot metal pole and her rechargeable drill with the star screwdriver bit attached in its chuck. She did not want to retrieve the precious products while it was still light outside, but this had to be done now because as much time as possible was needed for delivery in the evening.

Fortunately, her backyard was very secluded and because of the high wooden fence, adjacent neighbors could see very little of her property unless they came right up to the slats to peer in. It was obvious there was no one around, so she went to work removing the eight screws which held down the wooden landing platform outside her kitchen door.

The canny creature propped up this plywood piece with the metal pole by having its base up against the inside of the hiding space and jamming it into the U-shaped metal handle, attached by her to the underside of the wooden landing a few weeks before. She was now able to reach down to where all was hidden and took hold of one of the two large cartons which contained the jewelry. She heaved it up and carried it into the house putting it down on the living room floor. Ariella returned for the second carton, brought this in and went back again for the box which contained the various disguises.

She walked out one more time, disengaged the metal pole from the handle, and leaving it in the secret compartment, lowered the platform back into position. It was temporarily tightened in place with just two of the eight screws, then she came in, locked the kitchen door, and closed the living room curtains so no one from outside could see in. With white cotton gloves on her hands, it was time to get started.

Over the next hour and a half, Ariella divided the jewelry into six different lots: For each, there were eight watches, the same number of diamond rings, necklaces, earrings, gold chains, and so on. Trying to be fair, she balanced the stacks as best as possible with similar-sized items. A seventh pile was created for her. If the police came asking, it would be important she too received some recompense from a 'Good Samaritan'. In case they were to confiscate it, her assortment was much smaller than the others.

Besides the seventh lot being hers, in addition, Ariella kept back about one-third of the total haul. She figured her grandmother's pieces were valued at more than $500,000 and what the other six victims would receive could be worth at least $150,000 for each. Because she had no idea what Barnwell stole from them, the hope was that whatever they got would make up for some or more of what was lost.

Ariella went into the kitchen and came back with a handful of large zip-top bags. Every pile filled six of these bags. She took the boxes purchased in the morning, being 8" deep by 10" across and 16" wide, and these were assembled with clear packing tape. Before too long on her living room carpet there were six corrugated cartons all the same size, each containing six poly bags filled with glitzy goods. A seventh was also there and this one would be addressed to her.

With the white cotton gloves remaining on her hands, she went into the study and turned on her computer. An information note was composed, seven copies were printed, and one was to be placed in each box. These letters were addressed individually to the six people, and one was directed to her. Other than a name change, they read as follows:

Dear Ms. Margaret Searle,

It is our understanding, in the recent past you were cheated or in some way robbed by Mr. Huntington Barnwell of the Fourth Street

Jewelers and Gold Exchange. Our Group of Justice Seekers became aware he was doing this to people in the area and decided we would no longer allow it to continue. While many people were victims of his treachery, there were a few such as yourself who suffered a substantial loss. Please accept this package as a means for you to at least get back part of what you may have lost. If this is too much, you might wish to donate to a worthy cause a portion of the excess from the proceeds received should you sell any items.

Sincerely, The Justice Seekers.

Important: Please tell no one about this carton. If word gets out, the police could well confiscate this jewelry and similar packages from other recipients. If they come calling, it will be best for you to deny receiving this because they might take it (and who knows, keep some of it for themselves.) Put it into a secure place and do not get a safe deposit box in a nearby bank. Rather go out-of-town to do so. Wait at least 6 months before you decide to dispose of anything and then only sell one or two items at a time. Again, only deal with pawn shops or similar stores which are out of the area. It may be best not to unload any goods online.

From her computer, Ariella made a label relating to the name and address of each person and made one for herself. Below this information, it read:

HIGHLY CONFIDENTIAL.
To be opened ONLY by the person whose name is printed here.

She would try to deliver these personally and could then explain the details of the enclosed letter. But if a parcel was to be left at someone's house because they were not there, then the note on its own would suffice. Each address label was matched to the name on the letter inside. As awkward as it was wearing the cotton gloves while assembling and closing the boxes with the clear packing tape, she certainly did not want to leave her fingerprints behind which would show up very well on sticky tape or on the back of self-adhering labels!

Six of the seven packages were carried to the Chevy in the garage. Some were put on the passenger-side front seat and others on the floor of the car. From the carton of disguises, out came the hairpiece for the 'Mandy' look, a grey wig with long hair, and an attachable short grey beard. She also took the pair of black-framed glasses and the other more delicate pair of red-framed glasses.

The remainder of the jewelry was consolidated into one large, corrugated container, sealed shut, and together with the box of disguises was carried out the rear door. She undid the two screws which were holding down the wooden landing, lifted it, and propped it up with the metal pole. Picking up the two cartons, these were put back where they belonged. She put the metal pole down inside the secret space and lowered the large wooden cover. Using her rechargeable drill, the plywood piece was screwed down tightly with all eight screws.

The balance of the haul was now hidden away, all of which was justifiably hers. The Heistess became an Heiress.

Once back inside she took off her gloves and with a knife, cut the tape to open the package which was addressed to her. Every zip-seal bag was handled by her, putting her fingerprints on all four of them. She opened the wall safe and inside it, placed the plastic bags and the note addressed to her. If the police came, her story would be that she found it on her front porch and locked the contents away. The empty box was left in her garage where it could easily be seen. Her feeling was the authorities would only be suspicious if her fingerprints were *not* on the box, the plastic bags, and the note.

This sorting and packing began around four o'clock and it was now five thirty, almost time to go on her night's mission. Ariella again did an online search for the telephone number of the Atlantic Consolidated Insurance Corporation in New York City and wrote this on a piece of paper. Using the burner phone, she called the number. It was now Friday evening, and a recording could be heard instructing after-hours callers to leave a message. She said nothing and simply ended the call, then cleared her computer's search history.

Ariella went into her 'Word' program and created in a large font, the information which would be left on the Atlantic Consolidated phone system that night, and in the wording the Toyota's license plate number was included. This message was printed on paper and placed in her pocket. The Heistess then removed from her computer the letters written to the other victims, she also deleted the carton labels and the message just typed regarding the insurance company.

It was now time for the 'Mandy Moore' disguise, but this time she would use the name 'Jane Bradford'. Ariella put on the short black wig, darkened her eyebrows, and added the brown contact lenses, but left off the beauty spot. When at the police precinct with Roger, the report from the officer who stopped her early in the morning of July 4th, referenced this beauty mark. She did not want it to be referred to again by any of the people being called on.

Like before, to cover her fingerprints, Ariella painted the underside of her fingers with New Skin and waved her hands around to allow the solution to dry. All packages could now be handled in front of the recipients and none of her prints would be left in their homes. She could not take the chance someone might call the police after her departure.

Into a paper shopping bag went a flashlight, the black-framed and red-framed glasses, and the grey wig-and-beard disguise. She left her regular cell phone at home, so there would be no GPS tracking or record of being out of her house or what her destinations were that night. Ariella took a hard copy of the *List of Ten Suspects* so she could have with her the details of the six people receiving the packages.

Miss think-of-everything, gathered up two old, small hand towels from the laundry closet, grabbed the burner phone, and a $10.00 bill from her purse. Ariella took her driver's license with her and $250 in cash, plus some additional money in case of an emergency.

She went to the garage and picked up the dealer license plates and a screwdriver, and put these into the trunk of the car next to the spray bottle with its muddy mixture and the 4" paint brush left there earlier. Then, getting into the red-and-black Chevy, she placed the $10.00 bill into the center console where it would be handy for when it was needed. It was almost six o'clock as she drove away.

◆◆◆◆◆

Looking at the *List of Ten Suspects*, Ariella decided to go to the person who lived the longest distance away as the first call. Twenty-five minutes after leaving her house she got to the home of Mrs. Margaret Searle. Using the burner phone, she dialed the number. A female voice answered.

"Is this Margaret Searle?" The astute actress's English accent sounded very distinguished.

"Yes, it is. Who is speaking?"

"My name is Jane Bradford, and I am with a citizen's group called The Justice Seekers. We help victims of crimes."

"I have not been hurt by any crime." Margaret had some concern in her voice thinking this was a type of scam.

"Well, our records show you were swindled out of a lot of money by the Fourth Street Jewelers and Gold Exchange."

"Oh yes, we were taken for over $100,000 but there is no way you or anyone else can help me. My husband is very ill, and we urgently needed whatever cash we could have obtained for our jewelry and gold coins. But our stuff is all gone, and we are really struggling now." Sounding frustrated and almost desperate, she added, "By the way, that exchange owner recently got robbed and it serves him right!"

"My group broke into the store and took many valuable items to provide to people who were cheated out of their money by Mr. Barnwell. I have about $150,000 in jewelry to give you, if you are willing to accept this."

Without hesitation Margaret replied, "Of course we will take it! We cannot cover our medical bills and we are about to lose our house! When can you get this to me? Wait, is this a trick or a con? Is this real?"

"I assure you it is no hoax. I am parked outside your house right now. Will it be okay if I come inside to see you?"

"Yes… well… all right. You may come in." Margaret sounded scared and skeptical, and one could not blame her.

Ariella picked up the appropriate box and walked down the brick pathway onto the front porch. She was about to knock when a silver-haired lady opened the door.

"Please come in." Mrs. Searle stared past her to make sure that no one else was about to barge in.

Once inside, Ariella followed from the hallway into the living room. It was sparsely furnished with old, well-worn furniture. The woman told the visitor to please call her Maggie and asked her to sit down. It was at that point Ariella noticed an overweight old man standing at the entrance to the living room, holding a baseball bat.

"It's okay George, this young gal means no harm! Now what do you have in that box you are holding?"

Other than carrying it in, the benevolent beauty did not want to run the risk of her fingerprints appearing on the box or its contents or have the packing tape lift the New Skin off her fingers. She handed the carton to Maggie who opened it immediately and placed the polybags on the living room table. The lady and her husband could see the bags were stuffed with diamond rings, watches, pendants, and more.

"Is this legal?" Her eyes were wide with amazement.

"No, it is not legal!" The English accent sounded somewhat authoritative.

"The Justice Seekers whom I represent, broke into Barnwell's store to help his victims get compensated for what he stole from them. There is a note in here and I would ask you to please read it carefully. It suggests you keep a low profile and do not sell anything locally. If you wish to dispose of some things, do so only a few items at a time. Tell no one about my visit or that you even have this jewelry. Hide it in a safe place."

Ariella could see tears coming to the sweet woman's eyes. Even her husband seemed to be tearing up.

"Oh, my child, bless you! We thank you from the bottom of our hearts."

"The police might find out that customers such as you received a package like this one. If they ever come to question you, please deny you ever got this."

"Don't you worry, we will keep this all safe and secure and we will never tell a soul. An officer was already here grilling us, but he could see we had not a bit to do with the break-in and I am sure he won't be back."

Ariella stood up and gave Maggie a hug, nodded to George, and then left. It was 6:50 p.m. when she was once again in her car and on her way to the next address on the list, the home of Miss Lyn Eccles. Not ten minutes later the red and black Chevy was parked outside a rather old three-story apartment building. Ariella made a call from the burner phone and a female's voice answered. The conversation was not too different from the one with Maggie some thirty-five minutes earlier. Soon she was ringing the bell.

When the door opened, the Heistess was surprised to see a woman in a wheelchair, who was likely in her early thirties but looked much older.

"Hello, Miss Eccles, I am Jane Bradford." The English accent sounded very charming.

"Please call me Lyn and do come inside." From her sitting position, Lyn shook Ariella's hand, closed the door, and wheeled herself into the dining room. "What is this about you bringing back my family heirlooms?"

"Well, what I have here is almost certainly not what was taken from you. This is random but very valuable jewelry that my group took in the recent burglary at the Fourth Street Jewelers and Gold Exchange. This could all be worth around $150,000." The box was handed to Lyn who opened it and then proceeded to put the various zip-top bags onto her dining room table.

Lyn's face lit up. "What? $150,000! I think you have just saved me. As you can see, I am handicapped, I was born with a defect that makes walking difficult but not impossible for me. With my wheelchair I can get around reasonably well and I am able to drive in my specially equipped vehicle. However, my father doesn't have much money and lives two hours away. When my mother died a year ago, my dad gave me all her gold and silver assets including her diamond ring and other sentimental items." She stopped to take a breath.

"Go on," said Ariella, now beginning to realize from the first visit and this time again, that her 'Robin Hood' actions were very important.

"My father said, to help sustain myself I should sell some of the items. I do work, you know... I provide computer-based copywriting for a few companies, but this is all freelance and my income is very sporadic. I did not intend to sell everything, but when that thief Mr. Barnwell came here, he insisted on taking my stuff to evaluate it. He then claimed it was not worth much and he paid me very little for what I know had a value of perhaps $120,000."

Ariella reached over and held her hand. She could see tears beginning to well up in Lyn's eyes. "The group with which I am affiliated has heard similar stories from others." She was now thinking of Maggie Searle and her own nana.

"As I said, you have saved me. When everything got stolen, I dared not tell my dad. If I told him, being the hothead he is, he would have shot Barnwell or something like that. He is very protective of me and endured a hard life because of my condition."

Ariella discussed the note which was in the package and then added, "Please hide it all carefully and never admit to the police if they come calling that I was here, or you were given anything like this from anyone."

"My father made me open a safe deposit box when he gave me my mother's gold necklaces, diamond pendants, and other items of value. I will get everything locked away there. Do not worry, there is no record of me having this bank box. The invoice for its annual fee goes to his address so no one knows I even have a secure place where I can stow what you have brought me, before I sell some of it."

They spoke for another couple of minutes then gave each other a hug. Ariella walked to the door to leave.

"How can I ever thank you? Where can I find you in the future? I would love to have you as a friend."

"I need to remain anonymous for now. But do not worry, one day I will be in touch with you when my associates and I are sure this has blown over. I am pleased to be of help." Then it was all about going downstairs to the badly painted red car with its black racing stripe.

The time was seven twenty-three and the next address was not too far away. She stopped outside a modest home at 425 Farrell Avenue. Looking at the slightly overgrown lawn and the peeling paintwork on the house, she called the telephone number and spoke to Byron Landers.

Within two minutes, Ariella was in his living room. Byron was an elderly man whose wife passed away a few years back. He had all but outlived his retirement money and, like Maggie Searle and Lyn Eccles, was in dire financial straits. He could barely keep up with his debts and other obligations. Barnwell stole from him about $140,000 in coins, watches, diamond rings, and other items.

Ariella's discussion with him went much along the lines of the first two stops. Byron Landers was overwhelmed by what this gracious gal brought him. The same "you have saved my life" sentiment expressed by the other two, was again told to her.

By seven fifty she was on her way to the home of Frank and Cathy Hollister. Here too was a couple who could hardly make ends meet and after hearing their story, they were left with their gift of joy.

A short while later she arrived at Vera Appleby's apartment and could not believe this was another person who was down and out like the others. Yet again, Ariella was able to give an old lady hope for the future.

It was almost ten minutes to nine and time for the sixth and final home which was located at 22 Pinebrook Street. The sky was starting to darken earlier than usual because of the cloudy conditions. She called first, and a few minutes later was standing on the porch of the house belonging to Miriam and Stan Connolly. They very cautiously opened the front door and after a brief discussion, decided to let her in.

Ariella listened to their situation about Barnwell robbing them of over $250,000 in jewelry and other items. While they did not appear to be too badly off, she was able to deduce Hunt's dastardly actions put a large dent into their retirement assets. During her talk with them, Stan said he needed to go to the bathroom.

But he was not headed there. He slipped out the back door and walked to the front gate, hoping their guest would not spot him in the low-light conditions outside. He scribbled down her license plate number and thought, "If this Jane Bradford is running around with a fortune in jewelry, why does she have this awful badly painted car?"

Stan Connolly took a snapshot of the auto with his cell phone and told himself this woman needs to be investigated. He was well-connected at the local precinct.

It was 9:18 p.m. when Ariella left their home, pleased that over the past few hours, she was able to right some of the wrongs caused by the unscrupulous jewelry store owner.

After she drove away, Miriam and Stan discussed the visitor. Stanley picked up the zip-seal bags and took it all to the well-hidden safe in the floorboards of his study. The way the floor opened, the safe was undetectable. As they were instructed, the couple felt they would deny that anyone dropped off a box of valuables at their home, if the police ever showed up. Except Stan was about to call them!

About fifteen minutes later, Miriam went to the bedroom to get ready to go to sleep. Stan meanwhile went downstairs and called his friend who worked at the Averton P.D. Yes, he and his wife were handed a fortune, but this woman, with what could be a fake British accent, should be found and arrested, especially if she was part of the gang which stole the jewelry. Ever since the break-in took place, everyone in the immediate area was on edge, not knowing if their homes or businesses were about to be pillaged.

"Hello Leyland, this is Stan."

"Oh hi, old buddy! What can I do for you?"

"I noticed a strange suspicious car prowling around our neighborhood, you know, the Pinebrook Street area."

"Did you get a good look at it?"

"Oh yes, I have some details and I will text you a picture because this car stopped briefly outside our house. It is a red two-door small Chevy with a black racing stripe. The license plate is O84 EBC. I even got a good look at the woman driver. She is white, has short dark hair, and wears what might be red-framed glasses."

"That is great information. A red two-door Chevy with a black stripe will be easy to find especially since we have some street cameras on main roads in the area."

"Great! Glad I could be a good citizen."

Stan decided not to provide more details such as her height, slender build, and that she had brown eyes. This type of detail would not be something anyone could see from simply glancing at a person who was driving through a neighborhood. He didn't want Leyland to know she just dropped off a pile of bedazzlements at their home. But now all was hidden away, so he did not care if they arrested her and then found she was part of a larger theft ring. He might even get the reward being offered. Now that would be fantastic!

After texting a picture of the car to Leyland, Stan walked to the living room to watch a couple of boring television shows.

◆◆◆◆◆

Ariella arrived at a nearby fast-food restaurant in downtown Averton and went to the drive-up to get a burger, fries, and a soda. From there, she went to the 'skid-row' part of town. This is where the homeless, derelicts, and drug pushers tended to hang out. Driving slowly, first down one narrow road and then up another, the Heistess was hoping to find a specific person to make a phone call for her. Every now and again an individual would stumble out of an alley or would look up from the large piece of cardboard on which they were lying.

After turning onto Carson Lane, she noticed a tall man pushing a shopping cart in the middle of the street. He was walking not too far from the corner which intersected with a main thoroughfare, and this was good for making a quick getaway if needed. The red and black Chevy stopped, and he turned around to look at it.

"Perrdon mayy, I need yearr' help." Ariella's broad Scottish brogue was the accent this time. With the New Skin shielding her fingerprints, the fast-food bag was held out the window with its tasty dinner inside. He saw it and came scurrying over.

She continued, "Heer, this is feerr yeeu. What's yearr name?" He had a weathered but kindly face with hazel eyes.

"My name is Timothy," he answered promptly. "I like your accent. Are you from Scotland?"

"Aye! I hail froom Sco'land! I am visiting feerr a wee period, just a cooople o' weeks." The more misinformation that could be put out there, the better it would be if anyone ever dug into this part of her plan. "Tell mayy, can yeeu' rreeed?"

He smiled. "I used to be a schoolteacher before drugs and alcohol cost me my wife, my children and my life." His words were a bit slurred. The liquor still had a hold on him.

Ariella thought, how sad for this man, but was pleased he could read and that he was a little drunk. He would likely remember very little by the following day.

"I ceean pay yeeu' $250 if yeeu' leave a message on someone's phone feerr mayy. This is tooo help sooolve a crraime."

"You will pay me $250? Sure, I can assist you! What do you want me to do?"

As he stood next to her car window on this potholed road, Ariella did not feel there was any real danger. The engine was running as she looked ahead and in the rear-view mirror, noticing there was no one else wandering around. Timothy took the paper with its specific wording, set up in large twenty-four-point type. She shone her flashlight onto the paper to help him see properly because the streetlights only provided minimal visibility.

"Oh, nice big lettering, I can easily say what is on this sheet," he said smiling. "Here we go." In his gruff, slurred, and stumbling way, he did a test run of the few lines which were well prepared.

"Goood. Now let mayy' call this pear-son and yeeu leave the voice-meell."

She dialed the New York City number for the Atlantic Consolidated Insurance Corporation and listened while the after-hours message introduction started and ended. Ariella did not want Timothy to hear the name of the business, but as soon as the beep sounded, she handed him the cell phone and he once again read from the piece of paper:

"*This is a message for Mr. Renfrew. The New Jersey jewelry store robbery was done by… done by the owner and a female accomplice… I was able to see them doing it on the night of July 3rd. I saw them putting some of the jewelry in the trunk of a white… a white car and I even got the plate number. It is K14 YRW.*"

Ariella purposefully made the wording sound like it was coming from someone who knew a bit about the break-in but did not know too much about the Insurance Company by not addressing it to 'Mr. Hillman'. She also made sure the date being stated was the night of July 3rd, the time when the Subaru was not at her house. From this recording, the police would soon have Barbara's license plate number.

The first time Timothy read the script in the practice run it was fine, but this time he was unsure and hesitated a bit more due to nervousness. Now that the message was read, she took the phone and pushed the red button to end the call.

"Do you want me to do it over?" he asked, embarrassed because of the way he faltered.

"Oooh nooo! Yeeu weeeer pear-fect! Heeer is $250 fer yeeu! Thank yeeu fer yearr help."

Holding the bag of food and the unexpected cash he thanked her and walked away. Ariella started moving the car forward but stopped after about twenty feet. She got out and put the burner phone on the ground by the left front wheel then got back inside and rode over it. After that, the crushed plastic pieces were retrieved, and the Scottish lass drove away.

She briefly thought, "I did the accent quite well! Edinburgh and Glasgow, here I come!"

Her tasks for the night were almost done, but there was one most important visit, and this was a special venue on Bridge Avenue.

It was close to ten o'clock when Ariella turned from Carson Lane onto Second Street and began driving to Bridge Avenue which was close by. Suddenly she noticed the flashing lights of a police cruiser in her rear-view mirror. This car was quite far away but the officer was alerted by the desk sergeant at the precinct, who had just spotted the red and black Chevy on one of the few cameras which existed in the downtown area.

Ariella yelled out loud, "Are they after *me?* How can they know what I have been up to tonight? Who would have told them?" Then it occurred to her, this easily recognizable automobile probably appeared on a monitoring device.

The cruiser was currently about eight blocks back, but it was going at a high rate of speed and was of course gaining on her. To have any hope of escaping she needed to get to her next vital destination, which was just over two blocks away and it seemed Ariella might not make it there before the cops were able to stop her. This time she very well could be caught.

CHAPTER 23

While Ariella was visiting the victims of Barnwell's treachery and giving out packages of plenty, Hunt and Barbara were meeting again as they continued with their affair. He arrived at her apartment, they hugged and kissed, and then she put a small dinner together. Barnwell brought along a bottle of wine and filled two glasses with part of its contents.

Before too long they were sitting down to eat and that is when she brought him up to date about what had transpired since the shopping bag was left in the flowerpot. Barbara told him she met with Ariella this past Tuesday night here at her apartment and how her guest appeared to be very anxious and scared of the police. Barbara explained, this nervous nellie strongly denied having any connection to the break-in and admitted being questioned the day before at the precinct regarding new information that came up, and her lawyer was present at the interview.

"I think they grilled her about the jewelry which they discovered on her porch. I believe having a lawyer there to help her, is what has kept her out of jail... for now. I am under the impression with the strong evidence which was found on her property it is only a matter of time before she is arrested."

Hunt nodded. "Yes. I agree. It will be great when they bring charges against the bitch. Even without the goods which you planted it is my belief she took part in this crime perhaps with a group of smart, professional thieves."

Barbara was pleased to hear him say that, for she was convinced *he* was somehow involved, and that he ransacked his own place of business. In her mind, although Ariella spoke at one point about getting all her grandmother's goods back by breaking into the store, Barbara was not certain her close acquaintance did this. Well at least not on her own.

"Don't worry, honey," said Barbara, "I am sure because of what was found at her house, they are really watching her now. Since she is most likely in cahoots with a theft ring, they must be gleaning all kinds of information off her cell phone and from emails."

"We have to get this resolved. The police must make an arrest soon because I need to get the insurance money."

"So, my love, what gift did you bring me tonight besides the wine?" She changed the subject and now put on her soft sexy voice hoping Hunt would be showering her with more bright adornments.

From his jacket pocket, he took out a little box. In it were a pair of diamond earrings and a gold necklace with a platinum octagon containing a large emerald, surrounded by smaller faceted green chips. "Here sweetheart."

Barbara cried out with a delightful "Wow"!

As soon as Hunt secured it in place, he kissed her. She wanted him for the money and gifts, and he wanted this attractive twenty-something as his girlfriend, or at least as one of his girlfriends! She continued tolerating him being such a revolting character, to get as much as possible out of him for as long as she was able to do so.

◆◆◆◆◆

Also, at six-thirty on that same Friday evening while Ariella was making her deliveries and while Barbara and her lover were having dinner at her apartment, Roger Riley was still in Philadelphia where he had been since Tuesday, working at his one major client, QP Holdings Incorporated.

The main focus of this company was that it operated in the rock-crushing industry, and it owned three quarries. Two were in Pennsylvania and one was in Ohio. Right now, they were in the process of acquiring a $15 million per year family-owned stone mining business in West Virginia and Roger had piles of work to do regarding finalizing the deal.

But he also enjoyed coming to Philadelphia for his girlfriend of two years, twenty-six-year-old Sheila Rhodes. Her multi-millionaire father, Anthony Rhodes, owned this very successful company. Sheila was in no way attractive… and was definitely no oil painting! But she came from an immensely wealthy family so what was lacking in beauty she more than made up for in money. Ever since the handsome and charming Roger met her, he pursued her due to the potential 'Pot-of-Gold' he could gain if they ever got married.

Sheila loved it, because being seen with this stud at the many functions which she attended, was a great morale booster for her. But once Roger met Ariella, confusion reigned. Should he go after money and eventually a very plain wife or a sexy beauty who had not much by way of assets?

The QP Holdings acquisition was going to be a big payday for him. He could well earn over $75,000 in legal fees and this was vital income for him. His small one-man-show law firm in New Jersey was not generating enough for him.

Roger, like many young professionals in their mid-thirties, was living way beyond his means. His costly BMW was leased, he resided in an expensive apartment and dressed to the nines. He hinted at marriage with Sheila a couple of times, but she ignored him on that subject. Besides, her parents did not like him, and they told her to be careful because all he might be interested in was the family fortune.

Anthony Rhodes gave some of the legal work for this acquisition to Roger with much trepidation and only at the insistence of Sheila who was recently put onto the Board of Directors of QP Holdings. Anthony was not keen on his daughter's boyfriend, and while this fellow might be reasonably competent, he was just too suave, and too slick. But Anthony finally gave in, just to appease his daughter.

And now at the end of the day, Roger arrived at Sheila's large rooftop apartment after working in the QP corporate offices for many hours. She got the barbeque ready on the outside verandah and set a table for two with a good bottle of wine. Roger was asked to grill the steaks and he was happy to do so.

He liked cooking and was looking forward to dinner with this wealthy woman and then romping in bed with her. But as had happened lately, while making love to his Philadelphia girlfriend all he could do was imagine he was with his New Jersey nymph.

Sheila was keeping busy in the kitchen when she saw Roger's phone on the table. Her curiosity caused her to start scrolling first through his phone calls and then his text messages. She noticed that contact with an 'Ariella Gerson' came up frequently – in fact, way too often. Sheila wrote down the name and phone number and decided to Google this female, to find out what this was all about.

After having dinner together, Sheila and her beau ended up in bed for an evening of mediocre lovemaking.

CHAPTER 24

That Same Friday Night, July 15th at 10:04 p.m.

The police cruiser was going after Ariella, who was driving like crazy to an important locale on Bridge Avenue. Again, her rear-view mirror showed there were two cars on Second Street a few blocks back, both going in her direction. One had already slowed down and was pulling over to make way for the hot pursuit, but the flashing lights had not yet reached the other one. This helped to obscure the red and black Chevy just a bit.

The officer giving chase was directly in touch with the precinct. "I am quite far behind a red two-door with a black racing stripe which is likely the vehicle reported in the Pinebrook Street area, the one with the fake license plates. This could be the same car that was seen on some of our downtown cameras, and it just turned out of the drug-infested Carson Lane. I am currently going south on Second Street."

"Stay on it, Oscar. This is a woman driver so use kid gloves when you apprehend her because the department does not want to get sued over some false accusation. We are sending backup, but that is still a couple of minutes out."

"Ten Four, I will catch up to this offender soon."

Ariella turned off the Chevy's lights, knowing this was an older model and hoping the lights would not remain on while the car was in motion like they do on newer autos. This assumption was correct. Relying only on sparse and not-too-bright streetlamps to see where she was going, driving became difficult. However, Bridge Avenue was now very close, and the ambient low-light conditions were providing her with some semblance of cover.

Ariella activated her turn signal to show the car would be going left, hoping the pursuing officer would see the left-turning flasher from way back where he was. She braked a bit to slow down then pulled her foot off the brake and cancelled the turn signal, swinging to the right instead, still going faster than ever to take the corner.

By not using her brakes rounding the corner, this prevented the brake lights from coming on, and hopefully, the policeman who was about four blocks behind, would not realize this dull-colored car made a right onto Bridge Avenue and not a left turn. There was still one other auto in between them, and that driver was now in the process of slowing down to let the siren-blasting vehicle pass him.

As the ravishing racer took the high-speed, wide turn, the Chevy's tires squealed in protest and the car lurched violently, coming close to rolling over. It went totally to the other side of the road barely missing the sidewalk curbing. What a relief to see there were no cars parked or any coming the other way.

She made it around the corner and was now tearing toward the critical Bridge Avenue venue. The Chevy was one hundred yards out, then fifty, then twenty-five and now it was at the automatic car wash. Ariella forced the steering wheel hard to the right and entered the property still going way too fast, but braking at the last second, screeched to a stop by the wash-bay control panel. It was 10:06 p.m.

She grabbed the $10.00 bill placed by her in the center console earlier, and poked this note into the money receptacle which immediately swallowed it. She pushed the button for a high-pressure full-service carwash, which would end with a rinse and forced-air drying procedure. Immediately the conveyor mechanism began pulling the Chevy inside. At that moment a siren could be heard and then it started fading away as the police car steered to the left from Second Street onto Bridge Avenue. Her turning-signal ploy worked, and it sent the cruiser in the wrong direction. But even with this brief reprieve there was no time to lose.

The gushing water of the carwash together with the five-brush system made of heavy neoprene material, rapidly dissolved the water-based Tempera paint mixture, cleaning it off entirely, and at the same time, the license plate alterations disappeared.

The dark-hair wig was pulled off and stashed under the seat as the washing cycle was completing itself. Now the pressurized air-blowing stage began. A short while later a virtually dry, silver Chevy emerged. Ariella jumped out taking with her the two hand towels. Looking at the license plates, she noticed the changes painted onto these a few hours before were now washed off so the fake numbers and letters of O84 EBC now reverted to C31 FPO the Buick's original identification.

She went over the lower extremities of the car with the towels. Then she opened the trunk, grabbed the muddy mixture spray-bottle and the 4" paint brush, and slammed the lid closed. Going with the spray action quickly, Ariella went around the whole car, but most especially its lower parts 'dirtying' it all up. Then she poured some of the bottle's contents onto the 4" brush and flicked this over the areas just covered. The real objective for doing this mud-work was to disguise the license plates. Ariella needed to make these difficult to read, but in order not to arouse suspicion, the rest of the car had to be somewhat grimy looking, like it was all filthy with street gunk.

By applying the brown mixture in a targeted way, the identification was partially camouflaged, so the C31 was sort of visible on both plates, but the FPO was almost impossible to read. This way the police would not be able to track the numbers and letters back to the Buick or even realize at a quick glance these did not belong to this auto. The other reason for adding muck throughout was she needed it all to look dirty enough so it would not appear too clean. Ariella did not want anyone to even think this was the same red and black Chevy they were pursuing, and the color had somehow been rinsed off.

Barely three minutes after the washing and drying ended, the mud spraying was complete, and she hopped back inside. The feminine faker put on the long-haired grey wig and attached the wiry grey beard by its strip of chin adhesive and elastic bands looped over her ears, then the black-framed large-lens glasses were added to round out the disguise.

After starting the engine, a right turn put her onto Bridge Avenue, and then at First Street she turned left, which got her going in the direction of Woodward's Auto Center. However, sharp-eyed officers were very much out and about and were looking for a red and black Chevy Cruze with fake license plates and a woman with dark hair at the wheel.

It was therefore not surprising when after a minute of driving along First Street, Ariella saw in her rear-view mirror stroboscopic lights rapidly approaching. She slowed down and drove closer to the edge of the road to let him pass. In no time the police vehicle was almost upon her, and he turned off his emergency beacons not wanting to waste time stopping her.

He hovered at the same slower speed behind her for about thirty seconds while calling it in.

"Benny Halpen here. What color did you say the Chevy Cruze is that everyone's looking for?"

"It is a two-door, red with a wide black stripe and it has false designation numbers and letters of O84 EBC. There is a woman driving with short, dark, hair and red-rimmed glasses."

"I am behind a silver two-door same make and model, but its reference is C 31… and the rest of it is too dirty to read. I cannot really see the driver from back here, but it looks like it could be an older, grey-haired man."

"Not to worry Benny. The color of the auto is wrong and the bit of identification you can see tells me it is not the right car. The driver also does not match the description of the person we are after. Leave it alone and keep searching for a chick in the red and black coupe."

"Copy that." Officer Halpen passed Ariella and as he did so, he glanced at the driver, and communicated one more time, "Hey it's Benny again. Even though it is dark outside, I can see the operator of this silver Chevy is an older man with grey hair, grey beard and large, black-framed glasses."

"For sure this is not who we are after, Benny."

The prestidigitator smiled as the lights began swirling again and then disappeared down the road in front of her. Before too long she arrived at Woodward's Auto Center, and driving around the back to where Harry said he would leave the Subaru, parked the loaner car under a lean-to shelter.

She got out, opened the trunk, took the dealer plates, and grabbed her screwdriver. Then Ariella removed the Buick's markers and attached the dealer ones in their place. The trunk of the Chevy was closed, and the screwdriver and Buick's plates were put back into the Subaru. Taking the crushed burner phone pieces, these were carried to the edge of Harry's property and tossed into the trash dumpster which belonged to the next-door enterprise.

From inside the Chevy, Ariella picked up the spray bottle with its muddy contents, the red ladies-style glasses, and the dark hairpiece from under the driver's seat. She took the flashlight, her garage door remote control, the 4" paintbrush, and the two hand towels, and put all these items into the Subaru. Under the front floor mat were her keys which Harry left there as arranged. Ariella removed the black-framed glasses and yanked off the grey wig and beard and threw these onto the passenger seat of her vehicle.

From the glove compartment, she took a piece of paper and scribbled a note to Harry apologizing for returning the car in such a dirty condition and for not filling the gas tank. This note was placed with a $20.00 bill for gas, together with the key under the front floor mat of the Chevy. She knew he would not mind about the griminess because he would never reprimand her. All he ever wanted was to win her favor.

The Heistess got into her sedan and drove away just as it started raining, and soon it was really pouring. If the rain had started an hour or more before, the paint would have washed off the doctored car when she was not ready for this to happen, and her mission would have been compromised. Whew!

Ariella arrived home close to eleven thirty, and driving into her garage, got out of the car. She left the screwdriver, her flashlight and the Buick's license plates in the garage, and the spray-bottle with its muddy mixture was poured out in the garden, and then it was thoroughly washed. She stuffed the glasses, the two wigs and the beard into a kitchen drawer with the intent to hide these away sometime over the weekend. The brown contact lenses were removed.

After making a cup of tea, she ate a few cookies, gave Purdy a little more food, and then the burned-out beauty went to bed for a well-deserved rest. Her undertaking was now complete. All that remained was for Barbara to get caught and when they arrested her, Hunt would likely be incriminated as well.

CHAPTER 25

It was a rainy Saturday morning in Philadelphia and Sheila Rhodes was working on her computer doing a Google Search for someone named Ariella Gerson who lived in New Jersey. The evening before she saw texts on her boyfriend's phone which seemed to be very suggestive, indicating a relationship between him and this female. There appeared to be many phone calls between them.

Her delving revealed this woman worked for a technology firm that created sophisticated electronics for some top-level clients. There were also pictures online of Ariella at the company's Holiday Party from the end of the previous year. Sheila, being an ugly duckling, stared in disbelief at this amazing beauty.

She suddenly felt very threatened. A further search on Linked In provided her with even more information about her rival. Having the phone number and being a pushy person, Sheila had no qualms about calling the gorgeous starlet to find out more.

Ariella was in a warm-up suit in her study paying bills from her computer. Suddenly the phone rang. She could see it was a Philadelphia area code, and for sure it must be Roger calling from his hotel.

"Hi there," was her enthusiastic greeting.

"Hello, is this Ariella Gerson?"

It was a woman's voice which Ariella was not expecting and did not recognize. Very tentatively she said, "Yes, it is. To whom am I speaking?"

"This is Sheila Rhodes from Philadelphia. You do not know me, but we have a mutual friend."

And from there the conversation between them became very interesting. They talked for a while, and it was mostly about the two-timing cad. Each was quite open with the other and before too long both realized 'Mr. Bigshot' was a playboy who would exploit women to gain whatever financial or sexual advantage he could from them.

They ultimately concluded he was using Ariella primarily to learn if she was involved in a store robbery, so he could claim a large reward from an insurance company. In Sheila's case, he was latching onto her with the hope he could make a lot of money doing legal work for her father. Perhaps he may one day marry her to benefit from her family's wealth.

The discussion ended amicably, and the philanderer's fate was now sealed. Ariella would call and tell him not to see her again because of his girlfriend in Philadelphia. However, she would be quiet about her knowledge regarding his affiliation with Atlantic Consolidated. The relationship needed to be cooled anyway, particularly after she learned about his connection to these insurance people.

Sheila would get QP Holdings to fire Roger on the spot and he would not be able to earn $75,000 for finalizing the acquisition. She knew her dad would drag his feet on paying the lawyer-scoundrel for the work already done. Sheila could almost hear Anthony Rhodes saying *"So, sue me!"*

She would tell her soon-to-be ex-boyfriend their relationship was over, and he was never to come and see her because she knew he had a romantic interest in New Jersey.

For the rest of the weekend, Ariella remained at home, and things were uneventful. Every now and again on Sunday, she thought about opening the secret space under the platform outside the kitchen door to hide the 'Mandy' wig, the grey-hair/beard disguise, the black-framed and red-framed glasses. But feeling a bit lazy, this was put off for now.

She thought about Barbara, and the evidence in the trunk of her car, just waiting for the fallout from the tip-off to Renfrew Hillman. Ariella felt at some point the following day when the message got retrieved, the police would swing into action. And so, they did.

CHAPTER 26

Monday Morning, July 18th at 9:30 a.m.

Two weeks had passed since Ariella took back what belonged to her from Hunt's shop. Now sitting in front of her computer at her place of work, she wondered what was happening regarding Friday night's call by the homeless man to the office of the insurance company. Little did Ariella know, much was already in motion like it was planned to be. But something else was afoot at Woodward's Auto Center.

Harry was away for the weekend, so he did not go in on Saturday morning, but now he was back at work and going over the Chevy, left in his parking lot. The keys were under the driver's side floor mat together with $20.00 for gas and the written note. He smiled as he read her message.

The rain did not wash off any of the dirt because Ariella parked it under the overhead shelter and thus the grime was still very apparent. But it did not matter that the car was a bit grungy because one of the mechanics would wash it soon. Walking around the rear of the vehicle something made him stop. The lower part seemed to have a mild, muddy appearance but the dealer license plate was completely clean. He looked at the plate in the front of the car and noticed the same thing. This had him somewhat puzzled.

When Harry opened the trunk, there appeared to be traces of red coloring and a tinge of black, and he found the same thing when opening the hood. As he wiped a damp cloth over these areas, the red and black smudges came off. When he poured water over the rim of the hood the hue immediately washed away. What was Ariella doing with colors that diluted in water, and why was the car dirty but not the license plates?

Harry went back into his office where the TV was on with the morning news. At that moment the announcer said that traffic control was looking for a two-door Chevy Cruze, red with a black stripe, and gave the license plate numbers and letters. Harry did not recognize these details. The reporter indicated no crime was committed but the vehicle had fake identification numbers and that is why the authorities were keen to find it. The newscaster went on to say the driver of the car was a woman, but the description they were giving on TV did not match Ariella's appearance.

Harry wondered if his pretty patron lent the car to someone. He did, however, believe his silver Chevy Cruze was the red and black car they were searching for, and that Ariella or a friend of hers was perhaps up to no good. He reached for his cell phone and dialed the number for the local precinct. With all her meticulous planning and execution, the one thing she forgot to do was to 'muddy up' the dealer license plates after exchanging these for the Buick's plates.

"Hello, is this the police? Harry Woodward here. I need an officer to come and look at something strange." He provided the address. The desk sergeant said someone would be there shortly.

◆◆◆◆◆

Renfrew Hillman arrived in his office in New York City at nine forty-five. As he sat down at his desk, his secretary Angelina came running in, eager to tell him what she heard on their communications system. "Mr. Hillman, you have *got* to hear this."

She pressed a button on his phone, and they listened when the recording began to play. Hearing the gruff voice of an older man which rambled on for about thirty seconds, caused them to smile at each other when the message ended.

"We must call the Averton precinct. This could be the news we have been waiting for."

"Yes sir, I will get you the number right away."

Within a minute Renfrew was talking to a policewoman in the local crimes division.

"Hello, my name is Hillman from the Atlantic Consolidated Insurance Corporation in New York City. We are the insurance carriers for the Fourth Street Jewelers and Gold Exchange. I need to speak to whoever oversees the case regarding the recent break-in at this store."

"Please hold sir. I will connect you."

The telephone on Leyland's desk buzzed and he was told that there was an important call waiting.

"Good morning, this is Detective Wakefield."

Renfrew Hillman introduced himself and his company and told about the message which was left sometime over the weekend. He played the recording, and when Leyland heard about Barnwell having a female accomplice helping him with the burglary, his face lit up. He now also had vehicle reference data relating to the commission of this crime.

"I am not sure how credible this tip really is," said Wakefield. "The person sounded drunk, he did not leave his name, and you are offering a reward. But we will follow up. I am sure you are as anxious as we are to find out who did this."

"We really hope you can get to the bottom of it. We are dealing with a potential $1.5 million claim, so retrieving some or all the stolen jewelry is extremely important to us."

"I will be back to you in a day or two and give you a progress report. Please give me your full company name again and your telephone number."

Renfrew recited this to him.

"I appreciate you calling, Mr. Hillman."

"Thank you and have a great day."

Wakefield thought about the tip for a minute or two. This robbery, possibly done by Barnwell and perhaps a girlfriend, seemed to make sense. He called Charles to his office and brought him up to speed regarding the conversation with Hillman. They had license plate information, meaning the owner of the automobile could easily be found.

"I do not think we should speak to Hunt directly," said Leyland. "I would like to call that woman who came here to go over the videotapes with us, who knew so much about every customer. Her name was Laura... something. She may be able to provide more background before we try to locate the owner of this car."

"I believe her name is Laura Kelly," said Charles.

"Yes, that's right, now I remember. If we call her boss, he might warn whoever committed this larceny with him. Also, since he is now a suspect, we do not want to provide any hint that we are considering him and his female co-conspirator as possible perpetrators of this crime."

"We must visit Laura Kelly because she should have all the records. If Barnwell is there, one of us can distract him while the other looks through the customer histories."

"Great idea! But first let me see who owns the car referred to in that recording. I also want to make a change to my *List of Ten Suspects*."

Wakefield went to his computer, and soon he had the name of the owner of the vehicle, Barbara McKenna. There was a home address, but he needed to have this confirmed. He then accessed the 'Word' file with the original list of ten names that Steve, Charles, and Laura had put together almost two weeks before. He deleted a name and added a new one in its place, Barbara McKenna. He typed in the local area code and fake phone details. This way he could get from Laura a home and work telephone number for their newest suspect without arousing suspicion, by having her data hidden among the rest. He printed the new sheet.

"Charles, I am ready. I know a few things about Ms. McKenna, but now we can learn a lot more, like where she works. Let us drive over to Fourth Street immediately."

It was just past eleven o'clock when they arrived. Things appeared to be quiet and there were no clients present. Laura was standing in the main sales area when they walked in.

"Good morning Ms. Kelly."

"Good day to you, sir." She seemed pleased to see them. She was hoping they were making progress on the case because all the employees had been very nervous since the theft occurred. "How may I help you?"

"You have the records of every client, right?"

"Yes, we do. As you know I am very organized!"

Leyland took out the modified list of names. "You might recall identifying certain individuals who were very upset with Mr. Barnwell when you were with Steve Parker and Charles Weston at the precinct recently?"

"Oh yes, we did consider a number of people."

"I need to double-check three of the residences and two of the phone numbers. My officers are following up on these, but they seem to be slow in getting results. They are unable to contact some of those customers because they may have changed their home locations."

He handed Laura the list, highlighted in three places. For two of these addresses, she showed him what was on her computer, and they looked correct. "Maybe these folks moved away and that is why you could not find them."

"Okay, we can track them down I am sure," said Leyland with a smile. "Now what about this one, we have the phone details which seem to be wrong, and we have an apartment locale requiring confirmation. We also need a place of work and a landline number if you have it. He was of course pointing to Barbara's name.

"Let me see on the "M" alphabetical reference in my computer. Oh, here it is, Barbara McKenna. Well, the area code is right, but I have a different home phone number for her than what you have." Laura gave this information to Leyland.

She confirmed the residence was correct and wrote down where the individual was employed. Laura did not seem to be aware this name was not originally flagged by her back on July 6th when she was helping Charles and Steve.

Weston asked if Hunt was there, hoping he was not.

"Oh no. Mr. Barnwell does not come in on Mondays and nor do any of us. We are normally not open on a Monday, but since the break-in, we are trying to do extra business to start recouping some of our losses and that is why we are here today. This week he will not be working until Wednesday."

Leyland was pleased to hear Barnwell would not be in until mid-week. It was likely Laura would not let Hunt know he and Charles were there asking for Barbara's details.

"Well, thank you for your help, Ms. Kelly." He sounded courteous and appreciative.

"Anytime! I hope you find out soon who did this and how they got in and out."

"I am sure we will." Charles smiled at Laura while exiting the store.

They left and drove back to the precinct, now armed with what was urgently needed. It seemed this was obtained without raising any suspicions. They called Captain Morley and asked him to arrange a warrant.

◆◆◆◆◆

Back at Woodward's Auto Center, a policeman arrived to respond to Harry's phone call. But, at the last second Harry decided not to get Ariella into trouble. If she did anything illegal, he didn't want to know about it.

"You know officer, I thought my lockbox with cash in it was missing but I just found it. So sorry for the false alarm."

"Not to worry Mr. Woodward. I am glad all is okay here at your place of business."

◆◆◆◆◆

It was 1:30 p.m. that same Monday afternoon, when Wakefield and Weston presented themselves at the company where Barbara worked, and they were shown to her office by the receptionist. Within minutes tongues were wagging all around the place as to why two detectives wanted to talk to this employee. Some people speculated it might be business-related or maybe a drunk driving incident. But others felt this could be something more sinister.

They sat down in front of her desk. "Let me get right to the point," said Wakefield after introducing himself and Charles. "We have received a tip from a reliable source that you were involved in the robbery at the Fourth Street Jewelers and Gold Exchange."

Barbara looked stunned. Her head was spinning. "I have not stolen a thing, and I have never broken into any place, ever!" She was indignant, almost shouting. Had Hunt turned on her? Did he put them up to this?

"We have a warrant." Charles handed it to her. "We will need to search your vehicle and your apartment. Did you drive to work today?"

"Yes, I drove in, and my car is in the parking garage next door." She took the warrant, looked at it, then handed it back. Barbara was horrified when it suddenly occurred to her that if her home was searched, they would find all kinds of golden goods, the various gifts Hunt had given to her over the past two years. How was that going to be explained?

"Please take your purse and keys, then come downstairs with us so we can go through your automobile." The detective sounded stern and intimidating.

She said, "I need to use the ladies' room." Once inside, Barbara called Hunt, but he didn't answer, and it went to his voicemail. Not wanting to leave any details he was asked to get back to her as soon as he heard the message.

When she came out of the bathroom, the three of them took the elevator down to the ground floor. Barbara was startled to see two policemen in uniform waiting in the foyer. All now walked in the direction of the three-story garage which was located adjacent to the building they were in and were shown where her Toyota was parked.

"This is my car. You will find nothing in it which could tie me to the burglary at that jewelry place."

"Have you ever visited the Fourth Street Jewelers and Gold Exchange?" asked Wakefield while he verified the license plate. It matched the numbers received from Hillman.

"Yes, just once. I sold them some small gold chains and a few bracelets a couple of months back." She tried to sound vague and to make it appear there was very little connection between her and the store.

"Do you own any expensive watches, necklaces, diamond earrings, gold coins or other similar stuff of high value?" Leyland was laying the groundwork in case they should find such things in her possession.

"No, I do not." Barbara's mind was now racing. At home there were many valuable items from Hunt. "Wait! At my apartment I have a few diamond pendants and costly earrings. But fancy watches, I have no need for these. I use my cell phone to tell the time and I do not own any gold coins."

"Good. Now tell me, do you keep your auto secured at all times?"

"Oh, absolutely. With the random vehicular thefts going on in the area these days, it is *always* locked, even when I am at home."

Okay, good information. Are you the only one who has a key to your car, and does it have an alarm?"

Barbara was puzzled at the questions, but she answered them anyway. "I am the only one with a key and yes, it has an automatic alarm. I have a spare key-fob, but it is at my residence hidden in a very safe place."

"Thank you. Now please unlock the doors."

Putting on latex gloves, the two officers proceeded to thoroughly go through the sedan's interior. They looked under the seats, in the console, in the glove compartment, around the door pockets and beneath the floor mats.

"The articles we are looking for sir, are non-existent." The policeman glanced at everyone as he straightened up.

"I told you there is nothing of value here. I was not a party to that robbery!"

Leyland ignored her comments. "Let us check in the back." He was hoping this would not be another dead-end as was the case with so many other leads. He shuddered as he remembered how he was tipped off about there being spoils of the crime in a flowerpot and after he emptied it out, there was zero to be found there.

Pulling on a small lever on the driver's side, one of his men popped the trunk open.

Barbara stood by as the search continued. They came across the T-Shirt and the work papers, but that was all. Then one of the officers lifted the carpeted plywood piece which covered the spare wheel and gave a low whistle.

"Sir, look!" He opened a bag that was nested there.

Leyland and Charles immediately moved in closer. They were staring into a shopping bag, and clearly visible in it were all kinds of jewelry items including gold coins, watches, diamond necklaces, bracelets, and many rings. No doubt deeper in a lot more would be found.

Wakefield spun around, grabbed Barbara by the arm and pulled her toward the back of the Toyota. Finally, he had what he wanted for almost two weeks, some tangible evidence, and an actual suspect!

"What is all of this? You told us that you own no coins, no watches no diamonds!"

Barbara stared into the trunk completely dazed. "I… I… I do not know where this came from. This is not mine!"

"You very clearly stated to me, to all of us…" he waved his arm in a gesture of inclusion toward the two police officers and Charles, "You told us your car is always locked, that it has an alarm, and only you have a key. You either robbed the Fourth Street Exchange on your own, or you did it with the owner, or you are part of a gang!"

"I have no idea how this got here. Someone is trying to set me up!" She was mortified. Now fear turned to complete puzzlement as Barbara realized the large shopping bag was the actual one she took to Ariella's home. Surely the authorities already had these goods in their possession. Why was all of this not in the evidence locker at the police station? How did this get here and what the hell is going on?

And then real trepidation began to set in when Barbara started to understand how careless she was when leaving the shimmering collection in the flowerpot. She did not use gloves that night, and everything was grasped with her bare hands when Hunt gave it to her, and when she rifled through it to take some items to keep, and again when leaving the bag at Ariella's house. "How could I be so stupid!" She cursed her own carelessness.

And as she was thinking along those lines, Charles said, "Let me dust this all for fingerprints. It will only take me a minute to get my crime lab kit from our cruiser and then we will know if this was planted by someone else or not."

"Good idea." Leyland was determined to keep the momentum going and if this woman was involved, he wanted to arrest her here and now.

Charles ran quickly to retrieve what he needed. He donned his latex gloves and within a few minutes was working on the bag as it lay in the trunk where they found it. "We have a few good prints coming up here. At a quick glance, it seems there are two different sets." He sounded pleased with what he discovered. Then he reached in and took out a gold Rolex watch and dusted this on its face.

"I have some very clear ridges showing here." With his portable fingerprint scanner, Charles went over the shopping bag and the Rolex. This was the same equipment used in Dora's apartment on Friday July 8th.

He now turned to Barbara, "Give me your hands." She meekly complied. He did an electronic analysis of her fingers and in less than 20 seconds his suspicions were confirmed. "I have a match to you," he said looking directly at her. "There is also evidence of another person on this bag. Large fingerprints, possibly a male."

"Ms. McKenna," began Leyland, "You are being placed under arrest for the break-in at the Fourth Street Jewelers and Gold Exchange on the weekend of July 4th. You have the right to remain silent…" He finished reciting her Miranda Rights as an officer put cuffs on her wrists and led her sobbing to their squad car.

While being taken away, she kept asking in her mind, "How did this get into the trunk of my car? It *is* always locked. I *am* the only one with a key. Why was all of this not found at Ariella's house on the night they searched there? I saw them on their way immediately after I left it on her porch."

She was now terrified and in total shock, having found herself in the very situation she had planned for Ariella.

As the door of the patrol car closed, Barbara heard the detective say in a gloating voice, "Finally we have a solid suspect. We will bring this case to a rapid conclusion."

Charles was carrying the jewelry evidence and Leyland called the police impound lot to arrange to have the Toyota towed to the crime lab's garage. They would need to process it thoroughly to see if it would reveal anyone else's prints and to make sure this was not a set-up as Barbara stated. He also needed to see if others were in this automobile like members of a larger theft ring.

When arriving at the precinct, they allowed her to make one phone call and she called Hunt. This time he answered his phone and was told about the arrest and what was found in her car. She whispered to him these were the very items placed in the flowerpot by her.

In a quiet voice, Barbara explained that somehow this bag of merchandise ended up in her trunk, with her fingerprints all over it and possibly his as well. "Hunt, this Gerson woman set me up! I do not know how and when she did it but the police at this moment think you and I robbed the store together. They will be coming for you next!"

"That witch, Ariella!" He screamed out loud. "I will get even with her. I have her home address and I will be waiting there for her today when she gets back from her place of employment!"

Hunt assured his lover he would call his lawyer and get her out of jail soon, possibly by tonight. However, he had no intention of helping her get released just yet. He was confused. Did she really do this and somehow get the alarm code from him? It was written down in his store and at his home.

Was Barbara part of a gang? Was she in league with Ms. Gerson? The more he thought about his girlfriend being set up and how this could come back on him, the more furious he became. Barnwell went to the safe in his house where he kept a firearm. It was an unregistered 9mm Glock 26 which he purchased from a desperate client. His intent was to go to Ariella's house that evening, kill her, and then make it look like a suicide... the suicide of someone guilty, who recently ransacked a store.

◆◆◆◆◆

Charles and the two officers went to the suspect's apartment. It was a small place, so it took hardly any time for them to find all they were looking for. They were back at the precinct just before five o'clock with a carton full of jewelry.

They sat Barbara down and asked if she wanted a lawyer and she said no. The thought crossed her mind to call her mother who was a practicing attorney, but she decided not to, because that could cause some family problems. Leyland asked her to please explain where all the valuables had come from since they were found in her apartment and in her car.

Sobbing, Barbara began to relay a lot of information to Wakefield, Weston, and Captain Morley. The two-year affair with Hunt came up and how during this time he gave her money, watches, diamond rings, and other gifts. She told them how Ariella Gerson stormed into Barnwell's store about six weeks back and engaged in a heated argument with him.

Leyland nodded. This part of the story matched what Hunt told them when he said she was a disgruntled customer. Ariella admitted to the police she was mad at Hunt and confronted him because he stole from her grandmother.

Barbara took a sip of water from the bottle Charles gave to her and then continued. She enlightened them as to how she and Ariella became friends, and that Ariella on several occasions spoke about getting even with Hunt.

Captain Morley held up his hand, "Do you think Ms. Gerson was involved in this crime?"

"There were times I thought she was and there were other instances when I felt she wasn't. From what Barnwell told me, he is puzzled as to how anyone got in and out of his place. The back door is always bolted shut and the entrance door is equipped with two different locks. The shop has a good security system including a time recorder. This would show the exact minute anyone turned off the alarm, entered the store, and then re-armed it when they left. To me, Ms. Gerson is just another regular girl with a steady job and is not overly smart. I do not believe she is responsible for this burglary."

"So, you think this was done by experts, by perhaps a well-experienced band of thieves?" Leyland inquired.

"I think it was done by sophisticated bandits, or Mr. Barnwell did it. He has a huge walk-in vault, full of jewelry which might all have come from this so-called break-in."

Startled by these details, they nodded in agreement.

"Okay, please go on." Morley urged her along.

"I have found Ariella has been acting quite normally on the couple of times we have been together since the theft. Being so calm and quiet, and not showing any signs of nervousness, tells me she was not in any way involved. But there is one thing baffling to me."

All three perked up and paid more attention to her.

"I am embarrassed to say I planted evidence at Ms. Gerson's home to try to pin this break-in on her. I placed a shopping bag with jewelry in a flowerpot on her front porch in the early morning hours of yesterday, Sunday, July 10th. Leaving this stuff there was something Hunt and I decided I should do because he was anxious for the insurance money. With your people having no one in custody yet, and since she was such a strong suspect, we were hoping you would find the goods and arrest her. It was Barnwell who tipped you off."

"Yes, I know," said Leyland. "He called me and we went right away to Ms. Gerson's residence. This was the second time we looked, but again we didn't find anything. I searched in that earthenware pot and found no jewelry in it."

Barbara kept going, "As I said, I put it there just after midnight.

The house was in total darkness, and she *must* have been asleep. I drove away and parked nearby to see what would happen and I saw the police cars arriving not long after. How did that exact bag with incontrovertible proof of the robbery, disappear from Ariella's porch and turn up next to the spare wheel of my car a week later?"

Leyland said, "To reiterate, we were at her house very soon after I received the call. Now that you have told us this, I cannot understand how Ms. Gerson knew those items were placed there and how she was able to get rid of everything so quickly. There was no time to hide the stuff. Where could she have put it, especially since we all searched there so thoroughly, including emptying out the flowerpot? We may have to call her in again. In the meantime, we will need to get Mr. Barnwell here to be questioned by us. Planting evidence is a serious crime, and he is as involved as you."

"Detectives, I do not want to sound too repetitive, but I am still confused by all of this. I cannot believe how that treasure tote, filled with what Hunt gave to me and which you found in my car, *is* the exact bag of goods I left at Ms. Gerson's house on July 10th. How did it suddenly disappear and why did your people not find it that night? What made the same package end up in the trunk of my Toyota? I have told you my vehicle is always locked, it has an alarm, and I am *the only person* with a key fob. From what we saw, mine are the only fingerprints on this bag and the others are probably those of Mr. Barnwell."

"Ms. McKenna, what you have said does not surprise us. This is the strangest case we have ever dealt with, and your statement today only adds to the big mystery. How did one or more persons break into the Fourth Street location, get past its sophisticated alarm system, mysteriously cover the camera lenses without being seen, make their way through a locked front door, or get in and out of a bolted back door, steal $1.5 million in jewelry and get away without leaving a trace? There was also evidence at the scene of others being there, who were never there! Even a dead man was in the store taking valuables from Barnwell!"

Charles now chimed in. "I am beginning to believe in ghosts! We all know Ms. Gerson's grandmother died because of what was stolen from her which we understand was a meaningful number of high-worth heirlooms. I think it is her ghost driving this crazy case. If doors were never opened and since we found no holes in the ceiling, the walls, or the floor, and no ladder was there, only a ghost could have got in and out leaving absolutely no sign of how it was done!"

They all looked at Charles with incredulity. Not one of them said a word. There were no explanations for anything, and a ghost so far was the only plausible hypothesis that seemed to make sense.

"There is even more to this mystery." Leyland sounded very serious. "Earlier today one of my officers again followed up with people on my *List of Ten Suspects*. These were disgruntled customers scammed by Barnwell. One by one they eventually admitted to us that someone stopped by their homes this past Friday night and dropped off a large amount of jewelry to compensate them for their losses. We have also tried to call Ms. Gerson in this regard but have been unable to reach her so far. Maybe she too has received a compensatory parcel."

He then added, "At this point we are considering allowing these individuals to keep what essentially is theirs. But they all describe a woman, perhaps in her mid-thirties with short straight dark hair and brown eyes, wearing red-framed glasses and who spoke with an English accent. Do you know anyone who meets this description?"

"No, I do not." Barbara also seemed mystified. "That certainly does not describe Ms. Ariella Gerson."

"Why would a group of gangsters, after pulling off a daring, risky, and well-executed heist, decide to allow one of their female members to give away hundreds of thousands of dollars in jewelry to these victims?" It was a rhetorical question from Leyland, and everyone just stared at him.

"And here is where the story becomes very strange again." His tone was solemn as he glanced around the room. "How did this person know who these victims were? One of the recipients informed us this woman was driving a two-door Chevy which was red with a large black stripe, and it had a fake license plate. A short while after we were told about this, we saw the car on a downtown camera. An officer in a cruiser nearby was notified and before too long he spotted the coupe, and began a hot pursuit. This auto then disappeared somewhere near Bridge Avenue. Multiple police cars converged on the area at around 10:10 p.m. this past Friday night. We have *never* seen this vehicle again. Like POOF! The British woman and her red and black car have vanished!"

Morley said, "Daily this case becomes more insane."

"Ghosts! I tell you. Ghosts!" Charles was wide-eyed.

Barbara suddenly looked at her watch. It was 5:30 p.m. "Detective Wakefield, I nearly forgot about something."

"Forgot about what?"

"When I arrived here at the precinct, I was allowed to make one phone call. I called Hunt Barnwell and explained what was going on, and how the bag of evidence I placed at Ariella Gerson's house ended up in my Toyota. I asked him to hire me a lawyer to help me get out of here. He sounded furious and said that he was going to wait at Ms. Gerson's house and be there when she got home from work today. I am afraid he will do something rash. He has a bad temper."

"Does he own a firearm?"

"Yes, I believe he owns a handgun."

◆◆◆◆◆

Ariella was able to leave her office a little earlier than usual, and as always, the commuter bus dropped her a couple of blocks from her house at ten minutes after five.

Walking past a black Cadillac parked on the other side of the road, she didn't notice there was a person inside. When its occupant saw her approaching, he ducked down, and the car's tinted windows also helped to obscure his presence.

Changing from her work clothes into Capri pants and a pink blouse, she tidied the kitchen and while doing so, discovered the dark hairpiece, the grey-haired wig with its beard, and the two pairs of glasses, all stuffed by her into a kitchen drawer on Friday night. These were meant to be put away sometime over the weekend. She thought it was best to do this now, because who knows if the police will suddenly show up here again like they did before?

The time was five-twenty when Ariella gathered up the disguises and went into the garage to get her rechargeable drill which still had its star screwdriver bit installed in it. Taking this with her and proceeding out the back kitchen door, she kneeled on the 4' x 4' plywood piece, undid the eight screws which held it securely in place, and slid these into the pocket of her Capri pants. Ariella walked down the three steps and standing at ground level raised up the wooden cover, like one would lift the hood of a car.

The large, corrugated container which had in it the balance of what was held back from the heist was of course still there, untouched. Her break-in drone plus two others, and all the electronic parts were in a smaller carton on the concrete base of the hiding place. She reached inside and grabbed the metal pole to prop up the platform and hold it open.

The wigs and glasses were placed into the box of disguises and then she climbed inside the large area where the jewelry was so well stashed and squatted down on the concrete floor. This solid pad extended under the three wooden steps and was also part of the walkway alongside this secret compartment. Ariella took her cell phone out of her back pocket, not wanting to bend it or break it while she was in this crouched position and placed it on top of the box which contained the drones.

The lovely lady could not resist looking at some of the haul one more time, so she opened the large carton and removed a bag of several top-of-the-line watches and gazed at these in wonder. Then out came two emerald-studded necklaces with fine gold chains. A zip-top with some awesome diamond rings got her attention. Their sparkling beauty was amazing.

Suddenly the doorbell rang, which startled her, and then she remembered that UPS notified her they would be dropping off a package.

The golden-haired girl immediately jumped outside the concealment space, picked up her rechargeable drill which was lying on the top step, then reached in and put this onto the concrete base alongside the large open carton of jewelry. The metal pole was moved out of the way and the coverlid was slowly closed. At that moment she realized her cell phone was on top of one of the boxes. Oh well, it wouldn't matter to be without it for a minute. Ariella ran up the three steps and walked over the unsecured laminated wood, then went down the passage to her entrance hallway. The person out there was ringing the doorbell again.

She unlocked the door and opened it. To her horror, there right in front of her stood Hunt Barnwell with a smirk on his ugly face. In his right hand, he had a gun, and this was pointed directly at her. Ariella was in utter shock, expecting a delivery person, and now the man who bilked her grandmother out of a fortune and who very likely caused her nana's premature death had found his way to her house!

Fortunately, she was quicker than him, and slammed the door shut, then twisted the deadbolt closed. At that moment Ariella realized the kitchen door was unlocked but more important, the critical plywood piece shielding the precious robbery spoils, was loose! She did not expect someone to show up at her home while the cache was unsecured. If Barnwell ran to the back, he could very easily discover the storage space, find his stolen items, and have her arrested!

But worse, there was no way to call for help because her cell phone was left under the landing.

Instead of going around the house, using the butt of his gun, Hunt smashed the small, fixed windowpane on the side of the front door. He looked through the opening in time to see Ariella flying down the passage and he shot at her once, and then fired again. She screamed as one of the bullets hit the left side of her waist, and then warm blood began to trickle down her hip.

The horrified Heistess yelled out loud, "Oh no! He has come to kill me!"

Hunt's hand went through the broken window, and he turned the deadbolt to open the door, cutting his arm on a glass shard in the process. Ignoring the deep gash, he moved rapidly into the house and then rushed down the passageway after her.

Ariella fled through the kitchen and out the back door over the loose decking and down the steps. She lifted the platform and squeezed inside the space, letting the plywood drop down above her. What had been the best hideout for the loot from the heist was now a life-and-death shelter for her. In total darkness, she grabbed for the U-shaped metal handle in the middle of the panel, originally installed to make it easier for her to raise and remove this covering.

Hearing his loud footsteps above her, she pulled down on the handle, not wanting Hunt to realize the landing was unstable. The platform was now shaking and flexing as his overweight body walked across it, then he tramped down the steps. Things were quiet for a moment and Ariella surmised he must be looking around the backyard to try to spot her.

Then she heard him cursing "You stupid bitch! I will get you! You will not leave here alive today!"

Letting go of the handle and feeling for her phone, her hand found it on the drone box, but she dared not make a call to 911 or he might hear her. She turned the flashlight on. The eight screws in her pants pocket were digging into her thigh because of her being in this crouched position and these were causing added pain. The fearful femme could hear him talking loudly as he stood close to her hiding place.

"Where are you?" Then he started to walk up the steps going back into the house to see if he could find her inside.

As Ariella grabbed the metal handle to hold down the platform again, her phone slipped out of her hand and fell onto the concrete.

With a popping sound, its glass face cracked. "Oh no!" was her discon-
certed whisper. She continued to hold onto the handle so he would
not feel any movement under his feet. Once he was inside the house
Ariella let go of the handle and tried to call 911. It no longer worked as
a phone but fortunately, the flashlight was still operating.

An idea came to her. Create a weapon! Managing to maneuver
her hand into her pocket, with difficulty she retrieved three of the
screws, hoping to quickly fashion a piercing defensive tool. With her
phone flashlight still lighting up the dark space she was able to carefully
tear a strip of corrugated board about 6" long and 3" wide, from the
flap of one of the cartons, and taking the three screws, pushed these
through the cardboard, spaced about ¾" apart. Then folding the
cardboard to cover the heads of the threaded spikes, her right hand
closed over it, so each of the three sharp stems protruded out about an
inch, from in-between her fingers.

Ariella was now armed like a leopard with claws, waiting to strike
if necessary! In the cramped area illuminated by her cell phone, she
was able to look at her wound. With her adrenaline rush, there was
hardly any awareness of pain, but now her left side was really starting
to hurt, and blood was dripping quite steadily onto the concrete base.
There was really nothing that could be done about it because there was
no way to stop the bleeding.

Suddenly she heard Hunt approach the back door again. He had
checked out every room in the house and decided his quarry was either
in the backyard or somehow ran around the side of the house and
escaped. Once again, she grabbed the metal handle to prevent any
movement as his heavy walking thumped on the plywood platform
above her. This time at the bottom of the steps he stopped, was quiet
for a moment and then he uttered words which terrified her.

"I know you are under the landing here." His voice sounded
gloating and menacing. "I can see blood oozing out onto the concrete
path. Either you come out now or I will start shooting through these
wooden steps into the space where you have concealed yourself."

She hesitated, and then said, "Okay, I will come out." Her phone
was in her bloodied left hand, and she tried again to dial 911. But
before Ariella could attempt this, he rapidly raised the platform and
knocked the phone out of her hand.

"No! You don't call anyone!" He didn't notice the screws sticking out from in between the fingers of her right hand when she rose from the hunched position. He said, "Today you are going to die!"

At gunpoint, Barnwell made her step out of the secret space. Gazing inside at the open carton of jewelry, his next words were, "Well, what have we here? So, you were the one who broke in! You are a thieving, conniving bitch! I don't know how you did it, I cannot figure out how you made your way in or out, but you robbed me of more than a million and a half dollars and now you will pay for this!"

"You stole a fortune from my grandmother and from others. I got it back, and I have helped various victims of yours as well!"

She was now standing on the concrete walkway, and he was holding up the wooden panel with his left hand. In his other hand was his gun which was pointing toward the ground. He seemed mesmerized by the sparkling pile in the large open corrugated box.

With him distracted for the moment and with both his hands occupied, now was the time to act. Ignoring the throbbing pain in her side Ariella spun to face him straight on and with lighting speed she brought her right arm up and raked the weapon down the side of his face, starting from the top of his forehead above his left eye and past his cheek, using as much force as possible.

Hunt was taken completely by surprise and shouted out in pain as he dropped the platform which miraculously fell perfectly into position, closing the hiding place. Ariella took off, attempting to get across the back lawn, with the goal of getting around the house and out to the street in front.

BANG! BANG! He wildly fired two shots at her, and both missed. She was terrified and screaming. Hunt was reeling in agony and could not see properly out of his left eye which was covered in blood. Ariella was not able to run very far before stumbling and falling onto the grass. Weak from loss of blood, she only made it to about fifteen feet away from him. He held onto the railing of the steps to steady himself.

The Heistess now lay there half crawling on her stomach, trying to get away, but it was futile. She was starting to pass out and in her dazed condition saw him aiming his gun at her, this time very carefully and deliberately.

Again, there was a loud gunshot, BANG just as her mind started drifting out of awareness. And then another BANG from gunfire rang out. The pain from the wound in her side was now more excruciating than ever. She murmured, "He has shot me again… I am dying."

Those were her last thoughts before completely losing consciousness. Ariella was bleeding to death and would die soon unless she got urgent medical help. But there was none to be had. The only other person in her backyard was Hunt with hate in his heart, a badly injured face, and holding a 9 mm automatic.

CHAPTER 27

When Barbara told the three men at the precinct that Barnwell was going to pursue Ariella and that he owned a gun, they jumped up from their chairs in the interview room.

Leyland called out to Captain Morley, "Hold her here, don't let her go anywhere!"

He ran to his office, took his firearm out of a locked cabinet, and accompanied by Charles, tore down the stairs and jumped into a squad car which they commandeered from a female officer, about to go out on her rounds. Charles immediately got on the radio and called for backup to meet them at Ariella's house. He grabbed Leyland's cell phone and began reading off the address to the dispatcher, so those following would know where to go.

With lights flashing, sirens blaring, and running many red lights they rushed through the streets with one goal in mind, get there before Barnwell does. Nine minutes later, upon arriving at their destination, their vehicle screeched to a halt. Wakefield and Weston all but tumbled out and raced across the walkway. When they got to the front door it was wide open and they could see the shattered side window.

As Leyland started running down the passageway two gunshots rang out. These were coming from the general direction of the backyard. The detective rounded the corner to the kitchen in time to see Hunt holding unsteadily onto the railing at the bottom of the wooden steps with his gun pointed downward at someone on the ground. Half his face was covered in blood. The detective catapulted his muscular frame toward the door with his right arm outstretched and a pistol in his hand.

"Police! Drop the gun!"

Barnwell turned and changed his direction. He was now pointing his Glock at Leyland and then pulled the trigger.

Wakefield heard a 'thwack' as the slug hit the siding of the house close to his left ear. He fired back. Years of training at the range allowed for an accurate shot to land into the armed assailant's upper torso, finding its target barely one second before Barnwell could shoot again. His body lurched slightly backward, his face showed a look of disbelief and then he fell to the ground.

Leyland ran over the unsteady platform and literally jumped down all three steps at once, kicking Hunt's gun away and running over to where Ariella was lying on the grass. She was bleeding profusely from a wound on her left side. Leyland felt a very weak pulse and she was unresponsive.

"Call an ambulance," he shouted at Charles who had just emerged out of the kitchen.

"They are on their way, I summoned two of them when we arrived, and I heard the gunshots."

"Is Barnwell alive?" asked Leyland, half turning his head to where Hunt was lying. Charles made it down the wooden steps and was now kneeling by the fallen store owner.

"Yes, he is." The words were redundant as both heard moaning and some indistinct babbling coming out of his bleeding mouth.

"How is Ms. Gerson?" Charles asked with concern.

"I don't know. Barely breathing. She has hardly any pulse. Where are those damn EMTs? Charles, use your cell phone and take as many pictures as you can. Climb up onto the landing outside the kitchen door for the best perspective. We will need to remember exactly where these two were, later when we try to piece together what happened here."

Leyland now realized the young lady was clutching something in her right hand, and it seemed to have three sharp spikes sticking out. He pried her fingers open and found a piece of folded corrugated cardboard with three 2" long screws inserted into it. There was blood on them. A weapon? Jumping up, Leyland scurried over to where Hunt was sprawled out, and that is when he saw Barnwell's glaring injury. His badly lacerated face showed three distinct gash lines from his forehead almost down to his chin, as though he was clawed by a large wild cat.

"Good girl," Leyland said gently. "You fought back against a man with a gun… what an ingenious spur-of-the-moment idea."

He then ran back to Ariella and continued to put pressure on her wound, trying to stem the bleeding. In the meantime, the crime lab expert began taking a whole bunch of photographs with his cell phone camera. He followed Leyland's instructions and took some from the elevated position not noticing the plywood on which he was standing was unattached and shaky. It was ten after six when two distinct sirens could be heard approaching.

Charles dashed around the side of the house to the front entrance of the property. When the first ambulance arrived, he directed it to go over the lawn into the backyard. Then he signaled the second one to do the same.

Two police cruisers showed up and Charles sprinted over to the officers and instructed one to stand by the front door and not to let anyone in. Another was to remain near the fence to prevent people from going behind the residence. The other two were to keep onlookers, neighbors, and news or TV reporters off the property. They were ordered to put up crime-scene tape everywhere and then he ran around to the back.

Ariella was already on a stretcher and being put into one of the ambulances.

"Get in! Go with her!" Leyland waved at Charles.

"Okay. Yessir! By the way, all is under control out front. Four of our guys are there keeping everyone away."

"Good work!"

He scrambled into the rear of the vehicle alongside an orderly who put Ariella on a drip. The EMT cut away part of her shirt and started treating her wound. Charles held the patient's hand, which was so cold to the touch it startled him.

The driver began backing up toward the front of the house with help from a policeman. He reversed further onto the lawn and with a sharp right turn drove forward onto the asphalt and was now facing the entrance. The wheels were spinning as the emergency van roared out onto the street with sirens shrieking and lights ablaze.

A large crowd of neighbors gathered, and a few literally jumped out of the way to avoid being struck by the speeding demon. They could not believe the gun shots and the commotion in their normally quiet neighborhood.

Hunt was now securely on a stretcher and the EMTs were putting him into the second ambulance.

"Please tell them at the hospital I will be sending someone to guard his door because as of now he is under arrest for the attempted murder of me and also Ms. Gerson," said Leyland to the driver as he began reversing out of the backyard. In less than a minute the badly wounded store owner was on his way to get critical medical care.

Leyland called the four policemen together who were standing near the entrance gate. "I want two of you to stay here until midnight.

At that point when your shift is over, I will arrange for at least one new replacement to take over. I do not want anyone on this property because this is a major crime scene. I am not sure whether the two people who were shot will live or die. Understood?"

A chorus of voices answered, "Yes sir!"

He continued, "Charles Weston from the crime lab who was just here, will return tomorrow morning to gather evidence. Morrison, I want you and Jackson to not let strangers onto this property. Patrol it and walk around the back often. Guys, you are not to touch anything, please! I must take a few more pictures in the backyard and inside the house. I know from previous visits here the homeowner has an indoor cat. I will need to find it and make sure it has food and water."

"Sir," began Morrison. "My brother-in-law owns a glass repair business. Would you like me to call him to come by and fix the broken window by the front door?"

"That will be fine, but not until Charles tells you tomorrow, he is done with the crime scene. I will close it now with cardboard and masking tape. Thanks for the suggestion."

And with that, two officers departed and the other two remained behind.

Leyland needed to start getting some initial evidence as part of figuring out exactly what happened, and a huge surprise was in store for him! First, it was a trip into the bathroom to wash Ariella's blood off his hands. Then he walked to the front door and stood there surveying the scene. Through his head went the following thoughts…

Okay, so Barnwell rang the bell, and Ms. Gerson answered the door. She somehow realized who it was and therefore did not let him inside. He then broke the side window, unlocked the door, and let himself in. She must have run down the hallway, and he fired at her, perhaps twice.

The detective walked through the passage and saw a bullet hole in the wall at the end. He continued surmising…

I guess one of the shots struck her and is likely lodged inside her. I see blood droplets starting at the kitchen entrance and thus I can gather she was hit while still in the house.

These droplets are now going out the door over the landing. Wow, this base feels loose and unstable. Yes, this red trail goes down the steps to the side, and now they have stopped.

Wakefield was standing on the walkway staring at the thigh-high large plywood sheet. When looking down at his feet, he observed a pool of almost-dried blood that appeared to have come from under the area behind the steps. When attempting to lift the wooden landing piece, to his amazement it came away very easily. He raised it from the edge closest to him with the back part remaining against the house, and holding it up, everything inside was visible.

There was a lot of blood on the concrete base, and his guess was Ariella hid in there. Then his eyes went to the large cardboard carton which was literally overflowing with jewelry. Leyland could not believe this, and then said out loud, "Oh my goodness! *She is the one!* The suspicions so many of us had were absolutely correct!"

He wondered for a moment if she did it all on her own or if this act of larceny was done with accomplices. He again began verbalizing, "What a pity this lovely lass will have to spend many years in prison. Between Ms. Gerson and Ms. McKenna, and the evidence we have found in possession of both, I believe we have identified at least two of the gang members and we may have solved this case."

But then in his mind, doubts began arising. "Perhaps Ms. Gerson was not part of a theft ring but was given all of this by the *Good Samaritan* who was doing the rounds making other victims whole? But maybe not, there is far too much of the stolen property here in this carton."

Then he noticed that a small piece of cardboard from one of the carton flaps had been torn off. "So that is why she was clutching a section of corrugated board with screws in it. She was evidently hiding in here and made a sharp raking tool which was very successfully used on Barnwell when he discovered her. What a brilliant idea! By slowing him down just a bit until Charles and I arrived, she might well have saved her own life."

Wakefield spotted the fractured cell phone on the concrete floor and figured she was unable to call 911 because her phone was broken. He now propped up the plywood platform with the metal pole which Ariella left in the secret space. This allowed him to pull another box toward himself.

Inside this second carton were a few wigs used for disguises. There was a third box containing a small four-rotor drone, a controller, and an FPV headset. There were also two other battery-powered flyers and some assorted electronic parts in the box. "Could this be how it was done?" Then he immediately mouthed the words, "But if so, how did you get this bird-burglar into the store and how did you get all the jewelry out? This craft has no claws or hooks attached to it."

Leyland hoped she would live and not die. He had to know how *The Perfect Crime* was committed. Reaching for her broken cell phone, it went into his pocket, and he also picked up the rechargeable drill, which was lying on the concrete base, then the wooden platform lid was closed. He went into the garage and found a box with 2" steel screws like the ones on the cardboard in her hand. He grabbed a few and went back outside. Using the drill with its screwdriver-bit, he secured the platform firmly into place, then walked back into the kitchen to get a plastic shopping bag.

Taking this to the backyard, the detective found Hunt's gun which was still on the lawn, a short distance from where the vengeful man fell after being shot. Using the shopping bag as a 'glove' Leyland picked up the gun and then turned the bag inside out. The Glock was now well preserved as evidence.

At that moment it started to rain, softly at first and then it began to really pour down. Barely making it into the kitchen before the deluge got worse, he went to the garage, where the extra screws were put back into their correct box. The rechargeable drill was left on the workbench.

Finding a corrugated carton in the garage together with a cutting knife and a roll of masking tape, he went over to the front door and temporarily closed the area of the damaged windowpane. He said out loud, "At least the cat won't be able to jump out of the house and hurt itself in the process."

Ariella's cell phone was obviously broken, but Charles or Steve should be able to retrieve most or all its information.

It would be interesting to know if she was part of a band of bandits in league with Ms. McKenna or if she was a sole operator. "Ms. Gerson *must* be part of a sophisticated group," he said boldly. "Her phone will reveal a lot to us. But, on the other hand, maybe she had nothing to do with the break-in."

Going back into the house and after searching around, a terrified Purdy was found hiding under a bed. Leyland coaxed him out and then carried him downstairs. After opening a couple of cupboard doors he discovered an open bag of dry cat food and added a handful to Purdy's bowl. He also made sure the water dish was full. He then emptied the kitty's box and added fresh litter to it.

"I will see you tomorrow morning, little fella," he said affectionately to the now-purring feline. Leyland was not all 'macho detective', there was a softer side to him, and he happened to really like cats!

He locked the back kitchen door and came out front to talk to the two police officers who were standing on the porch out of the rain as they guarded the house. He called the precinct and arranged for one new replacement to come at the midnight shift change and then for another to be at the house the following day until four o'clock. Hopefully, by then Charles should have all the evidence needed from this crime scene and the windowpane will have been replaced.

It was around eight fifteen when Wakefield put the Glock into a second plastic bag and then said goodnight to the two policemen. Holding Hunt's gun under his jacket Leyland ran through the deluge and got into the squad car to drive to the hospital. Although he searched Ariella's house twice, interrogated her, and had her pegged as a top suspect, he still held a fondness for her. Like most other men he was taken by her attractiveness and intelligence.

Being with her on the lawn in the backyard earlier, brought him closer to this skillful thief. Even after Ariella was put into the ambulance and when walking around the house surveying the crime scene, the detective was somehow filled with a strange admiration for this brazen beauty.

While driving to the hospital he called his associate and his first question was, "How is she?"

"I do not have good news." Charles sounded quite morose. "She has flat-lined twice and lost an enormous amount of blood. The doctors are holding out little hope of a good outcome."

"Oh no! Don't tell me that. Listen, I am on my way, and I can be there in ten or twelve minutes."

"Don't rush. I see it's pouring outside and there is no need to hurry in this bad weather. There is nothing you can do, and the medical personnel are providing whatever care they can. The good news is that the bullet which they removed did not strike any vital organs."

"Well, okay. I will be there soon." He felt Charles was right. There was no point putting on lights and sirens and endangering himself and others, just to see sooner what Ariella's status was.

When Leyland arrived at the medical facility, the guard in front let him park in a Fire Lane near the entrance.

He walked inside and up to the reception desk.

"May I help you?" The lady with a Spanish accent smiled at him. Her badge showed her name, Juanita Nomura.

"I am here about Miss Gerson, gunshot victim, brought in about two hours ago and still in the E.R. What floor will she be on?" He pulled his jacket aside slightly so the receptionist could see the police badge on his belt.

Juanita looked at her computer. Then with an ashen face and in her Spanish accent said, "Miss Gasson? Gunshoot? I be sorry Señor, lady… no make it. She jus' pass' away, a few meeenuutes ago."

He was shocked. "I am talking about Miss Gerson… who came in by ambulance in the past couple of hours?"

"Si, Señor. It says here she die' from bad wooon' after being shoot. The doctors try' very har' but in the end, they could no' save her. Mi simpatia hacia usted."

Leyland could not believe it and turned around as tears began welling up in his eyes. Devastated, he walked over to one of the soft padded chairs in the waiting area and sat down, putting his head in his hands. His mind was racing. It is so tragic that she should die at the hands of a pig like Barnwell.

This brilliant and kind-hearted beauty figured out how to rob a jewelry store and not leave a trace as to how she got in or out. Evidence was very cleverly staged to throw everyone off track. She gave away a fortune in jewelry to other victims of Hunt's treachery and made herself whole by keeping what he took from her grandmother. One could argue this all was rightfully hers as it was for the others. But now that she has died, what is the good of this treasure?

Well at least there will be no suffering by her spending the next few years in prison. The evidence is overwhelming that she alone or with others, committed this crime. However, with her passing away, no one will ever know exactly how the break-in was done, how an amazing robbery was pulled off.

He spoke almost inaudibly, "And Barnwell? I wonder if this monster will survive. He should have died, not her."

◆◆◆◆◆

It was earlier that evening at 8:00 p.m. when Captain Morley went to where Barbara was being held in a small jail cell at the police station. After the other two had rushed out, Morley did not continue with the interview. He ordered an officer to take her to the cell in which she was now sitting.

"I am afraid you will have to remain here overnight."

"What? I thought Hunt Barnwell was sending his lawyer over and I would be able to go home!"

"Well, Ms. McKenna, I guess he did not make those arrangements for you and now there are complications. Ms. Gerson was shot by Mr. Barnwell. She is in hospital, the outlook is very bleak and she could die at any minute. Barnwell was shot by the police, and he is in critical condition. I wish you had told us earlier he was pursuing Ms. Gerson and that he owned a firearm. We might have got to her house in time to prevent anyone from getting injured or killed."

Barbara was stunned and did not know what to say. Captain Morley left her and walked to his office upstairs. It was time he went home for the day.

She sat there petrified, verbalizing out loud, "What if Hunt dies? Who will take care of me? Where will I find the money to hire a lawyer to defend me? They have evidence found in my car and more in my apartment, and everything was given to me by Hunt. But how will I be able to prove I did not steal these items from Barnwell's store?"

She began thinking about what if Ariella died. Although she was spying for Hunt, Barbara still had a lot of feelings for Ariella, and now reminisced about the enjoyable times they had together when out for drinks or for dinner. She curled up on the awful mattress, pulled the two scratchy blankets over her clothing, and cried herself to sleep.

CHAPTER 28

Leyland was sitting in the waiting area of the Hospital. His mind was numb with disbelief and sorrow. Suddenly his cell phone rang, and it startled him out of his fugue state. He noticed it was Charles calling him.

"Where are you? I expected you up here fifteen minutes ago."

"I am downstairs in the reception waiting area. I felt there was no point in me coming to the E.R."

"Yes, I know I said there was nothing you could do for her, but at least you should be here so you and I can talk. We need each other at a time like this. I am on the fifth floor."

"Okay. I will come right up. You are correct, we should be there to support one another right now."

Wakefield got into the elevator, and on the fifth floor, the doors opened. He was normally not a demonstrative person but upon seeing Charles, he walked right up and hugged him. Charles was caught a bit off guard but then hugged the detective back.

"I cannot believe this happened." Leyland's tone was somber. "I just wish Barbara McKenna had told us about her lover earlier. If she did so, the two gunshot victims would not be here, and nor would we."

"Absolutely. I have been thinking the same thing." His voice was choking with emotion.

"That poor girl. She must have been terrified when that bastard burst into her home and started firing his gun. I wish we could have arrived there sooner."

"We did our best," said Charles. "We got to the house as quickly as we could. If Barnwell survives, we will make sure he never sees the light of day again!"

Wakefield nodded in agreement, thinking Hunt will be tried for the murder of Ms. Gerson and the attempted murder of a police detective. Because he and his crime-lab partner were on the scene as it was happening, no matter how good a defense team that gun-toting store owner hires, there will be no way a prosecutor would let him wriggle out of this one.

At that moment a doctor in scrubs came walking out of the E.R. "For the first time things are looking a bit better.

I am pleased to say that finally, the blood transfusions seem to be working. The condition is still very grave, but at least there is a glimmer of optimism that only fifteen minutes ago we did not have."

"I do not think you should be wasting your time and talent on a low life like Barnwell. Just let him die." Leyland had a look of disgust on his face.

Charles immediately chimed in, "You've got this wrong! He is talking about Ms. Gerson. It looks like there is now a small chance of her surviving. There is a slim possibility she may recover!"

Wakefield's mouth dropped open, "You mean she is still alive?"

"Well, yes." Charles seemed to be puzzled. "When you and I were talking on the phone as you were driving here, I didn't say she passed away."

"No, *you* did not. But the receptionist downstairs… when I asked about Ms. Gerson… she told me that the gunshot patient Ms. Gerson had died!"

The doctor suddenly interjected, "Wait a minute… we had three shooting victims brought in today. One passed away about twenty-five minutes ago. Her name was Angela Gasson. I believe our receptionist got the two names confused and I am so sorry. I apologize on behalf of Ms. Nomura. English is not her home language."

Leyland could not believe his ears. This news was very encouraging. Ariella was still alive! He walked over to a chair in the hallway and sat down. Charles came over to him.

"I had no idea you thought she died, it's no wonder you remained downstairs in the waiting area. Yes, it looks like she might make it." It was his turn now. He pulled Wakefield out of the chair and gave him a big hug. Both men had tears of hope and faith in their eyes.

At this point, the two went and got a cup of coffee from a vending machine. They returned, and sat quietly in the hallway outside the E.R. About forty-five minutes later the doctor came out and told them Ariella was critical but stable and they would now be moving her from the E.R. to the Intensive Care Unit.

When the nurses wheeled her by, on her way to the ICU, she appeared deathly pale and drawn. There were tubes everywhere, and an oxygen mask hid much of her face. Both men were thinking she was so beautiful and vibrant the times they saw her before, even though she was mad at them for searching her house and for questioning her. But now it looked like Ariella had been to hell and back… and one could say this was the case.

They heard that Barnwell was also in the ICU, and the doctors were not sure if he would survive the night.

A short while later Wakefield and Weston drove back to the precinct, and once there, they locked Hunt's Glock away as crime-scene evidence. After discussing some aspects of the past few hours, they tidied their work areas, then each got into his own personal vehicle and went home.

◆◆◆◆◆

It was Tuesday morning at 10:08 a.m. and Leyland, Charles, and Captain Morley were at the precinct discussing the events of the day before. They decided to let Barbara go home but told her not to leave town.

They heard that Barnwell died during the night, and Barbara broke down in tears upon hearing this. She was more worried about her future and what was to become of all the valuables taken from her home by the police. She did not know if they were going to charge her with anything regarding the jewelry in her car, what was found at her apartment, as well as the planting of evidence at Ariella's house. Other than her low-paying job, she had nothing else.

But being young and attractive, before too long she would most certainly find another sugar daddy. Barbara was genuinely upset to hear about Ariella being in critical condition and that it was Hunt who shot her. She soon began to realize if Hunt did not die, he very likely would have gone to jail for the attempted murder of her friend and for shooting at the detective.

The two pals from the precinct drove once again to Ariella's residence. It had started raining the previous evening just as Leyland finished fastening down the platform. The rain was so intense at times, that all the blood at the base of the hiding place on the concrete walkway was now gone. Both men understood a lot of the outside evidence would not be there by the time they got to the house, and they were not wrong. Fortunately, this morning the sun was shining.

Charles thanked Leyland for suggesting he take photographs in the backyard the evening before. "I am sure the rain washed away any blood trails from the landing, the steps, the walkway, and the lawn. But at least we have a record of exactly where each person was positioned on the ground." Charles took a deep breath. "Even though we were both there, it is hard to remember fine details. There was so much going on, a lot of it now seems like a blur to me. My cell phone pictures will provide an excellent recap of it all."

When they arrived, they were greeted by Officer Juan Ramirez who was on duty. He reported all was fine since his shift started at midnight, and he was now working overtime because his replacement was running late.

Both men thanked him for being there and offered to make him a cup of coffee. Before too long they brought him his hot beverage and gave him some cookies from the kitchen to snack on. Ramirez was pleased and said he did not mind staying on duty a bit longer than anticipated.

Going over the inside of the house with a fine toothcomb, Charles tried to re-create exactly what happened there. Leyland shared his own thoughts about how Barnwell smashed his way in and fired twice at Ariella, missing her with one shot but hitting her with the other. Charles agreed with this basic theory and said he would study the scene more closely to verify this supposition.

He dug the bullet out from the wall at the end of the passageway and removed another from the siding outside the kitchen, the one which nearly hit Leyland. With the metal detector, he found two more rounds on the lawn in the backyard. These were from Hunt firing wildly at Ariella.

Leyland handed the broken cell phone to Charles and after tweaking it for a few minutes, despite its cracked glass, he got it operating again. They looked at the call history and all the texts for the past two months and found nothing incriminating, no string of successive communication to one or more suspicious people. They now concluded she was not part of any break-in gang. Leyland said he would take the phone with him and get it repaired.

Charles called Officer Morrison who was there the previous day and told him his brother-in-law could now come and replace the window glass because he would be done shortly with the crime scene inside the house.

While Weston was busy doing his thing in the hallway, the kitchen, and outdoors, Wakefield spent a lot of time walking around and sitting in the living room, lost in thought. He refilled his coffee cup several times. Going over and over in his head was something of a moral dilemma, what he should do regarding Ms. Gerson?

Thinking about it, he realized Charles very likely was not aware of the blood on the walkway the night before due to all the commotion.

Even if he did see it, or if the blood appeared in any of the pictures, no one would necessarily know it seeped out from under the landing. This could well have come from either Ariella or her assailant simply standing there since both were injured and bleeding. Hunt no doubt saw the contents of the large carton when he discovered where Ms. Gerson was hiding. This meant he and Leyland were the only two who knew about the cache of jewelry. But because Barnwell was now dead, that left Leyland as the one person who knew she might have perpetrated this burglary.

What went through the detective's mind was this: Hunt was an unscrupulous and corrupt individual who robbed, swindled, and stole from countless customers over the years. Some of the most aggrieved people were given a form of recompense by Ariella. She was also a victim and her repayment lay under the platform outside her back door. The jewelry in her possession was rightfully hers and was perhaps of a similar value to what was taken from her grandmother. To any other detective or insurance investigator looking into this case, there was no evidence, not a stitch of it anywhere, that the blue-eyed blonde was involved in stealing these goods.

This was for sure an inside job carried out by the store owner. One could argue that Hunt placed the finery-filled bag in Barbara's car after removing it from the flowerpot on the porch. He was the only other person who knew about the evidence being planted at this house, and if anyone had access to Barbara's car it would be her lover.

So, Wakefield kept asking, why should he penalize someone so badly injured and ruin her life? Barnwell was the only robbery 'victim' and the items taken from his store were certainly a lot less than what he expropriated from so many others over the years.

The insurance company would not issue funds on this claim, so it wouldn't be hurt. The company would not pay on the policy especially if the police concluded since they could not prove otherwise, entry and exit must have been through the front door by someone with keys and who knew the alarm code. Most certainly a crime committed by the proprietor.

The detective imagined that Hunt's father would come out of retirement to run the store which would not go under because of losses from the heist. It was a highly successful operation and with the unscrupulous Hunt out of the way and not skimming money every week, before too long his father would generate enough profits to cover any 'refunds' given by Ms. Gerson to herself and to other victims.

Leyland decided not to arrest Ms. Gerson. He would never remind himself about seeing the hiding place, and therein a carton filled with spoils from the robbery. There was no jewelry at her house and no drone. As far as he was concerned Ms. Gerson did more good than harm. That lying, cheating, scum of a man, Barnwell, caused his own demise. But even more compelling was that there was no way to prove Ms. Gerson did it. A couple of wigs and a drone do not mean she broke in anywhere. Maybe the robbers asked her to give some jewelry to other victims while handing her a larger share. Leyland knew he could prove nothing in court.

It was noon when the window repair man came to replace the glass pane. The next officer arrived to watch the house and Wakefield told him the crime scene was now released, and he was to remain until his shift ended at four o'clock. Ariella would not be home until at least the weekend, so patrol cars would be in the area often until she returned because an empty house is a temptation to thieves. Leyland undertook to come by every day to take care of the cat.

By three twenty he and his crime lab associate finished their work at the house. After locking up, they drove back to the precinct. On their way, they stopped at Pulsar Electronics, a cell phone repair store. Wakefield handed Ariella's phone to an eager young techie who said the cracked glass could easily be replaced and that it would be ready in a couple of days.

Leyland got back into the car, and the two continued their discussion about the events following the break-in. They decided their police report would show this would be classified as an *inside job*. Barnwell did it and there were no other accomplices. They recalled how Barbara informed them Hunt had a huge walk-in vault, packed with jewelry, and that is where the spoils of this crime ended up.

There was no evidence anywhere about a gang of thieves or to show that either Ms. McKenna or Ms. Gerson had anything to do with this larceny. They decided they would return to Barbara all the jewelry which Hunt had given to her over the past couple of years, and everything found in the trunk of her car, placed there without question, by Barnwell.

◆◆◆◆◆

It was now Thursday afternoon, July 21st at 12:40 p.m. and four days since Ariella was shot by the man who robbed her grandmother. Leyland decided to visit her and see how she was doing. On his way, he went into Pulsar Electronics to pick up the repaired cell phone and paid the $125 cost. Once at the hospital, a nurse accompanied him to the room where the shooting victim was recuperating. She was now out of the ICU and in a private ward.

The two went in and found the patient busy reading a magazine. Her recovery had been quite remarkable considering she almost died just a few days before.

"I have a visitor for you." The nurse spoke in a happy, upbeat voice and stayed there for a moment before leaving.

Ariella's face lit up briefly as the caregiver came in but then the smile was gone upon seeing who walked in behind her. Ever since regaining consciousness and clearing her mind, she was petrified about what the authorities would do regarding her antics, feeling sure they found the hiding place, the jewelry, the drone, and the wigs. At this stage they would have realized it was she who committed this crime.

Ariella felt that even if they did not discover the valuable cache, Barnwell certainly knew where it was hidden, and he must have taken everything back and told them.

"Miss Gerson," Leyland began in a gentle voice, pulling up a chair and sitting down. "I am pleased to see you are awake and doing so well."

"Good afternoon, Detective Wakefield." She was very worried as to why he was there and didn't know what to say.

"You gave us all quite a scare."

"What do you mean? How did you know I was here?" Ariella understood that sooner or later the police would show up and place her under arrest. She was completely in the dark as to what happened at her house because the hospital staff was unaware of the events, and this man was her first visitor.

Leyland began to realize Ariella knew nothing, so he started to fill her in on the details, explaining how they were interviewing Barbara because of evidence found in her car, and then she told them Hunt was going after Ariella and he was armed with a gun.

"By the time we got to your house, Mr. Barnwell had already wounded you with a bullet in your left side. The two of you were out in the backyard, and that is when we heard him firing twice more.

Thankfully he missed, as you were trying to scramble away. Fortunately, I managed to get off an accurate shot which brought him down."

"Is he dead?" she asked with her eyes now wide open.

"Well, he was rushed to this hospital like you were and yes, he died. But you are alive and that is the best outcome."

"So, are you here to take me into custody?" Ariella was thinking they had found her hiding place and all the spoils.

"Arrest you? No, Ms. Gerson, why would we do that? We have never found any evidence connecting you to the theft. Heaven knows we searched your home twice!"

She chimed in, "That you did!" Then she thought about the plywood lid slamming closed when Hunt let it go, but it wasn't secured in place. Did Wakefield not yet discover what was stashed under the platform? Is everything still hidden away like it was before? She was a bit bewildered, and suddenly very encouraged.

"We are certain this whole thing was done by Mr. Barnwell alone. It is very likely he planted the evidence in the trunk of Ms. McKenna's car, and we have just informed her that she too is no longer considered a party to this robbery. We have closed the file on this case."

Ariella stared at him in disbelief. For the past four days while recovering here in the hospital, she was very concerned about losing all the jewelry, and that she would be locked up and spend years in prison. Now the detective just told her the store owner was dead, and the case was closed!

"I must say, what an ingenious improvised weapon you made with the cardboard and three screws to fend off your attacker. I believe that saved your life. You obviously incapacitated him and he was only able to fire wildly and miss hitting you. This also delayed Mr. Barnwell just enough for me to arrive on the scene and shoot him. Incidentally, your cat is fine and is being well taken care of, and I am sure he is keen for you to come home. By the way, what is his name?"

"His name is Purdy and thank you for having someone look after him. I have been anxious about my cat, and I was thinking maybe he was put into an animal shelter. Who is feeding him for me?"

"Well… I am. I go in every day to give him his wet and dry food and to clean out his litter box. When you were taken to this hospital, I temporarily taped up the broken window. It has now been properly fixed. I heard you are due to go home on Saturday and I will be happy to drive you there. It is the least I can do to make up for all the accusations and searches of your house."

Ariella was surprised at the detective's sudden change of attitude. Why was he being so nice? "Well, thank you for looking after Purdy for me. I appreciate you offering to drive me home, but I am sure an Uber car can take me back."

She was beginning to feel very uneasy about this new-found friendliness and his attention to her. She had no interest in a sixty-year-old man! What could he be up to? Does he know more about the robbery than he is letting on and will he hold this over me until he gets what he wants out of me?

He looked at his watch. "Oh, I see it is just past one o'clock and I have arranged for a special guest. Someone will be here to visit you any moment now."

"Another caller? Do I know him? Is it your buddy Charles Weston from the crime lab?"

The door to the ward opened and a female came in. She appeared to be in her mid-thirties, tall and quite attractive with brown eyes and dark, wavy, shoulder-length hair.

"Ariella," Leyland began. It was the first time he ever addressed her by her given name, "I want you to meet Charlotte, my daughter. I know you have no close family here, and I have concluded that Barbara McKenna absolutely let you down and she is no ally of yours. You deserve a genuine friend and in fact, you are in need of a good family. We would like you to be part of ours and we would be delighted if you will accept our invitation."

The tall, attractive visitor walked up to the hospital bed, and Ariella was now looking at them in astonishment.

Charlotte gave her a gentle hug and after holding back for a moment, the hesitant Heistess hugged her back. Leyland could see the tears welling up in Ariella's eyes.

"My daughter is a pediatrician, and on most weekends, she volunteers like I do, at a local orphanage. We enjoy helping children who are in difficult circumstances. By the way, if you do become part of our clan, you will gain yet another sister, Holly, and two married brothers Michael and Dennis, and their wives and children. My wife Marjorie will tell you we are a noisy bunch at Thanksgiving!"

Her perception of Detective Wakefield changed completely. It appeared he was a fine man with a great family and immediately Ariella wanted to belong with them. She too was interested in helping young children who had very little in their lives and who were starved for love. She no longer wished to be all alone, and now having been given a new lease on life, it was her intention to live it to the full.

Leyland stood up. "Charlotte, I must go. But before I do, give me a minute with Ariella."

"Sure, Dad." She walked out the door and waited in the hallway. He went over to the bed, and whispered into the ear of the Heistess…

"Justice has prevailed. Barnwell got what he deserved. I have heard through the grapevine that a few people on my 'Disgruntled Customers List' have each received a windfall by way of a box full of jewelry. You have done the right thing and I respect and admire that. You helped others get back what was stolen from them, and you have restored what became desperate lives. You also now have back what he took from your grandmother."

Ariella stared at him in shock. There was disbelief in her cerulean eyes. "So, you know… you know everything?"

He nodded and then spoke further, holding a finger up to his mouth, "Shhhhh! Let me continue. No one else in the police department is aware of this. It is time for you to get on with your life. I have not figured out how you did it, leaving no trace of how you got in or out. Or maybe you did not do it, because I cannot prove you broke in anywhere. There were no tools or implements to be found at your home indicating that you committed this theft. I have been solving crimes for many years and at no time have I ever been mystified by a scenario like this before, where there was no obvious point of entry or exit. I have never been confronted with a situation where cameras in a store were recording, and then there was nothing, where one moment we were pursuing a red and black car and in the next minute it completely disappeared."

Ariella smiled, and Leyland smiled back.

He held up his hand and added, "You have my undying admiration for pulling this off… if you even did it. This is not 'The Perfect Crime' but it is 'The Perfect Retribution'. Justice has been served, and you are a remarkable young woman. In fact, I might be calling on you to help me out in the future if I come across any puzzling cases which need unraveling. You have an ingenious and creative mind which thinks in many directions."

As he began standing up, she grabbed his hand and squeezed it. And then she started sobbing. Her tears were from the relief of it all being over, his kindness, his understanding, and now Leyland inviting her into his fine family.

Charlotte came back into the room and sat on the chair next to the bed. She handed Ariella a tissue.

"By the way," said Leyland as he took something out of coat pocket, "Here is your cell phone. I had it repaired for you."

"You found my phone? Is it fixed? Thank you!" She took it from him and looked up again at his beaming face.

"I am going now." He made his way to the door. "I will leave you two sisters to catch up. By the way, Ariella, I just want you to know, the eight screws are in place, all is sealed down tight, and I left your rechargeable drill in your garage on the workbench."

■ ■ ■ ■ ■

About the Author

Alexander (Lex) Sloot was born in South Africa. He grew up in that country and obtained all his schooling there including a college education majoring in business and commercial printing. He is a classically trained pianist, having started piano lessons at the age of six. He studied classical piano for many years, attending various music schools and academies in South Africa. Piano playing and classical music continue to be an important part of his world today.

In 1974 Lex married his wife Jennifer, and at that time, he set up his first company which provided printing and marketing services to a corporate client base. Lex successfully sold this small business in South Africa when he and Jennifer immigrated to the United States in 1978.

A year later Lex and Jennifer started their company (Printmark) in Stamford, Connecticut specializing in promotional printed products. Over the course of the next few years, they acquired a few small companies, each time improving the production capabilities of their original business. One such acquisition was in Pennsylvania, paving the way for Lex and Jennifer to ultimately move to Northeastern Pennsylvania in 1992. At this point, their operation changed and began to produce and market promotional reflective safety products.

The company continued to grow as Lex developed countless new products and processes. In 2009, he sold the reflective products business and focused on the commercial rental properties that he and his wife owned. At that time, they started an outdoor advertising Digital Billboard Business (Media Center LLC) which has become a thriving enterprise.

Lex holds dozens of US Patents. He is an inventor, photographer, writer, artist, public speaker, and amateur theater actor. He serves on many Community Boards, particularly Non-Profit Organizations. He frequently gives talks at area Schools and Universities. He is the author of two books on Philosophy and Life Skills: *The TOOLS to XEL* (Excel). This title is derived from his first and last names spelled backward, and his other book is titled *VIABILITY... The Essence of Existence*. And now, *The HEISTESS* has made its debut.

■ ■ ■ ■ ■